THE HOMECOMING TREE

BRUCE HENNIGAN

Book Cover Design by ebooklaunch.com

"The Homecoming Tree" lyrics by Bruce Hennigan copyright 2018.

Standing Tree Books, an imprint of

613media,LLC

10911 Sanctuary Shreveport, LA 71106

www.613media.com

This is a work of fiction. The characters portrayed in this book are fictitious unless they are historical figures explicitly named. Otherwise, any resemblance to actual people, whether living or dead, is coincidental.

Author's website www.brucehennigan.com

All scripture quotes are from the New King James Version of the Bible.

www.homecomingtree.com

❀ Formatted with Vellum

PREFACE

In 1993 I wrote a play entitled "The Night Gift." The play departed from previous productions by being set in a more urban setting as opposed to the usual rural settings of most of my plays. My dear friend, Larry Robison asked me to create a duo of cantankerous old men like Waldorf and Statler of the Muppets. Thus, Mr. Collinbird was born. His character, meant to be played for pure comic relief, also played a pivotal role in the story. Midway through the play about a group of office workers trapped in a penthouse office on Christmas Eve I wanted to change from a comical mood to a more serious mood. The characters shared their most memorable Christmas. When Mr. Collinbird stood up, everyone groaned in anticipation of more corny, comical stories. Instead, he told the very poignant story of being thirteen and going out into the woods to cut down a Christmas tree because his father had not yet come home from the attack on Pearl Harbor. The scene that followed is recreated in "The Homecoming Tree" and proved to be one of the most powerful scenes in "The Night Gift."

After the first night's performance, Larry brought four men up to me. They wanted to meet the man who had written and directed the play. I nervously introduced myself unsure of what would follow. It turns out these men were veterans of World War II and wanted to thank me for honoring veterans on Veteran's Day. Yes, the performance had taken place on November 11, and I had not intended for that short scene to be a testimony to our servicemen. God, it seems, had intended this to happen. And, one of the men had been at Pearl Harbor! The next night, Larry once again brought someone to meet me after the play. An elderly lady with tears running down her cheeks told me the following story.

"My brother died at Pearl Harbor, and I have been mad at him and mad at God ever since. But, tonight, you allowed me to tell my brother goodbye and find peace for the first time in decades. I also was able to make peace to my Maker."

I was stunned! God had taken a short, seven-minute scene from a play I had written and used it to honor and change the lives of people I had never met! God humbled me that day, and I realized the power of God's story.

Later Larry Robison asked me a question. "Bruce, when are you going to tell that boy's story?"

"What boy?" I asked.

"The old man when he was a child from 'The Night Gift.'"

And so began the process of thinking and praying about Daniel "Collinbird's" story. I had chosen his name based on the first four verses of "The 12 Days of Christmas." Mr. Collinbird's friends were Mrs. Partridge, Mrs. Turtledove, and Mr. Frenchen. I would change Collinbird's name in the future versions of his story.

In the years that followed, I descended into a deep dark depression. Out of that experience came the first book on depression, "Conquering Depression." In 2012 Mark Sutton and would update that book as "Hope Again: A 30 Day Plan for Conquering Depression". I took a break from drama, and it wasn't until 1999 I started thinking about the story of the young boy and his tree.

My parents, Lena and Slayton Hennigan were fabulous storytellers. The stories of their lives together living through the Great Depression and World War II always fascinated me as a child. I asked my parents and my brother, Ronald to come to the house in 1999. For my parents' sixtieth wedding anniversary, I converted their old photos to old-fashioned slides. We sat around the dining room table with a video camera pointed at the slide screen. Starting with my parents' childhood, I had them tell their story from the 1920's up through the 1950's. I spent a great deal of the time exploring their lives at the beginning of World War II.

My father dreamed of being a farmer, but after having two children and almost starving on the farm, my mother persuaded him to move them to the big city of Shreveport. They leased a house on Buckner Street. After the war began, their many relatives availed themselves of my parents' hospitality. Mothers and children whose husbands had been shipped overseas moved into the house on Buckner Street while the mother found a job. Their house functioned as a boarding house with an ever-changing array of characters. I based my story on their lives in Shreveport at the beginning of World War II.

The story of the young boy cutting down the tree had surfaced in my subconscious. When I was eleven, I decided to go out into our pasture and cut down the family Christmas tree. My father worked long hours at the Post Office during the holidays, and I determined to become the "man of the house." The tree I cut down also toppled over and almost took my head off! In fact, if God had not sent a wind to cause me to lose my balance and fall to the side, the tree trunk would have killed me when it shot backward as it fell. Only while writing this story did I realize how close I had come to death!

The play, "The Homecoming Tree" debuted in November 2005. Unfortunately, my mother had passed away in August 2004, and she did not get to see her story on the stage. But, my father helped paint the flats for the set and recorded one of the 1940 era songs for our "commercials" played during scene changes. My brother by this time was homebound with COPD and did not get to see the play.

After the play premiered to a fabulous reception, I began the process of converting it into a novel. The story has changed some in the process with the addition of the character of "Ray" as my every-man. After working through the story, I rewrote the play to resemble the story of this novel. One day, I hope to produce the new version of the play, and I'm working on a musical version.

I hope you enjoy "The Homecoming Tree." In the cynical, hopeless, angry environment of the twenty-first century, this story is a breath of fresh air. This story reminds us of a time when good and evil were clearly defined; when sacrifice meant something far different from having to turn off your cell phone during dinner; when men and women rose to the challenge of ridding this world of the heinous evil of totalitarianism and genocide. It is a story of the "Greatest Generation," and I have learned much from that story. I hope you do, too.

Bruce Hennigan
    October 2018

❦ I ❧

Headlines The Shreveport Times
   November 22, 2001 -- Thanksgiving Day
   Shreveport, Louisiana

A surplus of coins, perhaps compounded by Americans emptying their change jars in the softening economy, has prompted the U. S. Mint to begin layoffs.

NASA's Mars Global Surveyor has taken its 100,000th picture of Mars.

Ben Laden search intensifies. "Enemies hide in sophisticated cave complexes located in some of the most mountainous and rugged territory. These hideouts are heavily fortified and defended by fanatics who will fight to the death." President George W. Bush said. "Afghanistan is just the beginning in the effort to fight terrorism."

No. 1 on this year's list to be thankful for is Barksdale Air Force Base, which, time after time, has proven invaluable to our nation's military. B-52 bombers from Barksdale in recent days have helped break Taliban rule in Afghanistan. In the immediate moments following the terrorist attacks of Sept. 11, Barksdale was the first stop for President George W. Bush.

Entrepreneurs are taking seriously the city's strategy for people to live, work and play downtown. At least two new residential projects are underway. New nightclubs and restaurants are planned downtown in the Red River Entertainment District.

Former Airline High School and LSU golf great David Toms won the U. S. Men's Open and two other golf tournaments this year.

The Veteran's Memorial was unveiled on Clyde Fant Parkway, adding more public art to the downtown Shreveport riverfront. Against the backdrop of a nation at war in Afghanistan, the memorial honoring veterans from our area takes on greater significance.

The long-awaited movie adaptation of "Harry Potter and the Sorcerer's Stone" opens today at Tinseltown, Bossier Regal Cinema, and Bossier 9. Pixar's latest, "Monsters, Inc." also opens today.

Two of Northwest Louisiana's biggest holiday attractions — Rockets Over the Red festival and Christmas in Roseland — kick off the local holiday spirit into high gear this weekend.

In spite of residents being nervous about flying in today's war climate, flights in and out of Shreveport Regional Airport reported passenger loads at 80 - 90 percent full although 20 fewer flights than last Thanksgiving are scheduled.

Local businessman, Roy Anderson, vice chairman of Collinsworth Industries, is to be honored as the Arklatex businessman of the year in next week's annual Louisiana Business Consortium meeting.

Wednesday, Nov. 21, 2001
Shreveport, Louisiana

. . .

"WAR IS HEAVENLY!" ROY ANDERSON THREW BACK THE LAST OF HIS scotch.

"Indeed, sir." Isaac Cheatwood stood stiffly in the office doorway, his thin, cachectic face etched with shadows. Anderson cleared his throat and studied his reflection in the penthouse office window before him. He touched a hint of a double chin with his index finger and frowned. Time to get back to the fitness center.

"Have you closed the deal?" He turned and regarded his Chief Financial Officer.

"Yes, sir." Cheatwood ran a hand through his thinning gray hair. "Purchasing the old ammunition plant six months ago was a genius move."

"I knew eventually we would end up in a war over terrorism. It's been so long since we had a good, old-fashioned war. Always good for the economy."

"In the long run, sir." Cheatwood smiled, and his thin lips stretched over his stained teeth.

"In the long run, Isaac. But, in the short run, have you met with the board?"

"Yes. I had to twist a few knives in some select wounds, but they caved." Cheatwood's pale eyes filled with a predatory gleam. "When will you tell Mr. Collinsworth he just lost control of his company?"

"He's in Hawaii for his annual family get together. Let's wait until after Thanksgiving. It will make a nice Christmas present." Anderson smiled. "I'm now CEO?"

"And Chairman of the Board." Cheatwood rubbed his bony hands together.

"And, you made sure you received that nice bonus?"

"Of course, sir. In spite of the downturn in the economy, as the CFO, the board agreed that I deserved that bonus."

"Yes, you do." Anderson leaned over his desk and glared at Cheatwood. "What secrets are you keeping about me?"

"Secrets?" Cheatwood shrugged. "Like your trip to the Caribbean? Sir, I would never betray your secrets."

"Good." He turned back to the window. "My driver should be here any minute, and I'll be off to the airport." He paused and exhaled. "And, I need you to get my lawyer to finish those divorce papers for me. I have a prenuptial agreement with my wife. She'll regret signing it."

"Yes, sir. I'll get right on it."

Anderson waved a hand. "You can go, Isaac."

"Yes, sir. Oh, and have a Happy Thanksgiving."

Thanksgiving. Anderson cracked his neck to relieve the tension. He was good at lying. It was a necessary skill for any ambitious businessman. But, lying to his family had been, well, challenging. He pulled on his overcoat and retrieved his luggage from the corner of his spacious office. There was a much larger office across the hall belonging to the founder of the company, Daniel Collinsworth. It had a lovely view of Red River, and by the time he returned from his island getaway, the office would be his!

His cell phone rang, and he flipped it open and glanced at the caller ID. He swallowed and calmed his nerves.

"Hello."

"Roy, I tried to explain this to David, but he just doesn't understand." His wife's voice came through the speaker.

"Now, Deb, we talked about this earlier this morning. Tomorrow is Thanksgiving, and I have to fly to Dallas in an hour. I'll be there by 5, have this emergency meeting with the stockholders and be back in Shreveport by ten tomorrow." He said calmly.

"But, flying is not safe." His wife said.

"Security is tighter than ever, honey. I will be more than safe. The meeting is about changing the direction of our manufacturing line to help the war effort. I can't turn my back on my country." Oh, how easy the lies formed on his lips. He licked them and closed his eyes. Somewhere in the back of his mind, a voice screamed. What you're doing is wrong! Then, the image of his secretary rose up from the warmth of his memories and the voice was smothered by the promises of her embrace.

"Can you at least talk to David? Make him understand? Tell him that you love him?"

Anderson massaged his temple. "Don't you think that will upset him more? I'm in a hurry, dear."

"Just one minute? Please?"

"Okay." He steeled himself to lie to his son. He glanced at his watch. His secretary had gone on ahead and should even now be checking into that beach house on St. John.

"Dad?" Anderson winced as the young voice came over his cell phone speaker.

"David? How's my big boy?" He asked, and his heart raced. He pushed back nausea. He could do this. Hadn't his father lied to him as easily when he was young?

"Why are you going out of town? When will you be back? Will you bring me a prize?"

Anderson looked down from the penthouse office suite over the cityscape beyond. For a moment, he gazed through his reflection with that annoying double chin. In his mind, Roy Anderson was much younger; much thinner; someone who could win over the young, voluptuous Fannie Mitchell who would be waiting for him on a warm beach. "I have an emergency meeting in Dallas, son. I'll be back by tomorrow in time for Thanksgiving dinner." The words rolled off his tongue. "And, yes, I will bring you a prize."

"I made *you* a prize," David said. "I put it in your overcoat pocket."

Anderson froze, and his breath clouded the window before him. "You did?"

"Did you find it?"

Anderson placed a hand in the pocket and pulled out a hard object made out of roughly carved wood painted with sloppy swirls of blue and white. A round head with a halo drawn in blue sat on top of a triangular body. Two eyes stared at him above a smile on the face of an angel. Wings spread out from the body.

"It's your guardian angel. We made in art class." David said. "Like that angel in our favorite movie. You know, the one with George Bailey. We can it watch tomorrow night, can't we? We always watch it on Thanksgiving night."

Anderson felt his eyes grow moist. He shoved the angel into his pants pocket and wiped angrily at his eyes. "Yes, we will. It's nice, David. I have to go and catch my fight."

"Okay, Dad. Love you."

"Me too," Anderson said hoarsely. He snapped the phone shut and slid it into his coat pocket. This is about *you*. This is what *you* deserve. Don't be George Bailey and find yourself trapped in dull, old Bedford Falls, Roy. Your time is NOW! He drew a deep breath as thoughts of his son faded in the wave of anticipation that overwhelmed him. He glanced down at the street in front of the office building as his limousine pulled to the curb. Someone got out of the back seat. An elderly man stepped up onto the far curb, a fedora perched on his head, his face turned up toward the office building. Even from thirty stories away, the eyes of Daniel Collinsworth seemed to focus on him. He stepped back from the window. What was Collinsworth doing in town? He was supposed to be in Honolulu.

Anderson grabbed his luggage and hurried from the office, down the elevator and out the front doors of the Collinsworth Building. A tall, thin man in black stood next to the open door of the limousine. Anderson paused in the cold, crisp air.

"You're not my driver."

The man took off his hat and bowed. "Mike at your service. I'm afraid Manuel has the flu."

"Mike? Did you just drop off Mr. Collinsworth?"

Mike glanced over his shoulder. "Yeah, he asked for a ride before I came to get you. He just walked into the park."

Anderson exhaled a plume of angry breath into the cold air. "What is he doing in town?"

"He didn't say, Mr. Anderson. Now, if you'll hop in. We wouldn't want to be late for your flight."

Anderson swore beneath his breath and looked at the open door of his limo. All he had to do was climb in and take off. But, what if Collinsworth knew about the board meeting? What would he do while Anderson was off on an island beach with the new love of his life?

"Mike, give me a few minutes. I have to speak to him."

As Anderson hurried around the limousine, snow began to fall from the leaden sky. He pulled his coat tightly about him and felt the angel slip from his pocket. He paused on the edge of the park and watched the angel tumble into the grass. He almost left it behind but in a moment of weakness, grabbed it out of the grass and tucked it back into his pants pocket. Guardian angel? He hoped he didn't have one. What he was about to do was not in the realm of angels.

Anderson hurried down a brick pathway into the deep, dark woods of Collinsworth Park. He had never been here. It was far too dangerous. Muggers and dope heads and gangs infested the park. No place for a businessman in a fancy overcoat and expensive shoes. He hurried up the path winding his way through darkening shadows filled with quietly falling snow. He rounded a turn and ahead, a huge open clearing stretched. A park bench sat in the center of the clearing and crouched on the bench sat Mr. Daniel Collinsworth. The old man looked up at him from beneath his fedora. His eyes glowed with angry fire.

"Why would a man lie to his son on Thanksgiving?"

Anderson stopped dead in his tracks. "How did you know?"

"Your wife called me this morning. She wanted to know why I, the director of the board of Collinsworth Industries, would call an emergency stockholder meeting the night before Thanksgiving. She wanted to know why you had to fly to Dallas tonight. She said that your son cried when he found out. How old is he now? Five? Six?"

"Seven." Anderson wiped the snowflakes from his face. "What did you tell her?"

Mr. Collinsworth leaned back on the bench and tapped a finger on his cane. "I didn't tell her about your secretary. I didn't tell her about the flight to the Virgin Islands you have scheduled this afternoon instead of to Dallas. I didn't tell her about the affair that you've been having for the last month."

"And I didn't tell her that the Board of Directors had an emergency meeting *this* morning and ousted me as the chairman of the board and installed you not only as the chairman of the board but as the CEO of Collinsworth Industries."

"It was Cheatwood, wasn't it" Anderson hissed. "I knew we should have hired a new CFO. What do you have over him? He's been feeding you information hasn't he?"

"Isaac and I have had our differences in the past, but unlike his grandfather, the man still has some scruples," Collinsworth said.

Anderson brushed snowflakes from his hair. "Let's face it, Mr. Collinsworth. You're old. You're ancient. Why would we allow an eighty-year-old man to run a company like ours?"

"I'm 72. Ronald Reagan was president when he was my age."

"Beside the point." Anderson glared at him. "You're supposed to be with your family in Honolulu for your annual gathering. Isn't this the year that they celebrate the 60th anniversary of the attack on Pearl Harbor?"

"My flight was delayed. Snowstorm." He stood up and paced around the bench. In spite of his age, he was remarkably agile. "Roy, you are a very good businessman. If you had waited a few months, I was going to ask you to be the next CEO of this company. I don't have any doubts about your ability in business." He paused and pointed his cane at Anderson. "But, you leave a lot to be desired when it comes to your morals."

"Morals are old school," Anderson said. "It's a new century. If you want to get ahead in business, you have to lie and cheat with the best of them, or you'll be left behind. Don't tell me you never told a white lie?"

Mr. Collinsworth stiffened at the accusation and rammed his cane tip into the ground. "I pride myself on my honesty, Mr. Anderson. Ask any businessman I've dealt with, and they'll tell you I'm as honest as they come. See, that's because of my scruples, my morals, my upbringing." He tapped the ground with his cane. "The reason this park hasn't gone under the bulldozers is because this is where I grew up. I played in these hills. The very foundation of my life and my family is soaked into this ground."

"Mr. Collinsworth, do you see that building over the treetops?" Anderson pointed to the high rise across the street from the park. "Thirty years ago, that was the largest building in Shreveport, Louisiana. When you built it, it was a paragon of modernity. But over the years it has become nothing more than a testimony to your failing leadership. It's time for new leadership to take over your business and that is exactly what I'm about to do. You see this park around me?

Soon all these trees will be leveled to the ground. A new gleaming, shiny, high-rise office building will arise on this ground. Don't worry. We'll make certain after we tear down your building we put something useful in that space. Probably a parking garage."

Mr. Collinsworth lifted his cane and pointed it at Anderson's chest. "What happened to your heart? When I hired you, you were a strong young man with an unwavering sense of morals. You were a deacon in the church. You gave money to the Salvation Army. You played basketball with some of the underprivileged kids in this neighborhood. What is it that you forgot, Mr. Anderson?"

"I haven't forgotten how to get ahead in business Mr. Collinsworth. If you want to get ahead, you have to play the game. Collinsworth Industries is sitting on the newest drone technology, and that is what will be needed as we go to war."

"Drones in the future will be used to relieve men and women of going into dangerous places like forest fires or disaster zones from hurricanes. You know how I feel about war!"

"So black and white! You've got see the world in shades of gray, Mr. Collinsworth. It's not just a world of good and evil anymore."

Collinsworth stepped toward Anderson and touched the tip of his cane to his chest. Anderson took a step backward. "That's the problem with your generation. You quickly throw away the past! You think you can learn nothing from it. Even after the September 11 attack, you refuse to learn! How long did our country turn to God? About six weeks, I'd say, and now it's business as usual." He glared at Anderson. "Look at what you are throwing away, Roy. A wife that has been loyal and loving to you for years. A young son who idolizes you. Businessmen in this community who look up to you. You're throwing all that away for a young, feisty secretary. I can tell you that your story has played out a thousand times over a thousand years. Five years from now, she'll be taking the money from you and leaving you high and dry. How old are you now?"

"I'm 35, Mr. Collinsworth."

"Not too young for a midlife crisis. You see, the problem with you Roy is you forgot the good things of your past. The only thing worse than nostalgia is amnesia."

Anderson shoved the tip of his cane away from his chest. "Mr. Collinsworth, it is time to move on. What I do with my private life is none of your business."

"Son, it is my business because we're one big family at Collinsworth Industries. I haven't forgotten my past. My family has been there for me for all these decades. I set the standard for this company. We care for each other like an extended family. And now you want to throw all that away so that you can transform this park into a brand-new high-rise building. And with what? War profiteering? I heard about the abandoned ammunition plant. Son, this war isn't like previous wars."

"Really?" Anderson snorted. "You're proving my point. Drones and cyber warfare are the future. And, our company is no longer all about media and computer programs and art software. When you moved into hardware, it was only a matter of time before we got involved in these kinds of advances."

"You've been so busy keeping your eyes on your secretary; you haven't been paying attention, Roy. I had a plan for building a cybersecurity center out by Barksdale. But, you squandered the money on an old ammunition plant. Now, who is outdated?"

Anderson swallowed and cleared his throat. It was a good plan; he had to admit. But, too late. "Well, too late now. My plan will work, Mr. Collinsworth."

"Yeah, it's worked well so far today, hasn't it? Listen, why don't we spend some money and transform this park into a place where families can come and play and spend time together in the heart of this city? New lighting. New security. Landscaping. Our families will sorely need that in the coming days. Trust me. I know."

"I will not waste money rebuilding this park. Families can find their way to get back together." Out of the corner of his eye, Anderson saw someone in dark clothing moving along a path through the forest. From behind a tall tree, a man stepped into the clearing.

"Mr. Anderson, you're going to be late for your flight," Mike said.

"I don't think Mr. Anderson will make it out of here today. If they canceled my flight, they cancelled his too."

"I'm flying east, Mr. Collinsworth. No problem getting to Atlanta.

The storm is coming in from the west." Anderson nodded towards Mike. "I'll be there in just a minute, Mike. Go keep the car warm."

Mike disappeared into the trees, and Mr. Collinsworth moved away from the park bench toward the center of the small clearing. He paused before a brass plaque placed in the ground. "Why did you follow me into the park when you came out of the building a while ago?"

"I wasn't expecting to see you in Shreveport."

"And yet, you followed me up here into this park. Want to know why? The entire time I was walking up that path to this park bench I was praying for you. You felt the prayers, didn't you? Or, was it just your guilty conscience?"

Anderson sniffed. "Really? You expect me to believe God made me follow you into this park?"

"Yes. I was praying for your family's future; that you wouldn't forget the man that you were in the past. Reminders from the past are very important just like this plaque. You know what this plaque is, don't you?"

"Some kind of reminder of your family, I'm sure," Anderson said. "I've never paid much attention to this park other than its potential."

"Used to be a very important tree right here." He touched his cane to the brass plaque.

"No one climbs trees anymore," Anderson said.

Collinsworth frowned and looked upward into the snow-filled sky. "My father was quite the pilot. Flew for Chennault before World War II. Our house is right down the hill there. I still live in it. Oh, his generation was the best generation we ever had in America. You could learn a thing or two from him, Roy. Yep, you could learn a thing or two. If you were open to learning from the past." He turned and glared at Anderson. "You see, Roy, that's my prayer for you. Don't forget the right choices you made to get you to where you are today. God has richly blessed you, and you've forgotten that. If you don't pay attention to God, He might have to knock your flat on your back to get your attention. You'll have your own September 11 surprise. My prayer is that when He does, you'll realize what's going on, and you will learn your lesson."

"Only thing I will learn is how to turn your failing company into a top Fortune 500 industry, Mr. Collinsworth. Now if you'll excuse me, I have a flight to catch."

As Anderson turned, the figure in black stepped out from behind the tree. "Mike, I told you I'd be there in a minute." But the man in black was not Mike. A ski mask covered his face.

"Well if it ain't Christmas come early." He said. "Now if you gentlemen will empty your pockets, I'll be on my way."

"How dare you attack us in my park!" Mr. Collinsworth shouted and crossed the clearing with surprising agility. He lashed out at the man with his cane and caught him on the side of his face. The man cursed and then turned back and pulled a black pistol out of the pocket of his hoodie. He slammed it across Mr. Collinsworth's face, and the old man fell onto the snowy ground. Blood trickled from his temple. Before Anderson could react, the man stepped between him and the old man and pointed the pistol at his face.

"Really like that nice fancy coat you got there. Take it off and put it on the bench nice and slow."

Anderson's heart raced as he slowly shrugged out of the overcoat and draped it over the bench. "Let's just stay calm, okay?"

"Take off that jacket, too. That'll look real nice on me at the country club. That's right, lay it right there on top of the big old nice fancy coat. You know what? I like that watch you got on. Not one of them fake Rolexes is it?"

Anderson glanced at his watch, and before he could say anything, the pistol touched the skin between his eyes. "Off with the watch and lay it on the coat. I'll have that fancy diamond wedding ring, too. Those diamonds on your belt buckle? Go ahead and take that off and throw it on the pile. And then follow it with your wallet. And, your tie."

Anderson piled everything onto his coat and shivered in the cold when snow began to fall down the back of his neck. "You got what you want. So, get out here and let me take care of the old man."

"Sounds to me like I did you a favor the way you were talking to him. Now, you're going to take off your shoes. Look like they're about my size."

Anderson started to protest, but the gleam in the man's eye was maniacal. He slipped off his shoes and threw them on top of the jewelry. His feet froze through his wet socks.

"Don't you worry about the old man. You'll be stripping him next. Don't you try anything or you'll be pushing up daisies."

"Really?"

The mugger took a step back and rolled up the jewelry into the coat packing it into a nice, neat bundle. "Really. I've always wanted to say that. I'm just a little bit old school."

The tree behind the mugger rustled, and Mike stepped into the clearing. The mugger whirled and pointed the pistol at Mike and pulled the trigger. Anderson was not sure what happened next. Mike seemed to blur: seemed to glow with an inner light, and his hand went up in a gesture of defiance. The bullet stopped in midair and fell to the ground. The mugger dropped the bundle and backed up. Then, he reached out a hand and grabbed Anderson's shoulder. He hugged Anderson against his chest with his arm locked around Anderson's neck. Anderson felt the cold barrel of the gun press against his temple.

"I don't know how you did that. But, you need to get on out of here, or this man gets it!"

Mike's eyes glowed, and he lifted a hand toward the mugger. The pistol slid off his head, and Anderson felt the mugger struggle with the pistol as if it were being pulled from his hand. An explosion sounded in his ear and filled his head with an echoing pain. Pain lanced across the right side of his forehead. The blow was so strong it threw him back against the park bench, and he rolled onto the ground. Something warm trickled across his temple and into his right ear. Gray sky yawned above him and snowflakes settled on his face.

Mike appeared in the periphery of his vision and gestured with his hand toward the mugger. The mugger lifted into the air and flew across the clearing and into a tree. Mike squatted down and took off his cap. He studied Anderson for a few moments and then looked to the side as if listening to someone. He nodded and looked back at Anderson's face.

"Mr. Collinsworth is going to be all right. Now, someone who loves you has prayed for you today. And, my Master has just told me how I could make sure that prayer is answered. You're not going to like it, Roy. No, not at all." He tilted his head and looked over his shoulder toward the sky and nodded. "Yes, sir. If that's what you want, I'll give it a try." He looked back at Anderson and reached down with his hand and touched the wound on the right side of his forehead.

"Don't worry it was just a grazing blow. You're going to be fine, Roy. Unfortunately, you're going to suffer from that amnesia that Mr. Collinsworth talked about a while ago. You're going to forget all about this life. But you're going to see another life. Pay attention and see what you might learn from the past. I'll see you on the flip side."

Mike's hand strayed across Anderson's face, and his index finger and his thumb touched his eyes. Light exploded behind Anderson's eyelids, and he fell through a vortex of smoky snow. The universe wheeled, sunsets and sunrises flashing like strobe lights. Stars and comets, planets and meteors, and a bright kite-tailed star of blinding luminosity fell through the darkness gathering around his mind.

Anderson blinked and found himself standing in total darkness. His pants sagged and his cold, wet socks hugged his feet. Melting snowflakes dappled his freshly starched shirt. A pinpoint of bright sunlight cast a shadow before him. In the distance, he saw his secretary standing on a beach in a bikini. Over his shoulder, he heard a voice. He whirled and saw his son cradled by his kneeling wife. His son's tears fell into the darkness, and he turned bright luminous eyes in Anderson's direction.

"Where's Daddy? Why isn't he here?"

"I don't know where he is, son." Anderson's wife looked up from their child and her gaze settled on him, filled with untempered fury and fire. "We need to pray for his safe return."

Anderson stumbled forward and reached out a hand toward them. Something crimson and hot ran over his right eye, and he screamed in pain. He grabbed at his face and pulled away a blood-stained hand. The darkness spun into a vortex, sucking him down into oblivion where mind and memories separated and his past flowed away like a flooding stream.

In the smothering darkness, Anderson fell and thudded against hard concrete. His head bounced, and stars danced in the darkness overhead. The stars spun and radiated into long, sparking wires as a trolley passed by trailing the sharp odor of ozone. He blinked in confusion as the sound of big band music rolled over him from the open door of a nearby drug store. Tobacco smoke filled the air as a man stepped out of the store and tilted his fedora back on his head. His teeth clenched a pipe, and a Christmas wreath hung from his arm. A tall man in a black overcoat with a familiar cap on his head joined him.

"Sorry about this, Roy. Or, should I call you Ray?"

"Mike?"

"Mikey. I'm a cab driver here, Ray."

"Is he going to be okay?" The pipe smoking man asked. "I can call a policeman over."

"That won't be necessary." Mikey smiled at the man. "He's a friend of mine."

"Ah, too much of the sauce?" The man stoked his pipe and shrugged. "I'll leave you to it." He walked away, and the pipe smoke swirled behind him in the cold air. Mikey leaned over him again.

"And, I'm afraid I have to take your memories. Hope you can make this work for you." He touched Anderson's throbbing, bloody temple and the darkness drank him. Anderson's mind melted away, fading into a warm, cloistered darkness and everything he knew was being sucked into a tiny, black safe. Mikey slammed the door, and he spun the dial. Ray's mind was gone, empty; nothing remained. He managed to roll over onto his side and watched the cab driver slide into a black car with a bulbous hood and drive off.

He slowly stood up and stumbled down the sidewalk. A wide street stretched from right to left. Buildings towered over the street. They were vaguely familiar. Cars passed by him trailing steaming exhaust in the cold air. But, they were wrong; all bulbous curves and fins. A trolley rolled by powered by a rod that stretched upward to the network of sparking electric wires spanning the street. People bustled all around him in overcoats and furs and fedoras. He stumbled back into a cold brick wall. At the head of the street, a church towered with huge white columns. Where was he? This was, home? But, no it wasn't home! It was different. He rubbed the crusting blood from his face. He stumbled down the sidewalk to the nearby trolley. The back door opened with a whiff of ozone. He climbed the steps and collapsed in the back seat. The trolley trundled down the street. He looked up into the frightened face of a little girl clutching her mother. Her eyes filled with fear.

"Mommy, what's wrong with that man?"

The woman reached up and pulled on a string, and the trolley lurched to a halt. The driver hurried down the aisle toward her. "Hey, lady, what's the emergency?"

"This man." She pointed at Anderson.

The driver jerked with shock at the sight of Anderson. "Hey, what's up with you? I don't let no violence take place on my trolley. You gotta get off. Now!"

Anderson opened his mouth to protest, but the driver already had him by the arm. He pulled him up out of the seat and shoved him toward the door. "Get out! Now!"

Anderson stumbled down the steps and fell onto the sidewalk. The cold melting snow burned through his shirt and his hand fell onto his pockets. He teased the hard lump out of his pocket and held it up. As he rolled over onto his side, through blurry eyes, he studied the tiny angel. An angel? It felt warm in his hand, and he shoved it back into his pocket. He must not lose it. Why? He didn't know. He only knew it was important. Maybe a link to the emptiness that filled his head?

Who am I? His mind was a blank page. A firm hand took him by the shoulder and rolled him onto his back. He looked up into the face of a boy in a bright red shirt. He had a tattered white star sewn over his chest. He wore a fading red mask around his bright, blue eyes and carried a square shield with red and white stripes.

"Gee, Buster, who is this?"

Another boy leaned into his field of vision. He wore an old-fashioned leather aviator hat and goggles. "I'm not Buster, Cap. I'm the Midnight Menace."

"Forget that, Buster. This man is hurt. He's been shot." The first boy pushed his mask up into his blonde hair.

"Maybe he's a Nazi spy." Midnight said. He held up his wrist and spun a dial on a watch-like device. "I'll decode the secret message, Captain Freedom."

Captain Freedom pushed the boy's wrist away. "Buster, this is not a game. Let's get him to the house and see if we can help him. He's no spy."

Midnight bent closer. "Hey, mister. Who are you, anyway?"

He opened his mouth to answer and realized he had no idea who he was. He was empty and tired and sleepy and wanted nothing more than for the pain to go away and for sleep to come. The man sank into the waiting darkness and slept.

❦   2   ❦

Headlines – The Shreveport Times
    November 20, 1941 – Thanksgiving Day

Armed plentifully with American weapons manned by some 750,000 imperial troops plus the royal navy, the British have opened a new triple-threat offensive by land, sea, and air against the Axis in Libya.

The "hostage terror" sweeping nine Axis-occupied countries in Europe has resulted in the death of more than 100,000 persons, and disappearance and imprisonment of countless other thousands.

War between the United States and Japan would be long and arduous, despite the optimists who go about the country voicing assurance that a few bombs on Tokyo or a few shells against Japanese warships would give victory within a few days or even hours according to a retired admiral.

Palais Royal will have it's after Thanksgiving sale tomorrow beginning at 9 A.M. Bright new dresses start at 3 dollars and untrimmed coats at 10 dollars. 300 new smart hats range from 1 dollar to $1.98! Suede high hill shoes are on sale for $3.15!

Don't miss Barbara Stanwyck and Henry Fonda in "You Belong to Me" at the Majestic theater tonight. For times phone 2-6735.

Today's top hit is "Chattanooga Choo Choo" by Glenn Miller and His Orchestra with Tex Beneke and the Four Modernaires.

Too busy to cook on Thanksgiving? Morrison's Cafeteria is featuring Family Night. Roast turkey, dressing, and cranberry sauce is 25 cents. Broiled Spanish mackerel with cole slaw is 22 cents. Grilled Salisbury Steak and French Fried potatoes are 18 cents. Mince pie, with hard or Brandy sauce, is 10 cents. Fresh pumpkin pie with whipped cream is 8 cents. Fresh coconut cake is 7 cents. Open from 5 to 8 P.M. Happy Thanksgiving!

Barksdale Field officers will be wearing a new insignia starting today. A demi-griffin with outspread wings stands guard above an azure shield with a clenched fist holding seven shafts of lightning. Each shaft of lightning represents one of the seven phases of instruction and preparation for trainees.

Live tonight on the Centenary College Campus don't miss the New General Motors Parade of Progress Exposition! It's absolutely free! Here you will see the famed "Circus of Science," an eye-opening panorama of the possibilities of the future in the home life of 1960!

The Byrd Yellow Jackets and the Fair Park Indians will clash this afternoon in the tenth renewal of their annual duel on the Louisiana State Fair gridirons. A crowd of 10,000 is expected to witness this classic high school football game. Admission 25 cents and 55 cents. Adult and reserved seat tickets are on sale at Evans Sporting Goods, Bacon and Edwards, and Glenwood Drug for $1.10.

Bing Crosby has invited two special guests to help him celebrate Thanksgiving in the "Music Hall" tonight on NBC-KTBS at 8 o'clock. That's 1480 on your radio dial!

The man opened his eyes, and every muscle in his neck ached. He found himself lying on a cot in a dark room. A cold draft chilled him to the bone. The air smelled of baked rolls and roasting turkey and his stomach growled. In the distance, he heard big band music playing. He blinked, and as his vision cleared, he made out a desk in the center of the room and book-filled wooden shelves on the walls. A man in a black coat shuffled through the books. He held an angled, dark green flashlight and played its pale beam over the books.

"It's got to be here somewhere. Find it, Dad says. Do this, Lazarus. Do that, Lazarus. Get me a cup of coffee, Lazarus. Go sneak into Collinsworth's house and find it, he says." He muttered to himself.

The man sat up painfully on the cot, and it creaked under his weight. "Lazarus" spun around, and the flashlight clattered onto the wooden floor. The downturned brim of a fedora hid his face. He fumbled for his coat pocket and pulled out a pistol. It shook as he pointed it at the man.

"Put your hands up. I mean, stay there. I mean reach for the stars." He said in a trembling voice.

"Hey, Cap, let's go check on our prisoner." Someone said beyond the room's open door.

Lazarus glanced through the door toward the other room. He snatched the flashlight from the floor and hurried to a nearby open window. He slid through the open window and disappeared into the cold outside. He pointed the pistol at the man one more time. "You keep your trap shut, or you'll be eating lead, hear?" He said and his breath steamed in the cold air.

The man tried to stand up, and a wave of dizziness passed over him, and he slumped back onto the cot. Where was he? Who was the man with the gun? He reached up and touched a bandage on his forehead. Had he been shot? But, by who? By the man who had just climbed through the window? He closed his eyes and tried to sort through the confusion as two boys came into the room.

The boy in the red mask from earlier rushed across the room to the open window and pressed his gloved fists to his hips.

"Who dares to trespass on the inner sanctum of Captain Freedom?

I'll find you filthy Nazi scum if it's the last thing I do." He bellowed at the top of his lungs.

The other boy in his aviator cap and goggles held out his hand, and a golden ring flashed in the meager light of the living room as he clamped his hand over the other boy's mouth. "Hey, don't wake up our prisoner! I am The Midnight Menace, and I am here to find the plans to the secret formula the Nazis are preparing to put all of Europe to sleep. I'll use my secret decoder ring to decode the secret formula."

Red mask shoved the other boy's hand from his face. "Wait a minute, Buster! You can't be The Midnight Menace right now. He's a good guy, and I need you to be Captain Freedom's arch enemy, the Crimson Skull. Our prisoner works for the Crimson Skull, and you are here to take back the secret plans hidden in his pocket."

Buster was rail thin and wore a tattered black sweatshirt with a clock face sewed onto the front. He raised his aviator goggles and sighed. "I'm NOT the Crimson Skull, Daniel! I'm The Midnight Menace. I'm one of the good guys! I've got the secret decoder ring and the secret squadron decoder badge. Gee, I'm tired of being the bad guy. Every time you want *me* to be the Nazi."

Daniel poked Buster in the chest with a gloved finger. "And every time, Buster, you want to be the hero. Sometimes, we gotta have an arch villain!" He pointed at the man. The man on the cot blinked in confusion. Was he a Nazi? A villain? Somewhere deep within, his soul burned with shame. He wasn't entirely innocent, but for the life of him, he couldn't remember why.

Buster backed away and pulled off his aviator cap in anger. His dark curly hair stood on end with static electricity. "My hero is not a villain. He's the best! He doesn't need a shield. And, America isn't even in the war, so we don't need a Captain Freedom!"

Daniel pushed his red mask up on his head. His bright blue eyes flashed with anger. "Uncle Lonnie says we will be in the war real soon."

"Well, my Dad might be wrong," Buster said.

"You just don't want him to have to go off to war. You want him to stay here." Daniel replied.

"You'd like that wouldn't you?" Buster poked Daniel in the chest. "Then, you'd have the only Daddy in town with a war medal."

"And, it's gone, okay? He lost it." Daniel frowned.

"Let me show you why I'm a hero." Buster reached up to the third shelf on the right and pulled down a huge book. He laid the book on the desk and opened it. "This is no ordinary book. Instead, it's a book safe containing a hidden compartment." Buster reached into the book and pulled out a bright, shiny disc of metal attached to a ribbon.

"Here is your Dad's medal! Now, would an arch villain have found that medal for you? Huh? No more Crimson Skull, Daniel. I'm the Midnight Menace from now on. We can get Keith down the street to be the Crimson Skull."

"How did you find that?" Daniel took the medal.

"I was looking for a book one day, and I found this. It has a hidden compartment. At first, I thought it was some kind of secret formula that would make us superheroes. But, instead, it's just a bunch of papers." Buster rummaged through the contents of the book and pulled out a large folded sheath of papers. He laid the papers aside and pulled out a dark wad of material wrapped in wax paper.

"Yeah, but that's not as swell as this is. Look what else I found." Buster opened the wax paper bundle and revealed a dense collection of brown fibers.

"It looks like cow manure," Daniel said.

"It's chewing tobacco, dunderhead." Buster tore away a handful of the tobacco and held up to Daniel's nose. "Here, try some."

Daniel pushed his hand away. "I don't want to put that in my mouth. It stinks!"

Buster smiled and held the tobacco just inches from his mouth. "Oh, you're just a big sissy. A real superhero chews tobacco so he can spit all the way across the room." He put the wad in his mouth and began to chew. "Now watch," Buster mumbled as he puckered his lips to spit.

Buster's eyes widened as he looked toward the door to the library. Another man walked into the room. He was a tall, dark-haired man dressed in a flannel shirt and khaki pants. His piercing, brown eyes traveled over the room and took in everything in seconds. The man straightened painfully and rubbed his head.

"I see you're feeling better."

"Where am I?" His own voice was a stranger.

"You're in my house. I'm Frank Collinsworth." He put out his hand, and the man studied it as if it were a snake.

"I don't know who I am." He whispered.

Frank Collinsworth lowered his hand. "I thought as much. Give me a minute, and I'll explain." He turned his attention to the boys and Daniel gasped and tried to stand in front of Buster.

"What are you boys up to?"

"Hey, Daddy. Uh, we were just playing Captain Freedom and the Midnight Menace." Daniel said. His bright, blue eyes strayed for a moment to the other man and then back to his father. "That man is our prisoner. He's working for the Nazis and the Crimson Skull. His partner climbed out the window."

Frank glanced at the open book safe, and he walked over and stepped between the two boys. His hands came to rest on each boy's shoulder. "You've been reading those comics, again? I thought I told you that stuff would rot your brain."

"*Mommy* said it would rot your brain. You told me I could read them." Daniel said.

Frank glanced through the open library doorway. The man noticed the lights were now brighter in the living room and the dining room beyond. A woman appeared from the door to what must have been the kitchen and crossed to a table in the far corner. She placed a tray of food on the dining room table.

"Let's just keep that between us, OK?" Frank grinned. "Now, what have the two of you gotten into?"

Daniel pointed to the open book, and his eyes widened when he saw Buster's desperate expression. Buster's cheeks bulged and his eyes watered.

"Uh, Buster found this book when we were playing. He thought it was a secret vault for a formula to defeat the Nazis."

Buster nodded nervously as his eyes bugged out of his head. Frank smiled and studied the boy's expression.

"Well, Buster, that's good work finding a secret hiding place." Frank slapped Buster on the back. Buster lurched forward, and his cheeks collapsed. His swallow was loud, and his eyes watered even more. His face paled, and he grabbed his stomach. He glanced once at Frank and Buster and ran from the library.

Daniel's smile faded as he looked back nervously at his father. "Daddy, Buster tried to get me to chew some of that tobacco, but I didn't."

Frank picked up the wax paper. He studied the dark shreds of tobacco and then lifted them to his nose. He inhaled, and a contented look came over his face. "I wouldn't mind taking a bite or two myself. But, I promised your mother, I would quit. That's why I put it here in my hidden treasure box."

Daniel's eyes widened in surprise. "But, if you quit, why didn't you just throw it away?"

Frank lowered the tobacco and reluctantly closed the wax paper around it. "Let's just say I was hoping one day she might change her mind."

"Why did she make you quit?"

Frank put the tobacco back into the book and put the papers on top of it. "Ever kiss someone who's been chewing tobacco?"

"Yuck! I don't kiss girls. You know that. They're yuck."

Frank grinned and sighed. He reached over and ruffled the boy's blonde hair. "One day, you'll change your mind. And, close that window. That draft can't be doing our friend any favors." Daniel closed the window and Frank motioned to a chair by the desk. "Sir, why don't you come over here and have a seat."

The man shuffled across the library and collapsed into the chair. "Do you know who I am?"

"No, sir, I don't. The boys brought you inside an hour or so ago. Said they found you on the sidewalk. Looked like you had been beaten up and robbed. I called the police, but they had no report of a missing person."

The man nodded and touched his forehead. It stung, and he gasped. "I don't remember a thing."

"Gosh, Dad, he doesn't even know his name?" Daniel asked.

The man glanced at the boy in his Captain Freedom costume. "The only name I remember starts with the letter R. Robert? No. Richard? No. Maybe Ray?"

"Then we'll call you Ray," Frank said. "Is that okay?"

Ray nodded. "Feels almost right. So, where are we? I mean what city?"

"Shreveport, Louisiana." Frank leaned toward him. "Does that name ring a bell?"

"No, sure doesn't."

"Well, you're at the Collinsworth boarding house. At least it's a boarding house while I'm away on missions."

Daniel held up the medal so that Ray could see it. "My Daddy went on a secret mission and saved a bunch of his buddies."

Frank reached over and plucked the medal from Daniel's grasp. "It was pure luck, Daniel."

Daniel drew a deep breath, and his bright, blue eyes gleamed with pride. "Daddy, tell Ray how you got the medal again."

"He needs a last name so that you can call him by his formal name." He glanced at Ray. "Any idea what your last name is?"

Ray blinked as he searched his memories. "I've got nothing."

Daniel pointed to his shirt. "Well, you've got a castle on your shirt."

Ray looked down at a green castle monogrammed just above his shirt pocket. "Yeah, that's the logo for, uh?"

"Logo?" Frank said.

"A symbol for a company that makes this shirt." Ray concentrated until his head hurt. "A castle, uh, what is it?"

"How about Mr. Castle?" Daniel said.

Ray sighed in frustration. "I guess that is as good as anything."

Frank looked at his son. "You need to call him Mr. Castle. Not Ray. That is showing respect."

"Okay, Daddy" Daniel nodded at the man. "Golly, Mr. Castle's never heard the story. And, I want to hear it again."

Frank glanced at the medal, and something foreign moved across his face. "It's just it seems awful flashy for such a little thing I did."

"Saving four men isn't a little thing, Daddy."

Ray watched the loving, adoring gaze the boy had for his father. Something ached within him. It was a yawning emptiness and a sense that he was missing something. Was he a father? Did he have a young son like this?

"Daniel, you're just twelve. You wouldn't understand. Saving those men was just my job."

"Your father has every right to be proud." Someone said from the door to the library.

Ray glanced over at the door to the library. The woman he had seen in the dining room was standing in the door. She was shorter than Frank, and her bright green eyes glittered with excitement. She wore a simple cotton print dress covered with a frilly apron, and her dark, curly hair was piled up on top of her head.

"I see our visitor finally woke up." She walked across and reached out and put a cool hand on Ray's forehead. "At least you don't have a fever. I might have to give you some castor oil later."

"Don't let her do it, Mr. Castle!" Daniel ran around the desk. "That stuff is awful."

"It cured your cough, young man."

"Ann Lee, healthy or sick, you don't dare cough after a dose of castor oil," Frank said.

Ann Lee stood up and put her hands on her hips. "Just ignore them, sir. So, what's your name?"

"I'm not sure." Ray felt of his forehead. It did feel a little warm. "I don't remember anything."

"We've decided to call him Ray Castle," Daniel said. "Sounds like an alter ego. Hey, what if he's a real superhero?" He said the last words out loud with his hands planted firmly on his hips.

"Daniel, calm down. I'm sure Mr. Castle probably has a headache to go with that wound on his head." Ann Lee frowned. "So, you don't remember who attacked you?"

"No, I don't. I don't remember much of anything."

"Well, give it some time. You can sleep in here on the cot until you get back on your feet."

Ray glanced at his cot. Sleep on a cot? How dare she tell him he was going to sleep on a cot! He drew a deep breath and pushed the sudden arrogant anger away. Where had that come from? He was lucky to have a roof over his head. He looked back at Ann Lee.

"That will be just fine."

Ann Lee nodded. "I'll try and find you some clothes before dinner.

In the meantime, why don't you listen to Frank's story? I just love to hear him tell it."

"I just did what any man would do."

"Sounds like you're a real hero," Ray said.

"Gee, you're right, Mr. Castle. Dad's the best hero around."

Ann Lee put an arm around her son's shoulders and straightened his hair. "Not just any man can fly like Frank. You should have seen him the first time he climbed into that old crop duster of his. It's like he was born to fly an airplane."

Daniel smiled at his father. "That's why you quit farming, isn't it Daddy? Because of the flying?"

"Yeah, I had to learn to fly to keep the boll weevils off the cotton. And, then once I learned, it got into my blood." He pushed the book safe behind him, and Ray realized he was trying to get it and it's chewing tobacco out of Ann Lee's sight. "But, I'd still be on the farm if General Chennault hadn't of given me a call."

"Frank knew General Chennault when he lived here in Louisiana. He knew what a good flyer he was." Ann Lee smiled.

"Tell Ray, uh, Mr. Castle, about China, Daddy." Daniel sat on the floor next to the desk chair.

"Oh, son, I don't want to talk about all that."

"Go ahead, dear. He'll never grow tired of hearing it." Ann Lee said, and her eyes twinkled. "And, neither will I."

Frank sat in the desk chair and cast a desperate look at Ray.

"Don't look to me to rescue you. I'd like to hear it, too. It might help me with my amnesia." Ray said.

Frank started talking and took them thousands of miles away.

❧   3   ❧

POSSIBLY LATE SUMMER OR EARLY FALL, 1941 --
SOMEWHERE IN BURMA

"Lieutenant Collinsworth!" The door to the ramshackle shack flew back on its rusty hinges. The sergeant ran into the room and almost knocked over Frank's small desk.

"What it is, Hap?"

Hap pulled off his cap and pointed through the open window at the dusty dirt airfield outside. "Four of the guys took off this morning in a transport plane."

Frank stood up and walked over to the open door. He glanced out at the P-40B Tomahawk sitting under the trees. Sometimes he wondered about Chennault's sanity for putting these untrained men out here under these conditions. And now, four of them had taken a transport plane. It was common for the men to take off and fly practice loops around the cluster of shacks and tents that passed for headquarters. But, he had specifically given them the day off to take the station wagon into the nearby town for some R&R.

"Why did they do that?" He turned to Hap.

"I don't know, Frank. But one of the Chinese spotters said the airplane crashed about twenty miles east of here. And, a villager saw two Japanese soldiers holding them at gunpoint in that open field just outside his village."

"I know the field you're talking about," Frank said.

"The villager also saw some Japanese reconnaissance teams in the area. They could be in trouble. You want me to tell the Old Man?"

Frank looked across the way at the lecture hall, as it was called. General Chennault was preparing for his daily lectures. "No, just tell him I took a plane out for a test spin. Those guys probably thought they could take out the Japanese recon party on their own. I give them high marks for their spirit but low marks for their common sense."

Frank grabbed his aviator cap and goggles and ran to the nearest airplane. A Chinese mechanic helped him climb up onto the wing, and he slid into the cockpit. He pulled a picture of Ann Lee out of his flight jacket pocket and wedged it next to the speedometer.

"Don't worry honey. I know I promised I wouldn't be flying into combat, but I've got to find those four men. I know you'll understand." Then, he glanced upward at a blue sky as brilliant and bright as a robin's egg. "And, Lord, I don't know why you decided to make me a pilot instead of a farmer, but be with me today. Help me find those men." The ship hurtled across the bumpy dirt airstrip and into the sky.

Frank studied the horizon and made out a thin column of black smoke to the east. That would be the crash site. And, he knew the field the villager was talking about. If he came in from the east, he could surprise the Japanese. But first, he had to do something he'd never tried before. Frank knew the sound of every airplane engine in the Japanese fleet. He had trained himself to listen for the sound of approaching Japanese bombers or Japanese Zeroes. Now, he needed to make his airplane sound like a Zero.

He adjusted the fuel mix and throttled the engine down just a bit. The dull roar changed ever so slightly. The average person wouldn't know it had changed. But, the Japanese soldiers would recognize the sound. They would think Frank's airplane was an approaching Zero.

The smoke column drew closer, and Frank sank lower to the ground until the shadow of his airplane chased him across the hills and trees. Just like flying his crop duster back home.

Frank flew through the column of smoke and caught a brief glimpse of the transport in the trees. They had tried to land and didn't make the field just ahead. Suddenly, a huge tree appeared in front of him, and he knew the field was just on the other side. He would have to miss the tree and take the Japanese by surprise.

He cocked his guns and heard a dull click. He had no ammunition! He had been in such a hurry; he had grabbed an airplane that hadn't been reloaded. Now, what would he do? The huge tree was growing nearer. He stomped on the rudders and pulled the airplane into a right angle to the ground, the wheels brushing the branches of the tall tree. He hurtled out into the field and saw the two Japanese soldiers staring at him; the four Americans crouched on the ground. One of his men took the distracted Japanese by surprise and subdued them as Frank righted his airplane and swung around in a huge arc. The four men were jumping up and down with the two Japanese down on the ground. He landed the airplane on the rough, bumpy ground of the field.

Louisiana Slim greeted him as he climbed out of the cockpit.

"Frank! Are you a sight for sore eyes!"

Frank looked over his shoulder at the other three men, J. D., Moses Malone, and Wally. "No time for that. There's a recon group coming soon. We've got to get out of here."

Moses shook his head. "How do you reckon on getting us all in the one-man cockpit?"

Frank frowned and glanced around at the open field. "Well, we'll have to try something else. Wally, run back to the transport plane and get some rope."

"What?" Wally's mouth fell open.

"Hurry." Frank watched as the man ran across the field. "J. D., you get up here on the wing, close to the fuselage."

J. D. blinked. "On the wing?"

"You want to stay around and have rice with the Japanese?" Frank slapped the wing. "Moses, you get on the other side. And Louisiana, you climb up there by J. D."

Wally returned, gasping for breath with two coils of rope. "Frank, tell me you ain't thinking what I'm thinking you're thinking."

Frank took the ropes. "Get up there by Moses."

Frank strung the rope around the nose gear and handed an end of the rope to each man. "Tie this around your shoulders and make sure it's tight."

J. D. wound the rope around his back. "Frank, you sure this will work?"

Frank climbed into the cockpit. "No." He fired up the engine and began taxiing for the far end of the field. He didn't have much time, and he wanted to take off at the end of the field away from the tall tree. But, the shout of a Japanese soldier appearing at the tree line changed his mind. He gunned the engine and headed for the far end of the field.

The extra weight of the four men held the airplane down, slowed his acceleration, and he upped the fuel mixture and threw the throttle all the way open. He glanced briefly at the four men clinging for dear life on the wings, but he had to concentrate on that tall tree.

The whine of bullets filled the air as the recon party burst out of the trees far behind him. If he were lucky, they would be out of range. Luck? There was no such thing as luck, in Frank's book. He glanced at the tree in front of him, impossibly tall and blocking his exit from the field. God, he prayed, I need your help.

Out of nowhere a gust of wind rushed across the field, and he felt the airplane lift off the ground. With mere inches to spare, he brushed the top of the tree and soared into the sky.

＃ 4 ＃

“Wow! That's swell, Daddy. See, Mr. Castle, my Daddy's a real hero!” Daniel jumped up from the floor. His face was red with excitement, and his eyes widened with joy.

Frank smiled and ruffled the boy's hair. “Son, I was just doing my job. And, if God hadn't of heard my prayer, I wouldn't be here today.

“He heard my prayer, too.” Ann Lee said quietly. “Now, Daniel, out of that Superkid outfit and wash up for dinner.

Daniel frowned and pulled his red eye mask back down off his head. “Mommy, I'm Captain Freedom. You don't even know your superheroes.”

“That's because I don't read that trash. It's a waste of ten cents. You can go to a movie and get a coke for that much money.”

“But I can only see the movie one time. I can read the comics over and over.”

“You should stick to literature.” Ann Lee said.

Daniel pointed to a book lying next to the door to the library. “Like those romance novels, you like so much.”

Ann Lee blinked and picked up the book and placed it back on the shelf. “Well, these books are *historical* romance novels. They educate while they entertain me.”

Daniel seemed deep in thought for a moment, and then he smiled. "I learn a lot from my comic books, too. Almost as much as you learn from that radio show, you like so much. What is it called, Daddy?"

"The Guiding Light."

Ann Lee smoothed down her apron and adjusted her hair. "Well, I'm not here to talk about me. I'm here to get Daniel to get ready for Thanksgiving dinner. I'm sure our guest is hungry."

Ray felt cold and sweaty. Something was very, very wrong. After hearing the story about China and the exchange that had just occurred, his mind felt fuzzy. "What year is this?"

Ann Lee frowned and put a hand to her mouth. "Oh, my, Frank. It's worse than we thought."

Frank came around the desk and put a hand on Ray's shoulder. "It's November 20, 1941. Today is Thanksgiving day."

Ray paled even more and felt nauseous. What year was it supposed to be? How could it be any other year but 1941? He swallowed nervously and ran his hand through his sweaty hair. "It just doesn't seem right. It's like I've heard all this before. It's not supposed to be 1941. What am I going to do?"

"You're going to stay here until you're better." Frank looked into his eyes. "Understand?"

"Why are you doing this?" Ray asked.

"Doing what?"

"Taking care of me. You don't even know me."

Frank stood up and glanced over his shoulder at Ann Lee. "Because, it's the right thing to do, Ray."

Ray shook his head. No one did something because it was 'the right thing to do' anymore. They always had an ulterior motive. The thought was a cold, hard spike through his brain. What were these people really after? He cast a wary eye at Ann Lee. "Well, thank you, then."

Frank patted his shoulder again and reached out and pulled Daniel over toward him. He looked at Ann Lee. "Honey, I'd like just a few more minutes with Daniel. He and I need to take a little walk before dinner. Is that OK?"

Ann Lee glanced down at Daniel and sighed. She started to say something more to Ray, but she closed her mouth and crossed her arms over her chest. "Sure. It's going to be at least another hour before we eat."

"Thanks. Daniel, why don't you go put your costume up in your room and get your coat and some warm gloves."

Daniel pulled away and turned to look at his father. "OK, Daddy. Can Buster come?"

"No, this is just between you and me."

"Am I in trouble? 'Cause it was Buster who got that chewing--"

Frank's hand darted out faster than sound and clamped over Daniel's mouth. He looked up sheepishly at Ann Lee. "You're not in trouble, son. Now run along."

Ann Lee watched her son run from the room. "And don't let me catch you playing those comic book characters again."

Daniel paused in mid-stride and assumed a heroic pose with his hands on hips. "But, Mother, Captain Freedom is a hero. He fights injustice and evil. He's just like Daddy."

"Your Daddy is a real hero, and he doesn't need a cape and a shield. Now, run along."

Daniel broke his pose and ran into the living room and up the stairs. Ann Lee turned to her husband, and her gaze fell on the book on the desk behind Frank. She started to reach around Frank for the book, but he caught her hands in his and pulled her close to him.

"Ann Lee, thank you."

"For what, dear?"

"Well, for being here for the kids when I was away."

Ann Lee looked over at Ray. "Frank, not in front of Mr. Castle."

Frank seemed to have forgotten Ray was there. He smiled weakly. "I don't mind if Mr. Castle hears what I have to say. He needs to know what a wonderful woman you are."

Ann Lee pointed to the corner of the library. "Maybe Mr. Castle would like to wash up in the bathroom. It's right over there, Mr. Castle."

Ray stood up slowly and walked over to the bathroom. He closed the door but left it cracked open. In the mirror above a pedestal sink, he saw Ann Lee and Frank drawing closer together in the library. Their love for each other was obvious. Did he love someone? Was he married? He glanced down at his left hand. No ring. But, there was a hint of a groove around the base of his ring finger. He blinked in confusion and watched the two people in the library.

Ann Lee looked down at Frank's chest. "You were only gone for a few months. And, you promised me you wouldn't be flying into combat." She glanced back into his face. "Of course, I could be angry with you for saving those men. But, Daniel is right. You are a hero."

Frank sighed and released her hands. He rubbed his jaw and shook his head. "I'm just an ordinary man. I never set out to be a hero. All I ever dreamed of was running my farm. Now, here we are in the big city of Shreveport. We don't own a farm anymore, but we own this old, drafty boarding house and take care of half of our relatives."

Ann Lee placed her hands on his chest. "Well, your father left it to you, and I couldn't see us staying on that farm while you were always up in the air. You couldn't get much plowing done behind the stick of an airplane."

Frank chuckled and sat in the desk chair. "I guess I never was much of a farmer. But, I'm worried about you. It's such a burden on you having to take care of all these folks."

"Frank, they can't stay on the farm any more than we could. At least here in the city, they can find work. I know this old Depression is coming to an end, but times are still hard for them. Besides, the rent they pay helps make ends meet. The Army Air Corps doesn't pay that well."

Frank pulled her down into his lap. "You know something, my dear, there isn't an angel on the face of the planet more caring than you."

Ann Lee glanced at the bathroom, and Ray stepped back further away from the mirror. "Oh, Frank, you always know just what to say."

Frank touched her hair and her face with his hand. "I just want you to have some time to yourself. In fact, I have a surprise for you. Soon, you'll be spending a little time in an exotic location."

"What?"

Frank took her hands in his. "I told you I would be leaving tomorrow for a couple of weeks. It's a secret mission. The Army Air Corps wants me to do some more training."

Ann Lee frowned and tried to pull her hands from his grasp. "But, you promised me you wouldn't go back to China!"

"I'm not going to China."

Ann Lee glanced at his face and then shook her head in horror. "You're not going to Europe are you?"

"You know we're not in the war. Yet. I'm not going to Europe, honey. But, you have to keep this a secret, OK?"

"Okay. So, where are you going?"

"Hawaii."

Ann Lee straightened in shock. "Hawaii? You mean the island?"

"Yes, honey, the island. Hickham Field needs help training pilots."

"But, won't it be dangerous?"

"In Hawaii?" Frank smiled. "That's the last place in the world the enemy would attack. That's why we're going there. It's safe. And, beautiful, like you."

He reached forward to kiss her, and Ann Lee pushed him away. "When will you be back?"

"I'm leaving Sunday, and I promise I'll be back by Christmas. And then, after Christmas, you and I are going to have that honeymoon we never had. I'm going to take you back to Waikiki beach and put you in a grass skirt and watch you do the hula."

Frank pulled her close, and his lips met hers. Ray looked away and shut the door quietly. He examined the face that looked back at him from the mirror. It was the tired, bruised face of a stranger. Frank had mentioned Hawaii and something tickled at the back of his brain. The year 1941 and Hawaii had some connection. But, what was it? He clenched his fists in frustration at his amnesia. Would it always be like this? He had the sudden sense of danger and foreboding for the two people in the library. Just moments before, he had been suspicious of their motives. And, now, he was afraid for their lives. Why?

Ray opened the door and stepped out into the library. A tall, young woman was standing in the library doorway. She had long, curly dark hair that hung to her shoulders. She wore a pink wool sweater and a short skirt.

"Mommy, can I talk to Daddy, please?"

Ann Lee extricated herself quickly from Frank's lap and straightened her apron. "Sure, Rachel. How long were you standing there?"

"Oh, I just got here. I didn't see the two of you smooching or anything."

Ann Lee cleared her throat. "We weren't smooching."

Rachel stepped into the room and grabbed her mother's hand. "Well, you ought to be. Daddy is going somewhere next week on a secret mission. He needs all the smooching you can give him."

Ann Lee pulled her hand away from her daughter. She looked at Frank for help. He just smiled. "Now, Rachel, it is not proper for a young lady like you to say such things."

"Sorry, Mother."

Ann Lee hurried around her daughter and paused in the doorway. "Now, I've got to go finish the turkey and dressing."

Ann Lee left the library and Frank closed the book on the desk and hurriedly put it safely back in an open slot on the bookshelves. "What is it, Rachel?"

Rachel glanced at Ray. She started to say something and then looked back at her father. Frank realized her uneasiness.

"Mr. Ray Castle." He pointed to Ray.

"We think," Ray said, happy to be thinking of something other than the uncomfortable paranoia of a few moments before. He sat down on the shaky cot. "So, you're Frank and Ann Lee's daughter?"

"Yes, sir." She put out her hand, and he shook it. "Unlike my crazy brother, I have good sense. Which is why I'm here." She held out a piece of paper to her father. "I need you to sign this."

Frank took the paper and studied it. "What is this?"

"Oh, nothing really." Rachel shrugged. "Just a piece of paper giving me permission to enter a contest."

Frank looked up at her. "What kind of contest?"

"A singing contest. At the radio station." Rachel said quickly.

"I see. Have you told your mother about this?"

"No, Daddy. You know she wouldn't approve."

"But, it says here you have to be eighteen."

"I will be eighteen. In six months. Please, Daddy. You know I don't want to spend my whole life here in this dismal old house. Do you think I want to grow up to run a boarding house like Mother? I've got dreams and hopes. I want to make something out of myself."

"So, you think your mother and I have wasted our lives?"

"No, I didn't mean that." Rachel stomped across the room. "It's just that I want to make something of myself. I want to sing. I want to act. I want to be a movie star."

Frank got up from his desk chair and came over to Rachel. He put his hands on her shoulders and turned her to face him. "There's been a lot of young women who had the same dream. Dreams can change as you grow older."

"Well, that may be so. But right now, the only thing that is important to me is to be in that singing contest."

Two girls appeared at the doorway. Rachel glanced at them. "Daddy, you remember Penelope and Gwendolyn."

Penelope was the shorter of two dressed in a dark sweater and a dress with a black French beret on her head. Gwendolyn was the taller of the two, dressed in a flowing dress with a red scarf around her neck. Her hair was blonde and lustrous, and she looked like a young movie star.

"Mr. Collinsworth," Gwendolyn ran to Frank and pulled him away from Rachel. "You simply must allow Rachel to enter this contest. The three of us are going to be a team."

"A team? Playing what? Basketball?" Frank said.

Penelope took his other arm. "No, in Hollywood. I'm the artist, and I will design all of Rachel's posters."

Gwendolyn flipped her hair over her shoulder, head held high. "And, I am the fashion expert. I will design all of Rachel's gowns. She will saunter right down Hollywood Boulevard and dazzle all of the stars from Cary Grant to Clark Gable."

Penelope pulled Frank toward her. "And, when she accepts her Oscar, I will design the invitations to the exclusive ball after the festivities."

Gwendolyn strutted across the room as if walking down the red carpet. She held out her hand to Penelope.

"Here's my invitation."

Penelope took the imaginary envelope and studied it. "Are you sure?"

Gwendolyn laughed out loud and patted her hand against her throat. "Actually, I don't need an invitation. I am the glamorous Gwendolyn Miller, fashion consultant to the stars. Surely you recognize me?"

Penelope squinted as she looked Gwendolyn up and down. She smiled. "Oh, forgive me, Miss Miller. Of course, our good friend Rachel Collinsworth is waiting for you at her private table. You may go right in." As Gwendolyn passed her, Penelope stopped her and said, "And, save me a seat."

Gwendolyn sighed. "Is Cary Grant here yet?"

Penelope spied Ray. She ran over to him. "Here he is." She pulled Ray to his feet. "He arrived moments ago with Katherine Hepburn and Ava Gardner." She put her arm around his and smiled at him. "Of course, he didn't ask for *you*. But, he invited *me* for an after-dinner dance."

Gwendolyn opened her mouth to protest, and Frank cut her off. "Enough, girls. You made your point. This is not Cary Grant.

"At least we don't think I am," Ray said quietly and tried to smile. Was he famous?

"This is Ray Castle. A new visitor to the Collinsworth boarding house." Frank glanced at Ray. "I don't suppose you remember having daughters?"

"I don't know, Frank. But, I think you've lost this mission. If I were you, I'd sign the release."

Penelope released Ray's arm and ran to Gwendolyn. The two of them jumped up and down. "I told you it would work," Penelope whispered to Rachel.

Rachel glanced at the clock on the mantle of the small fireplace in the library. "Oh, Daddy, there's going to be an announcement of the contest any minute. Can I turn on the radio in here? I don't want Mother to hear it."

"Sure. Go ahead."

Rachel hurried over to a small radio set on the bottom shelf and turned on the power. She fiddled with the dial and static was interrupted by the abrupt sound of voices and music as she moved up and down the numbers. She paused, and the strong, clear sound of an announcer echoed through the room.

"And now, live from the studios of KTBS in Shreveport, Louisiana it's the Hour of Stars featuring the Voice. Here he is right now, the Voice." The announcer on the radio had a small, thin voice that echoed through the room but the voice they heard next was deep and resonant.

"Thank you. That's Lloyd Parker announcing the program tonight, folks. We have a special evening for you with some great entertainment coming to your radios. Isn't that right, Lloyd?"

"Today is a special day, isn't it?"

"That's right. Today is that day all turkeys love to hate, Thanksgiving Day, 1941. We have a fantastic line up of music you listeners will be grateful for. And, later a brand-new episode of the newest adventures of Captain Midnight. But, right now, we are proud to announce the fifth annual Piney Woods Holiday Singing Contest sponsored by your local Big Chain Grocery Store, the first supermarket in the South. Come to Big Chain and find it all in one easy location."

Rachel was beaming and pointed excitedly at the radio as the Voice continued. "Here it comes."

"Our contestants have one more day to turn in their applications before the contest begins next week. The first prize is a position on the singing circuit of our nation's newest service organization, the USO. Our winner will get to tour the United States for the next year, meeting, greeting, and entertaining our men in uniform."

"See Daddy; you won't be the only person in the military. It's the chance of a lifetime!" Rachel turned off the radio. "Please?"

Frank sighed. "Okay, I'll sign the papers, Rachel. I want you to have the chance your mother never did."

Rachel started clapping and then paused as she slowly stood up. "What? Surely Mother didn't want to be a singer?"

Frank pulled out a fountain pen and signed the paper. "Not really. She wanted to be in the movies."

"The movies? My mother?"

Gwendolyn came over and put an arm around Rachel's arm. "See, Rachel, darling. I told you that you were a natural. So, Mr. Collinsworth, what happened to keep Rachel's Mother from becoming a movie star?"

Frank folded the papers and handed them to Rachel. "The silent movies had come to an end and talking movies came out. Let's just say that your mother's speaking voice was about as good as her singing voice. Rachel, you've heard your mother sing."

Rachel cringed. "Oh, yes I have."

"So, she gave up her dream of being in the movies to raise a family." He took Rachel's free hand. "Honey, I just don't want you to forget who you are along the way. God has made you a sweet, lovable young lady and I wouldn't want to see that change."

"Thanks, Daddy." She leaned over and kissed his cheek. Penelope and Gwendolyn followed her out of the library. Frank smiled at Ray.

"Well, you've put off the inevitable long enough."

Ray shook his head. "The inevitable?"

"Meeting the residents of the boarding house. Prepare yourself." Frank motioned toward the library door. Ray stood up shakily and followed him into the living room.

The living room was a large, high ceilinged room with a fireplace on the far wall opposite the front door. A portly elderly man sat in a large stuffed chair. His thick, white hair was an unruly mess on the top of his head. He wore a red undershirt and black pants held up by bright green suspenders. A small pair of reading glasses sat on his nose allowing him to read the newspaper. On the couch next to the old man, a small compact woman knitted. Her gray hair was pulled up into a bun underneath a net. She wore a green dress and a similar pair of reading glasses. A medium height man in brown pants and a white shirt was pacing before the fireplace. He had short, red hair and puffed on a pipe. The fragrance of the pipe smoke played against the background aroma of turkey and dressing. Ray's stomach growled with hunger.

Three tiny women sat in rockers in front of a large upright radio. At first, Ray was convinced they were triplets. But, as similar as they were in dress and appearance, there were small differences. All three women wore pale, white dresses and shirts that buttoned up to the neck. They each had salt and pepper hair pulled up into tight buns on the top of their heads. They were staring off into space and slowly rocking to the tempo of the music playing over the radio. A big band orchestra played "Hark the Herald Angels Sing." Angels? Was there something in one of his pockets? Before he could follow the thought with action, it slipped away, and he massaged his face in confusion. His vision blurred and he blinked until it cleared.

In the corner of the living room opposite the front door from the dining room, Rachel and her friends sat at a small concert piano. Rachel had a piece of music perched in front of her and pecked away at the piano keys. The door to the kitchen burst open, and a tall woman with blonde hair and wearing a bright red party dress strutted into the room. Perched on the top of her head was a garish, bright green hat upon which sat a cardinal.

Ray gasped when he saw the woman. Her complexion was the color of cream, and her eyes were a piercing blue. Her blonde curls bounced around the base of her hat as she moved around the living room in the tight red dress. There was something immediately familiar about her and Ray felt his heart race. Did he know her? The woman glanced at him, and her eyes moved up and down his rumpled clothes in an appraising fashion. She wrinkled her nose in distaste and turned back to the other occupants of the room.

"Well, how do you like my new hat?" She said. Her voice was high pitched and a bit screechy. Ray winced. Maybe she wasn't anyone he knew. But, for a second, he heard the sound of waves lapping on the beach and the distant music of the Caribbean.

The old man glanced up over his newspaper. "Looks like something you found up in a tree. Are you going to wear that thing out in public?"

The woman sitting next to him slapped the man's arm. "Lawson, don't talk that way to Peggy Lou. She can't help it if her taste in hats is outlandish." She cut her eyes over the top of her reading glasses. "Of course, you would never catch me in that hat."

Peggy Lou put a hand on her hip and pouted. "Now, Aunt Wimpy, this is the latest craze in hats. I found it down at Palais Royal. It only cost one dollar."

Another woman entered from the kitchen carrying a tray of rolls. She was shorter than Peggy Lou and slightly plumper. Her face was plain but honest, and her hair was a limp mass of curls. She placed the rolls on the table and chuckled. "You wasted a whole dollar on that

hat? You could have bought a dozen eggs and a gallon of milk for that much! No wonder you can't pay the rent to Ann Lee as you should. What's gotten into you wasting money like that? It doesn't grow on trees."

"That's right, Sue Carol." Lawson glanced over his shoulder. He pointed his arthritic finger at the newspaper. "It says right here in the newspaper that bread is 4 cents a loaf, milk is 34 cents a gallon, and eggs are 60 cents a dozen."

Aunt Wimpy glared at him over her reading glasses. "That's the only way you would know how much food costs! Let me remind you that it will be our turn to work in the kitchen soon. And, you better not break any of those eggs." Aunt Wimpy turned her attention to Peggy Lou. Her gaze roved over the hat on her head. "Peggy Lou, how much do you make an hour down at the Saenger Theater?"

Peggy Lou placed a perfectly manicured fingernail on her lips. "You can tell Uncle Lawson that I make 30 cents an hour. And, they should pay me more! Taking up tickets is hard work. They're showing that Roy Rogers movie, "Jesse James at Bay" and the line was around the block! Why last night, I broke a nail!" She held her finger up to examine it.

Sue Carol appeared at her side and straightened her food-stained apron. "You don't know what hard work is, Peggy Lou! You should have to work in that kitchen helping Ann Lee and try to raise two children."

The man with the pipe stopped pacing and pointed his pipe at Sue Carol. "Sue Carol, calm down. I bet she got the money for that hat from one of her boyfriends."

Sue Carol smiled. "You're right, Lonnie. And, she probably dumped him as soon as she got the dough."

Peggy Lou's mouth opened in shock, and she glared at Sue Carol. "I bought this hat with my hard-earned money to impress the love of my life."

"The love of your life?" Lonnie chuckled. "How many does that make?"

Peggy Lou put her hands back on her hips. "I'll pretend I didn't hear you say that. In fact, he will be eating with us tonight. I wanted to look nice for him because I think he may be the one!"

Frank waved his hands to get their attention. "Folks, I want you to meet our guest, Mr. Ray Castle."

Lonnie crossed the room and shook Ray's hand. "You're the unfortunate soul that was assaulted, right?"

"Yes, sir." Ray reached up and touched the bandage on his forehead. "And, before you ask any questions, I can't remember a thing."

"And, he means it. Doesn't even know who he is." Frank said.

Ann Lee appeared down the stairs carrying a box. "Mr. Castle, I found something for you. Why don't you come with me to the library?"

Ray turned away from the uneasy stares of the people in the room and followed Ann Lee into the library. "That was awkward."

"I'm so sorry for that."

Frank stepped into the library with Ray and studied the box in her hands. "Those are my father's clothes."

Ann Lee nodded. "Yes, Frank. I kept them after he died. Just in case. And, now, we can use them. Now, Mr. Castle, I've got some water heating in the reservoir in the kitchen and in about thirty minutes it'll be hot enough to put in the washtub. Frank, will you go get the washtub from the back porch and put it in the library bathroom."

"Reservoir?" Ray asked. "You don't have a water heater?" A fuzzy image danced in his memory, and he blinked. Where had that come from?

"We have a kerosene water heater from the Holyoke Heater Company, but it's over twenty years old," Frank said. "We just put the reservoir on the stove."

"But, there are so many people in the house. How do they take a bath every day?"

"Every day?" Ann Lee laughed. "I'd like that, all right. Especially those boys. No, Mr. Castle, we rotate the hot water. A bath a night for each resident. Now, when the water gets hot, I'll fix your bath for you, and you can soak before we eat. Thank goodness Frank's father added that indoor bathroom to the library. It's become our emergency bedroom for unexpected company. Like you!"

"The bathroom is a little drafty and cold, I'm afraid," Frank said. "My father wasn't the best builder around."

Ann Lee had opened the large cardboard box and pulled out a collarless white shirt. "I think you and Frank's father are about the same size."

Ray wrinkled his nose. "Smells kind of musty. Why don't you fluff the clothes up in the--" He paused at a loss for the next words. What was he talking about? Ann Lee and Frank were looking at him with a puzzled expression on their faces.

"Fluff them up?" Frank said. "You mean put them out on the line?"

"Oh, we can't do that." Ann Lee shook her head. "It's cold and misty outside. I think it's clearing up, but right now they'd get wet. I tell you what I can do. I'll hang this shirt and a pair of pants in the washroom and turn the fan on them. At least that will get rid of the musty smell." She placed the shirt over her arm and lifted a beige pair of pants from the box. "Now, you go on back in the living room and don't let those people intimidate you. They're all bark and no bite."

Ray swallowed nervously and followed Frank into the living room. Aunt Wimpy stood up and placed her knitting on the couch. "Mr. Castle, you come right over here and sit beside me on the couch."

"That's right, Mr. Castle, we're happy to welcome you to the boarding house. Just so long as you don't expect to sleep in our bedroom." Uncle Lawson grumbled.

Aunt Wimpy slapped Lawson's arm. "You hush up, old man. Mr. Castle will sleep wherever Ann Lee says he does. She runs this boarding house, not you."

Ray sat on the couch and glanced nervously around him. "Thank you for being so understanding. With my amnesia, I'm not sure about anything."

One of the women sitting beside the radio stood up. "My good sir, perhaps we can be of service. What do you think, sisters?"

The woman in the middle rocker nodded. "Perhaps you are correct, Ophelia. After all, there was that time the Colonel struck his head while fighting with Teddy Roosevelt."

The third woman patted her sister on the arm. "You are correct,

Theophila. The Colonel's mental instability was handled very well by our ministrations."

Lonnie leaned against the radio. "Just who was the colonel?"

Ophelia straightened her white sweater, and a shocked expression crossed her pale features. "Why, my dear Lonnie, the Colonel was our dear departed father. He fought bravely with Teddy Roosevelt. Surely you know your history?"

Theophila stood up and tapped Ophelia on the shoulder. "Ophelia, not everyone is as literate in the historical facts as we are. Don't blame Lonnie for his lack of education. After all, he is but a humble workman at the Post Office."

Lonnie opened his mouth to protest, and Sue Carol's laughter cut him off. "I think you had best quit while you're ahead, honey."

Evelia leaned forward and was able to reach over and place a thin, bony hand on Ray's shoulder. "Mr. Castle, I think your mental difficulties would be reversed by a liberal dose of the Remedy."

Uncle Lawson sat forward and lowered his newspaper. "The Remedy? You girls have a new batch of the Remedy?"

Aunt Wimpy nudged him. "Stop it! You can't have any of the sisters' 'Remedy,' Lawson."

"Our Cousin Bubba in Blanchard assures us he will have a case of the base for our Remedy by next week," Ophelia said.

"And, once we add our special mixture of herbs and minerals to the base, we will have over a dozen bottles of our elixir, Lawson," Evelia said.

Lawson glared at Wimpy and winked at Ray. "Mr. Castle, the Remedy will cure whatever ails you."

"More like you don't care about what ails you after a liberal dose," Wimpy said.

Frank lifted a flight jacket off the coat rack next to the front door. "I think we should postpone any discussion of the Remedy, sisters, until Mr. Castle's bruises and swollen muscles have subsided."

Ophelia nodded and eased back into her chair. "Perhaps you are correct, Frank. I believe we can discuss this further with Mr. Castle next week."

"Perhaps Cousin Bubba can double our shipment. What do you think sisters?" Evelia said.

The three sisters nodded and began talking among themselves. Lonnie eased past the sisters and joined Frank at the front door. "Frank, where are you headed?"

"I just put on a big pot of hot water for Ray and then Daniel and I are going to take a little walk before dinner," Frank said as he pulled on his flight jacket.

'Do you mind if I talk to you first?" Lonnie glanced over his shoulder toward Sue Carol.

"No, go ahead."

Lonnie tapped the pipe against his chin. "There's a rumor you're leaving tomorrow."

"I am."

"Mind telling me where to?"

"I can't Lonnie. It's a secret." Frank pulled on his pilot's hat.

Lonnie sighed and clamped the pipe in his mouth. "All these dad burned secrets! I suppose you'll be over there fighting those Nazis, right? That's what I ought to be doing."

Frank glanced at Ray, and there was something foreign and painful in his gaze. "Lonnie, don't wish for the war to come to us too hard. We'll be in it soon enough."

Ray felt a chill. The war was coming. It was going to be bad. It was going to consume the world in its chilly grasp. Once again, the images shimmered in his memory. Goose-stepping soldiers marched across the emptiness of his memory followed by the searing image of a huge mushroom-shaped cloud. He shook his head and rubbed his tired eyes.

Lonnie strode away from the front door, his fists clenched in frustration. "And, I can't wait for us to get into this war. I'm just itching to get my hands on a gun and—"

Sue Carol stepped in front of his pacing figure, and he lurched to a stop. "Lonnie, calm down. You're already serving your country down at the post office."

Lonnie sighed and glanced around the room. Everyone was looking at him. "I just can't abide sitting around waiting for the war to come to us. They killed over a hundred of our boys when that German U-Boat sank the *Reuben James*. Most of the country ignored it. We should have gotten into the war then."

Sue Carol looked over her shoulder, and Ray noticed the small boy in the middle of the living room floor for the first time. He had to be five or six years old. He wore a cowboy shirt, blue jeans, boots, and a red cowboy hat on his head. He had a plastic belt with holsters for two toy guns around his waist. He was building a corral out of Lincoln Logs.

Ray drew a deep breath at the sight of the boy. His heart raced, and his mouth was dry. Something about the little boy was familiar but also disturbing? Was that how he felt? Disturbed, yes. But, more than that. He felt something deeply troubling. Shame? Guilt? His hand drifted to his pants pocket, and he pulled out the object he had thought about just moments before. He stared at the small, wooden angel. It had been a gift. From who? Sue Carol's voice broke his reverie.

"Lonnie, please, calm down. You're scaring Little Lonnie."

Little Lonnie jumped up and ran across the room to Ray. "Hey, mister. What's that?"

The boy was leaning against his knee. He smelled of peanut butter and little boy sweat. His eyes were clear and watery, and a trickle of snot ran from his nostril. For a moment, the boy's face morphed, changed into the face of another boy. Ray closed his eyes as Little Lonnie took the angel from his hand.

"Gee, mister, this is an angel. Look, Mommy, the mister has his own angel."

Ray opened his eyes and drew a deep breath. "Yes, Little Lonnie, it was a present from someone."

"Who?" Little Lonnie asked as he studied the angel. He wiped his hand across his lip and smeared snot on the angel.

"Little Lonnie, let me have Mister Ray's angel. I'll have to clean it up for him." Sue Carol reached over Ray's shoulder and took the angel from the boy. "I'll go rinse it off in a minute, and we'll put it on the mantel above the fireplace to dry. Is that okay, Ray?"

"Yes," Ray whispered as Little Lonnie kept staring at him.

"Hey, Mister Ray, your angel can ride on my train."

"What train?" Sue Carol asked.

"The one Santa is going to bring me. Daddy, isn't Santa going to bring me a train set?"

Uncle Lawson tapped his newspaper. "Says right here in the paper that the number one most wanted toy this Christmas season is the Raggedy Ann Doll, not a train set. I'll bet Santa can't afford to bring you one of those."

Little Lonnie marched over to Lawson and lifted the bottom of the newspaper. He ducked underneath it and stared at Lawson. "I don't want no doll for Christmas, Uncle Lawson. I'm no sissy. Am I mother?"

Sue Carol hurried around Lawson's chair and picked up Little Lonnie. "No, Little Lonnie. You don't listen to Uncle Lawson." She glared at Lawson. "Of course, Santa is not going to bring Little Lonnie a Raggedy Ann Doll, you old fool." She smiled back at Little Lonnie. "Yes, honey, Santa will bring you a train set. How could he not? You're the biggest boy on the planet."

Lonnie tucked his pipe into his shirt pocket and took Little Lonnie out of his wife's arms. "That's right. I'll make sure Santa brings you that Lionel train set you've always wanted."

Little Lonnie smiled and pushed his hat up onto his forehead with one of his pistols. "I hope so. I need my train so I can ride out west and get Jesse James and his gang. Pow! Pow! Daddy, are you going to go blow up some bad guys?"

"No, he's not Little Lonnie," Frank said. "He's staying right here in Shreveport and making sure all those important letters get to the President of the United States. And, to Santa. Right, Lonnie?"

Lonnie lowered Little Lonnie to the floor. "Right."

Daniel appeared on the stairs. He was wearing a brown coat and a pair of wool gloves. "I'm ready, Daddy."

Frank pointed to the door. "Let's go, Daniel."

Uncle Lawson lowered his newspaper. "Now, where in heaven's name are the two of them going? It's nearly dinnertime. I don't want them to hold up our dinner."

Aunt Wimpy thumped him on the ear with her finger. "I can hear your stomach rumbling. Wait a minute. That's not your stomach. It's your bellyaching! Now hush up, old man."

Ann Lee closed the door after her husband and son disappeared into the approaching twilight. "Don't worry, Uncle Lawson. You'll get fed."

Uncle Lawson looked over his reading glasses at Ray. "See what you have to put up with around here?"

"I'm grateful to be here at all, Uncle Lawson."

Aunt Wimpy poked Lawson in the ribs. "See, you old coot. Mr. Castle has the right attitude. You should be grateful on Thanksgiving Day."

Uncle Lawson rattled his papers. "I am grateful. But, remember the reason we pay our rent on time is so we can eat on time!"

Ann Lee grimaced and stepped up behind Lawson's chair. "Uncle Lawson, you've been late on your rent three months in a row."

Aunt Wimpy smiled once at Ray and reddened. "Oh, Ann Lee, you know it's because our pension check got lost in the mail. Don't listen to Lawson. You take your time getting dinner ready. Some of us are still thankful you have this boarding house for us to live in."

Uncle Lawson pushed his face deeper into the newspaper. "I didn't say I wasn't thankful. But, I would be thankful if you'd get your daughter to shut up with that piano plinking and put my favorite song on that new phonograph."

Rachel stopped playing notes and turned to glare at Lawson. "We're not listening to that song again, Uncle Lawson."

"If we have to hear 'I'm Walking the Floor Over You' again, I'm walking out that door," Penelope said.

Gwendolyn flipped her platinum hair over her shoulder. "And, have you seen what Ernest Tubb wears? A cowboy hat and a string tie. How ghastly!"

"It's not like this all the time, Mr. Castle." Ann Lee said. She turned toward the piano. "Now, girls, there's no need to be impolite. Watch your manners. Uncle Lawson is a tenant. If he wants to hear his song, then play it."

Penelope sighed. "Well, for just a few seconds."

Gwendolyn covered her eyes. "Well, I'm closing my eyes, so I don't have to see him in those hideous country clothes."

Penelope crossed the room toward the upright radio. She opened the tilt-out front of the tall, wooden radio cabinet to expose the phonograph table. She lifted the needle and placed it on a record on the turntable. It started to turn, and the scratchy, slightly wobbly sound of music took the place of the radio program. The three sisters shook their heads in dismay as the song, 'I'm Walking the Floor Over You' filled the air with its strident notes.

Uncle Lawson lowered his newspaper, and a huge smile plastered his wrinkled face. He handed his newspaper to Aunt Wimpy and jumped up out of the chair. He pulled his suspenders away from his chest in time with the music and began to dance a jig on the floor. He joined Ernest Tubb in singing with an out of tune voice. Ray found his hands over his ears while the remainder of the people in the living room grimaced in pain.

Sue Carol hurried across the room and jerked the needle off the record. "Now, who's singing off key? We've heard enough of that. I think we ought to play some Benny Goodman."

Rachel pointed to the sheet music on the piano. "But, I wanted to practice, I mean, hear this song."

Sue Carol placed her hands on her hips. "Rachel, we're paying tenants just like Uncle Lawson, and we have just as much right to hear our song as he does."

Ophelia stood up from her rocking chair. "May I take this moment to remind everyone that my sisters and I are the ones who purchased this radio-phonograph for our collective entertainment needs."

Theophila stood up as her sister sat down. "Yes, thanks to our unprecedented profit margin on sales of the Remedy we were able to purchase this amazing new 'Beam of Light' radio-phonograph for only two hundred thirty-five dollars." She ran a gloved hand along the side of the upright radio.

Ray noticed that most of the residents of the room were mouthing the sisters' words as they spoke. They had heard this before.

Theophila continued. "No needles to change with subsequent longer record life and, of course, stroboscope control."

Evelia stood up and joined her sister by the radio. "And, Sister, do not forget the Philco automatic record changer and new tilt-front cabinet with the built-in super aerial system for excellent reception of our classical music."

Ophelia stood up and joined them. "With, of course, a beautiful hand polished walnut cabinet."

Lawson popped his suspenders one more time and collapsed into the embrace of his chair. "Yes, we are well aware of your sophisticated radio, sisters. You remind us every night."

Wimpy punched him. "And, who gave good money for Remedy so they could buy that radio?"

Ophelia smiled and closed the tilt front cabinet on the phonograph. "Well, will you excuse us for asking if we could hear some Beethoven? My sisters and I have been deprived of such genteel music since the day we arrived at this charnel house."

Ann Lee's brow wrinkled in puzzlement. "Charnel house? What is that?"

Theophila placed a gloved hand on Ophelia's arm. "My sister is referring to the ancient practice of butchery wherein cow carcasses stripped of their skin were hung in the air to dry. Now, Sister, I find your metaphor somewhat lacking. Perhaps you should choose a more appropriate phrase."

Evelia nodded. "Yes, Sister, such as insane asylum. The day to day bedlam that swirls around we three Southern Belles is much more akin to the goings on at such a place."

Ophelia nodded as she sat back down in her rocker. "I believe you are correct, Sister. I stand corrected, Ann Lee. Forgive me for my characterization. I should have referred to your home as an insane asylum."

Theophila patted Ophelia's hand and moved to her rocker. "Now, Sister, we don't want to be condescending. Let's choose a more positive sounding designation."

"A sanitarium?" Evelia said.

"Yes, perfect. A sanitarium, then. Now, can we please hear some chamber music?" Evelia reached for the radio dial.

"You can go flush the new indoor toilet in the library and hear that chamber music." Uncle Lawson said.

"Why I never." Ophelia put her hand up to her mouth. Her two sisters moved in unison to do the same.

"And, you never will." Uncle Lawson said and then started laughing out loud.

Sue Carol looked at Ann Lee. "Why in the world did you ever agree to let them live here?"

"They're our aunts, in case you haven't forgotten." Ann Lee said. "And, they bought us a radio."

Lawson peeked over his newspaper at Ray. "You figured out the cast yet?"

"Is everyone here related?" Ray asked.

Sue Carol looked at Ray. "Sometimes it gets so confusing, Mr. Castle. Ann Lee married my brother, Frank and I married Ann Lee's brother, Lonnie. I don't know what got into us."

Ann Lee glanced at Ray and grinned. "Sue Carol, you've got to admit that Frank was handsome."

Sue Carol wore a look like she had just smelled a skunk. "He's my brother, Ann Lee. I remember when he had no teeth and brayed like a mule."

Uncle Lawson pointed over his shoulder toward the piano where Rachel was once again picking out notes on the keyboard. "That's what that caterwauling over there sounds like when your youngin' is trying to sing. Sounds like the love call of a donkey."

Lonnie pointed his pipe at Lawson. "Recognized it right off, did you?"

"Oh, leave a man alone. I've got a newspaper to read." Uncle Lawson hid behind his newspaper again.

Lonnie walked over to the three sisters. "You can listen to your Beethoven until Bing Crosby comes on."

"Bing Crosby?" Evelia looked stricken.

"His show tonight is a 'Music Hall' special Thanksgiving show with Raymond Massey and Jinx Falkenburg."

"Jinx?" Rachel jumped up from the piano. "Jinx is on tonight? She is my model."

"She's a model, all right!" Lonnie grinned. Sue Carol punched his arm.

"Who's Jinx Falkenburg?" Ray asked.

"You've never heard of her?" Rachel asked. "Why she has been on the cover of hundreds of magazines. She is not only a model, but she is an actress."

"And her face is on dozens of billboards advertising that beer." Ann Lee said. "I don't think it's right for my daughter to want to model herself after an actress who advertises beer."

"Oh, mother. She does so much more than that. Why there's talk of her joining the USO entertainers." Rachel stopped suddenly and put her hand to her mouth.

"USO? What's that?" Ann Lee asked.

"The United Service Organization." Rachel said. "It's this new organization that works with the government to go around and entertains the troops. You know, build up their morale."

"A cold can of Rheingold beer would certainly do that." Lawson laughed. "Or, a little dose of the Remedy. Eh, sisters?"

"Okay, that's enough about the Remedy." Wimpy punched him again. "I, for one, would love to hear Bing Crosby sing."

"Too bad we can't *see* Jinx," Lonnie said.

Sue Carol grabbed his arm. "What's wrong with you?"

"Nothing," Lonnie said. "One day, mark my word, we will be able to see those shows as well as hear them."

"Of course you will," Ray said. "On T.V."

"Tee Vee?" Lonnie asked. "What's Tee Vee?"

Ray opened his mouth to answer. He glanced at the radio. Something was missing. "Uh, I don't know. Don't listen to me. Sometimes, I get confused."

Ann Lee appeared beside Lonnie. "Don't worry, Lonnie. Sisters, remember, we had this conversation earlier? You've listened to classical music most of the day."

"Well, there was that interruption earlier by that game," Ophelia said.

Evelia shook her head with a dismayed look on her face. "That outrageous affair pitting poor teenage boys against each other."

"Ruffians!" Theophila nodded.

"That was the Byrd versus Fair Park football game." Lonnie clamped down on his pipe. "And, we had to change the channel before the game was over so you could hear the Moonlight Sonata!"

Ophelia beamed. "Yes, and wasn't it lovely?"

Evelia put a hand on Ophelia's arm. "Sister, we did agree that we would share this radio set. It would seem our beloved, genteel classical music will be pre-empted by those coarse, immoral stars of Holly-wood." She paused and smiled. "Excepting, of course, Mr. Crosby."

Evelia dabbed her nose with a lace handkerchief. "Very well. We will relinquish our control in favor of Mr. Crosby."

Ray noticed Peggy Lou primping in front of a mirror hanging on the wall just beneath the stairs. Peggy Lou motioned to Sue Carol to come over.

"Sue Carol, is my lipstick smeared?"

Sue Carol studied the woman's face. Her lips were bright red and seemed crusted with lipstick. "No. Did you use the entire thing?"

Uncle Lawson glanced over the top of his paper. "Then go put a sack over your face."

Aunt Wimpy dropped her knitting and slapped the man on his arm. "Lawson, that is enough. You don't have to be so cantankerous. Did you drink your prune juice this morning?"

Uncle Lawson glared at her. "We're not talking about my insides. I'm hungry. Isn't it almost time for Thanksgiving Dinner?"

Ann Lee shook her head. "Just as soon as the turkey is done. I don't think you'll starve to death. Now leave Peggy Lou alone."

Peggy Lou pouted her lips and glanced once again in the mirror. "Thank you, Ann Lee. He just doesn't understand how hard I work to make sure my natural beauty is showing."

The doorbell rang and Ray, for once, was glad to see the tit for tat end. His head was swimming trying to keep up with the conversation. Ann Lee glanced over her shoulder at the door, and Peggy Lou hurried across the room.

"I'll get it. It's probably my new boyfriend."

"New boyfriend?" Sue Carol asked.

Lonnie settled onto the other couch. "It is Thursday, you know."

Ann Lee headed for the kitchen. "What does that have to do with it?"

"A new day, a new boyfriend."

Ann Lee paused at the kitchen door and shrugged. "I think Mr. Castle's water is ready. Tell Peggy Lou's boyfriend I'll be right back." She disappeared into the kitchen.

Peggy Lou opened the door, and two men stepped in. The first man was small and slight in stature and as thin as a skeleton. He wore a black suit and a small, red tie. His limp, oily hair was combed back away from his sallow complexion. He had watery, dark eyes that seemed to dart around the room taking in everything. A pencil thin mustache sat on top of his thin lips. Ray blinked. He looked incredibly familiar. For a second, the image of a similar face flashed in his memory. But, the image was gone as quickly as it came.

The other man was smaller with reddish blonde hair and a youthful face. He wore the same black overcoat Ray had seen earlier when he had been in the library. The young man's eyes fell on Ray, and his face registered his shock and surprise. Ray looked away unsure what to do or say. He had no idea what the young man had been looking for, and for all he knew, he had been a part of Daniel and Buster's game.

The first man raised his eyebrows and ogled Peggy Lou. "Oh, my sweet, gorgeous Peggy Lou. If you don't look like the cat's meow. Come here and give me a squeeze."

Peggy Lou leaned into him, and the man hugged her tightly and planted a kiss on her cheek. Lonnie stood up from the couch and pointed his pipe at them.

"Wait a minute. I know you. You're Esau Cheatwood."

Esau released Peggy Lou but kept his arm possessively around her waist. "That is correct. And this is my son, Lazarus."

Lazarus peeked around his father's figure. "Glad to meet you. How did you know who we were?" He glanced once at Ray.

Esau slapped Lazarus on the back of his head. "He didn't recognize you, you brainless idiot. He recognized me! I'm the celebrity here." He turned his thin smile back toward Lonnie. "You must have seen my picture in the paper yesterday. I was awarded a contract by a huge oil and gas company to handle their account."

Lonnie shook his head. "Actually, there's a picture of you in the bathroom upstairs."

"What?"

"Frank told me your father owned this house before he sold it to Frank's father. Isn't that right?"

"That is correct."

"Well, your father must have left some photographs of you in this house from before you moved. Probably back when you were in high school. There's a picture of you upstairs, and someone drew horns and a goatee on it and labeled it 'Satan.'"

Esau's face reddened, and his eyes twitched as he glanced around the room again. "I never heard of such."

Lazarus took off his coat and hung it on the coatrack. "My grandfather probably did that to Daddy's picture. Daddy and Grandfather never did get along. Daddy never forgave him for selling the house to someone outside the family. Isn't that what you always said, Daddy?"

Esau's face reddened even more, and before he could speak, Ann Lee appeared from the kitchen with a large pot of steaming water. "Come along, Mr. Castle. I'll get your bath ready."

Esau glanced over at Ray. "You have a new tenant?" Esau's glittering eyes roved up and down Ray's clothes. "You look like something the cat dragged in."

Ann Lee stopped midway to the library. "Someone shot at Mr. Castle and left him on the sidewalk. We took him in until he recovers his memory."

Esau cut his eyes in Ann Lee's direction. "Amnesia, huh? Sounds awfully convenient. Not that I want to disparage your guest's status, but you realize he could be trying to hoodwink you."

Ann Lee sighed. "Mr. Cheatwood, I am well aware of how devious a man can be to get his way. I've read quite a bit about you in the newspapers. But, you are Peggy Lou's guest tonight, so I will refrain from telling you that I trust this man far more than I trust you. Now, Mr. Castle, come with me."

Ray's breath had quickened, and his heart raced at Esau's words. He fought for control and followed Ann Lee into the library. She closed the door behind her and led him into the bathroom. It was, indeed, drafty and colder than before. The temperature outside was falling close to freezing, and the room wasn't much warmer. Frank had carried a wide, metal washtub and it sat in the corner. Ann Lee took a rubber hose from under the sink and attached it to the small faucet above the sink. She ran some cold water from the sink into the washtub through the hose and struck a match to light a small gas heater in the corner of the room.

"Now, that will heat up the room in short time, Mr. Castle. When you're done, just turn it off to save money. Once the tub gets about six inches deep, pour this boiling water in, and it will be just right. There are towels and a rag in the shelf over there. Once you've taken off your clothes, put them outside the door. By then, I'll have your clean clothes waiting for you. Take your time and soak your muscles. We won't be eating for another thirty minutes or so."

Ray nodded and glanced around the room. "So, where's the shower gel and shampoo?"

Ann Lee opened her mouth and paused in puzzlement. "The what?"

Ray felt that eerie feeling of confusion and paranoia. What had he said? Shower gel? What was that? "I don't know, Mrs. Collinsworth. I'm liable to say just about anything."

Ann Lee pointed to the sink. "There's soap at the sink. Now, remember, don't let the water get any deeper than six inches or it'll be too cold." She opened the door to the bathroom and disappeared into the library.

Ray slipped out of his clothes and was shocked at the sight of huge bruises on his pudgy sides and back. He looked at himself in the mirror once again. He did not recognize the dark-haired man with the bruised and swollen face that looked back at him. He leaned into the mirror and looked deep into the eyes of his reflection. Who was he? How did he get here? He sighed and put his clothes outside the door.

He turned off the faucet and lifted the huge pot of steaming water and poured it into the tub. He stepped in and sighed as he settled into the warm embrace of the water. His aching muscles relaxed, and his skin began to sting. He wrinkled his nose in disgust. He smelled horrible. He took the rag and soap and scrubbed himself clean and washed dirt, sticks, and dried blood out of his hair careful to not dislodge the bandage. When he was finished, he got out of the water and was pleased to see the room had indeed warmed up as Ann Lee had promised.

Ray opened the door to the library and spied a pile of clothing sitting on the floor. He picked up the clothes and separated them. An old pair of boxer shorts with a hole over the right butt cheek was a little loose on him. He put on the white, cotton collarless shirt and it was soft in spite of its musty odor. He pulled on the worn, brown pants with patches over the right knee and left thigh. A pair of suspenders completed his ensemble. He sat on the commode and pulled a pair of dark wool socks over his feet and then slid his feet into a pair of worn, work boots. They were a bit snug, but he would manage. He stood up and glanced at himself in the mirror again. He combed his unruly dark hair back out of his face with his fingers and took the bandage off. The bloody gouge beneath was crusted with dark clotted blood. He placed the gauze back over the wound and pressed the adhesive tape in place.

In these clothes, he looked different. He looked like he belonged here in this house with these strange people. But, as strange as they seemed, they were the only people he knew. He reached up and pulled the chain on the hanging light bulb and turned out the lights in the small bathroom. A blue glow came from the space heater. He leaned over and twisted the knob on the side to turn off the flow of gas. The room descended into silence and darkness.

He opened the door into the library a crack and heard voices. Esau and Lazarus were in the library with the door closed to the living room. Esau held a small flashlight in his hands. It was the same flashlight Lazarus had used earlier when he had come into the house.

"Do you realize what you almost did in there?" Esau shook the flashlight in Lazarus' face.

"It just fell out of my pocket. I was going to tell them—"

Esau slapped the young man on the side of his head. "Tell them what? When are you going to learn to keep your mouth shut?"

Lazarus cringed after the blow. "That hurt. I was going to say I had used it to look for something. I was only telling them the truth."

"We don't deal in truth, Lazarus. We deal in perception. Understand? Now, did you find the deed?"

"No, Dad. Those two boys came into the living room, and I had to sneak out the window." Lazarus rubbed the side of his head. "And, that other fellow saw me but I don't think he recognized me."

Esau shook his head in disgust and began looking around the

library. "I know it is in here somewhere. My father always kept his valuables in this room. In a safe, I think. So, it is reasonable to think that Mr. Collinsworth did, too. We have to find that deed."

Lazarus followed his father as he walked along the wall covered with bookshelves. "But, the house belongs to Frank Collinsworth."

Esau paused and poked his son in the chest. "Have you been listening to a thing I told you before we got here?"

Lazarus seemed to be deep in thought for a second as he rubbed his chest. "Yeah, you said to make Miss Peggy Lou feel really special so that you could cozy up to her."

Esau raised the flashlight as if to strike his son and then shook his fist in anger. "I'm talking about the deed! See, this house should have been mine and all the property with it, and I want it back. There has to be a deed somewhere. We find the deed and sneak it out of here. Then, the house and the property both become mine."

The door to the library opened, and Peggy Lou peeked in. "Esau, you're ignoring me. I got this hat just for you."

Esau shoved the flashlight into a clear spot in the bookshelves and pushed his way around Lazarus. "And, honey, it is the cat's pajamas. You look swell. Why don't you go find us a place at the table, and we'll be right there?"

Peggy Lou smiled at him and went back into the living room. Esau turned back to his son and crossed his arms as he thought. "Now, Lazarus, I'll keep buttering up Peggy Lou. If we can't find the deed on our own, I'll see what she knows."

"Sure, Dad."

They left the library, and Ray stood alone in the dark bathroom. What were the two men up to? Were they looking for the deed to this house? Did they plan on taking it away from Frank Collinsworth? Why? His mind filled with strange possibilities.

"I *would have handled it differently. Making a move on the woman was a wise choice.*"

A voice echoed in the bathroom behind him. Ray whirled and for a second saw something dark hulking in the corner. His heart raced, and he fumbled through the air for the pull cord. He finally snared it and the room filled with light. The bathroom was empty.

The voice echoed outside the door in the library. *"If Esau weren't such an idiot he would realize all he has to do is go to court and asked for a review of the succession. That would have placed the deed into the hands of the court before anyone could sign it."*

Ray threw the bathroom door open and bounded into the library. No one was there. Was he hallucinating? Where had the voice come from? More importantly, where had these thoughts come from? He understood them. They were options he would have considered under the same circumstances. He stepped into the bathroom to turn off the light and for a second caught a glimpse of his face reflected in the mirror. His eyes were obscured in shadow, and for a second he saw another man lurking in the shadows behind him. He whirled, but the small bathroom was empty. Who had he seen? Just a shadow? He knew beyond a shadow of a doubt the shadow man was a conniving, devious man with no soul and no conscience. That man was no different from Esau Cheatwood.

Ray paused at the door to the living room and peeked through the cracked door. The occupants of the living room were now sitting around the dining room table. A huge, carved turkey occupied the center of the table. Ann Lee was pacing around the table with a worried look on her face.

"Where are Frank and Daniel? They were supposed to go for a short walk."

Uncle Lawson reached for a roll and Aunt Wimpy slapped his hand. "Not yet, old man."

"Well, this is a fine kettle of fish! Now that the turkey is done we can't eat until the other turkey is found." Uncle Lawson growled.

"The turkey is already at the table!" Aunt Wimpy said. "Lawson, would you just sit back and be quiet. They'll be back, shortly. Won't they, Ann Lee?"

Ray closed the door on the idyllic scene. It was straight out of a Norman Rockwell painting, whoever he was. After hearing the voice of the shadow man, he was so confused, and he felt so out of place. Perhaps he could take a short walk and see if anything outside triggered his memories. He could volunteer to find Frank and Daniel. He spotted a coat hanging on the desk chair. He pulled it on, and it felt warm and snug. He opened the door to the living room and noticed Esau and Lazarus standing at the front door.

"Don't you worry, Mrs. Collinsworth," Esau said. "I grew up in these woods. Lazarus and I will go find them." He pushed his son out the door and closed it behind him.

Ray backed into the library and shut the door. He didn't trust Esau any further than he could throw him. Wait! Lazarus had climbed out of the library through a window! It might be best if he went after Esau and Lazarus and kept an eye on them until Frank and Daniel got back. It was the least he could do for all that the Collinsworths had done for him. He retrieved Lazarus' flashlight from the shelf, slid open the window, and painfully climbed out into the frosty evening.

✣ 6 ✣

Ray stood on the dark front porch of the Collinsworth boarding house and tried to decide where to go. Esau and Lazarus had already disappeared into the surrounding trees, and all Ray could see from the front porch where the endless array of tree trunks disappearing into the distance. A long driveway wound its way up a sloping hill to the front of the house. If he held his head at just the right angle, he could make out the lights atop some of the taller buildings in downtown Shreveport through the branches of the trees. For a second, a towering building shimmered in his memory and then blew away like snowflakes in the wind.

Ray turned on the flashlight and covered the lens with his hand to keep the light at a lower level. He followed the porch around the side of the house and made his way down a stairway to ground level. The air was cold and moist with the rain of the day, but when he looked up at the night sky, he saw thousands of stars glittering in the blackness of space. A pathway worn in the dead grass led away from the house into the woods. He heard voices farther up the hillside, and he took the pathway deeper into the pine trees.

The pathway wound its way through the tree trunks, and Ray made out the voices of two men not far away. He saw the glimmer of a lantern and stopped as he spied Frank and Daniel Collinsworth in a small clearing. A large tree stump sat to one side of a green evergreen tree in the center of the clearing. It was slightly taller than Frank. The lantern sat on the stump and cast eerie shadows in the gathering night. The clearing seemed familiar. For a second he saw an image of an old man hunched over a cane sitting on the stump. He paused in confusion and tried to hold onto the thought. No, it wasn't a stump, it was something else. What? It slipped away like an eel.

"Boy, it's getting colder out here," Daniel said, rubbing his hands together.

Ray leaned against a tree and tried to gather his thoughts. Maybe he shouldn't interrupt this private conversation. Maybe if he listened and didn't interrupt they might say something about him they wouldn't say to his face. They might be hiding something about him. After all, they had come into the woods to talk. What were they hiding? Some deep, dark secret about Ray? He shivered, and the hair on the back of his neck stood on end. He whirled, and the long, lean shadows of the trees disappeared behind him into darkness. For a moment, he thought he saw a pair of glowing eyes and the shadow of a man. The shadow man! That's what it was! He shook his head in confusion and turned back to the clearing.

Frank Collinsworth looked up at the sky. "Yep, son, even though it is clear right now, I think a winter storm is coming. Feel that wind picking up?"

Daniel nodded, and his breath was thick and steamy in the cold air. "Daddy, you haven't said two words to me since we started out into these woods. Are you mad at me?"

Frank shook his head. "No, son. I have a lot on my mind. You see, Sunday I'm leaving to go help get our soldiers get ready in case the United States goes to war."

"You won't be here for Christmas?"

"I know it's a shock, son. But, I'll be back before Christmas. I promise. I'll be gone for a few weeks."

"Where are you going?"

Frank walked over and put a hand on his son's shoulder. "Well, I can't tell you. It's a secret."

"Gee whiz, a secret mission? My Daddy is on a secret mission! Just like Captain Freedom when he went after the Crimson Skull."

"Well, I'm not going into enemy territory. So, you needn't worry."

"You won't be rescuing anyone?"

"Not likely, son. I'll just be showing some recruits how to fly their airplanes."

Daniel had walked around the clearing and paused beside the stump. He bent over and picked up something from the dead grass. He held up a rusty ax. "Hey, Grandpa's old hatchet is still out here by that stump."

Frank took the old ax from his son and studied it. "Yeah, my Daddy put that ax in that stump before he died." Frank moved the lantern and sat on the stump. "My daddy moved here to Shreveport long ago and left me with the farm. I guess I was too pig-headed to see that farming wasn't a way to make ends meet during the Depression."

"Why did he leave the farm, Daddy?"

Frank studied the ground and seemed to be far away. "When my mother got sick, he moved them here so she could go to the Schumphert Sanitarium and that is where she died. A year passed, and my Daddy must have known he didn't have long left to live the day he brought me out here. Funny how a man can sense when the end is near. Anyway, he had this small cypress tree in a bucket and that old ax."

Daniel pointed to the tree in the center of the clearing. "You mean this tree right here?"

"That's the one. Daddy had a tradition passed down to him by his father and his father before him. On the day a son was born, the father would plant a new tree in the forest. And, the day the son was big enough to cut down the tree and bring it back by himself was the day that boy became a man."

"So, you planted this tree the day I was born?"

"Sure did."

Daniel looked back at the ax. "What happened to Grandpa?"

Frank touched the ax with a finger and sighed. "He had a heart attack."

"So, he was right about knowing he was going to die?"

"Yep." Frank's voice was a bare whisper.

Daniel looked away from the ax, and there was a hint of a tear in his eye. He wiped it away and looked over at the tree. "Daddy, why are you showing me this tree today? I'm only twelve. I'm not old enough to be a man, yet."

Frank stood up and took his son by the shoulders. "Well, Daniel, I've got a feeling in my bones. I think a worse storm is coming than this cold wind blowing."

Daniel pulled out of his grasp and whirled around to face him. "Daddy, don't say that! You're scaring me."

Frank reached for his son, and he backed away. "Daniel, we've got to face reality. The United States is not going to stay out of this war much longer. Soon, we'll be right in the middle of it. And, when that happens, my country is going to need me. I won't be at home to help take care of your mother and your sister. So, I'm giving you a mission."

Daniel paused in his retreat and the expression on his face lightened. "A mission? What kind of mission?"

Frank crouched down, so he had to look up to his son's anguished face. He took the medal out of his pocket and held it up. "You're going to be MY hero, Daniel." He pinned the medal on Daniel's shirt. "You see if something happens and I get . . . delayed, I want you to be the man of the house."

Daniel backed away with a look of horror on his face. His hand strayed to the medal. "Daddy, I don't want to be the man of the house. I just want you to stay home."

Ray realized he was holding his breath and he had to look away from the painful scene in front of him. For some reason, he knew exactly the pain that Frank was talking about. A great and horrible evil was coming, and he knew it. He felt it in the air and saw the ravage and damage it was going to do to this family. He gasped for breath and fought for control. The feeling of dread was worse than the fear the shadow man drove into his heart. In the clearing, Frank grabbed his son and crushed him to his chest in a tight embrace. Ray felt tears stinging his cheeks, and his heart ached.

Frank pushed his son gently away and studied his face. "Daniel, we don't have any choice in the matter. There's evil that's sweeping over the world; a huge, dark shadow that has to be stopped. Listen, Captain

Freedom works hard to defeat the Nazis, right? Wouldn't you like to be like him?"

"Daddy, you're talking about something real, not a comic book. I don't want you to go. And, I don't want to be a man, either. That old tree can just grow and grow forever. I'll never cut it down. Never!" He stomped away and turned his back on his father.

Frank looked over at the tree and then back at the stump. "I'm sorry you feel that way, Daniel. But, we don't have much choice when it comes to growing up and taking charge. I never asked to be a pilot. My whole life, there have been twists and turns that brought me to where I am today."

Frank sat on the stump and picked up the ax. "God saw the path I needed to walk. His plan for my life was different than the plan I had for my life. I had always dreamed of being just a simple farmer like my father. Sometimes I long for the simple life of a farmer, plodding along behind the swaying backend of a mule pushing the plow into the earth, watching the corn grow. But, things didn't happen that way. I learned to fly. I liked it. I was good at it. And, if I had stayed on the farm, those four men I rescued would be dead."

Daniel glanced over his shoulder at his father. "That doesn't make me feel any better."

Frank took the ax and thudded it into the soft wood of the stump in one fluid motion. The sound echoed through the trees. "I know. One day you'll understand. One day you'll stand here and realize you have a choice to make. I had to make my choices to follow the path that God chose for my life. And, I'm glad I did. Daniel, just make sure you make the right choices for the right reasons." Frank stood up. "Now, I'm going to head on back to the house. Thanksgiving Dinner should be ready. You coming?"

Daniel shook his head and kept his back turned to his father. He touched the medal hanging from his shirt. "No. I want to be alone for a bit. I'll come on in a minute."

Frank reached out and almost touched his son on the shoulder and then he turned and made his way down the path back toward the house. Ray slid around the tree trunk out of Frank's sight as he passed him in the darkness. Something on the other side of the clearing moved out of the trees and Ray watched Buster peek out from behind a tree trunk. His face was pale and his eyes sunken.

Daniel was oblivious to his cousin, and he ran over and kicked the tree stump in anger. His face twisted in agony and hopped around in pain holding his foot.

Buster stepped into the clearing. "That was a stupid thing to do."

"Buster! What are you doing out here?"

Buster hugged his stomach. "Trying to get over my green stomach. That tobacco made me sick."

Daniel lowered his foot to the ground and tentatively walked on it. "Serves you right for sneaking into my Daddy's things."

"Wait a minute! You were looking, too. If you hadn't of been so yellow, you would have tried it."

"I'm not a coward! Leave me alone!"

"Sorry. I heard what your Daddy told you."

"Yeah, so what?" Daniel shrugged.

"I know how you feel." Buster sat on the stump. "My Daddy talks all the time about going over and kicking some Nazi's bottoms. I don't want him to go, either."

"Yeah, I guess we're in the same boat. Only, your daddy won't be gone soon."

"I know that. But, one day, he will go." Buster stood up and looked off into the trees. "Hey, somebody's coming, and I don't think it's your Dad."

Daniel squinted in Ray's direction, and he ducked behind the tree. Esau and Lazarus Cheatwood stepped out of the woods not far to Ray's right and entered the clearing.

"There you are. The whole clan is waiting at the table to partake of Thanksgiving Dinner, and the two of you are playing Tarzan." Esau drawled.

"Who are you?" Buster asked.

Daniel nudged him in the side. "He's Aunt Peggy Lou's boyfriend."

"She has a new one?"

"It's Thursday, ain't it. Your Daddy says she has a new one every day."

Esau's mustache crawled as he frowned. "I can assure you two young men that my relationship with Peggy Lou is much deeper than you think. She is the apple of my eye."

Lazarus slapped his father's back. "And the core of your spirit."

Esau glared at him. "Don't try to be too creative, son. You might hurt yourself. Now, if you youngins will head on back to the house, we can get our dinner underway."

Daniel and Buster shrugged and ran off down the path right toward Ray. Ray stepped back out of the way, and they never saw him as they passed. Ray started to follow after them, but he glanced one more time at Esau and Lazarus. Esau was studying the stump and the surrounding trees and took out a small notebook from his coat. He turned slowly as he surveyed the clearing.

Lazarus watched his father with interest and Ray decided to keep hidden. Lazarus motioned to the trees. "So, this is where your buried treasure is?"

"That's right. Somewhere in these woods, my father buried a fortune."

"And, that's why you need to find the deed, right? So you can get the property back?"

"That's right." Esau closed his notebook. "And, when we get into this war, the man with that treasure will get richer."

Lazarus suddenly frowned. "But, don't we need to give it to the government so they can use it to fight the war?"

Esau slid the notebook into his pocket and slapped his son on the back of his head. "No! And to think you are my son. You must have gotten your brain from your mother's side of the family. They were all daft! No, when we get into this war, the armed forces are going to need things."

"Yeah, like rations and coffee and cigarettes and posters of Lana Turner!" Lazarus rubbed his head.

"I'm talking about tanks. And airplanes." Esau stalked across the clearing. "And battleships. And jeeps. Son, we are going to use that treasure to make our fortune. Oh, son, it's the American way to squeeze every penny out of our resources when we sell them to the needy. The good old, capitalistic, American way."

Lazarus nodded. "Greed!"

Esau nodded enthusiastically. "Avarice!"

"Riches!"

"Stocks!"

"Bonds!"

Esau slapped his son on the shoulder this time. Lazarus cringed for a second and then smiled in appreciation of his father's admonition. Esau smiled broadly. "You're catching on. Now, when we get back to the house, you have to look around for that piece of paper. You almost got caught this morning, but I know it's somewhere in the Collinsworth library. I'll continue to woo the attention of Peggy Lou for as long as it takes for us to stay in the house until we find that deed. Got it?"

"Yes, sir. You know, I like Miss Peggy Lou. Are the two of you getting married?"

Esau turned his nose up as if he had stepped in something foul. "Heavens no! Once we find that paper and claim this treasure for our own, then I'll drop her like a hot potato."

Ray watched them leave. He stepped into the silent clearing and retrieved the lantern Daniel had left behind. He felt something stir behind him. He glanced over his shoulder, and his shadow stretched behind him. He jerked back toward the comfort of the lantern's light.

"*You feel it, don't you?*" A voice whispered harshly behind him. He closed his eyes, and his heart raced.

"Who's there?"

"*The real you. The forgotten you. Think about it. You understand them. You are like them. You get it.*" The voice continued.

Eyes still closed, Ray cringed as a cold mist flowed over his shoulders. "No! I'm nothing like them. Nothing!"

"*You know I'm right. Their plans excite you! Stop and think. You have nothing. You are no one. How will you survive? Think about his plan. If you help him out, there might be some reward in it.*" The voice grew stronger, and a cold breath chilled his right ear.

"No!" Ray whispered weakly.

"*It wouldn't be so bad to have a plan, now would it? Only the strongest will survive, and the weak will falter. You need a plan. Just think about it.*" The voice slowly faded, and the cold mist fell away.

Ray opened his eyes to the warmth of the lantern and turned. The clearing was empty. There was some truth to what the shadow man had said. He did have to survive. But, he didn't want to hurt the people who had reached out to him. Either way, he couldn't get the sound of that voice out of his head.

Ray's stomach growled loudly, and it startled him. He was hungry. Survival? He had no idea if tomorrow he would have a meal and a roof over his head. Time to consider the shadow man's words. Just consider them, he thought. He started down the path to fill his stomach with Thanksgiving turkey.

❧

WHEN RAY ENTERED THE LIVING ROOM, HE FOUND EVERYONE seated at the dining room table. Ann Lee motioned to an empty chair next to hers.

"Come on, Mr. Castle. We saved you a place at the table."

Ray paused behind the empty chair and slowly took off his coat. His face warmed with shame. He did not belong at this table. These people were total strangers to him. Why did he feel this way?

"I'm sorry, Ann Lee. I'll wait in the library for some leftovers."

Esau nodded. "Smart choice."

Peggy Lou poked his arm. "Don't say that, Esau. It's Thanksgiving."

Frank stood up at the head of the table and motioned to the chair. "The sooner you have a seat, the sooner we can eat, Ray. Everyone is welcome at our table."

Ray slid into the seat. "Thank you."

Frank motioned to Lawson. "Uncle Lawson is going to say grace. Or, at least read a prayer he saw in the newspaper. Lawson?"

Uncle Lawson nodded and held up his folded newspaper. "Well, ya'll go ahead and bow your heads. I'm going to read this prayer by Clarence Hawkes, the Blind Poet of Hadley, Massachusetts who has been sightless for 59 of his 72 years."

Everyone bowed their heads and closed their eyes. Ray kept his eyes opened and watched the people gathered around the table sit in silence.

"God of peace and not of passion, Full of mercy, truth, and love. Let us turn from earth's commotion, And look this day to Thee above. Let us turn from earth's dark rancor, And from thoughts of bitter strife. Let us pluck out hate's dark canker, That would blight human life. Let us for all mankind pray For peace and love Thanksgiving Day."

Lawson paused and cleared his throat again. "Show us how to lead in concord, How to banish human strife, How to heal the wound that's rancored, How to lead in Christian life."

Ray cut his eyes to Esau. The man's gaze was directed across the room toward the library and the clear, predatory glare of his eyes sent a chill down Ray's spine.

"Save the race from its inventions, Bid all turbulence be still. Fill mankind with good intentions,"

Here Esau grinned and licked his lips. For a second, his eyes cut toward Ray, and he winked. Ray looked quickly down at his plate.

"In obedience to Thy will. God bless our land, for it we pray. And all the world Thanksgiving Day. Amen." Lawson looked up and smiled. "Now, we can dig in!"

❈   7   ❈

Headlines The Shreveport Times
  Saturday, November 22, 1941

*Japanese American negotiations for a Far Eastern settlement were at a standstill
tonight. Tokyo's special emissary, Saburo Kurusu and Ambassador Kichisaburo
Nomura were not among the callers at the state department during the day, nor
was any appointment made for the resumption of the conversations tomorrow.*

*Tanks are maneuvering in a strange land battle in North Africa. The British
armored legions and their Nazi rivals navigate the desert sands by star and sun
sights and radio beams as sailors find their way about the wide seas.*

*Save today on Christmas gifts! "Elgin" bicycles equipped for boys or girls are on
sale for $25.50 at Sears. Shop today from 9 a.m. to 9 p.m.*

*Beware the cough that hangs on! Creomulsion relieves promptly because it goes
right to the seat of the trouble to help loosen and expel germ laden phlegm. Tell
your druggist to sell you a bottle of Creomulsion!*

"She's a baby" to the lads in Guy Lombardo's orchestra, for off the air she's fifteen-year-old Jean Miller singing parody solos and duets with Kenny Gardner on the Lombardo program on CBS-KWKH tonight at seven o'clock.

Monroe man is held on draft count! An American born German with a swastika and the word "Hitler" tattooed across his chest was charged here today with violating the selective service act by not having a registration card.

The annual Tulane – L.S.U. Freshman football game, which serves as an appetizer for the clash between the varsity teams, will be played Saturday afternoon. The varsity aggregation will collide at New Orleans the following Saturday.

❧

"**D**ad? Dad? Where are you?"

Ray wandered through a dense fog that spilling out of leafless trees. Pale light diffused through the limbs. He tried to peer through the fog. "Son? Is that you?"

In front of him, a small shadowy figure hurried across the path and disappeared into the fog. "Dad? Dad?" The tiny voice echoed through the forest. Ray stumbled down the path. He stretched out his hands into the thick fog. Had he heard his son?

"Ray? Mister Ray?" The voice was closer now, and the figure moved toward him through the fog. It emerged into view. Pale blue eyes stared at him from beneath a shock of blonde hair. A red mask partially obscured the boy's face.

"Son?"

The mask lifted. "No, Mister Ray. It's me. Daniel. Wake up."

Ray sat bolt upright on the cot and gasped for breath. Daniel Collinsworth stood over him. "What? Who? Where?"

"Gosh, Mister Ray. I didn't mean to scare you." Daniel pulled his mask back over his face. "It's just Mom said to tell you breakfast is ready. And, if you wait too long, Uncle Lawson will eat it all."

Ray's breathing slowed, and he stood up. He was in the library. Sleeping on the cot. In the Collinsworth boarding house. In a tattered pair of old pajamas that once belonged to a dead man. Why had he thought he would be anywhere else? The dream of the boy in the fog was fading. "Thanks, Daniel. I'll just wash up in the bathroom, and I'll be right there."

"Swell!" Daniel started toward the door and paused. He turned back. "If you don't have anything to do this afternoon you can go with Buster and me to the new Roy Rogers movie. It's at the Saenger theater, and Peggy Lou got us some free tickets. It's called 'Jesse James at Bay.'"

"Roy Rogers? I remember him. Has a horse named Trigger."

"Yeah, that's right."

"Okay, I'll think about it."

Ray stepped into the bathroom and took care of his business. He washed his face and slicked back his hair. He stared at the eyes looking back from an unfamiliar face. He half expected the shadow man to appear behind him. He didn't. He slid into his pants and shirt from the day before and pulled on socks and shoes. He had spent most of Friday in the library. Every time he entered the living room, he felt out of place. But, by Friday night, his new "family" made him feel more comfortable. Perhaps it had been the absence of Esau and Lazarus Cheatwood. Peggy Lou and Esau had gone to a nightclub to dance. Ray napped most of the day as he recovered from his head wound.

Uncle Lawson was already finished with breakfast and sitting in his leisure chair. His face was hidden by his newspaper.

"Ray?" Ann Lee said as she stood up from the table. "There's some scrambled eggs left and Sue Carol's famous biscuits. And, some fig preserves."

"No bacon though." Wimpy stood up from her plate. "Lawson gobbled it all down."

"That's okay." Ray sat next to Lonnie and felt his stomach rumble. "I have to watch my cholesterol."

Lonnie leaned away from him. "Your what?"

"Cholesterol," Buster said through a mouth full of eggs. "We studied that in biology last week."

Ray spooned scrambled eggs onto his plate and snared a biscuit. "Any gravy left?"

"Yep." Daniel sat on the other side of him and handed him a bowl. "Mom makes the best gravy in the state."

Ray ladled gravy on his biscuit. The eggs were wonderful, filled with flavor and cooked just right. Not like the eggs he was used to. He paused in mid-chew. What kind of eggs was he used to? He ignored the thought and finished his meal. He wiped his mouth and slurped some coffee. "Well, it's no skinny latte, but that coffee is good, and that is the best breakfast I think I've had in a long time."

"Skinny what?" Lawson said from his chair.

"Lot A?" Lonnie said. "Hmmm. Maybe you sell used cars?"

"I am NOT a used car salesman!" Ray blurted out and then blinked furiously as the strange thought faded.

"Sorry," Lonnie said. "I didn't mean anything by it."

"No, I'm sorry. I just don't know where some of these things come from. It's like little bubbles coming up out of the deep, and they are just tiny glimpses of my lost memory."

Ann Lee took his plate. "Not to worry. Now, it's your turn to wash the dishes, Ray."

Ray glanced up at her and bit his tongue. He hadn't washed dishes since his childhood. Or had he? Where had that thought come from? He suddenly saw himself standing before a huge metal table with a rubber-clad circular opening before him. Middle school students were sliding their lunch trays at him. Food bounced and covered his rubber apron. Some of it got on his face. They glared at him. They laughed at him. But, he had to wash dishes while he was at school. He got his lunch for free. It was the only way he could afford it, his father had told him.

"Ray? Ray?" Ann Lee said gently. "Are you okay?"

Ray shook his head as the memory rapidly faded. "I just recalled a memory. I was washing dishes at school when I was a kid."

"Then you ought to be good at it." Sue Carol said as she came out of the kitchen. "We all have to do our share of the chores."

The front door opened, and Frank Collinsworth stepped in. He shrugged out of his coat. "Getting cold out there. They say it might snow."

"Where have you been, Daddy?" Daniel asked.

"Had a meeting at Barksdale at 0600 hours, son."

"Breakfast?" Ann Lee asked as she hurried up to him and kissed him on the cheek.

"No, I had some lovely powdered eggs and spam at the officer's club. Ray, how are you this morning?"

"Fine, it seems. Although I think I'm on kitchen duty."

"Nope," Franks said. "You and I are going to have a little talk on the back porch."

"Lawson!" Wimpy called from the table. "Looks like you're up for dishwashing."

Lawson slapped his newspaper into this lap. "I don't think so. We cleaned up last night after dinner. Besides, I'm reading this article about a 70-year-old who married her 25-year-old student."

"What?" Lonnie stood up.

Lawson pointed to the paper. "Over in Fort Worth says right here a 70-year-old missionary is marrying a 25-year-old theology student. Says right here that they don't care what people think about their age. Theirs is a marriage made in heaven."

"Wish mine had been." Wimpy stood behind him. "Now, get up and let's get to it."

Frank laughed. "Lawson, next time it's your turn, Ray will fill in. Won't you, Ray?"

Ray sighed as he followed Frank toward the back porch. "Sure."

Frank opened the back door off the living room and motioned outside. Ray stepped out onto a partially enclosed back porch. Frank followed and shivered. "What's on your mind?"

Frank motioned to the walls of the porch. "I'm enclosing part of the porch to make another bedroom. Lawson and Lonnie are helping me at night. I'm leaving tomorrow for my secret mission, and I need to talk to you."

"I was expecting as much."

"Ray," Frank paced across the porch, "I've worked with hundreds of men over the past few years. I've got a pretty good sense about when someone is a bad apple or not. I have a good feeling about you. Don't know why. Maybe it's just the good Lord telling me to trust you." He paused and turned his intense blue eyes on Ray. "Can I trust you, Ray?"

Ray tried not to think about the shadow man. "I hope your intuition is right, Frank. I don't remember a thing about my past. But, for some reason, I feel like I need to fit in here. It feels like this should be my home." Ray chased away thoughts of the shadow man. "I might be keeping secrets, but if I am, I don't know what those secrets are, and I don't know why I would be keeping them." Ray looked away. "The fact is, I don't know where I belong right now."

"Well, I'd like you to stay on for a while until you get your memory back. But, that means you'll have to pull your weight. I don't expect you to get a job right off. But, I talked to Ann Lee and there a lot of chores you could help out with. Have you had any experience in construction?"

"I don't know."

Frank walked over to him and held out his hands. "Let me see your hands."

Ray placed his hands in Frank's hands. Frank turned them back and forth. "Well, you have a well-manicured hand, Ray. No callouses. I don't think you're used to hard labor."

Ray pulled his hands away and studied them. Frank was right. "I guess not."

"Well, you'll soon build up lots of callouses. Lonnie will tell you what needs to be done next. We need to finish out the walls for the enclosed porch and put up some insulation and plaster. Then, you can paint it. Shouldn't take you but a week or so." Frank took Ray's arm and turned his attention toward the backyard.

"Now, you see that tree back there? It fell during the summer, and I had a friend come over and cut it up into three-foot logs. What I need you to do is split those logs into fireplace size pieces of wood. Daniel's chore after school is to stack the firewood. Yours is to split it."

Ray felt his face warm. How dare this man tell him to split firewood! That was menial labor! That was – he closed his eyes and pushed the thought away. "Split the logs?"

"Ray, I can't let you stay here free of charge. We're barely making ends meet now even with everyone paying a paltry rent."

Ray drew a deep breath. "You're right. I don't like to accept charity. Or pity. I'll do my best."

"I'll get Lonnie to show you how it's done. But, take today and tomorrow to recover and start on Monday." He held out his hand.

Ray glanced at it and then shook it. "I will, Frank."

Frank leaned closer. "I have a very bad feeling about this mission."

Ray raised an eyebrow. The feeling of dread and oppression surfaced again, and he swallowed. "I'll do my best, Frank. But, it seems you've already been a hero once on a secret 'mission.' What's so different about this one?"

Frank looked over Ray's shoulder back into the house. "Let's go for a walk." He hopped down off the back porch and led Ray around the side of the house. They reached the front sidewalk and Frank pointed to a path that led up into the woods. "I need to tell you something important."

Ray sighed. Should he tell Frank he had overheard his conversation with Daniel in the woods? Not now, the voice whispered in the back of his head. He's keeping secrets so you should too! Ray shook his head to chase away the thoughts and followed Frank into the woods. They made their way up the path to the top of the wooded hill, but Frank did not veer towards the clearing with the tree. Instead, he paused at the apex of the hill and turned to point toward the city a few blocks away.

"Take a look, Ray. The Commercial National Bank is the tallest building downtown. Seventeen stories. Air conditioning, if you can believe it. The elevators work on their own without operators. Shreveport is growing in leaps and bounds. We've got servicemen and their families moving into Bossier City to work at Barksdale Air Field. It won't be long until we're in the war." He picked up a rock and tossed it into the trees below him.

"What's your point, Frank?"

"You came from somewhere out there. I don't know where. You don't know where. Your memory has all your secrets locked away. Truth is, I haven't been totally honest with my wife and kids." He studied Ray's face. "For some reason, I feel I can trust your judgment. I can tell you the truth about the mission where I received the medal. It's important you know the truth about me, Ray." He stepped closer and his gaze bored into Frank's. "Because I'm trusting my family around you for the next few weeks until I get back at Christmas. I need to know you can keep my secrets so when the day comes, and you have back your memory, I can keep yours. Understand?"

"I guess."

"I joined the Army Air Corp about the same time as a man named Claire Chennault. He's a native of Louisiana. Best pilot I've ever seen behind a joystick. He used to fly his biplane with his two buddies as the 'Men on the Flying Trapeze.' Beat me to the punch. I had two buddies who were ready to do the same act at an airshow in 1937, but after we saw Chennault, we backed out. I joined the Army Air Corp right after we moved here. One of my buddies was a test pilot for the P40. He invited me to visit the test site. Sorry, I can't tell you where." Frank laughed. "It's another secret I have to keep. That airplane is incredible. What power! It's a bit unwieldy in the air but it is fast and powerful, and I could nosedive out of the sky with blistering speed. While I was at the test site, I learned all I could about the P40."

Frank moved over to a fallen tree and sat on the log. "About six months ago I got a call from Chennault. And, this is where you have to be quiet. If you repeat what I'm about to tell you, I'll deny everything and tell people you're crazy. Because that's how crazy this story is."

Ray sat beside him. "Go on."

"Chennault has been in China for the past few years trying to help them form an air force to combat the Japanese. You don't hear much about it in the newspapers or the newsreels, but the Japanese are beyond brutal to the Chinese. They live by the three 'them alls.' Kill them all. Loot them all. Burn them all. Chennault came to Washington D.C. a few months back and met with some Army Air Corp people. Turns out FDR wants Chennault to help out the Chinese, but the U.S. can't appear to take sides. So, the U.S. gave about 50 brand spanking new P40's to Chennault, and he sent out a call for pilots. Ray, there's a lot of us pilots who are hankering to get into the war. Almost a hundred signed up along with almost 200 support personnel."

"So you joined up with Chennault?"

"No, it would mean resigning my commission with the Air Corp. But, my buddy who flew the P40s is now high up in the Army Air Corps leadership, and he volunteered me to visit Chennault and make sure he knew how to fly the P40. Kind of silly. Chennault can fly anything with wings."

"It was really a spy mission, wasn't it?" Ray said.

"Spy is a harsh word. They just wanted someone independent to get an eye on the operations. That was me. I couldn't tell anyone where I was headed, Ray. Took me days and days to get across the Pacific on a Dutch cruise ship. I had to pretend to be a newspaper reporter. Then, more time in trains, cars, and rickshaws until I arrived in British controlled Burma, right on the border of China. The British were willing to risk an uneasy truce with the Japanese to help Chennault and the Chinese government."

Frank wiped his mouth and shook his head. "What an operation. Hot, humid, mosquitoes as big as hawks. Mud and rain everywhere. And who should I run into but my old flying acrobatic buddies, Ziggy and Rocko."

"Ziggy?" Ray said.

"Robert Zigfield. Like the Zigfield of Zigfield Follies?"

Ray shook his head. "Not familiar."

"Yeah, amnesia. Right. And Rocko was Anthony Rockford. They were my trapeze guys on the acrobatic tour. Both of them would strap themselves to the wings of our biplane and stand straight up while I did rolls. They were looking for adventure and signed up for the American Voluntary Group. The AVG, the name for Chennault's little air force."

Frank sighed. "As good as it was to see them, the place was so depressing. But, right in the middle of this haphazard operation, Colonel Chennault was a figure of repose and strength. Not so most of the men. Some of them had no idea what they'd gotten themselves into."

"Like the four that got taken by the Japanese?"

Frank chuckled. "I couldn't tell Daniel the real story. Want to hear it?"

"Yeah."

LIEUTENANT FRANK COLLINSWORTH TAPPED HIS FINGERS ALONG TO the beat of "Boogy Woogie Bugle Boy" coming from the radio. The station was on the distant edge of Burma and broadcast by the British, so it was filled with static. But, the big band sound reminded him of home. He wiped sweat from his forehead and studied the notebook before him. He had made copious notes for the pilots on the nuances of flying the P40. Most of his tips were already known by Colonel Chennault. But, he had a few seemingly insignificant suggestions that might make the difference between a pilot getting shot down by a Zero versus the opposite. In spite of the shaky nature of his "mission," he had to justify his reason for being here.

"Lieutenant Collinsworth!" The door to the ramshackle shack flew back on its rusty hinges. The sergeant ran into the room and almost knocked Frank's small desk over.

"What it is, Hap?"

Hap pulled off his cap and pointed through the open window at the dusty dirt airfield outside. "It's Ziggy and Rocko."

Frank rolled his eyes and put his face in his hands. "What have they done now?"

"Well, they took a transport and drove up into the mountains."

Frank looked at Hap through his spread fingers. "Into the mountains? I'm afraid to ask, but why?"

Hap gazed at him sheepishly. "They wanted to hunt tigers."

Frank stood up, as his face warmed with anger. "Tigers? Hunt tigers?"

"Just got a radio call from them. Turns out they wandered over into Chinese territory."

Frank smacked his forehead. "Tell me it doesn't get worse."

"Uh, they were surrounded by a Japanese patrol, and they called for help then said they were smashing the radio. Can't let the Japanese know why two Americans were out hunting tigers." Hap wrung his cap in his sweaty hands. "Want me to tell the old man?"

Frank paced around the office. This was bad. No this was worse than bad. If the Japanese learned about the AVG and the growing Chinese air force and the presence of P40s, it could have worldwide repercussions. "The fools! No, don't tell Chennault just yet. Let me see if I can find them."

"With what?"

Frank paused and looked out his smudged and dirty office window. "Can't take a P40. But, there is that old biplane. I took it up a few days ago just for fun. I can land it just about anywhere." Frank whirled. "Go load up the guns on it and get it fueled. And throw a couple of ropes into the cockpit. I'll blow those two fools to kingdom come if I have to, so they don't talk."

"Frank, you'd blow up our own guys?"

"This is bigger than two rednecks hunting for tigers, Hap. Get to it."

Frank changed out of his uniform into a flower shirt over his pants. He shrugged into a leather aviation jacket with no markings. If he was captured, he could claim to be a lost newspaper reporter.

Outside his window, Hap was all over the biplane. The biplane was a Hawk IIs Curtiss F11C Goshawk sold to the Chinese air force in the late 1930s. Frank had flown one at Barksdale Air Field before the Army Air Corp switched over to Boeing P12. The biplane had a 600 horse-power Wright radial engine, single-leg cantilever main landing-gear units, metal, rather than fabric covered control surfaces, and armament based on two .30 inch fixed forward-firing machine guns supplemented by a hardpoint under the fuselage for the carriage of a 474-pound bomb. Hap finished getting the biplane ready, and Frank glanced toward the main building. All of the other pilots were in a teaching session with the old man.

Frank grabbed his aviator cap and goggles and ran to the biplane. He patted Hap on the shoulder. "If he asks, tell the old man I took it out for a test run." Hap nodded and motioned to a Chinese mechanic who helped Frank climb up onto the wing and into the cockpit. The airplane was an older model before the semi-enclosed cockpit had been added. As he settled into the seat and pulled on his cap, a sense of calm and wonder descended. This was what he was meant to do. He started the engine and felt the power of the airplane surge through him. He smiled as he turned the plane toward the landing strip. He pulled a picture of Ann Lee, Daniel, and Rachel out of his flight jacket pocket and wedged it next to the speedometer.

"Don't worry honey. I know I promised I wouldn't be flying into combat, but I've got to find those two men. I know you'll understand." Then, he glanced upward at a blue sky as brilliant and bright as a robin's egg. "And, Lord, I don't know why you decided to make me a pilot instead of a farmer, but be with me today. Help me find those men." He pulled his goggles over his eyes and the ship hurtled across the bumpy dirt airstrip and into the sky.

Frank flew low along the brushy hillside and up the mountain ridge toward Chinese territory. As he neared the mountain ridge, rain pelted his face. He flew right into a heavy downpour. Great! Things could get worse, it seemed. The biplane trembled and wobbled in the sudden gust of wind. But, Frank held her steady. He was used to flying into Louisiana thunderstorms, and this storm, as ominous as it appeared was pretty tame compared to those storms. This might actually be a blessing in disguise. The thunder and wind might hide his engine noise.

Below, through the driving rain and mist, he could barely make out the rutted winding dirt road Ziggy and Rocko had most likely taken up into the mountains. He almost wished they had encountered a tiger and the tiger had won! The road snaked across a ridge and descended the other side into a wide valley. He wiped the rain from his goggles and squinted into the gray morning overcast. Just ahead he saw the transport truck poised on the rise in the road. It sat at the edge of an open field of low growing grass. The Japanese had to be somewhere close by. But, what should he do? He cut the fuel to the engine, and it sputtered and died. He coasted silently across the open field. Grass had been pressed down by another transport vehicle, and the trail led to the far edge of the field. Ziggy and Rocko stood with their hands behind them just inside the tree line facing him. Four Japanese soldiers with their back to his approach had no idea he was coming. To the soldiers' right sat a Japanese transport truck. Frank wobbled the airplane wings and veered away to his right. Ziggy had seen him!

He waited until the airplane was almost down into the tree lines to start up his engine and he hoped and prayed the Japanese had not heard it. He gained altitude over the thick jungle and circled back toward the field. This time, he killed the engine and reached for his machine gun. He targeted the transport vehicle and hoped against all hope Ziggy and Rocko could read his mind. He grew closer and closer to the Japanese as they talked among themselves. His finger poised on the trigger and he motioned toward the truck when it seemed Ziggy was looking right at him.

Frank was close enough to see Ziggy nod and Ziggy threw himself against Rocko, taking both of them to the ground. The Japanese reacted, and Frank pressed the trigger on his machine gun control. The bullets tore across the grass and found the transport truck and its fuel tank. It exploded in a violent cloud of fire and smoke, and Frank flew right through the top of the acrid cloud of smoke.

He banked quickly and turned the airplane back toward the field, hoping he had enough remaining lift to clear the trees and land in the grass. His landing gear clipped the top of the trees, and he tore through the grass as his wheels bounced on the rough ground. He spun the airplane around with its last momentum and pointed it back across the field.

Already, Ziggy and Rocko were running across the field toward him. There was a problem. The airplane had a one-man cockpit. But, he had thought ahead. He hopped out and threw a coil of rope around the lower wing of the biplane close to the fuselage. He repeated it on the other side just as Ziggy and Rocko arrived.

"Frank! You're a sight for sore eyes." Ziggy gasped for breath.

"No time for me to chew you guys out." Frank pointed to the rope. "The old rodeo trick from our routine. Strap yourselves to the wings while I get the engine started."

Ziggy laughed and slapped Rocko on the shoulder. "Just like old times, eh?"

Rocko frowned. "We weren't getting shot at by Japanese, Zig. Let's get out of here."

Frank hopped back into the cockpit and started the engine. Ahead, he heard voices through the falling rain and thunder. More Japanese soldiers were coming! The propeller whirled, and he gunned the engine. "Boys, it's now or never."

The airplane began bumping across the field with the Japanese to his right. He saw their heads bobbing above the tall grass as they approached. Bullets whined nearby, but he was already a moving target. Ziggy and Rocko were prone on the wings, tied close to the fuselage and just as he reached the far tree line, the plane groaned under the extra weight and lifted from the ground. The landing gear clipped trees, but they were airborne. Frank banked once to the west and wiped the rain from his goggles to clear his vision. Ahead, the transport truck from the air base came into view. He grabbed his machine gun and pulled the trigger. The bullets found their mark and the transport exploded. He couldn't leave behind evidence of their presence. For good measure, he timed his approach and released the bomb from beneath the fuselage. As he turned toward the southwest, he caught the bright explosion as the bomb fell close enough to the transport to incinerate any remaining evidence of their visit. He glanced out of the cockpit at Ziggy and Rocko hugging the wings for dear life. They both gave him a thumbs up as he climbed out of the rainstorm and into bright, morning sunshine.

Frank laughed with exhilaration. As dangerous as this entire process had been, it gave him the rush of his lifetime. They had evaded the Japanese and blown up two transports in the process. And, Ziggy and Rocko were alive! A shadow passed over his face, and Frank glanced up into the sky. To his east and above him, a Japanese Zero had flown through the sunlight heading west. It was ahead of him so the chances it had seen him were low. The Zero was headed for Burma. Had their adventure given the Japanese cause enough to buzz the British in Burma? If the Zero flew over their base, they would see the P40s waiting for their eager pilots. A cold wave washed over Frank. He couldn't let that happen. He had to stop the Zero!

The biplane's maximum speed was around 200 miles per hour, and that was without two bodies lashed to the fuselage! He had caught only a glimpse, but chances were this was the newest Zero intelligence had discovered. If so, it had a maximum speed of close to 280 miles per hour and was much more maneuverable in a dogfight. Without thinking, Frank grabbed the machine gun control and fired off a flurry of bullets at the receding Zero before it could get out of range. It worked!

The Zero began banking back in his direction. Now what? He heard a pounding on the fuselage and glanced over at Ziggy. He was waggling his finger at his temple and mouthing, "Are you crazy!"

"Yes!" Shouted Frank as he banked back toward the clouds moving across the mountain ridges. He was safely inside the nearest gray cloud when the Zero finished its turn to head back in his direction. Rain lashed at the biplane, and the wings shook under the turbulence of the thunderstorm winds. In his mind, he visualized the Zero; saw it coming closer. If it stayed on course, it wouldn't enter the storm. He pounded the side of the fuselage and Ziggy glanced at him through squinting eyes.

Frank gave him the old signal for a barrel roll, hoping he would remember it. He gave the same sign to Rocko. He pulled back on the stick and aimed high into the clouds, pushing the biplane to the limits of its stalling speed. He ticked off the distance the Zero should have covered.

"Now!" He screamed and turned the airplane upside down. It curled on its side as he pulled out of the downturn and he felt the wings shudder with the increased speed. He righted the airplane just as they shot out of the cloud now a hundred yards lower than where they had entered. Would the Zero do as he predicted?

Frank grabbed the machine gun control and wiped the rain from his goggles as the cloud burst from around him and they shot into the sunlight. The Zero was coming right at them! He squeezed the trigger and let loose a volley of bullets and then executed another barrel roll. The Zero plowed through the space where he had just been and exploded into a fireball of flame and heat. Frank righted the biplane and looked over his shoulder. The disintegrating Zero disappeared into the moving storm cloud. He yelled in triumph and felt the wings shudder. Ziggy and Rocko were both pounding the airplane in joy.

Frank made it over the last ridge and followed the winding road traveled just a couple of hours before by the would-be tiger hunters. He felt something wobble and looked at Ziggy. The man was climbing up onto the top wing with the rope securely binding his feet. Rocko was doing the same thing. What were they up to? The fools!

Ziggy pointed to the approaching air base and gave the sign for the barrel roll. It would be just like their old acrobatic act; the one they had abandoned when they saw Claire Chennault's act back in the 1930s. What the heck, Frank thought. If both of them died, so be it. What a way to go. He tilted the airplane sideways until it was upside down just as they roared down the runway and over the main buildings. The entire company was out in the yard cheering and yelling and standing on the very top of the tallest building was Colonel Claire Chennault with his binoculars pressed to his eyes. Ziggy and Rocko pumped their fists as they hung upside down from the upper wings and barely missed Chennault by a couple of feet. Frank righted the airplane and banked around to make his landing.

❧

"Sounds like you were a real hero after all," Ray said.

"Yeah, the old man dressed all three of us down, but he couldn't ignore the fact I had managed to shoot down a Japanese Zero with an old biplane. He saw the whole thing from the roof. Chennault was no fool. He knew that what we had just done would do wonders for the morale of the Chinese air force and our pilots and crew. And, that was more important than Ziggy and Rocko's insubordination. So, we held a ceremony. Chennault pinned a medal on my chest. I actually met Chiang Kai Chek and his wife! Then, he pulled me into his office and told me to go home and tell the Army Air Corp to leave him alone. I got home about three weeks ago."

"Still, it was a good story for Daniel."

"Although not entirely true. I couldn't tell my family all of the truth. This war turns a man into a split personality. There's the good side of me that wants to love my family and be truthful with them. And, then there is the warrior side of me. That side of me that has to be willing to do whatever it takes to beat the evil in this world. And, sometimes, that takes a man down a dark pathway." Frank fixed his gaze on Ray. "I don't know which pathway you will choose to walk, Ray. I may not be here when your memory returns. If war breaks out and I don't get to come home when I want to, I'll need a man I can trust around my house to help protect this strange family of mine. Can you be a hero, Ray?"

Ray averted his gaze. In his mind he saw the luminous green eyes of the shadow man. "I won't deny that I probably have a dark side, Frank. Somebody shot at me. Why? I don't know. I'm hoping it was because I was doing the right thing."

Frank stood up and stretched. "Ray, there is a reason I took you in."

"Yeah, you said it was the right thing to do."

Frank nodded. "Let's head back down to the house. You promised to go to the movies with the boys."

Ray stood up and followed him. Frank's breath steamed in the cold. "Ray, when Ann Lee and I lived on the farm, the Depression had just begun. Men would wander up to the house almost every day. I looked them in the eye and tried my best to understand their motives. I wanted to chase most of them away. But, every time a wanderer showed up, Ann Lee would give them something. It might have been an old biscuit or a roast beef sandwich. We didn't have that much to give."

They came to the house, and Ray followed Frank up onto the front porch. "I asked Ann Lee why she did it." Frank looked into Ray's eyes. "Want to know why?"

"Sure."

"*Be not forgetful to entertain strangers: for thereby some have entertained angels unawares.* From Hebrews. Ann Lee always said one of those strangers might be an angel. And, she told me, Jesus always said what we did to the least of these we also did unto Him."

Ray almost squirmed under Frank's relentless gaze. "What's your point?"

Frank stepped closer. "I've told you my deepest secret Ray. Somewhere locked in that memory of yours are secrets you will not want to share. Are you an angel, Ray?"

Ray looked away, and for a second the voice of the shadow man whispered in his ear. "*Ah, secrets! The dust of darkness. You have leverage now!*" He closed his eyes and drew a deep breath.

"No, Frank, I'm no angel."

He felt Frank's hand on his shoulder, and he looked back into the man's deep, blue eyes. "Ray, we all have a dark side. If it weren't for that darkness in our soul, we would never long to do good. One day, after the need for secrecy, is gone, I'll tell Daniel the truth. But, for now, I have to be a flawed hero in your eyes only. I'm no angel, either. But, I'm hoping for everyone's sake that, like me, you are on the side of the angels."

Ray managed a smile. "I'll keep all of the secrets, Frank. You can count on me."

❧   8   ☙

Ray settled into the seat in the darkened movie theater. Daniel sat beside him, and Buster munched on popcorn on the other side of Daniel. The screen flickered in black and white.

"More newsreels?" Buster said. "Golly, I just want to see the movie."

"Shh!" Daniel said as he grabbed a hand full of popcorn from his own paper container. "They may say something about the Nazis."

The black and white image of a castle appeared with the logo "Castle Films" superimposed. Daniel punched Ray.

"Gee, Mister Ray, you may be a movie producer."

Was he? Ray dredged through his mind. "No, if I did, they would have better graphics."

"Graphics?" Buster leaned forward and stared at Ray. "What's that?"

"You know, C.G.I.," Ray said and then shook his head in confusion. "Never mind. I don't know what I'm talking about."

A title appeared on the screen. "The World's Biggest Bomber in the World Passes Tests."

Daniel poked Buster. "See what I mean? My Daddy could have flown that bomber on his last mission."

A crowd appeared and watched as a huge airplane taxied across the runway. "In Santa Monica, California," the narrator said, "the world's biggest bomber waits for its maiden flight. Compared to a pursuit plane, the big Douglas B19 looks and is tremendous." A large airplane with a bulbous nose and huge wings moved down the runway. "The giant has never been flown before. And everyone is tense as she starts to take off." The airplane accelerated down the runway and took to the air. "She's off easily and quickly. She'll be flying to a nearby Army field. Now, the flaps are down and the landing gear deployed." The airplane glided smoothly onto the runway with a bouncy landing. "Once more the wheels bounce and the largest and most powerful airplane ever built comes smoothly to Earth in a symphony of engineering genius."

B19? Ray rubbed his eyes. What about the B52? What was that? Again, his confused thoughts surfaced. The newsreel moved on alternating benign stories of a photographer on a California beach with stories of the British fleet sinking German subs. Throughout the newsreel, the boys cheered and their eyes stayed glued to the screen. Ray felt the anxiety surface again. Frank would soon be journeying to Hawaii far away from the European action depicted in the newsreels. But, Ray couldn't calm his growing certainty that bad things would soon happen. He tapped Daniel on the shoulder.

"I'm going to the restroom." He stood up.

"Hurry back, Mister Ray. The movie's about to start."

"Oh, no. There'll be fifteen minutes of previews."

Daniel glanced at Buster and back at Ray. "Mister Ray, sometimes you don't make much sense."

"I know." Ray sidled down the row of seats and the aisle to the lobby.

❧

"So, what did you think of the movie?" Daniel chewed on his popcorn as they walked through downtown Shreveport back toward their house.

"Well," Ray paused, "Let's just say it was awfully black and white. Not enough shades of gray."

Buster threw a piece of popcorn into the air and caught it in his mouth. "Shades of gray? What are you talking about?"

"He means it wasn't in color like 'The Wizard of Oz,'" Daniel said.

"No, that's not what I meant," Ray said as he thought about the conversation he had earlier with Frank. "It's just that in real life, good and evil aren't so cut and dry; not so black and white."

Daniel stopped and stared at Ray. "What's that supposed to mean?"

"Golly, are you saying that the Nazi's are good guys? Cause if you are, then it means you really are a spy." Buster said.

"No, of course not."

"But, the Nazis are bad," Daniel said. "Gee whiz, there ain't nothing good about them."

"Well, I have to agree with you on that. But, not everything in life is that clear." Ray said.

"Ok, so what you're saying is that if I think it's a good thing to rob someone, then I can go right into that Woolworth's store over there and pick me up a new flashlight and just walk out with it," Buster said.

"Buster, you've wanted that flashlight forever. You can't steal it. Stealing is wrong. Isn't that right, Mister Ray?" Daniel said.

"Yes, stealing is wrong." Ray fumbled for words. "Look, I don't know what I'm trying to say exactly. There are bad people in the world, and there are good people in the world."

"Like my father." Daniel nodded. "He's a real hero. He saved those men from the Japs."

"Yeah, and he knocked a couple of those Japanese soldiers in the head, didn't he?" Ray said.

"They deserved it," Buster said quietly. "I heard my Daddy and Uncle Frank talking about some of the things those Japanese did to the Chinese. I don't want to even think about it."

"You think what they did to the Chinese was right? That it was good?" Daniel asked.

"Well, no," Ray said.

"Mister Ray, you're making no sense at all. Either you're a hero or a villain. It's just that plain simple."

Frank drew a deep breath. He couldn't very well share Frank's real story with them. Every hero has a dark side, he wanted to say.

"And, what we have here, standing with you two impressionable young men is, no doubt, a villain." Someone said behind them.

Ray whirled, and Esau Cheatwood strode toward them. "You filling these boys' minds with your mumbo-jumbo, Mr. Castle. If that is your name." Esau drew himself up before them and glared at Ray.

"Of course not. We were just discussing a movie."

"I heard something about shades of gray. Good and evil."

"You should know," Ray said.

Esau stiffened. "What's that supposed to mean?"

"You're a businessman. All businessmen have to bend the rules to make a killing." Ray smiled. "Why, I bet you're cooking some kind of scheme right now to jerk the rug out from under some unsuspecting victim while smiling in her face."

Esau's lip turned up in a sneer. "Her? You talking about Peggy Lou? Well, listen here, if you think you've got a chance with my girl, you've got a few things coming." He reached out suddenly and poked Ray's bandaged forehead. Ray winced with the sudden pain and stepped back. He felt a trickle of warm blood run from under the bandage.

"Hey!" Ray shouted. "Keep your hands off me."

"Or what? You'll get violent?" Esau said. "Boys, did you ever wonder just why Mr. Castle was being shot at? I saw you come out of that cowboy movie. The cowboys in white hats were shooting at Jesse James, right? How do you two know that Mr. Castle isn't just as bad as Jesse James?"

"What's going on here?" A policeman in a dark blue uniform appeared behind Esau.

"Officer." Esau smiled. "Let me introduce you to a stranger in town who is hoodwinking these young boys and their parents. Go ahead and ask him for some kind of identification. Go ahead."

The officer raised an eyebrow. "I'm sure this man is just fine, Mr. Cheatwood."

"Well, look at the blood coming from under that bandage. Ask him how he got hurt. He was shot at, officer." Esau grinned.

The police officer studied Ray. "Do you have some identification?"

Ray wiped the blood on his hand onto his pants leg. "Uh, no. Fact is, officer, I don't even know what my real name is. I have amnesia."

"See!" Esau said. "I think you should take him down to the station and protect these innocent boys from his evil influence."

"I'm not evil!" Ray said. "I'm just confused."

"Golly, officer," Daniel stepped between Ray and the policeman. "Mr. Castle is just fine. He's not a criminal."

"Although he might be a Nazi spy." Buster glanced out from behind Ray.

"Hey!" Daniel shouted at Buster. "He's not a spy!"

The police officer took off his cap and scratched his head. "Maybe I should have you come down to the station, sir."

Ray started to agree when Esau interrupted. "Good idea. He's taking advantage of the Collinsworth family."

Ray blinked as his head began to throb. Pain lanced from the wound into the depths of his brain. "I'm not taking advantage of anyone. I hate being pitied and I don't take charity."

"Well, I know how we can decide this. I just saw Frank Collinsworth back there in the barber shop. I'd like a word with him." The police officer hurried away, and Esau turned a triumphant gaze on Ray.

"Say goodbye to your sweet deal, Mr. Castle. Not even Frank can save you from this one."

Ray clenched his fists and fought off a growing headache. Before he could speak, Frank and the police officer joined them.

"Ray?" Frank said. "Your head is bleeding? What happened?"

"Mr. Cheatwood hit him," Daniel said. "Right on his cut."

"I did not hit anyone," Esau said. "I merely pointed out that any man who has been shot must have been involved in some kind of nefarious deal and that this good policeman should take this stranger down to the station."

Frank glared at Esau. "No one asked your opinion, Esau. I'm betting everything was just fine until you poked your nose into things."

Esau stepped closer to Frank. "Like you poked your nose into my family's business?"

"Not in front of the boys, Esau."

"Why not? Shouldn't your boy know that your father stole that house and property right from under my nose?"

"Your father and my father were best friends. When your father died, he made the right decision in giving that house and property to my father. As I recall, he had thrown you out of the house when you tried to foreclose on your own father!" Frank's face was red with anger.

"All right!" The policeman stepped between them. "Enough of this. I don't care about some family feud. Frank, is this man staying at your house with your permission?"

"Yes." Frank rubbed his face. "And, on Thanksgiving Day when we found him on the front porch, I talked to the Sheriff, and he told me to keep an eye on him until his memory returned."

Esau chuckled. "There you go, officer. I'd call that collusion."

"Officer, may I speak to you for a moment?" Frank said.

They walked away, and Ray grimaced as the headache lessened but continued to pound away. Esau pulled his overcoat tighter around his lithe figure. "I think we're about to see the end of you, Mr. Castle."

Frank walked back to them and stood silently. Esau studied him and looked back and forth between Frank and Ray. "What did he say?"

"You can ask the officer yourself." Frank smiled.

"Where is he?"

"Putting a ticket on that car down the block. The meter ran out ten minutes ago. I noticed it when we left the barber shop." Frank pointed over his shoulder. "I wonder whose car that is."

Esau leaned to the side to look past Frank and swore. He ran down the sidewalk toward the officer. Daniel put his hands over his ears. "Gee, Daddy, if Momma heard me say something like that she'd wash my mouth out with soap."

Frank tousled the boy's hair. "You're right, Daniel. Now, let's get out of here before Esau comes back to give Mr. Castle more grief. I think I need a piece of apple pie."

❧

RAY FOLLOWED FRANK AND THE BOYS AND GLANCED UP AT THE bright sun. His headache was growing worse.

"Ray, in here," Frank said.

Frank and the boys led Ray into the Woolsworth department store diner on Texas Street. Bright, cheery Christmas tunes filled the air from a radio sitting behind the marble-topped ice cream bar. Silver tinsel hung from the ceiling in arches. Red and green foil bells hung from the tinsel. Almost every booth and table was full. Ray wrinkled his nose at the mixture of cigarette smoke and fried food. "I didn't think you could smoke in these places."

"Yeah, I wish that were true." Frank motioned to an empty table. "Ann Lee doesn't let anyone smoke in the house except for Lonnie and his pipe. I never smoked."

"But, you tried that chewing tobacco, right Dad?" Daniel plopped into a seat.

"Don't mention chewing tobacco." Buster leaned his head onto the table. "I was sick all night."

"You don't swallow it, Buster," Frank said. "You spit out the juice."

Ray massaged his eyes. "My head is killing me."

"You just need some coffee and a piece of Aunt Lorraine's apple pie," Frank said.

A portly woman in a stained apron hurried to the table. Her hair was short and salt and pepper in color. She wore a pair of small lensed glasses. "Frank! I missed you last week."

Frank stood up and hugged her. "Thanksgiving, Aunt Lorraine."

"Well, Slats and I missed you. Who is your friend?"

"Ray Castle."

"Oh, the amnesiac." Lorraine nodded. "Bet you didn't realize I knew such a big word."

"I'm sure that word is in your daily crossword puzzle."

Ray shook his head. "Slats?"

"Uncle Slats," Daniel said. "Dad, can I have a chocolate malt?"

Frank glanced at his watch. "We'll be eating supper in a couple of hours. Don't want to ruin your appetite."

"That boy's appetite never goes away." Lorraine ruffled Daniel's hair. "You're twelve now, right?"

"Yes, ma'am." Daniel smoothed down his hair.

"Well, I never gave you a birthday present. One chocolate malted coming up. Buster, what'll you have? A chewing tobacco shake?"

Buster straightened in his chair. "What? Who's been telling on me?"

"News travels fast around here." Lorraine nodded to Ray. "I heard Ann Lee calling the doctor on the party line. It didn't take long to put two and two together."

Ray sighed. "I'll try some coffee and pie, then. Maybe it'll help my headache."

Lorraine nodded and walked away. "She's my father's sister," Frank said. "Married my father's best friend. They call him Slats because he's so funny, he kicked the slats out of the bed on the day he was born he laughed so hard. That's what they say. Lorraine was the cook for Saline High School, and Slats was the janitor. She made homemade biscuits for the students every morning. But, the Depression got to them, so they retired and took the job of managing this diner about two years ago. As you can see, business is booming."

"And, her apple pie?"

"Best you'll ever eat. The recipe is a secret."

Lorraine returned with a tray of food. They each received a piece of golden, flaky apple pie. Buttery syrup oozed from the crust. Sugar crystals sparkled on the top pie crust. She passed a cup of coffee to Frank and Ray. She sat a tall glass filled with chocolate malt in front of Daniel. She put a hand on her hip.

"You never told me what you wanted." She said to Buster.

Buster shrugged. "I ain't got no money. I spent it on popcorn."

Frank shook his head. "Son, I'm buying. Get what you want."

Buster straightened and pulled his ever-present aviator cap off his head. His hair stood on end with static electricity. "I'll have a malt. And, a piece of the pie."

Ray put a bite of pie in his mouth, and it melted on his tongue. It was the most exquisite apple pie he had ever tasted! He closed his eyes and enjoyed the flavor as he chewed. He sipped the black coffee and waited. Surely the caffeine would kick in and stop his headache. But, instead, the minute the pie hit his stomach nausea overcame him. He stood up quickly. "Where is your restroom?"

"Back there." Lorraine pointed to the back corner.

Ray hurried through the crowded tables and barely made it to the bathroom stall before the contents of his stomach emptied into the toilet. He fell to his knees, and his head pounded even more. What was happening? The room began to spin, and he slumped back against the door of the stall. It opened, and he collapsed on the floor. The light burned into his eyes and he moaned with pain.

"Someone help me." He managed hoarsely.

"Ray?" Frank leaned over him. "You okay?"

"No!" Ray shouted. "My head! It's killing me."

The room swam in endless circles, and he fell into darkness.

$\maltese$ *9* $\maltese$

Headlines The Shreveport Times
    One Week Later, Saturday, November 29, 1941

The ominous Japanese-American situation reached a new point of gravity today with the capital's most authoritative quarters asserting in effect that this country's last word has been said as the question of peace in the Pacific depends upon Tokyo's next move.

A group of 34 landowners and taxpayers of the city of Alexandria through their representative in federal courts here yesterday sought to block the construction of two USO recreational buildings for military personnel in two of the city's parks.

The Tulane vs. L.S.U. football game can be heard on KRMD today at 1:45 P.M.

"Jimmy Davis and His Music," who now share their program with "Cousin Emmy and Her Kinfolks" will take the air 15 minutes earlier beginning today at 5:15 P.M. on KWKH.

"Sergeant York" starring Gary Cooper is currently showing at the Strand Theater. Prices are Main Floor, 50 cents, Balcony 40 cents, children 25 cents, and

colored 25 cents. Cary Grant and Joan Fontaine star in "Suspicion," currently showing at the Majestic Theater.

Independent Drug Store at the corner of Marshall and Milam is serving a special lunch, meat, two vegetables, salad and a drink for 24 cents. For supper meat, two vegetables, salad, and hot biscuits 30 cents. Served every day except Sunday. Phone 6150-6159.

Leading stocks dropped to a new low ground for more than a year in today's market as United States and Japanese relations appeared near the breaking point.

***

"It was a real bargain. I only paid $34.88 for it! I've been saving up my pennies for months now so we could get one. I can't believe Sears had that water heater on sale! Now, we can all have hot water whenever we need it."

"Between the kitchen and three bathrooms, you'll have to rotate everyone."

"I know. I got Frank to make out a schedule before he left for his secret mission."

Sniffles. Someone cleared her throat.

Ray winced as he opened his eyes. Even though the room was mostly in darkness, what little light came through the distant windows burned his eyes. "Where am I?"

"He's awake! Sue Carol, go get the nurse." Ann Lee leaned into his vision. "Ray, do you know who I am?"

"Yeah. An angel of mercy." He whispered. "No more apple pie, please?"

"Oh, it wasn't the pie. Doctor McKay said you had a concussion from the gunshot. Just took a few days before your brain began to swell. Now that you're awake, you must be getting better."

Ray slowly sat up in the bed and regretted it. The room swam, and he blinked his eyes.

"Take it slow and easy." Ann Lee helped him sit up on the side of the bed.

Ray studied the long room in which he found himself. There were a dozen beds arranged along the outer walls. Patients sat or lay in each bed. "Where am I?"

"The Schumphert Sanitarium, Ray. You're on the men's ward."

"I didn't get a private room?" He rubbed his head.

Ann Lee laughed. "Now, I know you're delusional. No one around here can afford a private room. Except maybe the mayor. Ah, here's the doctor."

A short, gray-haired man appeared beside Ann Lee. "Well, you finally woke up, Mr. Castle. I must say you are one lucky individual. I was afraid your brain swelling wouldn't go down." He put Ray through a dozen physical tests, flashing a penlight into his eyes and listening to his chest with a stethoscope.

"Did you do a CAT scan?" Ray asked.

Doctor McKay froze. "Mr. Castle, I'm not a veterinarian, if you must know."

Ray blinked. What was he talking about? "Sorry, I'm not making much sense."

"That's to be expected. Now, everything seems to be returning to normal. Excellent. I'd like to keep you one more night, and then Mrs. Collinsworth can take you back to the boarding house."

"Can Daniel come sit with Ray?" Ann Lee asked.

"How old is he, now?"

"Twelve."

Dr. McKay rubbed his chin. "I suppose so. But, only during visiting hours."

"How long have I been here?" A wave of weakness passed over him. Ray patted his stomach and listened to its growl. "I've lost weight."

"We have fed you through an I.V. and a feeding tube." Dr. McKay said. "Yesterday, you showed signs of improvement, so I pulled every-thing. I wanted to make your body push you to wake up and eat."

"Pulled everything?" Ray asked. He looked down. "Even that?"

Ann Lee put a hand over her mouth. "Oh, my. I don't need to hear this."

"Yes, I pulled all of your tubes, Mr. Castle. You've been in and out of a coma for a week now."

Ray's mouth fell open. "A week? Then, Frank is gone on his mission."

"I'm afraid so." Ann Lee said. "Now, about Daniel? He's out in the waiting room."

"Sure." Doctor McKay said. "He'll talk Mr. Castle's ears off, but that will be good stimulation for him." Ann Lee headed out of the ward.

"I am hungry. A week?" Ray said.

"And, we will start with soft food, young man." Doctor McKay said. "Your stomach has been mostly empty for a couple of days.

"Mister Ray?" Daniel ran to his bed. "Golly, are you okay? I thought we had lost you. I told Daddy that apple pie was loaded with too much butter and sugar."

Sue Carol laughed. "And, your chocolate malt wasn't?"

"Gee, I didn't even get to finish it."

"I'll buy you one when we get out of here." Ray said.

"No rich food for a couple of days after you go home, Mr. Castle. Now, if you'll excuse me, I'm going to listen to the rest of the LSU Tulane football game on the radio in my office." Doctor McKay turned and walked away.

"What day is it?" Ray asked.

"Saturday," Daniel said. He leaned toward Ray and motioned to his open jacket. "I brought some of my comics." He whispered. "But, we can't let Mom know. She's heading back to the house for a while and then she'll come back and get me when visiting hours are over."

Ray glanced over Daniel's shoulder. The doctor and Carol Sue were gone. "I think the coast is clear."

Daniel grinned and pulled three comic books out of his jacket. "Captain America is my favorite." He held up a comic book. On the cover, Captain America had delivered a right hook to Adolf Hitler. "He knocked the block off of Hitler!" Daniel tapped the cover.

"Yeah, I've seen this comic book. In a frame. In an office. In a very high building." He rubbed his eyes. "What am I talking about?"

"In a frame?" Daniel laughed. "Why would you put a comic book in a picture frame?"

"Because one day, these comic books will be worth a lot of money. They're collector's items, Daniel. You need to take very good care of them. They'll be worth lots of money. You'll see." Ray sighed as the strange memory faded.

"But, they're just comic books, Mister Ray."

"I know. But, Captain America is a symbol of everything that is truly American, right? Truth, justice, and the American way?"

"Naw, that's Superman," Daniel said. "I like Cap better. That's why I made up my own superhero. We need lots of heroes, like my Daddy, to defeat evil people like Hitler." Daniel leaned sideways and looked right into Ray's eyes. "And, Hitler's no shades of gray, Mister Ray. I'm sorry if you don't feel that way. He's evil, and he has to be stopped."

Ray felt that familiar sense of unease; of anguish; of foreboding. "I'm afraid you are right, Daniel. I don't know what I was talking about earlier. War is brewing all over the world."

"Uncle Lonnie says it's coming to America." Daniel studied the cover of his comic book. "Sometimes, Mister Ray, I get scared. Like when my Daddy has to go off on a secret mission. What if something happens to him?"

"You can't think about that, Daniel. Your Daddy is a real hero, and he'll be able to handle whatever is thrown at him." He tried to smile. "Why, he might get to punch Hitler's lights out one day. Imagine that!"

Daniel's gaze shifted into the distance. "He took me out in the woods the other day and showed me a tree that was planted on the day I was born. I think he was trying to tell me that one day I would be the man of the house." Daniel sniffed and wiped at his nose. "I don't want anything to happen to him. I don't want to be the man of the house!"

Ray watched a tear fall onto the cover of the comic book. The boy was in pain, and he had to do something to encourage him. But what? This was unfamiliar territory to him.

"Tell him to straighten up, or you'll give him something to cry about." The voice whispered in his ear.

Ray glanced over his shoulder. Shadows covered the corner of the ward on the other side of his bed. *"Remember what Dad did to you? For every tear, you got a stripe, remember?"* The voice whispered in his other ear.

Ray stood up quickly and backed up against the near wall. "Stop it! Leave me alone!"

Daniel fell back onto the floor, and his comic books slid under the hospital bed. "What did you say, Mister Ray?"

Ray pressed his hands against the cold plaster of the hospital ward wall. He closed his eyes. "I'm sorry, Daniel. I wasn't talking to you."

Daniel reached under the bed to retrieve his comic books. "Who were you talking to?"

"Bad memories," Ray whispered. "Some of them are trying to come back, and they're not good ones."

Daniel slid the comic books into his jacket. "Gee, Mister Ray, I didn't mean to get you all upset." He wiped tears from his eyes. "It's just that I'm worried about my Daddy. And this war. And Hitler. And the Japanese. They're coming from all directions."

Ray looked down at the boy standing before him, and for a second, another face swam into existence stamped over Daniel's. It was the face of a younger boy with blonde hair and blue eyes. The face faded and Ray sat on the edge of his bed.

"I'm sorry, Daniel. I don't know how to be a father. I don't know what to say."

Daniel nodded. "Well, if my Daddy were here he would hug me. So, I'll hug you." Daniel wrapped his arms around Ray's waist and embraced him tightly. Ray held his arms out to his side, unsure of what to do until he felt hot tears trickling from Daniel's face onto his shoulder. He slowly closed his arms around the boy and held him while he cried.

❧ 10 ❧

Battle tide at Moscow turned for Soviets, declare Russians. Nazi flight continues as Reds counter attack around the capital. Remnants of the elite German mechanized army routed from Rostov are fleeing to their doom in a Russian trap Soviet sources claimed tonight.

Spies and saboteurs in a vast anti-Fascist revolutionary movement were charged with attempting to assassinate Premier Mussolini, blowing up munitions plants and wrecking trains in which hundreds of Italians were killed.

Goldring's cordially invites you to a personal preview of advance fashions for cruise, resort and early spring presented on mannequins by Miss Sayre, New York stylist, in our salon de couture on the second floor Wednesday and Thursday from 9:30 a.m. to 4 p.m.

Idle cotton lands can produce food. Growing food crops for national defense may prove the salvation of the cotton farmer who has many acres of land made idle by acreage allotments according to the U. S. Department of Agriculture "food for freedom" program.

Motion pictures of the living body much clearer than the faint image of the present day fluoroscope are feasible said Dr. W. Edward Chamberlain of the invention of the electron microscope and the electronic television machine. He believes this revolutionary development is just around the corner!

Army faces a shortage of material; men are urged to apply. Brig. Gen. H. R. Harmon at Randolph Field, Texas said today that the army was faced with an imminent shortage of pilot material. "There is considerable apprehension that we may be near the point of exhaustion, but we feel that many young men are holding back. We wish they would come forward and join the air corps."

"Trouble is the easiest thing in the world to borrow, and it's one of the few things that can be successfully home-brewed," so sayeth the homespun philosopher, the Duke of Paducah on tonight's "Plantation Party" broadcast on KTBS at 7:30 o'clock.

The 1941 Gusher, the yearbook of Byrd High School, has been awarded a first place rating in the Columbia Scholastic Press association's Yearbook Critique and Contest according to Richard Huebner, faculty sponsor of the book.

❧

"**R**ay, your memory seems perfect when it comes to cussing," Lonnie said.

Ray leaned on the ax and fought for breath. "Sorry. It's just so frustrating."

Lonnie took his pipe out of his pocket and clamped it between his teeth. "If I cussed like that, my momma would come clean all the way up here from Castor and wash my mouth out with soap."

Ray glanced at his hands. Three new blisters had come up on his right hand. "I just can't seem to get the hang of it."

Daniel ran up behind Lonnie. He wore a flannel shirt over jeans and a corduroy jacket. "How's he doing, Uncle Lonnie?"

Lonnie raised an eyebrow. "We're gonna get mighty cold if it snows tonight."

Ray sighed and sat on an upturned log. "Sorry, guys. I don't seem to have all of my stamina back. Besides, there ought to be a better way. Some kind of machine that can split these logs."

Lonnie laughed and took the pipe out of his mouth. He pointed it at Ray. "Ain't no machine ever going to be able to do this, my friend."

"Hey, Uncle Lonnie, I'm done with today's homework, and supper's not ready yet so why don't you let me help Mister Ray?" Daniel said.

"Can't hurt. I'm going in and try to warm up some." Lonnie headed back into the house.

"Daniel, I just don't have the strength to do this. In my former life, I must have been a wimp."

"A wimp? What's a wimp?" Daniel asked.

"Me." Ray shrugged. "Just another meaningless word from my mysterious past. Look, about Saturday."

"What about it?" Daniel said

"Uh, in the hospital, you know." Ray avoided the boy's innocent gaze. "When we, uh, hugged?"

"Oh, yeah, and I cried?" Daniel leaned into him. "I won't tell anyone if you don't. Especially Buster."

Ray nodded. It wasn't exactly what he had been thinking. He was more concerned with his uncomfortable reaction to Daniel's embrace. What kind of father was he? If he did have a son, somewhere, what kind of relationship had they had? Or, rather, did they have?

"Let's forget about it, Mister Ray. It's Wednesday and three days since you got out of the hospital. I know you still feel weak, but, if I can split a log, you can split a log." He reached down and managed to stand a log on end. "Now, look here, Mister Ray."

"Ray. Just call me Ray."

"I can't do that. Dad wanted me to call you Mr. Castle so calling you Mister Ray is bad enough. Anyway, if you look at the rings of this tree, you can learn all about its life." He ran a finger across the rings in the end of the log. "What you got to do is find out something tragic that happened in the tree's life."

"Tragic?"

"You know like a forest fire or a disease. You know, trees get sick, too."

"Yeah, I know that."

Daniel studied the log. "Okay, right here. See this line? It crosses several rings? That's something that hit this tree pretty hard. And, the tree almost didn't get over it. It crosses a bunch of rings, so it took a while for the tree to get over it." Daniel stooped down and picked up a metal wedge. "Now, Mister Ray, once you see the tree's weakest spot, then you put this wedge up against it."

He placed the pointed end of the wedge against the line. "You line it up with this line because this is the log's weakest spot."

"And you always want to go for the weakest point," Ray said. A tingle ran down his spine. This, he understood.

"Yeah, attack this log at its weak point, and it will split right down the middle. Kind of like finding out what your arch enemy's weakness is."

"His kryptonite," Ray said.

"Yeah! Like Superman and kryptonite. Right." Daniel reached out his hand. "Let me see that ax."

Ray handed him the ax. He turned the blunt side of the ax down toward the wedge and gently tapped it until the wedge was seated in the line. "You got to be real gentle and slow at first. Kind of have to sneak up on the log."

Daniel stepped back and brought down the blunt side of the ax onto the wedge. The ring of metal hitting metal echoed through the cold air, and a crack appeared in the top of the log. "There, you see? Now that you've got a little crack in the log, you can go ahead and give it all you got. You start with a small crack and let it spread down into the log. Here," he handed the ax back to Ray. "Try it."

Ray lifted the ax above his head and brought it down on the log. The blunt side impacted the wedge and with a snapping sound, the log split in two. Ray smiled and laughed. "Take that, you log."

"That's the way, Mister Ray." Daniel smiled. He pulled something out of his pocket. "Here. These are my Daddy's gloves. You'll need them to help with the blisters."

The gloves were dark brown, and he ran his hand over the soft, well-worn leather. He pulled them on and winced as they touched his blisters. They fit perfectly, and the difference was staggering. He nodded at Daniel. "Daniel, thanks for being my hero today. I'll see how many of these logs I can split by the time supper is ready."

"Well, I'm going to go study a little bit. I got a 'rithmetic test tomorrow." He ran back to the house. Ray hoisted the ax on his shoulder and let himself bask in the glow of this accomplishment. It was small. It was almost insignificant. But, it was something he had never done, and now he had mastered it.

"Find that weak spot." A voice whispered behind him. He whirled. No one was there. Only the trees at the back of the Collinsworth property stretching away. *"Divide and conquer, I always say."* He whirled again.

"Stop it. I don't want to hear from you."

"You can't deny who you really are." This time the voice was right in his ear. He slapped at his ear with his gloved hands. He picked up the wedge and tapped it into another log. He slammed the ax down onto the wedge and the log split.

"I will not listen to you!" He shouted as he split another log. And another. And another until the darkness began to fall and the shadow man was silent.

❧

"Mrs. Collinsworth, that roast beef was better than anything I could have gotten at the Morrison Cafeteria." Esau Cheatwood tossed his napkin onto his empty plate. "I hope Peggy Lou is taking lessons from you."

Peggy Lou choked on a bite of bread and fanned her face with her hand. "Me? Cook? Oh, Esau, I told you I would burn water if I had to cook it."

"Boil it." Uncle Lawson wiped his mouth. "Mr. Cheatwood, if you are thinking about a future with Peggy Lou, I suggest you BUY Morrison's Cafeteria."

"Lawson!" Wimpy hit him with her napkin. "That's not a nice thing to say. I think Peggy Lou could become a good cook if she wanted to."

"Well, she might break a fingernail or two peeling potatoes." Sue Carol said.

Peggy Lou laughed. "Thank you, Sue Carol. Someone understands me."

"Perhaps, Mrs. Collinsworth, you have a special place you keep your recipes? Someplace secret?" Esau said.

Ann Lee looked around the table at her extended family and laughed. "Well, my recipes are no secret, Mr. Cheatwood. Most of them came from my mother, and I keep them in a small wooden box in the kitchen. My mother wrote them out on recipe cards."

"Well, Ann Lee, food as good as this deserves to be kept a secret." Esau winked at his son. Lazarus sat across the table and chuckled.

"What he means, ma'am is maybe you should throw away your mother's recipes." Lazarus paused and reached into his mouth and pulled out a half-chewed piece of roast beef.

"What?" Ann Lee gasped.

"Esau, you and your son, need to go back to Morrison's," Lonnie said. "The world is at war in case you haven't noticed, and the quality of beef here in the United States is suffering."

"That's right." Ann Lee nodded. "And, considering how much it costs to feed the tenants of this boarding house, I have no choice but to buy the cheapest cuts of meat. Now, if you would care to contribute to my food fund, Mr. Cheatwood, seeing as how you are showing up at just about every dinner lately, I might be able to afford a better cut of meat."

Esau placed his fork quietly beside his plate. "I'm am so sorry, Mrs. Collinsworth. I apologize for the brazen and uncalled for comment from my son. I am trying the best I can to teach him civility and diplomacy."

"What?" Lazarus said. "But, last night you said Mrs. Collinsworth's roast beef could be used for re-soling shoes."

Esau glared at his son. "This is what I'm talking about, you moron! You don't repeat everything you hear in front of strangers."

"I'd say you've worn out your welcome," Ray said. "Maybe you and your son should hurry on down to Morrison's before they close. You can leave Peggy Lou here with the rest of us civilized folk."

Peggy Lou glanced at him and did a double take as if seeing him for the first time. "Why, Mister Castle, I just noticed you've lost some weight."

Esau glared at Ray and slowly stood up. "Mrs. Collinsworth, I want to apologize for the rancor that has dampened the good spirits of this dinner. I will have some of the best cuts of beef delivered to you tomorrow." He jerked his head toward the front door. "My son and I will be leaving now. I'll leave you to the ministrations of this stranger in your midst. Coming, Peggy Lou?"

Peggy Lou tore her eyes away from Ray and slowly stood up. "Where are we going?"

"I feel like dancing the night away, sweetheart." Ray grabbed her hand and pulled her behind him as he motioned his son toward the door. He paused as Lazarus opened the front door. "Oh, by the way, Mr. Castle. What have you done lately to pay the Collinsworths for taking care of you for going on two weeks now? Are you paying rent? Purchased any food for them? Or, have you just split a few logs of firewood?"

Ray's faced burned with anger. But, before he could say anything, Esau laughed out loud. "Ann Lee, you need look no further than that cot in your library to find a laggard who is taking advantage of your good graces far more than you accused me of. Good night!"

Silence descended at the dinner table. Ray kept his gaze on the congealed gravy and potatoes on his plate. "Ann Lee," he said quietly. "I'm truly grateful for everything you've done for me. But, as much as I hate to admit it, Esau is right. I am a burden to this family, and I need to find a way to move on. There are some rooms available downtown in the Selber building, and I could probably find a job as a janitor somewhere." He drew a shuddering breath. *Janitor? That is so beneath me,* he thought. *I should be a captain of industry! I should be in charge!* He shook his head and chased the thought away.

"Nonsense." Ann Lee said. She looked around at the people sitting at the table. "Once you get your strength back, I have plenty of work for you to do. Much more than splitting logs. Frank and I talked about it. Like finishing the room on the back of the house. Until you get your memory back, we are going to do whatever it takes to help you get better."

Ray looked up at her face. He swallowed. "Why would you do such a thing? I'm a total stranger? For all you know, Esau could be right, and I could be a criminal. Someone shot me, for heaven's sake! I may be endangering the lives of everyone at this table. What if the person who shot me shows up at the front door?"

Ann Lee stood up and wrung her hands. "Mr. Castle, there are three strangers who have sat at this table in the past two weeks. Of the three, I feel much safer with you at the table than with either Esau or Lazarus. I can't put aside the feeling they're up to something."

Ray opened his mouth. He could tell her right now what he heard in the woods. *"But, then she would want to know why you hadn't told her sooner."* The voice whispered behind him. *"You hid something from her. You kept something dangerous to her family as a secret. She will not look fondly on that!"*

He closed his eyes and shook his head. Go away! He thought. He stood up and glanced around at everyone. "Thank you, Ann Lee. I just don't know what to think anymore."

"Gee, Mr. Ray, you've had a concussion and been shot and everything," Daniel said. "You'll be fine. Just wait, you'll see."

Ray nodded and walked away from the table, his head reeling. *"You're no better than Esau!"* The voice said. *"You're just as much a charlatan as he is. You've got your own agenda, and the sooner you admit it, the sooner we can get on with business."*

Ray stepped into the dark library and shut the door behind him. "Go away! I don't want to hear from you."

"Why?" The voice came from the shadows around him. *"Because it's true? You know it is. I'm just trying to help you remember who you really are. This kind and helpful persona you've adopted is not who you really are, Ray."*

"Shut up!" He grabbed his head and stumbled to the desk. He collapsed in the chair. "Leave me alone!"

"Golly, I'm sorry, Mr. Ray. I didn't know you wanted to be alone."

Ray jerked his hands from his face. Daniel stood in the open doorway. "No! Not you, Daniel. It's my thoughts. My confusion. It's like a voice in my head. A voice that belongs to someone I don't know. Someone who is not me." Ray stood up and paced around the room. "I don't know who I am, Daniel."

"Mister Ray, it sounds like you have an alter ego. You know, like Clark Kent."

Ray paused and looked at the boy. "Clark Kent is quiet and kind and bumbling and far from someone who would take advantage of your mother's good graces."

"Okay, why don't you come with me. I want to show you something."

"What?"

"Come on." Daniel led the way out of the library. Ray followed quietly, avoiding the gazes of the boarding house family. They walked up the stairs to the second floor. Daniel led him down the hallway.

"Is this where everyone lives?" Ray glanced in open doorways to bedrooms as they walked down the hallway.

"Yeah, the sisters have the largest room. Then, Uncle Lonnie the second largest. Miss Peggy Lou has the room at the end of the hallway. Buster has his own small bedroom off of his parents' room."

"What about Lawson and Wimpy?"

"Oh, they live behind the kitchen in a bedroom Daddy converted from the wrap around porch. And, Momma and Daddy have the master bedroom on the other corner by the library."

"Where's your room?"

Daniel jumped up and grabbed a rope and pulled down a set of attic stairs. "I have the coolest room."

"In the attic?"

"Yeah, come on." Daniel climbed up the stairs. Ray followed and ascended into a good sized room about 15 feet long and 12 feet wide. The ceiling was the peaked roof of the house and was covered with plaster. Two dormers pointed toward the front of the house. The slanted walls were covered with pictures and pages from magazines. A twin bed sat at the far wall. Around the walls of the room, rough wooden planks had been assembled into ramshackle shelves. These were covered with books and toys. In one of the dormers, a small cedar tree stood in the sunlight that filtered through the hazy window.

"What's a tree doing up here?" Ray asked.

"Oh, that's my Daddy's attic tree." Daniel shrugged.

"Attic tree? Why would you want to raise a tree in the attic?"

"I don't really know. Daddy never told me. He just comes up here once a day and pours water in the pot. When he's gone, I make sure it gets water. And, we turn it every couple of days, so it don't grow crooked."

Ray nodded in confusion. "Okay. Now, what have we here?" He took a small model of a tank from the shelf. It was made out of popsicle sticks. But, the attention to detail, even with popsicle sticks was amazing.

"That's Captain Freedom's tank," Daniel said. "But, Captain Freedom isn't in the comics. I made him up. He's *my* superhero."

Daniel ran over and pulled the ladder up and closed the door to his room. "Listen, Mr. Ray, what I'm going to show you has to be a secret, okay?"

"Sure." Ray put the tank back on the shelf.

"It's why I wanted you to come up here. But, you gotta swear you won't tell nobody. A pinky swear."

Daniel held up his hand and closed his fist with just his little finger held up in a curl. Ray looked at the boy's hand.

"I don't know what you're talking about."

Daniel rolled his eyes and grabbed Ray's right hand. He formed it into a fist and left his little finger sticking up. "Now, curl your finger. And put it around mine. Now hold on tight. Do you sweat to keep my secret and never tell anyone?"

"I swear."

Daniel moved his hand up and down and tightened his little finger. "It's done. You are sworn to secrecy, Mister Ray." He released his hand. Ray relaxed his fist and nodded.

"Okay. I promise I will not tell your secret. I'm good at keeping secrets, it seems."

"Why did you say that?"

"Because I can't remember any secrets from my past so I can't tell anyone."

"Okay." Daniel went behind one of the shelves where the slanted roof created a hidden space. Something hissed and scraped, and he pulled an old, dark green footlocker into view. "This was my grandfather's footlocker. He fought in the Spanish American war, I think. Daddy told me I could have it."

Daniel reached into his shirt and pulled out a key hanging on a piece of twine around his neck. He stopped and studied Ray. Daniel knelt before the footlocker and opened the locked hinge. He popped it back and opened the lid. He stood up and pointed at the contents. "Nobody knows I do this, Mr. Ray. Not even my Daddy. If Buster knew, I'd never hear the end of it."

Ray stepped over and glanced inside the locker. There were at least a dozen popsicle stick models of airplanes and tanks and vehicles. They surrounded a stack of writing tablets. The top tablet had a bright red cover with a North American Indian in full headdress in profile. In big, black letters the title on the tablet said, "BIG CHIEF." Daniel picked up the top tablet and handed it to Ray.

"Mommy thinks I spend my chore money on comic books. But, I spend it on these tablets."

Ray opened the tablet and gasped in amazement. The first page was covered with an intricate drawing of a car. But, it was unlike any car he had ever seen. At least, he thought he had ever seen! The outline of the car was flowing and streamlined. The star and stripes of the American flag covered a square on the driver door identical to the shield Daniel had designed. But, it wasn't just the design of the car that was amazing. It was the painstaking detail. And, this kid had drawn this on newspaper stock with a pencil. "This is amazing, Daniel."

Daniel shrugged. "There's lots more. I love to design things. Cars, tanks, airplanes, buildings. I trade some of them for comic books down at the Walgreen's drug store. Mr. Harrison likes my drawings, and he lets me have the comic books that nobody buys. Here." He took the tablet from Ray and leafed through the pages. "This is my design for Captain Freedom's headquarters."

The drawing was of a large, tall building with a cutaway on the side that revealed the interior. It was the design of the windows and cornices that blew Ray's mind. "Where did you learn how to do this?"

"Learn? I didn't learn. I just do it." Daniel shrugged. "See what I mean? If Buster knew I did this, he'd laugh at me all the way to school and back. And if my Mommy thought I was wasting time drawing, she'd really be mad."

Ray shook his head. "Daniel, you have an amazing talent. These drawings are absolutely stunning. You should be an architect. Or, design engines and cars."

"This is what I wanted to show you, Mister Ray. It's my secret identity. I hide my real self from everyone because they wouldn't understand."

"Daniel, this is your real superpower. Do you realize how fortunate you are to have this talent? You're a natural. Why you could be a captain of industry instead of freedom."

"Naw." Daniel took the tablet back. "I don't care about industry. I just want to help defeat the Nazis. It's the right thing to do."

Ray sat on the twin bed. "Daniel, you're a regular George Bailey, sacrificing your dream to help others."

"Who?"

Ray blinked. "Uh, I'm not sure who that is, but he did the same thing. Forgot his own personal dream to help others less fortunate than him."

"Gee, Mr. Ray, you understand then, don't you? See, when you get your memories back, you'll find out what your secret identity is. And, I'm betting it will be a good man who wants to help others and fight against evil and injustice just like Captain Freedom."

Ray felt his face grow warm. For some reason, his thoughts fought against one another. On the one hand, he saw the altruistic streak that blessed this young man. On the other hand, he saw the waste of a good talent that could amass a fortune if applied properly. Two sides of his nature waged a battle for his heart and soul. Was his secret identity that of a fiend? Did his hidden memories obscure the heart of a villain instead of a hero?

"Daniel, thank you for showing these to me." Ray managed to whisper. He cringed as a headache gripped his head. "I'm getting a bad headache. I think I need to go lie down and rest."

"Sure, Mr. Ray. But, my secret is safe with you, right?" He put the tablet back into the footlocker and closed the lid. The lock clicked into place.

"Yes, Daniel. It's safe with me." Ray stood up shakily and followed the boy down the ladder back into the house.

❧ 11 ❧

Headlines, Shreveport Times
    Sunday, December 7, 1941

F.D.R. appeals to Jap emperor. President Roosevelt has dispatched a personal message to Emperor Hirohito of Japan in the midst of darkening war clouds in the Far East.

The Red Army, smashing forward in powerful counter-attacks despite temperatures close to 20 below zero, was reported tonight to have brought the Nazi offensive to a standstill on key Moscow fronts.

Only 15 shopping days left so buy your Christmas Seals today. For 20 years Christmas Seals have financed extended research on the X-ray, which is the chief diagnostic method for tuberculosis.

Gifts From Hollywood! Special Make-up Set with Max Factor Hollywood Powder in a gay holiday box at Sears for only $3.55. Color Harmony Make-Up Set with correct makeup shades for "her" type. $6.55. It's thrilling to give her the gift she desires, a beauty secret of the screen stars created by Max Factor Hollywood!

On seven romantic islands of the Pacific ocean, the United States is now, under the veil of secrecy, throwing out a formidable string of new air and submarine bases. More than 100 men from the Shreveport area are leaving here to help build those bulwarks of defense.

Jack Benny gets a "big laugh" out of Fred Allen's "Star Theater," CBS-KWKH Wednesdays at 8 P.M. Benny who has his own show on NBC-KTBS Sundays at 6 P.M. takes his radio aboard a Pullman saying, "It convulses me." KWKH is 1130 on your radio dial, and KTBS is 1480.

Freddy Nagel and his orchestra will be appearing at the Zephyr Room in person featuring the lovely voice of Barbara Carroll. No cover charge and no minimum charge except on Saturdays (50 cents a person).

※

R ay slid the window up and down. "There. I fixed the alignment of the window pane and sanded down the sides so it won't stick anymore."

"Good job." Uncle Lawson growled from his couch. "You've turned out to be a pretty good handyman. And, you've put some weight back on."

Ray sighed. "Yeah, I guess somewhere in the past I must have been involved in construction." He glanced down at his hands. In the past week or so he had earned quite a few blisters and some rough callouses. His hands used to be pink and smooth, not the hands of a carpenter. "But, it must have been a long time since I worked on things. I didn't have callouses until I started working around the house." He glanced through the window across the front porch of the boarding house. Cars drove down the street in front of the house. A man and woman walked by pushing a baby carriage. "I seem to remember something about my father. He was a construction worker, I think." The sun came out from behind a cloud, and a shadow danced across the front porch. It stood just out of sight. He flinched. A voice echoed in his memory.

"You want to go to college, boy? That's not what a real man does for a living.

You gotta work with your hands, boy, not with numbers! Like I taught you! You turn your back on me, and I'll show you what a real man is like!" A meaty raised hand holding a hammer descended toward his head, and he ran.

Ray closed his eyes in pain and stumbled back from the window. The memory began to fade as he traced his finger along a scar at the back of his right ear. An old scar from his teenage days, he seemed to recall. Had his father hit him? He looked down at his empty hands.

"Ray? You okay?"

He whirled, and Uncle Lawson stood a few feet away. "Yeah, Lawson. I just had a memory."

"Good one?"

"No. Not so good."

"I got a lot of those, too." He returned to his chair. Lawson glanced at a clock on the mantle. "They ought to be home from church in a couple of hours. Now, Ray, remember, my lumbago is acting up, and that's why I didn't go. And, we listened to the Queensborough Baptist Church service on the radio."

"What if they asked what he preached on?"

"Just say, sin. Preachers always talk about sin."

Ray smiled as he crossed to the fireplace mantle. "Yeah, I don't think I was ever fond of church. Couldn't handle all that guilt." He glanced at the angel sitting on the mantle. He hadn't thought about it since the day Ann Lee had put it on the mantle. He picked it up and ran his finger over the smooth wood. It had been carved from a solid piece of wood. Had he carved it? No, the handiwork wasn't that of a seasoned professional. It was more like the work of an amateur. He put the angel back on the mantle.

"Lawson, I think I'll go for a quick walk before everyone gets home."

"Suit yourself. It's cold out there." Lawson muttered as he studied his newspaper.

Ray slipped into the old jacket that once belonged to the elder Collinsworth and headed out the front door. He started out on the sidewalk in front of the boarding house and made his way down Buckner Street to Fairfield Avenue where he caught the trolley to downtown. For a Sunday morning, the downtown was surprisingly busy. He set off down Texas Street away from the Red River. Glittering Christmas decorations had been placed on the street posts. People bustled about on their own private errands. Couples walked hand in hand toward the church at the head of the street.

Today is Sunday, and I'm not going to church. Shouldn't he be in church on Sunday? There was a nagging sense of loss when he looked at the tall, white columns on the front of the First Methodist Church at the head of Texas Street. He shook his head and turned into the Walgreens drug store and diner. The Woolsworth diner was closed on Sunday just like the store but the Walgreens drug store and diner in the Allen Building, had a huge sign "OPEN SUNDAY". Didn't Woolsworth realize how much money they were losing? No one closed stores on Sunday. He sat on a bench at the counter and glanced up at the menu.

"What'll be?" A man with a huge red nose leaned over the counter. He wore a paper hat over his greasy hair.

"Toast and two eggs over easy. And, coffee." Ray reached into his pocket and took out some change. Ann Lee had paid him a few dollars for the past two weeks of work. But, he wished he had a real job. For some reason, it grated on his nerves to be at the mercy of anyone else. He hated the idea of owing someone for his keep.

The man put a plate with two pieces of toast and two eggs in front of him and a mug of coffee. Ray ate the toast in silence and sipped at the black coffee. He had just placed his coins on the counter to pay for his breakfast when he spied three girls walking past the window of the diner. He jumped up from the counter and hurried to the door. He stepped outside into the cold air and watched Rachel, Gwendolyn, and Penelope hurrying down the sidewalk. What were they doing downtown? They were supposed to be in church.

Ray followed and stopped at a corner as they paused in front of a huge, brass door into a high rise building. Rachel seemed nervous and opened the huge door. The other two girls followed her in. Ray hurried up to the door and glanced at the brass sign listing the businesses inside. One listing was for the studio of radio station KWTT.

He smiled. Rachel was here for the singing contest! He stepped in through the door and Rachel was arguing heatedly with a woman at the front desk.

"I'm here for the contest."

"I'm sorry, ma'am." A short, dumpy woman was frowning at her from behind the desk. "But, you got to be at least eighteen to go up or be accompanied by an adult."

Rachel waved a sheaf of papers in the woman's face. "I've got the papers right here. My father signed them. I'm legal."

The woman shook her head. "I ain't going to believe it, little missy. I know your mother, and I know you ain't yet eighteen. You went to school with my daughter, and you're the same age."

Ray stepped up to the counter and put an arm around Rachel. "Perhaps I can be of assistance. I'm Uncle Ray. I'm staying with the Collinsworths, and I'm here to accompany Rachel."

Rachel's eyes grew wide, and Gwendolyn and Penelope squealed in delight. The woman looked like she had swallowed a canary.

"Well, in that case, I can't keep you any longer. Take the elevator up to the fifth floor."

Rachel was shivering as they stepped into the elevator. Ray nodded at the elevator operator sitting on a fold-out stool. "Fifth floor, please sir. You're looking at the next first place winner of the Piney Woods Holiday Singing Contest, Miss Rachel Collinsworth."

The man seemed unimpressed and closed the elevator door. "That's what they all say."

Rachel beamed at him. "Oh, Mr. Castle, that was the most swell thing anyone has ever done for me."

"Yeah," Gwendolyn almost swooned. "You're a regular Clark Gable."

"You came to her rescue," Penelope said.

Ray shrugged. "It was just pure luck. I was in the right place at the right time."

"It was the Lord making sure I could get in for this contest." Rachel said. "I've been praying and praying for the chance to sing this song."

Ray felt a bit uncomfortable at the mention of God and took his arm from around the girl. "Well, if you want to give him credit, I guess it's okay with me."

The elevator came to a halt, and they hurried out onto the floor housing the studios of KWTT. A tall, handsome man with dark hair was standing at the reception desk. He wore a nattily cut suit and smelled of cologne. He was clearing his throat as they walked up and his eyes were riveted on the blonde behind the desk.

"Tell me what you think, Ashley. This is what I plan on saying this afternoon. 'Welcome, ladies and gentlemen, on this Sunday afternoon, December 7, 1941, to the preliminary round of competition on the fifth annual Piney Woods Holiday Singing Contest. We'll have our first contestants just after these words from our sponsor, Big Chain Grocery Store.'"

The blonde actually sighed, and her eyelids fluttered. Rachel shivered beside Ray and gasped. "You're the Voice!"

The man blinked in surprise and finally noticed them standing there. "Of course I'm the Voice. Who else would I be?"

"Oh, you sound so grand!" Gwendolyn gushed as she leaned against the counter. "Like Orson Welles."

The Voice raised an eyebrow and cleared his throat. "I have much better diction than Orson. And, who are you?"

"I'm Rachel Collinsworth. I'm one of the contestants." Rachel said almost breathlessly.

The Voice smiled thinly. "Well, if you'll excuse me for just one minute, I'll come back and usher you into the studios." He turned abruptly and walked away.

Rachel jumped up and down. "I can't believe this is happening."

Ray smiled at the blonde and turned back to the girls. "What will you say when you mother notices you aren't in church?"

Rachel paled. She whirled to Penelope. "Are you sure you told your mother we would be staying at your house after church for lunch?"

Penelope nodded and pushed her dark hair back under her beret. "Don't worry, Rachel. I told her. I just hope she doesn't find out or I'll be in big trouble for lying to her."

Rachel reached out and took her friend's hands in hers. "You're my best friend, Penelope. If you do get in trouble, I'll tell her it was my fault. Mr. Castle is right. If my mother knew I was here at the radio station instead of being at church, she would lock me in my room. She just doesn't understand how important this contest is to me."

"Just remember me when you get to Hollywood. I want to meet Cary Grant. Oh, what a dreamboat!" Penelope said.

Gwendolyn brushed back her blonde curls. "Gary Grant? Give me Gary Cooper! I'd love to walk down the red carpet with him. He was a dreamboat in 'Meet John Doe.'"

Penelope ignored her and patted Rachel's hands. "Rachel, just relax. You're nervous because of the contest."

"I may get to sing today but there over twenty contestants, and I think over half of them have already tried out. Oh, here he comes!"

Ray glanced over his shoulder, and the Voice appeared from behind the wall. He was all smiles as he came over to Rachel. "Miss Collinsworth. Are you ready to sing for our preliminary judging?"

Rachel paled and bit her lip. "Oh, yes, Mr. Voice. I mean, Mr. The Voice. When do I sing?"

The Voice smiled and took her papers. "Well, it may be a couple of hours. What song have you picked?"

Rachel pointed to her papers. "I have my own song."

"You wrote your own song?" The Voice sounded skeptical.

"Yes, sir. It's called 'The Homecoming Tree.'"

"A rather unusual name."

"Well, my Daddy is in the Army Air Corps, and he went on a secret mission to Hawaii — Ooops, I wasn't supposed to say that."

"Don't worry. I won't reveal your secret." The Voice handed her back the papers. "I thought this was your father."

"Ray Castle. I'm a friend of the family and Frank is, well, indisposed so I'm filling in for him."

Rachel nodded. "He left the day after Thanksgiving, and he promised to be home by Christmas. So, I wrote a song about our Christmas tree. It will be his homecoming tree."

"Isn't it a bit early to have a tree?"

"No, not yet. But, we will have it up by the time he comes home for Christmas."

"That is very nice, Rachel. I look forward to hearing your song. Remember, the two finalists will get to sing live on the air on Christmas Eve. Let's hope you and your song make it."

"That would be a nice Christmas gift for my father."

The Voice motioned toward the door leading into the studio. "You may go in and make yourself at home. I'll get you when it is your turn. And, let's hope your father comes home soon."

The man walked away, and Rachel started toward the door. Ray leaned against the wall as a sudden feeling of fear engulfed him. He had a sudden and unrelenting feeling of dread. Frank would not be coming home. He knew it somehow. "Rachel, if you don't mind, I'll go back to the boarding house."

"Gee, that would be swell, Mr. Castle. Thanks a million for helping out." Rachel smiled at him.

"You're welcome, Rachel."

The girls disappeared. He glanced at the woman behind the desk, and she smiled.

"Ain't it grand?" She said.

"Yeah, it's grand."

Ray made his way back to Buckner Street and hung his old coat on the coat rack as he entered the living room. Uncle Lawson was sitting in his chair reading his newspaper. Ray cleared his throat to not startle the man.

"What is going on in the news today?"

"Good, you're back. Didn't want your little walk to delay lunch." Lawson said. "Well, there ain't much going on in the newspaper today. There's a whole bunch of Christmas ads. I can't believe they would start advertising Christmas this early! Today is only December 7!"

Ray felt a chill pass over him again, and he blinked. "December 7, 1941."

Lawson looked at him over his reading glasses. "Yeah, that would be the day."

Ray suddenly felt weak, and his heart was racing. Something about this day was important. Vitally important! He wracked his brain trying to remember why this day was so crucial. What was going to happen? But, in his continued frustration with his amnesia, he found nothing. Just a great, huge dark cloud of fear and anxiety that settled over him like a pall. He stumbled past Uncle Lawson's chair and settled onto the couch.

"Are you okay?" Lawson asked.

"Yeah, just a headache. Maybe I should have gotten up earlier and eaten breakfast." Ray felt sweat pop out on his forehead.

"Well, it's almost lunchtime now. I think Ann Lee has cooked up a roast." Uncle Lawson returned to his newspaper. "I hope this one is more tender than the last one that Esau Cheatwood dumped on us. A more expensive cut of meat, he said. Can't trust a word out of that man's mouth."

The front door opened and Aunt Wimpy came into the living room swathed in a long, brown wool coat. Her hair was pushed beneath a hat with a brown veil that came down over her face. "Lawson, you sure missed a good sermon today." She said as she took off her coat. Ann Lee followed her through the door and took off her hat and coat.

"And, that choir sounded so good. It almost made me cry."

Sue Carol followed her. "Just about anything makes you cry these days."

"If I could just hear from Frank. I haven't gotten a single letter since he left."

Lonnie appeared in the doorway dressed in a dark suit and a thin, red tie. "Ann Lee, he is on a secret mission, right? He can't compromise his mission. We can't expect him to write a letter when he's getting our soldiers ready to beat up on some Nazis." Lonnie loosened his tie and unbuttoned his coat. "So, Uncle Lawson, did you stay home from church so you could read the paper?"

"As a matter of a fact, I did learn something from the paper. Looks like Esau Cheatwood is keeping the company of some very important people."

Ray sat forward as Lonnie sat down beside him. "Mr. Cheatwood? Who?"

"Says here in the paper that he had dinner with the winner of the Louisiana Maneuvers. Fellow by the name of General George Patton."

Lonnie took his pipe out of his coat pocket and tapped it on his knee. "General Patton? Cheatwood had dinner with Patton? Do you know who he is?"

Uncle Lawson pointed to the paper. "Says here he was in charge of one side in the war games and he took Shreveport, winning the maneuvers on December 3rd."

Lonnie tucked his pipe into his mouth. "Patton is the best General we have right now. I would sure like to have met him. Instead, he had dinner with the sleaziest businessman in Shreveport."

Aunt Wimpy tapped Uncle Lawson on the shoulder. "Enough war talk, Lawson. You told me you were going to stay in bed all day."

"You know how my lumbago acts up. It's pretty painful today." He raised an eyebrow at Ray and nodded.

Ray cleared his throat. "That's right, Aunt Wimpy. Poor Uncle Lawson has been stuck in that chair all day. But, we listened to Queensborough Baptist Church on the radio. The pastor, uh, preached on sin."

A cloud of lavender engulfed Ray, and he looked up to see the three sisters huddle around the back of the couch. Their pale, powdered faces were etched with concern.

"My dear Lawson, if you would just take some of our Remedy, your back would stop aching," Ophelia said.

Theophila nodded in agreement. "That's is an excellent suggestion, Sister. Lawson already spoke to me earlier this morning about acquiring some of our Remedy."

Evelia touched Theophila on the arm to get her attention. "In fact, Sister, Sister and I procured a quart of the Remedy this morning and gave it to Lawson."

Theophila smiled. "Well, your back should be much better after taking some of the Remedy. How are you feeling?"

Aunt Wimpy glared at the three women. "He's probably feeling no pain! Lawson, I asked you not to drink anymore of that moonshine swill!"

Ophelia put a hand to her heart as if in great pain. "Now, Wimpy, you are mistaken in your characterization of the Remedy as swill.

During the dark days of Prohibition, our Remedy helped many a hapless wayward soul find solace."

Theophila nodded enthusiastically. "Yes, many a wayward soul. Why we owe our small fortune to the great success of our Remedy during those days. Our father passed on to us the secret formula."

Evelia put an arm around her sister. "And, it is not moonshine swill. It is the best medication for pain and suffering and--"

"Melancholy and consumption and headache and--" Theophila said.

"Lumbago known to man." Ophelia finished. "Would you like some to calm your nerves?"

Aunt Wimpy's face stretched in shock and dismay. "No, I would not! And, after partaking of the Remedy, Lawson probably feels a whole lot better, so he is going to help me out in the kitchen."

Uncle Lawson threw down his newspaper. "What? That's woman's work."

Aunt Wimpy grabbed him by the ear and pulled him up out of his chair. "Get in that kitchen and help me get Sunday dinner on the table you old coot or I'll call the sheriff and have him sniff around upstairs for your empty bottle of Remedy!"

Aunt Wimpy led him grimacing and complaining through the kitchen door. Ann Lee had disappeared up the stairs, and she now returned to the living room heading across the floor to Sue Carol. "Sue Carol, have you seen Rachel?"

Ray picked up Lawson's newspaper and tried to hide his face. It wouldn't be long before Rachel tried out for the contest.

Sue Carol was busy placing dishes on the dining room table, and she paused with a puzzled look on her face. "No, Ann Lee. I thought she wasn't feeling well before church."

Ann Lee shrugged. "She said she wasn't going to Sunday School, but she would be at the worship service. I didn't see her. I hope she's not sick."

Sue Carol placed the last plate on the table. "Maybe she went over to Penelope's house. Would you like me to call over there and check?"

Ann Lee nodded. "You're probably right. Go ahead and give her a call while I make sure Aunt Wimpy and Uncle Lawson don't burn down the kitchen."

Ray lowered the newspaper and sighed. The three sisters still stood behind the couch. He cleared his throat, anxious to change the subject. "You gals are becoming like the Baldwin sisters. You know like on the Waltons."

Sue Carol paused as she lifted the telephone receiver off the cradle. "The Waltons? Where do they live?"

Ray paused and once again the uneasy realization that he couldn't touch the memory filled him with frustration. "Uh, I don't know."

Ophelia raised an eyebrow in confusion as she settled into her rocker. "I did know Marybell Walker back in grade school."

Theophila nodded and put a hand her sister's arm. "I remember her. She whistled when she talked. She had that unfortunate gap between her two front teeth."

Evelia laughed. "We used to call her Sister Woodchuck. But, I don't recall any Waltons."

Ophelia nodded. "Other than Marybell, that is. Poor thing was a bit uncouth."

"How so?" Evelia asked.

"Why remember how she would take a sip of her milk at lunch and then spit it across the lunchroom through those gapped teeth? Very undignified." Ophelia said.

"Very, indeed." Theophila frowned.

A rumble came down the stairs, and Daniel and Buster ran into the living room decked out in their superhero costumes. Buster pulled his goggles down over his eyes. "We've got some crimes to bust and some Nazis to capture."

Daniel brandished his shield. "Yep, Captain Freedom never rests while evil looms in the world."

Buster put his hands on his hips and struck a heroic pose. "And, the Midnight Menace's secret squadron will soon save the world from Adolf Hitler. He's the scum of the Earth."

Daniel pulled his mask down over his eyes. "We'll be heroes like my Daddy."

Lonnie puffed on his pipe and watched as Little Lonnie knocked over his Lincoln Log house he was building in the middle of the living room floor and started over. "Maybe one day you two can be real heroes like General Patton. Imagine, he's right here in Shreveport. Now, there's a real war hero, boys. I can't wait to see those Nazis once Patton gets a hold of them."

Sue Carol put a hand over the mouthpiece of the telephone. "That's enough, Lonnie. I can't believe you keep talking like this when Daniel doesn't even have his father around."

Lonnie stood up and paced across the living room floor. "Frank is doing what a real man is supposed to do. He's fighting for our country not sorting letters to Santa Claus."

Uncle Lawson appeared through the kitchen door carrying a roasting dish filled with steaming roast beef and vegetables. A frilly, flowery apron covered his chest and ample belly. He wore two pink oven mitts, and he placed the roast beef on the table.

"Lunch is running a little late. But, here's your roast beef." He said grumpily. Ann Lee followed him out of the kitchen carrying a plate of rolls.

"Lawson, you look so cute."

Sue Carol frowned as she hung up the phone. She started to say something and then paused in shock at the sight of Uncle Lawson in his apron. "I think you ought to work in the kitchen more often."

Uncle Lawson put his mitts on his hips. "Don't get any ideas, sweetheart."

Aunt Wimpy came out of the kitchen with two bowls of steaming mashed potatoes. She was grinning from ear to ear. "Don't he look good in that apron? Reminds of the days we spent running the cafe in Saline."

Ann Lee stopped in amazement. "The two of you ran the cafe in Saline? I don't remember that."

Aunt Wimpy adjusted her snood. "Oh, honey, it was long before you were born. Then Lawson got sent over to Europe for the Great War."

Lonnie stopped his pacing. He looked the man up and down. "You fought in the Great War?"

"Yeah, I did. I was in the infantry."

Lonnie glanced over at Daniel and Buster. "I don't know who has the most ridiculous costume. I hope you didn't fight the Germans in an apron."

Aunt Wimpy laughed, and Uncle Lawson's face grew red with anger. Aunt Wimpy patted his arm. "Now, just calm down. We're only picking. Of course, you didn't wear an apron. But, when he got home, all he did was complain about his marching back and forth. His feet are flat enough he could put out forest fires with them."

Uncle Lawson pulled off his oven mitts and tossed them onto the floor. "Wimpy, don't be talking about my body like that. Woman, can't you keep your mouth shut?"

Aunt Wimpy picked up the oven mitts. "Well, your mother said all your guts settled in your feet. But, we know that isn't so, don't we?" She reached out and patted his huge belly.

Ann Lee suddenly grew pale and settled onto the couch next to Ray. She looked over at him, and a tear ran down her cheek. "All this talk about war and I haven't heard a word from Frank."

Sue Carol came up behind her and put her hands on the woman's shoulders. "I'm sure he's just fine. Wherever he is. God will take care of him. Just like he did when he went to China."

The front door opened and Peggy Lou entered. She wore a pale, woolen coat over a bright, red dress. Close behind her, Esau Cheatwood stepped through the door in a dark overcoat and a blue tie. His hair was slicked back, and his pencil thin mustache was particularly crisp. He carried a fedora in his hand. Lazarus slid in just in time as Esau slammed the door behind him. The young man was wearing a sweater vest and a red bowtie.

"And, I told General Patton not to worry about getting fuel for his tanks." Esau glanced around at the living room. "That's right, ladies and gentlemen. I had dinner with General George Patton. There's a real hero." He reached over to ruffle Daniel's hair, but Daniel pulled out of his reach.

"Did you see the way that woman in the pew behind us looked at me? She even called me a name." Peggy Lou shrugged out of her coat. Esau glared at Lazarus, snapped his fingers and pointed at Peggy Lou. Lazarus hurried over to catch Peggy Lou's coat before it could hit the floor.

"What did she call you?" Esau asked as he pulled off his overcoat and tossed it over Lazarus' head. The young man wandered around blindly until he ran into the coat rack by the door.

Peggy Lou took off her gaudy hat and patted her hair back into place. "A car lot. Imagine that. Why I don't look like a car lot."

Lazarus pulled the coat off his head, and his hair stood on end with static electricity. "I think what she said was a harlot, not a car lot."

Peggy Lou's face became still and very empty as if she were struggling to think of a reply. She relaxed and shrugged. "Well, I hear a lot, too. Those people in that church just don't know how to dress."

Esau put a hand on Peggy Lou's back. "I wouldn't worry one bit about it, Peggy Lou. You are the most beautiful woman in the world. A real brick."

"A real brick?" Ray laughed. "Why would you call her a brick?"

Esau glared at him. His upper lip crinkled as if he smelled a terrible odor. "Who jerked your chain?"

Ray blinked, and the room fell into dead silence. A shadow flickered at the window. He glanced over Esau's shoulder at a ghostly figure standing outside the window. *You going to let him talk to you that way? Huh? What's gotten into you? Where's your backbone?* A voice echoed in his mind.

Ray shook his head and looked away. "It just seemed a pretty demeaning statement to make to such a pretty girl. Peggy Lou reminds me more of a flower than a brick. That's all I'm saying."

Esau stepped closer to the couch. "Hey, back off there, Mister Amnesia. Peggy Lou is my girl. Go put your peepers on someone else."

Ray glanced at the shadow in the window. Maybe the mysterious shadow man had a point. He had taken about as much as he was going to take from Esau. Two green eyes appeared in the shadow man's head. One of them winked at him. Everything fell into place like a puzzle. Esau's weakness was Peggy Lou! His *angle* was Peggy Lou. Ray could play Esau's game just as well as Esau. And, if he could find the deed through Peggy Lou, then he would have the perfect bargaining chip. And, Esau would go down in flames!

Ray got up from the couch and walked around the back of it until he stood in front of Peggy Lou. "Well, Mr. Esau Cheatwood, you can't blame me for being attracted to the prettiest dame in town."

Esau slid between Ray and Peggy Lou, and his eyes were wide with shock. "Listen, here, Rudy."

"Ray. Ray Castle." Ray straightened his shirt and ran a hand through his hair. He leaned closer so that only Esau could hear. "And, I'm going to be a thorn in your side. May the worst man win."

"Are you two freeloaders staying for lunch, too?" Uncle Lawson interrupted them. "I don't know if I cooked enough for you and Tiny over there."

Lazarus was trying to get his hair to lay down, but the more he stroked it, the more it stood up with static electricity. "My name is not Tiny."

Esau raised an eyebrow as he studied Lawson. He reached over and grabbed Peggy Lou by the waist and pulled her close to him. "Now, Peggy Lou, here's what the best-dressed househusband should wear. Very frilly. Very pretty."

Uncle Lawson jerked the apron off and tossed it on top of his newspaper. "Oh, shut up and sit down. I think there's some fat back left in the kitchen for the two of you to chew on."

Esau rubbed his upper lip and glanced furtively at Ray. He grinned and sat beside Ann Lee. He patted her hand. "Ann Lee, you look so sad. I apologize for not giving you more advanced notice."

Ann Lee gently pulled her hand from Esau's grasp. "Apology accepted."

Esau licked his lips. "Have you heard from your husband? It's been quite a spell since he left for his military mission. I hope he has left you in proper shape in case any business has to be conducted on his behalf."

"Business? What are you talking about?"

"Surely he has told you where he keeps his important papers? Maybe in a safe somewhere?" Esau's grin reminded Ray of a possum.

Ann Lee glanced at Ray with a puzzled look on her face. "Safe? We don't have a safe in the house, Mr. Cheatwood."

Esau turned to study the walls of the living room. "No safe, huh? Then where does your husband keep your important papers? You know, your will, your birth certificates, your deed to this house? It's very irresponsible for him to leave you so unprepared."

Ann Lee stood up, and her look became even more distraught. "I really don't know, Mr. Cheatwood. Why are you asking?"

Lazarus had licked both palms and succeeded in smoothing down his hair. "Because he wants to know where the--"

Esau stood up and slapped the boy in the back of his head. His hair stood on end again. He turned back to Ann Lee. "I want to know that you will be well taken care of now that your husband is out of the country. You must be prepared in case--"

"In case what?"

"With the world in the condition it is in today, you never know what danger your husband is facing. He may be in harm's way, even as we speak."

Lazarus stepped forward and took a folded sheet of paper out of his pants pocket. "And, in the event that your loved one is indisposed, Cheatwood Insurance can take care of your every need. We have life insurance, disability insurance, and burial insurance."

Ann Lee's hand flew to her mouth. Ray hurried over to put his arm around her shoulders. She looked up at him helplessly. "Burial? Good heavens!"

Ray hugged her tightly. "That's enough from you two."

Lazarus looked up from his sheet of paper. "But, I was just practicing my speech. Dad is teaching me what to say to sell insurance to all the dopes coming into his office."

"Dopes, huh?" Lonnie clenched his teeth tightly on his pipe. "Why don't you two dopes head out of here and go find somewhere else to eat."

Esau glared at Lazarus and turned a worried gaze on Ray. He smiled and actually bowed his head in consolation. "Please, Mr. Britt and Mrs. Collinsworth, forgive my son his unbridled enthusiasm. He is only trying to better himself and learn the ins and outs of the business. Surely you can overlook his youthful enthusiasm?"

Ann Lee patted Ray's hand and sniffed. "I suppose so. But, what if you're right? What if Frank is in trouble?"

Esau brought his hands together in front of his chest and rubbed them together. "Then I am sure that Mr. Castle can lift your husband in prayer just before we eat."

Before Ray could respond, Ophelia hurried over to them. "Ann Lee, I discovered something in my sweater pocket just now. I was looking for my father's pocket watch. I keep it with me all the time."

Theophila joined her. "I thought I put father's watch in the armoire in our bedroom."

Evelia slipped between them. "Oh, no, Sister! Remember Sister took the pocket watch when Uncle Lawson arranged our meeting so that he could procure some of the Remedy. He said it was absolutely essential we meet him just after 8:45 this morning."

Theophila nodded. "Oh, yes, that is correct. He had to make sure the house was empty and assured us we would still have ample time to make Sunday School. In fact, Sister," she said to Ophelia, "I have father's pocket watch right here. You gave it to me so you could carry both quarts of the Remedy."

Aunt Wimpy slapped Uncle Lawson with the oven mitts. "BOTH quarts! Lawson! I ought to skin you alive!"

Uncle Lawson tried to fend off her feeble blows. "Now, Wimpy, it is good for my rheumatism and look," he jumped up in the air and clicked his heels together. "my lumbago is gone."

Ann Lee pulled gently out of Ray's grasp. "Never mind all of that, Uncle Lawson. Sister, what did you find?"

Ophelia held up an envelope. "Why, I believe it is a letter that was hand-delivered yesterday. I stuck it in my pocket and forgot all about it. How silly of me."

Ann Lee snatched the letter from her hand. She looked at and squealed in delight. "It's from Frank! A letter from Frank!" She paused and turned to glare at Ophelia. "You've had this since yesterday?"

Sue Carol hurried over and put her arm around Ann Lee. "Oh, never mind, Ann Lee. Open it and read it."

Ann Lee started to rip it open and then stopped. She looked over at Ray and frowned. "But, what if it's bad news?"

Lonnie put a hand on her back. "They deliver bad news in person, Ann Lee. A soldier would have come to the door."

"I guess we don't have to worry about bad news, Mrs. Collinsworth," Ray said.

Oblivious to the importance of the letter, the three sisters returned to their perches next to the radio. Ophelia started twisting the dial on the radio changing the station from county music to classical.

Uncle Lawson collapsed into his chair and his newspaper crinkled beneath him. "Don't play that classical garbage!"

Evelia continued to turn the dial. "Now, Uncle Lawson, we agreed that Sister could listen to the chamber music every Sunday afternoon."

Theophila nodded. "Usually we have finished lunch by now, and you are fast asleep on the couch. But, since as our chef you did not deliver lunch on time today, you will, no doubt be wide awake during the entire hour of music."

Uncle Lawson pulled his crumpled newspaper from beneath him. "No, I won't! That stuff puts me to sleep in a heartbeat. We better eat fast, or I'll wind up asleep in my pot roast."

Aunt Wimpy thumped him on the side of the head. "Let Ann Lee read her letter first. Go ahead, Ann Lee. Read it."

Ann Lee ripped open the top of the envelope. "Out loud?"

Sue Carol smiled. "Of course. We all want to know what is happening with Frank."

Ann Lee pulled out a folded sheet of paper and carefully unfolded it. Ray studied the expression on her face. He was expecting the worst. Why he didn't know. Instead, Ann Lee smiled. "My dearest cupcake."

Sue Carol giggled. "Cupcake? Oh, I love it. Frank is so romantic. Unlike someone else, I know." She elbowed Lonnie, and he backed away.

Ann Lee continued. "I know you are probably wondering what's going on over here in my little corner of the Pacific."

Lonnie slapped his hand against the back of the couch. "I knew it! He's in the Pacific, not Europe."

Sue Carol nudged him. "Hush! Let Ann Lee read."

Uncle Lawson rolled his eyes. "Yes, please let her read. The roast beef is getting cold."

Ann Lee's smile widened as she read the letter. "The days are warm and breezy, and the landscape is beautiful. I can imagine one of the red flowers of the hibiscus in your lustrous hair." She grew quiet, and a red blush came over her face. "Oh, my, I'll leave the rest of that paragraph for later. Ahem! Tell Daniel that I'm getting to fly some really big airplanes. I'm not only training, but I'm learning here at--" She squinted and showed the letter to Ray. "They blacked out the name."

Ray nodded. "Secret mission, remember?"

Ann Lee nodded. "Of course." She continued to read. "I'm planning on being home Christmas Eve so look for me. I'll be bringing you all very special gifts."

Ophelia stood up abruptly, and her hand went to her mouth. "Uh, Sister, did you hear what they just said on the radio?"

Lonnie glanced at her. "Sister, don't interrupt."

Theophila stood up also. "But, listen. Something has happened with the Japanese."

Ray's heart skipped a beat, and his hands grew clammy and cold. It was happening! Whatever the horrible, terrible thing was that he could not remember had happened. Evelia turned the volume on the radio as high as it would go.

"Forces of Imperial Japan have reportedly attacked Pearl Harbor in the American territory of Hawaii. Reports are scant and incomplete, but it appears the entire fleet in Pearl Harbor has been disabled. At dawn this morning, Hawaiian time, a squadron of Japanese airplanes carrying bombs attacked the American fleet in Pearl Harbor. We will bring you more news as soon as it is available. President Roosevelt has recalled his cabinet to the White House." The tinny voice of the announcer echoed through the suddenly silent house.

Ann Lee dropped the letter, and her hands flew to her mouth. "That's where Frank is. Pearl Harbor!"

Esau Cheatwood jumped up into the air and whistled. "That's it! We're in the war, now, son." He whirled and hugged his son. "We're going to make a fortune!"

Ann Lee put her hands to her mouth and stumbled. Ray caught her and lowered her to the couch.

"Ann Lee, just remain calm." Ray soothed her. His heart was racing, and his mouth was dry and papery. Lonnie's face was as red as a beet. Sue Carol was sobbing in Lonnie's arms. The two boys,

Daniel and Buster, were just standing there looking confused and lost. Little Lonnie kicked over his Lincoln logs again and sat down to rebuild them for the second time in the last hour. The three sisters were hugging each other, their powdery white faces riveted on the radio. Uncle Lawson's gaze was far away, and Aunt Wimpy slowly came over to him and put her arms around him. He stood like a statue. Peggy Lou was whimpering and turning slowly in circles like a puppy lost in the storm. Esau was beaming and pounding his son on the back.

"We're in the war, now. We're going to kick their tails all the way to China!" He paused as Ray glared at him. "What's eating you, Castle?"

"Ann Lee's husband is at Pearl Harbor, Cheatwood."

Esau shrugged. "Nothing we can do about that now, is there?"

The green eyes squinted in his mind. The shadow man screamed in anger. Something hot and fluid flowed through Ray, and he jumped over the couch catching Esau around the waist. They rolled across the floor into the dining room table. The dishes clattered, and Ray felt the hot gravy from the roast beef splash across his back. But, he didn't care. He wanted to pound Esau's face into the pavement. The two of them rolled and tussled across the floor until the coat rack fell on top of them.

Ray wrestled with Peggy Lou's coat and threw it off of him as he slammed his fist into Esau's face. Esau squealed like a pig and put his hands across his mouth.

"Stop! Stop it, you maniac!"

But, Ray felt the anger and the frustration build. This was bad. This was horrible. This was a defining moment in history, and this man had laughed and celebrated while thousands had died in Pearl Harbor. Strangely, he realized he had never cared about this before. He paused with his fist raised as the unfamiliar thought brought his beating to a halt. Before? Had he known about this before? How could he? It just happened!

A shadow fell over him, and he looked up at Lazarus just as he brought the roast beef dish down on his head. The dish shattered and roast beef and onions rained down on them. He fell back into darkness and pain.

RAY MOVED IN AND OUT OF CONSCIOUSNESS, LIGHT AND SHADOWS, silence and sound.

"Flash, Washington. The President announces Japanese attack on Pearl Harbor." He heard the Voice speaking from a great distance.

"Let me repeat this urgent news flash. The White House and the Navy Department report an attack by Japanese air forces on our naval base at Pearl Harbor, on the island of Oahu in the Hawaiian Island chain. We are trying to get all the details we can, ladies and gentlemen. We take you now to our foreign correspondent in Honolulu, Hawaii, Martin Worth. Come in, Honolulu."

Silence settled around Ray. He was sinking deeper.

"Come in, Honolulu." More silence.

"Come in, Honolulu."

"Yesterday, December 7, 1941, a day that will live in infamy," A different voice now. One from the past. But, how could that be? It was in the present. Wasn't that President Roosevelt? Darkness swam into cloudy light, and an old man sat next to him on a couch. Blood trickled from a wound on the old man's temple. His pale blue eyes were opened, and he stared off into space. It was as if the old man was talking in his sleep. Who was he? Why did he have a wound on his temple? Where was Mikey when you needed him? Mikey? Who was Mikey? Hadn't he stopped the mugger? But not before the man had shot him. Ray swam in clouds of confusion as the old man continued to talk.

"I remember it all. How could I forget? The surprise attack on Pearl Harbor was complete. The attack came in two waves. The first hit its target at 7:53 Hawaii time, the second at 8:55. By 9:55, it was all over. Behind them, they left chaos: 2403 dead, 188 destroyed planes and a crippled Pacific fleet that included eight damaged and destroyed battleships. It is rumored that a Japanese commander made the statement 'I fear all we have done is awakened a sleeping giant.' My family listened to the reports of the attack on Pearl Harbor on the radio. We saw the news footage at the newsreels at the movie theater. I imagined my Daddy as one of the brave pilots who actually made it into the air to attack the enemy. But, the truth was he was probably on the ground at Hickman Field and never made it into the air. In the days to come, we would wait anxiously for news from my father. But in the confusion and chaos after Pearl Harbor, the government was more concerned about entering the war against Japan and Germany. They didn't have time to track down one missing soldier. With only days left until Christmas, my mother, sister and I cared nothing about putting up Christmas decorations. We just wanted my Daddy to come home."

Ray saw smoke billow; flames consume shattered airplanes, wings, and fuselages with the red dot of the rising sun moving through the bright sky. The world shuddered and contracted around him as evil and death warred for supremacy in his life and the world. The image of a woman with blonde hair floated in front of his eyes. She reminded him of Peggy Lou, but she wasn't quite the same woman. A young boy ran across his vision chasing a small dog. The same old man who had been speaking floated across his mind. His face was swollen and bruised. Was the old man dying? They were all dying. The world was dying, drowning beneath a flood of blood. Ray swallowed and tried to cry out in horror.

"No! Don't let it be so! Stop it! God, stop it!" He pleaded, but the world continued to swirl around him nonstop. The old man's eyes opened, and he mouthed something Ray could not hear. Then, his features changed and smoothed and became the face of a young man.

"Mr. Castle, are you okay?"

Ray opened his eyes wider, and Daniel crouched over him. His bright, blue eyes were wide in amazement. "Daniel?"

"Gee, Mr. Castle, we thought you were a goner."

Ray sat up slowly, and his head swam. He was on a cot, but he was not in the library. Behind Daniel, the bars of a jail cell reached to a stained, paint flaked ceiling.

"Where am I?"

Ann Lee appeared behind Daniel as she stepped through the open door to the jail cell. "Oh, Mr. Castle, you're awake."

"Why am I in a jail cell?"

"You were in the hospital for a few days until the doctors decided you weren't going to die," Daniel said. "Again. You've got to stop showing up in the hospital."

"Doctor McKay said you couldn't stand another concussion. And, the reason you're in a jail cell is Mr. Cheatwood pressed assault charges." Ann Lee said.

"Against me?" Ray rubbed his head. Stitches scratched his hand. "I have stitches?"

"Sixteen!" Daniel said proudly. "Golly, Mr. Ray, you really showed them, didn't you?"

"Yes, and ended up in the hospital in another coma and the minute he started waking up, they moved him to jail!" Ann Lee said. "Remember that next time you want to hit someone, son."

"This isn't right," Ray said. "I'm the one who was hit with a serving dish."

"We tried to tell the judge that." Ann Lee said. "But, I think Mr. Cheatwood has some kind of special, uh, relationship with the judge."

"How long have I been out?"

"Three days," Daniel said. "They just moved you to the jail today. That's why we're here to bring you some clothes."

A man in a uniform stepped into the cell. "Mrs. Collinsworth, now that our prisoner is awake, you can leave."

"Deputy Wafer, can't you let him go?" Ann Lee pleaded.

"Sorry, that's not up to me." Wafer frowned. "Even though I think that Cheatwood feller got what he deserved. What with the war starting and all, we got a lot to deal with."

Ray froze. "Ann Lee! Have you heard from Frank?"

Ann Lee put a hand to her face and glanced at Daniel. "I'm sure we will hear something any day now."

Daniel's features darkened and he looked away into the corner. Ray sighed.

"I'm sorry I brought it up."

Deputy Wafer motioned to the door. "Now, if you will leave, I'll let Mr. Castle get cleaned up. He's been wearing those hospital pajamas for days."

Ray looked down at the gray pair of pajamas. "They brought me some clothes."

"Sorry, you'll be in prison grays until you leave. Then you can have your clothes."

Ann Lee reached out and took Ray's hand. "It's only for a few more days. The judge gave you seven days in prison. It'll be over before you know it."

Ray felt the heat build behind his eyes, an anger that was stoked by outrage. How dare they put HIM in prison? Why he would call, he would call—. The name skittered away like a stone tossed over the smooth surface of a lake. "My lawyer." He whispered.

"What did you say?" Wafer asked.

"My lawyer. I need to talk to my lawyer?" He shook his head as a headache seized him and he fell back onto the cot from dizziness.

"Who is your lawyer?" Ann Lee asked. "I'll call him."

"I don't know." Ray groaned. "Never mind."

After Ann Lee and Daniel left, Wafer took him to a cold communal shower. He washed dried blood out of his hair and scrubbed three days of stink from his body. When he was done, he dried off with a rough towel and put on the prison jumpsuit. It hung loosely on his body. He had lost weight again!

Wafer escorted him back to his cell. Other cells along the walkway held a dozen men. They were curiously silent as he passed. Why weren't they screaming in protest? Where were the catcalls and putdowns? Wafer locked him in his cell. "The doctor said you could have aspirin every six hours for the pain. Supper will be in an hour."

Wafer walked away, and Castle sat slowly on the cot. He felt something warm run down his neck and wiped away the blood. His cut was oozing.

"*Stinks, doesn't it?*" A voice came from the corner. He whirled and winced at the pain that came with the sudden movement. Something moved in the shadows and assumed the vague shape of a man. Luminous eyes glared at him.

"Who is there?" He whispered. Was he hallucinating?

"*You know who I am.*" The voice rasped. "*You just can't admit it. I hope this teaches you a lesson.*"

"What lesson?"

"You're getting weak. You're letting this family atmosphere soften you. You have forgotten who and what you are."

Ray looked away. Was it true? The anger simmered just below the surface. He desperately wanted to reach out and hurt Esau and Lazarus Cheatwood. They had beaten him at his own game.

"That's right!" The voice seemed closer now right at his ear. *"You let them win. It's time to wise up and get revenge. You can't let them win."*

Ray closed his eyes as the pain worsened. "Go away." He whispered. Then louder. "Go away! Now!"

Wafer walked into view. "Hey, Castle, keep it down."

Ray glanced up at Wafer and then looked over his shoulder. The shadow man was gone. He held out a hand. "I'll take those aspirins now."

❧ I 2 ☙

Headlines The Shreveport Times
Friday, December 12, 1941

Yesterday, December 11, Congress unceremoniously declared war on Germany and Italy following the American successes in the Pacific which found the nation's airmen sinking a Japanese battleship, a light cruiser, and a destroyer.

Private First Class Hal H. Perry, Jr. of Newellton was the first known casualty of the war. He was stationed at Hickam Field, Hawaii and was killed in the raids on the airport Sunday.

Tulane students told to continue studies normally. Continuation of study under the circumstances as nearly normal as possible was urged of the students of Tulane University today in a special communication from Dr. Rufus C. Harris, President.

Dy-Dee dolls just received in a new shipment to Rubenstein's are the miracle dolls that look and act like a real live baby! $2.98 to $10.98. With wardrobe $5.98 to $19.98.

With five simple words, "We are all in this" Winston Churchill proclaimed today Britain's proud determination to stand at the side of the United States and maintain at any and every cost the mighty barricade now thrust up across the world against the Axis marauders of Europe and Asia.

Your Country Needs You NOW! Let's Go! U.S.A. Keep 'Em Flying! Enlist Today! Your Regular Army is calling for volunteers! Men between 18 and 35 are needed for all of the Arms and Services. The Air Force wants thousands of young men, immediately! Come to the U. S. Army recruiting service in the Post Office Bldg. in downtown Shreveport.

Centenary Gents blew the lid off in the home schedule in a basketball battle with Magnolia A&M last night. The Gents successfully opened their campaign with a 50 to 40 wild scoring game.

The next few days were an unending string of hours and hours of boredom. Ray mostly slept as the pain lessened and the cut in his head healed. Five days after the attack, a doctor came to take out his stitches. When the doctor left, Wafer brought him his clothes. "Your time is up, Castle. I'm letting you leave early. Get dressed, and you can go. Your friends are here to pick you up."

Castle walked out of the courthouse into the bright, sunny cold morning. The streets were lined with bustling people. Cars parked along Texas Street. Lonnie waited on the sidewalk, stoking his pipe.

"Mr. Castle." He said, offering his hand.

"What's this?" Ray looked at Lonnie's hand.

"I want to shake the hand of the man who gave the Cheatwoods what for."

Ray shook Lonnie's hand. "Thanks, but I think they gave me the 'what for.'"

"Yeah, we tried to bail you out, but the judge must be in Cheatwood's pockets. You ready to go back to the house?"

"Ann Lee will let me come back?"

"Sure. You're a hero, Ray." Lonnie laughed. "Besides, you've got a week's worth of chores to catch up on. You're not getting off that easy."

Ray made it to the front door of the Collinsworth boarding house. He was a little short of breath from a week of confinement, but the fatigue was offset by the sensation of freedom. When he stepped into the house, he saw nothing had changed.

Uncle Lawson was reading his newspaper and Aunt Wimpy was knitting on the couch. The three sisters were crouched around the radio listening to a Christmas carol. In the near corner, Rachel and her friends were huddled around the piano, and Rachel picked out a tune on the keys. "I wish those girls were in school today. Why are they out of school?"

"It's a work day for the teachers and the students got a day off." Wimpy said.

"Well, they are working that piano for sure and it's working on my nerves!" Lawson said.

"Oh, girls, what will I do? This song just isn't working out like I want it to. It's missing something." Rachel said.

Penelope wore her ever-present beret, and she sat down beside Rachel at the piano. "It was good enough to get you into the contest."

"And, now I want to win the contest even more so for my Daddy." Rachel said.

"We'll help you, Rachel," Penelope said.

Gwendolyn was pacing around the piano. "I know what your problem is. Your clothes."

"My clothes? I just feel like the song lacks something. But, you're worried about my clothes?"

Gwendolyn smoothed the fabric of her dress as if she wore a slinky evening gown. "Your clothes will get you into the proper mood. I think you should wear a long evening gown with a pearl necklace. And we can get Mrs. Keller at the hair parlor to put a peroxide rinse on your hair."

Rachel turned back to the keys on the piano. "Gwendolyn, I don't own an evening gown! All I have is a pair of pajamas."

"You simply must catch the eyes of the judges. Your singing is good; I'll grant you. But, you've got to have the right posture." She walked over to the front door and spied Ray. She smiled and reached out to pinch his cheek. "Your color looks better today, Mr. Castle."

"Thanks," Ray said.

She entered the library and returned with three books perched on her head. She was carrying six more books, and she handed three to Penelope. Penelope grinned and put the three books on top of the beret. They began to walk carefully across the living room with the books poised perfectly on top of their heads.

"See how I walk with my back straight and my head held high?" Gwendolyn said.

Penelope followed after her. "And, we can recite a poem as we walk. Mary had a little lamb."

"Whose fleece was white as snow. It followed her to school one day." Gwendolyn continued.

"And Mary stubbed her toe," Penelope said as she tripped. The books flew across the room just as Ann Lee came in from the kitchen.

"What are you girls doing?" She asked.

Rachel tried to hide her music. "Oh, we're just looking at some old song."

Ann Lee saw Ray standing in the door and hurried over to him. "Mr. Castle, I'm so glad you're back home."

Home? The thought sent warmth through his chest. Was this place really his home?

"That was some blow on the head." Aunt Wimpy said, looking up at him.

"Yeah, I must have a really hard head to have lived through two concussions," Ray said.

Lonnie followed Ray into the living room and closed the front door. He shrugged out of his coat. "Lazarus is the one that should be arrested. He deserved to go to jail for the things he said after we heard about Pearl Harbor."

"I know. They were some terrible things to say. But, Lazarus had a point when he said you attacked him. The judge agreed, unfortunately. Mr. Castle, I appreciate you taking up for me, but you're lucky they didn't throw you in Sing Sing." Ann Lee turned abruptly. "Speaking of

Sing Sing, Rachel. What song are you trying to learn? Maybe I could help you sing."

Rachel paled. "Mother, maybe you should just let me sing the song."

"We've heard you sing, and—" Penelope nodded enthusiastically. She was cut off by a nudge form Rachel.

Ann Lee adjusted her hair and wore a hurt look. "Are you implying I can't sing?"

"Oh, Mrs. Collinsworth, it's not that you can't sing," Gwendolyn said. "It's just that you haven't practiced in so long. You wouldn't want to strain your vocal cords."

"Then you would sound like the Wolfman," Penelope said. Then, she let out a blood-curdling howl.

"What are you girls talking about?"

"You've never been able to sing, Mother." Rachel stood up slowly. "That's why you gave up your dream of being in the movies."

Ann Lee looked stricken. She glanced around at the others in the living room. They were all looking at her in anticipation. "Who told you that?"

"Daddy did. He said you dreamed of being in the movies until the talkies came out."

The room had grown very quiet. Ann Lee drew a deep breath. "I can't believe he told you that. Is that why you're singing?"

"What do you mean?" Rachel said.

"Because I couldn't? Are you trying to become a professional singer because your mother can't sing a note in a barrel?"

"No, Mother. I never said that." Rachel said.

"I've always told you I don't want you going into show business." Ann Lee pointed a finger at Rachel. "You should find a nice young man, settle down, and raise a family."

"In a drafty old boarding house? With relatives who can't pay their rent? You think that is how I want to spend the rest of my life?"

Ann Lee's eyes widened. "Young woman, you will not speak to me that way!"

"Just because you couldn't make your dreams come true doesn't mean you should try and ruin my dreams!" Rachel said.

Ann Lee whirled and paced around the room. "Dreams, dreams, dreams! You and your father all wrapped up in your silly dreams. Look where his dream of flying got him! If not for his dreams, we'd still be on the farm. But, instead, he had to go off flying! And now, we don't even know if he is still alive."

"Well, maybe if you had been more supportive of Daddy's dreams, he wouldn't have had to run off on some secret mission to Hawaii and leave us behind!" Rachel said as she followed her mother across the room.

Ann Lee whirled and slapped Rachel across the mouth. Rachel gasped and then ran out the front door. Penelope and Gwendolyn followed. Ann Lee froze, her eyes fixed on the hand that had slapped her daughter. Ray drew a deep breath. Sue Carol hurried over to Ann Lee.

"Ann Lee, it's not your fault Frank went off to Hawaii. You know that." Sue Carol hugged Ann Lee.

"I know. It's this war! It's destroying the world, and now it's destroying my family." Tears trickled down Ann Lee's cheeks.

"We are all feeling the effects of the war, Ann Lee. Lonnie and I can't have a civil word lately with him wanting to go join the Army." Sue Carol hugged Ann Lee tighter. "But, it's going to be OK. I just know it is. We just have to pray the Good Lord will take care of our families."

"It's been over a week since the bombing, Sue Carol. I can't stand much more of this."

Aunt Wimpy got up from the couch and crossed to Ann Lee. "I'm sure Frank is just fine. We haven't received any bad news."

Ann Lee shook her head. "Don't tell me no news is good news. I've tried everything. I've made a dozen phone calls. I've written letters. I even had Lonnie drive me over to Barksdale Air Field, and they wouldn't even let me through the gate."

"Mommy, what's wrong?" Daniel said as he and Buster came through the front door.

Ann Lee wiped away her tears and tried to smile. "Oh, nothing, son. I'm just worried about what to make for lunch. I think we have some bologna left for sandwiches."

"I heard you and Rachel fight. Where did she go?"

Ann Lee tried to smile, but it seemed forced. "Probably over to Penelope's house. She seems to be spending more and more time over there. I guess this old boarding house is becoming intolerable."

Daniel looked over at Ray, and their eyes met. He blinked and nodded as if he had decided something important. "If Daddy were here, things would be better, wouldn't they?"

Ann Lee reached out and put an arm over his shoulders. "Oh, honey, probably so. I'm doing the best I can to keep things together now that we're going to war."

"Ann Lee, you've always been the backbone of this family when Frank is away. You're strong. You can make it." Sue Carol said.

Ann Lee looked at Daniel and then across the room at Ray. Her eyes filled once again with tears. "But, what if? I mean if Frank doesn't?"

"Mommy, don't say it. Daddy will be home for Christmas. He promised." Daniel said.

Ray felt the old pain in his chest. A familiar and distant pain of despair and pessimism. Frank would not be coming home. He knew it.

Ann Lee's gaze faltered, and she looked away from Ray. "Of course, dear. He will be home."

Ophelia interrupted the gloomy conversation. "Now, Sister, that is a very beautiful rendition of *Adeste Fidelis*. I just love the classic Christmas carols." She reached over and turned up the volume on the radio.

"And, tonight, Sister, we can listen to our president as we celebrate the one hundred and fiftieth anniversary of the Bill of Rights. I hear Kate Smith is going to share the Golden Rules for Democracy." Evelia said.

"Well, forget that, Sisters," Lawson growled. "I want to hear Amos 'n' Andy. Besides the Golden Rules are right here in today's paper. Let's see." He adjusted his reading glasses. "One, do your part in defense of your country. Well, that leaves you sisters out unless you can ship some Remedy overseas." He laughed, and Wimpy punched him. "Two, Know the workings of democracy. Three, Be thoughtful regarding the issues of the day. Four, Protect your heritage, the Bill of Rights. Five, Try to understand the ways and ideas of others." Lawson glanced over his paper. "That one is for Esau Cheatwood. Six, help put the ideals of democracy into practice." He chuckled.

"What are you laughing at?" Wimpy asked.

"Oh, nothing. Just thinking about voting for some more Remedy."

Wimpy punched him again. "Get on with the Golden rules, you sot."

"Seven, promote freedom everywhere. Eight, beware of subversive propaganda. Nine, be friendly. Ten, Be courageous. Now, we don't have to listen to Kate Smith tonight."

Ray slipped out of his coat and hung it on the coat rack. "Those seem awfully idealistic if you ask me."

Lonnie walked over to the fireplace and grabbed a match from the mantle. He lit his pipe. "What do you mean?"

"I mean, who is to say what is subversive? What is propaganda? Sounds like the Golden Rules are propaganda."

Lonnie almost dropped his pipe. "That blow to your head must have been harder than you thought. You sound like one of those appeasers who think we can talk our way out of this war."

Ray opened his mouth to answer and then closed it. Why had he thought like this? The Golden Rules sounded so jaded; so unrealistic. The country had pulled together behind the attacks. But, how long would it last? Six weeks? Then, they would all be back to their daily grind and their cynicism. For a moment the image of two towering buildings with smoke billowing from their top floors appeared from the recesses of his mind. The image faded along with the memory.

Ray stopped and looked around him. Ann Lee and Sue Carol were frozen by the kitchen door, distressed looks on their faces. Even Lawson and Wimpy regarded him as if he had pledged allegiance to the Nazi flag. The sisters were whispering among themselves, casting furtive glances in his direction. Lonnie's face grew red as he stoked his pipe. Once again, Ray had said something that was inappropriate, out of sync with the mood of the country around him. But, he wasn't a patriot. Not like this. Sure, he was true to his country. But, things just weren't so cut and dry; so black and white. Or, were they? He raised his hands. "I'm sorry. I didn't mean anything by that."

"I hope not." Ann Lee said quietly. "My husband is risking his life for those ideals in that list. And so are thousands and thousands of American troops."

"You don't think America is worth fighting for?" Lonnie said.

"No, that's not what I meant. It just seems that it's hard to be courageous and friendly all the time. It's hard to understand the ways and ideas of others because they're probably hiding something." Ray said weakly.

"Are you hiding something?" Lonnie asked.

Ray looked around at his friends. His oddly familiar "family." A dozen raw and cynical thoughts crossed his mind. *"Go ahead and say them."* The voice echoed in his mind. *"They're a bunch of red, white, and blue losers who have placed their faith in the good old American dream and look where it has gotten them. In a war that will cost the lives of millions."*

He rubbed his head and chased the voice away. "I don't know what I'm hiding, Lonnie. I don't know who I am."

Ann Lee came to his side and placed a hand on his shoulder. "Well, we know who you are. You've been nothing but helpful the past few weeks. You've stood up to Esau Cheatwood and paid the price for it. You're Ray Castle, a man of honor and integrity. Don't give in to these hopeless feelings, Ray. Don't let them get you down."

Ray sighed and patted her hand. "Look at me. I'm the one who should be comforting you, Ann Lee. I'm sure once I've sorted out my thoughts, things will be better. Forgive me for being so negative."

"What we need is some Christmas spirit," Ophelia said.

Theophila smiled. "Indeed, Sister. We are remiss in our celebration of the coming Christmas season."

Evelia continued the thought. "I know of what you speak, Sister. Why there are no decorations about."

Theophila nodded. "No joy and happiness."

Ophelia glanced at Ray. "No mistletoe."

Ray shuddered and looked quickly away. Uncle Lawson rattled his newspaper.

"Wishful thinking. Says here in the paper that because of the war effort, fewer trees are being cut down for Christmas. You might have to get one of those new artificial trees."

Buster had joined Little Lonnie on the floor in the midst of a disassembled log cabin. He looked up in alarm. "Arty who?"

"Fake trees, son. Not real."

Little Lonnie shook his head. "But, we always have a real tree."

"I just love the smell of a real tree." Aunt Wimpy joined in. She was obviously trying to change the subject. "It makes the entire house so festive. And, it covers up Lawson's stinky feet."

"What? I soak my feet once a week."

"And bathe once a week, I know." Aunt Wimpy nodded and glared at him over the top of her glasses. "We have indoor plumbing with hot water now, and you could use a bath more than once a week. Fortunately, you don't do enough to break a sweat so you can last longer than most people."

Uncle Lawson tried to ignore her and went back to reading his newspaper. "There's new ornaments listed here in the newspaper. They come in a box set now. Looks like you can decorate your entire tree for $3. You know what I could do with $3?"

"Buy more Remedy?" Aunt Wimpy glanced over at the sisters.

"I can't possibly help put up the tree with my lumbago acting up," Lawson said.

Ophelia got up and came over to stand beside Ann Lee. "Ann Lee, how long are we to wait for the annual Christmas tree to be erected?"

Theophila joined them. "Yes, we usually celebrate the decorating of the tree with a little nip of the Remedy."

Uncle Lawson perked up and sat up straight in his chair. "In that case, I'll help put up the tree!"

"We usually wait until Frank cuts down a fresh tree. And, since he isn't here," her face twisted in sorrow and she started to cry. Sue Carol put an arm around her shoulders.

"There, there, Ann Lee. Don't be sad. Frank will come home. I just know it."

Ray cleared his throat. "Mrs. Collinsworth, I didn't mean to dampen the Christmas spirit. You've shown the true Christmas spirit to me since the day I showed up on your doorstep. I hope I haven't been too much of a burden."

"No, Mr. Castle." Ann Lee placed a hand on his arm. "It's helped keep my mind off the war. I am glad to see you back on your feet. You know, right after you ended up in the hospital, you talked in your sleep. Something about a bank in the Caribbean. Does that bring back any memories?"

Ray ran a hand through his thick, unruly hair and his body odor made him wrinkle his nose. A bank? It meant nothing to him. Nothing at all. "No, I don't recall anything about a bank. Whoo! I stink. And, I feel like I've been put out to pasture. I've only had one shower while in jail."

"You look like a tree full of owls." Uncle Lawson said. "You could use a haircut and a shave."

"And a bath." Aunt Wimpy said. "You can have Lawson's bath time. He's obviously not concerned."

Ray nodded, and Ann Lee pushed him toward the library. "Since we put in the water heater, Lonnie has put an old porcelain tub in the library bathroom. You can go soak for a while and get cleaned up."

Ray closed the library door behind him and drew a deep breath. What had gotten into him? Why had he said those things?

"Because the person who thinks those things is who you really are." The voice echoed in the corner of the library. He ignored it and ran hot water into a short, old cracked tub now occupying most of the space in the bathroom.

After soaking as long as possible in the heavenly hot water, Ray dried off and put on a fresh set of clothes. He looked at himself in the mirror of the library bathroom. The old clothing he wore although tattered and worn, made him look thin and wan. He glanced at his hair. The dark shadows in the library loomed behind him. A face appeared from the shadows. A clean-shaven, tanned face stared back at him. The hair was perfectly cut and layered. The reflection smiled at him.

"This is what you have to look forward to if you keep on this path." A voice hissed in his ear. *"Imagine spending a week in prison! You! Unheard of! You make sure the other guy gets caught. Not you! I mean, look at you! Unkempt.*

Unshaven. Smelling to high heaven. It's time to come back to me. Come back to who you really are."

Ray closed his eyes and leaned his head against the cold glass of the mirror. "Go away! Just go away! I'm confused enough as it is." He opened his eyes, and the face was gone.

❧ 13 ☙

Daniel appeared at the library door dressed in his superhero outfit. "Mr. Ray, I've got an extra quarter for you."

"What?"

"So you can get a shave and a haircut at Sam's Barber Shop." He held out his open hand. Ray stared at the quarter.

"I don't take charity, young man." He said harshly. He blinked furiously and rubbed his face. "Why did I say that?"

"We're all nervous as a cat on a hot tin roof, Mr. Ray. I understand."

Ray sighed and took the quarter. "You're right. I'm just confused by the blow to the head, I guess. Thank you, Daniel. I'll pay you back."

"Ah, don't think nothing of it." Daniel turned and started out of the library. "Just think of it as an early Christmas present. They close at five so you better hurry."

Ray followed Daniel to the living room. By the front door, he pulled on his coat and planted the worn fedora on his head. He headed out the front door and down the street to the trolley stop. He rode the trolley downtown and hopped out in front of Sam's Barber Shop. Men sitting around two barber chairs filled the shop. Most of them were studying newspapers, smoking unfiltered cigarettes and talking about the latest war news. "Chattanooga Choo Choo" played over the radio.

"I say we should never have ignored this war." One man said loudly around a cigar clamped in his teeth.

"Up until Pearl Harbor, I would have disagreed with you." Another man tapped his newspaper with his pipe. "But, I guess now we don't have a choice."

"They attacked us." A third man said from the barber chair. "Killed thousands of our sailors. We need to wipe them out!"

Sam, the barber, gently shoved the man's head back down onto the headrest of the chair. "Calm down, Charlie. I'm not finished with your shave."

Ray nodded at the men as he settled into one of the chairs. Sam finished up with Charlie as the talk of war continued. Ray felt uncomfortable sitting among these men. It was as if he were an observer from a different world and he knew how things were going to turn out. Sam motioned to him.

"You're next."

Ray looked at the other men. "What about them?"

"Oh, they're just here to tell Roosevelt how to run the country. What'll it be?"

Ray sat in the chair and took off his hat. "I need a haircut and a shave. How much will that cost?"

Sam put the drape around him and fastened it behind his neck. "Seventy-five cents."

Ray fished in his pocket. He had two more quarters to go with the one Daniel had given him. "That's all I got. I don't have enough for a tip."

"You were going to tip me?" He looked over at the men in their chairs. "Now, here's a real pal. A man with real class. He was going to tip me. That's more than any of you have ever done."

Some of the men laughed and then they continued their discussion of war news. Sam started trimming his long. "See you've had stitches up here. You must be the stranger down at the Collinsworth boarding house."

Ron looked up at the mirror in front of him and into the eyes of Sam, the barber. "How did you know that?"

"I recognize the clothes and the coat. I used to cut Samuel

Collinsworth's hair every week. That shirt you have on was one of his favorites."

"It fits me well. Ann Lee was kind enough to let me borrow them."

"Heard anything about Frank?" Sam asked.

"Nothing. Ann Lee is pretty upset."

"Well, Frank is a real hero. If anyone can survive that attack, he can. He's cut from good cloth."

A man appeared behind Sam's reflection in the mirror. He wore a long, black overcoat. His hair was slicked back, and his eyes were filled with mischief. *"Hanging out with the regular folk, are you?"* He said. Ray couldn't move his head to look away. The man laughed and rubbed his hand over his mouth. A gold watch glittered on his wrist. *"Well, well, I guess it was inevitable. Dad was one of these sad sacks, wasn't he? Only it wasn't the barbershop he visited. It was the local gambling joint. You remember, don't you?"*

The man's words cut through his amnesia. He saw a balding, overweight middle age man on his knees. The man's face glowed red with the flush of alcohol. His rheumy eyes cut toward Ray. "Here's how you do it, boy." He tossed dice onto the floor and rubbed his thick hands together. The dice clattered and came up a two and a one. The man's face slackened, and he fell back on his ankles. "No! I can't lose." He looked back at Ray. "This is your fault, boy! You're nothing but bad luck. Now, I just lost my paycheck. What will your mother think? Huh? You're worthless! I wish you'd never been born!" The man's whiskey-tinged breath played over him.

Ray sat forward with a start, gasping for breath. He glanced around. The well-dressed man was gone.

"You ok?" Sam asked. "You gotta be still, or I'm going to cut your throat with this straight razor."

Ray's breathing slowed, and he leaned back into the chair. "Sorry. I just had a horrible thought is all."

Sam nodded and continued to run the straight razor across his cheek. "Rat run over your grave? It's okay, son. You're probably still recovering from this cut on your head. Is it true?"

"Is what true?"

"You tried to take down Esau Cheatwood." Sam raised an eyebrow. The men around them murmured and nodded.

"Bout time someone put that crook in his place." One man growled.

"He's the one who made the bank foreclose on poor widow Jenkins." Another said.

"Ought to be tarred and feathered and run out of town." A third man said.

Sam leaned forward. "Looks like you have the makings of a hero, Mr. Castle."

"I'm no Frank Collinsworth," Ray said quietly.

"Heroes are in short supply right now," Sam said as the discussion moved on to football and the war. "There will be lots of panic for all of us coming down the road. We can't all be as strong as Samuel Collinsworth."

"What was Samuel Collinsworth like?" Ray asked.

"He was a good man. He had that farm down at Saline that he passed on to Frank. You see Frank's mother, Mary, got sick with consumption. Samuel realized he had to bring her here to the Schumphert Sanitarium for treatment. But, he couldn't go back and forth between here and the farm. So, he got a job with the railroad and bought that boarding house and all the property around it with money left to him by his father. His father was in the oil business, but Samuel never wanted to have anything to do with the business. He gave the farm to Frank and brought Mary to Shreveport."

Ray heard the sound of the razor 'scritching' against his beard. "What happened to Mary?"

Samuel appeared above him with the straight razor in his hand. "She lasted a couple of years. She died on the Christmas before Rachel was born. I hear tell Samuel brought home a little cedar tree in a bucket so he could decorate it for Mary. But, he was too late. Well, it wasn't long after that Samuel got sick, too. Frank moved to the city to take care of his father. He told his wife it was because he wanted to fly, but the real reason was to take care of his sick father."

The attic tree! That is why Frank had put the tree in the attic. And, why he had kept the thing alive. Growing in the attic had stunted its size, but it was still alive.

Samuel finished scraping the hair from Ray's face and neck and placed a hot, wet cloth over his lower face. The effect was wonderful! The heat and moisture soaked into Ray's skin. "Then, it wasn't a month after Daniel was born that he died of a heart attack."

"That was God's mercy if you ask me." One of the men said. "Heard he holed up in the attic sitting at a dormer looking out to try and see if he could spy Mary's grave in the cemetery down the street. I think he just gave up."

"That's how Frank ended up with the house and the property?" Ray asked.

Samuel sat him up and slapped witch hazel on his skin. The stinging, cool liquid made him wince until it settled into his taut skin. "I think Samuel deeded it over before he died."

Ray reached into his pocket and took out the change. Samuel shook his head. "Save that for a Christmas present. You don't have to pay me. Frank already took care of it."

Ray's mouth fell open in shock. "Frank?"

"Yeah. He came by here before he left and said if you came by to put it on his tab."

"That's Frank for you." One of the men said. "Just like his father."

Ray stood up and brushed the hair off his legs. He looked in the mirror. He liked what he saw. His hair was short and wavy, and his face looked clean and young. No double chin. He looked relaxed. Nothing like the tense, tight face of the shadow man. "Would you have done that, Sam?" His eyes met the barber's gaze.

"Done what?"

"Left the farm and put it all behind to save your wife?"

"What do you think the men of this city are doing right now? My son just got married two months ago, and he enlisted the day after Pearl Harbor. Just like his friends, he is willing to sacrifice it all to protect his wife and his family. Ain't that the most important thing in the world? Our family?"

Ray glanced back at the mirror. For a fleeting second his features were eclipsed by the reflection of the mirror man. Suddenly, he burned with shame. He knew in his heart he would never do such a thing. He would take care of himself long before he gave up his life for anyone, including his family.

"*There you go.*" The reflection whispered. "*Now, you get it.*"

For a second, the image of a dark haired woman with sad eyes floated through Ray's mind, and he saw, once again, a young boy holding a baseball glove. He shook his head and hurried out of the barbershop before the men could see the shame on his face.

Ray hurried down the sidewalk. His stomach growled. He should have grabbed a bologna sandwich. Or, he could stop at the Shreveport Club for lunch. He paused and glanced eastward on Texas Street. What was the Shreveport Club? It was back that way, wasn't it? He had a membership, didn't he?

He closed his eyes in confusion. Street lights and Christmas lights blinked all around him. Cars moved down Texas Street, and the smell of ozone wafted over him as a trolley trundled past. In nearby shop windows of Sears & Roebuck, festive and colorful Christmas displays gleamed with hope and promise for the future. Women and children gathered around the window displays in awe. This was their way of denying a war that would soon engulf the entire world. But, how did he know that?

Tinsel and garland hung from streetlights and across the street above the spiderweb-like tangle of trolley wires. He paused beside a window display. Santa waved in jerky movements. An animatronic. He shook his head. Another word that did not belong in this world. Why? A thin man in a long, wool coat and a fedora picked up a small boy and held him up to the window.

"Look, Daddy, Santa's waving at me." The boy squealed. His black hair stuck out from under a wool cap. His rosy cheeks glowed in the cold air. A woman holding a toddler girl with long, blonde hair smiled and steam issued from her mouth as she spoke.

"Don't you worry, Ronald. Santa's going to bring you and Gwen some sweet oranges and apples. Isn't that right, Slayton?"

"Yes, Lena, he will." The man put Ronald down and glanced at Ray. "Merry Christmas, sir."

Ray stepped back away from the placid domestic scene. This was not what he knew. It was not his life. His father, in the flashback, was far from the doting, loving father standing before him.

"Hey, mister?" The boy said. "Are you okay?"

Ray turned and hurried away from them.

"*Don't worry about the boy.*" Someone said. He stopped and whirled. Who had said that? He had left the family far behind. An elderly couple walked around him deep in conversation. A woman pushing a baby buggy followed. Where was he? Where was the shadow man?

"Shut up!" He hissed. "Just leave me alone."

"*Think about the blonde.*" A voice said behind him. He turned again. People moved toward him and away from him along the busy sidewalk. He backed up against the cold, stone wall of a storefront. Was he going crazy? Maybe it was the concussion!

"*Here's the plan.*" The voice whispered in his ear. He froze. "*Peggy Lou isn't playing with a full deck, but she is a looker. You can take her attention away from Esau Cheatwood and stop that man's plans. Have you forgotten? Listen, you've lost ground being in jail for a week. You've got a lot of catching up to do.*"

"Shut up!" Ray shouted and pressed his face into the hard, cold wall.

"Hey, buddy? Need a lift?"

Ray glanced over his shoulder. A man stood next to a cab. He wore a black cap and motioned to the empty cab.

"Do I know you?" Ray said.

"What's that supposed to mean?" The cabbie said.

Ray stepped closer and examined the man's bright, blue eyes and his dark uniform. He looked nothing like the mirror man. "I know you."

"Everyone knows me, buddy. I'm Mikey. Best cab driver in Shreveport. But, I can't say I've ever given you a ride in my cab." He smiled. "Maybe you've been getting Madeline to give you a ride. Now, she's a real pistol and all the guys like her driving style. The only woman cabbie in Shreveport. But, she's a little wild for my taste."

Ray looked away in confusion. He knew this man from somewhere but every time he tried to touch the memory, it slithered away like a scared lizard. He looked into Mikey's eyes. "Do you know who I am?"

Mikey raised an eyebrow and pushed his cap up off of his forehead. "Sure."

"You do?"

"Yeah, Mr. Collinsworth told me to look out for you. Said you'd fallen on hard times. No memory of your past, eh?"

"No." Ray felt bitter disappointment.

Mikey leaned against his cab and crossed his arms. "Well, mind if I give you some advice?"

"Go ahead."

"Sometimes, we tend to remember the person we've become and forgotten the person we're supposed to be. The good Lord has a plan for every man, and we tend to wander off the beaten path sometimes. Chase after that mysterious man we all think we can become." He stood up and leaned forward. "But, you know what?"

"What?"

"When we meet that other man and look in the mirror and think we've found the goose that laid the golden egg, we see a stranger. Don't be looking for the man you wanted to be, Ray. Look for the man you're supposed to be."

"How did you know my name?"

"Frank told me." Mikey opened the door to his cab. "Gotta go. And, the courthouse is two blocks down the street." He got into the cab and closed to the door.

"Courthouse?" Ray asked. "I just left there this morning!"

"Yeah, that's right. But, now you've got something besides jail on your mind, don't you? That's where you were headed, right? To check out something at the courthouse?"

"But, I never said anything about the courthouse." The cab pulled away from the curb. Mikey waved a hand and drove around the corner.

"Courthouse? Why would I need to go to the courthouse?" Ray shouted after the receding cab. He shook his head in confusion and pulled his coat more tightly around his shoulders. The sky was turning a darker gray, and the air was growing colder. He really should be heading back to the boarding house. But, there was something in the back of his mind about the courthouse.

"For once, I agree with my adversary." The voice whispered behind his right ear. *"Go to the courthouse."* A bright light flashed behind him.

Ray whirled. A couple had stopped in front of one of the display windows. The man wore a leather coat and a fedora. His girlfriend or wife wore a long, woolen coat and her hair was pulled back in a snood. Another man lowered his camera and held out a card.

"That was gorgeous, pally. Make a great Christmas gift. Give me a call, and the photograph will be ready tomorrow afternoon."

The man smiled at his girl and tucked the card into a coat pocket. The man glanced at Ray. "Hey, mister, you got a girl you'd like to have your photo made with? They make a great present. Who knows? You may be shipping off to the Pacific before Christmas. The photos make nice memories while you're away." He held out a card, and Ray took it.

"You've found a good angle, haven't you? Play on their fear." Ray said.

"Hey, pally, I'm just trying to make a living. 4F on account of my hearing in this ear." He pointed to his right ear. "Or, no hearing. Don't give me no grief. I'm just trying to pay the rent."

Ray put the card in his pocket. "Yeah, we all got an angle, don't we?"

The man winked. "Yeah, what's your angle, pal?"

Ray's face grew warm, and he hurried away from the man. An angle? What was his angle? Did he have one? Was he nothing but a con man like Cheatwood? The cold air burned in his lungs and light snow began to fall from the sky. He stopped and leaned against a stone wall. After catching his breath, he looked up at the courthouse he had walked away from just hours before. His angle on the deal was here. But, what was it? Like a shot of lightning, the memory erupted in his mind. The deed! He needed to find the deed.

The Caddo Parish Courthouse was a sprawling structure in the center of town with columns on the upper stories. Statues adorned each of the opposite entrances. He hurried through the doorway and paused just inside. A single security guard was drinking coffee next to a snack bar. Where was the metal detector? Metal detector? Why had he thought of such a thing? The security guard nodded at him.

"Afternoon, sir. Can I help you?"

"I'm Ray Castle. I'm living up at the Collinsworth boarding house. I just wanted to go down to the records room in the basement and check out the deeds for Mr. Collinsworth." How had he known where the records were kept? It seemed so natural as if this were his profession. "Say, you wouldn't know me, would you?"

The guard walked over to him and put a hand on his shoulder. "Sure do. Frank told me to look out for you. Said you might show up wanting to apply for a job. Go on down to the basement. I suggest the stairs. The elevator is running slow today."

At least the man didn't remember him from being released from jail! Just who had Frank talked to about him? He felt guilty about what he was about to do. If Frank knew he was looking for a bargaining chip with Esau Cheatwood over the deed to his house, he wouldn't have been so willing to recommend him to anyone. Well, there is a chump born every day, he thought. His face burned with shame at the thought. But once again it seemed so natural.

Ray made his way down the stairs and into the dark hallway of the basement. He paused in front of a door with a glass window. "Record Room" was stenciled on the glass. He opened the door and stepped inside. A high counter separated the small reception area from a huge room filled from floor to ceiling with wooden shelves. He had expected to find something else in the room. Some kind of machines, perhaps? With typewriter keyboards and glowing windows filled with information? He shook his head in dismay, and a small, stooped woman appeared behind the counter.

"May I help you, dear?" She said. She wore a golden bell on the lapel of her blouse. She was tiny and thin, and her face was sallow from days spent here in the basement.

"I'm Ray Castle. I'm doing some work for Frank Collinsworth. I need to check out some records from a few years ago."

The woman turned a huge logbook toward him and handed him a pencil. "Well, sign in, and I'll take you back to one of the work tables. I suspect you're talking about deeds and such? Sales and land transactions?"

Ray signed his name. "What is today?"

The woman pointed to a calendar on the wall. It showed a big "12".

He wrote down "December 12, 1941".

"You must be a landman. Looking for oil leases?"

Ray felt a trickle of familiarity with the term. "Yes, ma'am. But, I need to find out when a piece of property changed hands and who currently owns it."

The woman lifted the countertop at the far end of the counter and cleared a space for him to enter the records area. She led him back into the dark, dank and dusty rows of record books. She motioned to a long rack of logbooks.

"This entire bookshelf carries land transactions from up to twenty years ago." She pointed to a low wooden shelf with small drawers. "There are cards in there with the names of the sellers and buyers. It's not complete, but it will narrow down the month and year. Good luck. We close at four." She paused and sighed. "Sorry, I'm supposed to say we close at five since the war began. Lots of people coming and going on government business." She disappeared down the aisle.

Ray took off his overcoat and set to work. Neatly filed index cards with names typed on the top right-hand corner filled the card catalog and a description of the transaction and the date. He looked through them for Collinsworth and never found a mention. He made it through two more card catalogs. His head pounded with pain, and he sneezed. His stomach growled. He glanced up at the clock on the far wall. He had been there for over an hour and had made no headway. The deed was not registered or recorded.

Then, he recalled what Lonnie had said when he first saw Esau Cheatwood. "Your Daddy sold Frank's Daddy this house."

Ray went back to the card catalog. Such a transaction would have come when Samuel Collinsworth had moved to Shreveport long before Frank had come. What had Sam, the barber said? Mary lasted two years? Or, was it three? He went back twenty years in the card catalog and started looking for the name Cheatwood.

With only ten minutes left until closing, he found the card. He pulled it from the catalog and noted the date. He hurried over to the bookshelf and scanned through the dates scrawled on the spines of the logbooks. There! He saw it. He pulled the logbook down and thumbed through looking for the date of the transaction. He found it listed near the bottom of the page.

The transaction had taken place, but there was a notation in the last column. "Deed never filed. See tax logs." Ray mouthed the words and looked up at the clock. As if she had read his mind, the little woman appeared at the end of the bookshelf.

"Sir, we're about to close. I'm afraid you will have to leave for the day."

He closed the book and slid it back into its slot. He slid the card into his coat pocket. As he pulled on the overcoat, he thought furiously. He stopped at the counter.

"Can I ask you a question?"

The woman nodded as she turned off the lights in the record room behind her. "Sure. If it doesn't take too long."

"What would a notation mean if it said, 'see tax logs'?"

"Someone didn't pay property taxes. It means the property is open for probate."

Ray nodded slowly. "So, if someone paid the back taxes, what would that mean?"

"Well depending on the amount of taxes owed and the length of time they've been owed, that person could claim the property." The woman stepped out from the behind the counter. "You'll have to go upstairs and speak to the tax department. They probably know all about the back taxes on the property."

Ray nodded and followed the woman out of the office. He made his way up the stairs and out the door into the cold, bitter evening. So, the property could be had by paying back taxes. Did Esau know this? If not, then his information was a bargaining chip. He smiled, and the feeling was one of triumph. He felt a thrill, unlike anything he had experienced since he closed that deal with the board! Frank paused. The board? He had closed some huge deal. What was it? It was supposed to change his life forever! But, no matter how hard he concentrated on it, he couldn't resurrect the memory. But there was one thing he did know for certain. Whatever the deal was that he closed, it had come at a great cost to someone else. It had been a whole heap of hurt for the person who lost in the deal. And, for a second, his victory was eclipsed by guilt.

❦   14   ❦

Ray returned to the boarding house shortly before dinner. He hung his coat on the coat rack and heard a whistle. He whirled. Aunt Wimpy was ogling him.

"You clean up pretty good, Mr. Castle. If I were any younger and not married to this lump of meat, I'd be coming after you."

Ray's face reddened, and he chuckled nervously. "Why, thank you, Aunt Wimpy."

Ann Lee turned around from the dining room table and gasped. She shook her head. "For a moment there, I thought you were Frank, Mr. Castle. With your hair cut that short and the beard gone, you look a lot like him."

"Well, from what I heard about Frank today, we're nothing alike. Your husband is an amazing man, Ann Lee. I hope you hear from him soon."

The front door opened abruptly, and a man in a uniform was backlit by the sunlight. Ann Lee gasped. Sue Carol's mouth fell open in shock. Lonnie Britt stepped into the room dressed in an Army Corps uniform.

"Maybe it's time a real man went looking for Frank," Lonnie said.

Sue Carol rushed over to him. "Lonnie, what on earth have you done?"

"Sorry, I didn't tell you. I enlisted yesterday in the Army Air Corp, and they told me to come to Barksdale Air Field to pick up my uniform. I'm going to fly an airplane. I can't say too much. Loose lips sink ships, you know."

Sue Carol glanced over her shoulder at Ann Lee and Ray. Her face filled with desperation. "But, what about your job at the Post Office?"

Lonnie motioned toward Ray. "Ray needs a job. I talked to my supervisor. If Ray wants the job, it's his. You see, Sue Carol, I'm a real man, and I'm going to serve my country."

Little Lonnie looked up and ran over to his father. "Hey, Daddy, your clothes are all shiny."

Lonnie ruffled his son's hair. "That's right, son. I'm a soldier now."

"Not a very smart soldier, honey." Sue Carol picked up Little Lonnie and turned away from her husband. "Lonnie, how could you do this? You promised me you wouldn't go off and join the military."

"If I wait much longer, I'll be drafted. This way, I get to choose. Besides, I want my son to know his Daddy is going to be a real hero."

Uncle Lawson glanced at Ray and put his newspaper on the coffee table. He stood up and came over and pushed his face close to Lonnie's. "So, you want to be a hero, huh? Think that uniform makes you a hero?"

"No, Uncle Lawson. But, it's a start."

"You have no idea what you're getting into. If you had any sense, you'd listen to your wife." Uncle Lawson said. Aunt Wimpy put a hand to her mouth in surprise. What was Lawson up to?

Lonnie glanced nervously around at everyone and then drew up in a defiant stance. "I don't think this is any of your business, old man. Go back to your newspaper reading and your lumbago."

Uncle Lawson started to turn away, and he stopped and whirled back to face Lonnie. "Don't you talk to me that way, Louie!"

"Louie? My name is Lonnie. Are you getting senile?"

Uncle Lawson paused and looked around at the people in the living room. For a second his gaze met Ray's. "No. It's just that, well, Louie was a friend of mine. A long time ago. I guess I got your names mixed up."

"Oh, I suppose he was a real hero, huh?"

Uncle Lawson opened his mouth to speak, and then his face became pale. He turned away and silently returned to his chair. He studied the empty seat for a moment and then picked up his newspaper.

Lonnie hurried after the old man. "Well, you're just going to leave it at that? Call me Louie and then go back to your newspaper?"

"I got better things to do with my time than talk about the past. Besides, we're about to eat supper."

"Lawson, who was Louie? I don't remember a friend of yours named Louie." Aunt Wimpy said.

Uncle Lawson looked at the folded newspaper as if it were a stranger. "That's because he was dead when we got married."

"Dead? What happened?" Aunt Wimpy slowly stood up.

"I'm not talking about it. It's been twenty four years. It's in the past."

"Twenty four years? That would mean you knew him during the Great War." Lonnie said. "Was he in the infantry with you? You know, your flat feet and all?"

Uncle Lawson suddenly crumpled the paper in a violent gesture and tossed it across the room. He bolted up from the couch, and his eyes widened with anger, and his face reddened. "What would you know about war? You're still wet behind the ears. Thinking that uniform is going to make you bulletproof? You don't know the half of it."

"Well, then tell me!" Lonnie shouted.

Uncle Lawson took a step closer. "Fine! I'll tell you. You want to hear what it was like in the trenches? How we crouched in the holes like scared rabbits? You want to know what the artillery sounded like? How it thundered across the trenches and hit your eardrums like a bass drum? We couldn't hear a thing after that."

Uncle Lawson paused and looked away from Lonnie into some far distant land of dead memories and buried pain. "Silence. Total silence all around you because for a moment you're deaf. And then you feel your buddy tugging on your arm. You look over at Louie, and his eyes are as wide as can be and his mouth is moving, but you can't hear what he's saying. And then he pushes you down and brings up his rifle and there right behind you is an enemy soldier about to put a bullet through your back. And you see the rifle kick when it's fired, but you don't hear the explosion and the soldier behind you falls. Dead. Silent."

Uncle Lawson reached out and grabbed Lonnie suddenly for support. For a moment it seemed he was going to fall. Lonnie grabbed the old man's arm and held him up. Uncle Lawson's eyes were moist and red with horror and loss. "And then, I looked at Louie, his mouth moving, his eyes wide and there on his chest, a red flower blossomed like a rosebud. He looked down at it and just then the sound comes back with all the explosions, and the screams and Louie looked at me and said, 'Be good chap.' He fell on top of me dead as a doorknob."

Aunt Wimpy appeared on his other side and gently pulled him away from Lonnie. She put an arm around his waist. "You never told me about Louie, Lawson. Why?"

Uncle Lawson seemed to return to the present. He looked down at the floor. "There are some things a man can't talk about."

"Even to your wife?"

Uncle Lawson looked at her and fire returned to his eyes. "I said I didn't want to talk about it anymore!" He tore his arm out of her grasp and settled back into his chair. "Where's my newspaper?"

Aunt Wimpy gasped and put her hand to her mouth. Little Lonnie ran across the room and picked up the wadded up newspaper and brought it back to Aunt Wimpy.

"Uncle Lawson dropped his newspaper."

Lonnie looked away from his son and quietly walked out the front door. Aunt Wimpy took the newspaper and straightened it. She drew in a deep breath, and a false smile came over her lips. She turned to Uncle Lawson and handed him the newspaper.

"Thank you, Little Lonnie. Lawson, here's your paper, dear. Would you like some coffee?"

"Good soldiers always drink lots of coffee. Let's see what this war has in store for Lonnie." Uncle Lawson jerked the newspaper out of her grasp and opened it. "Well, says here that the Flying Tigers that Frank used to fly with did a grand job over China. In fact, Winston Churchill had some good things to say about them. *'The victories of these Americans over the rice paddies of Burma are comparable in character, if not in scope, with those won by the Royal Air Force over the hop fields of Kent in the Battle of Britain.'* I guess Frank ought to be proud of helping to train those men."

Buster was standing stock still in the middle of the room. His eyes were fixed on the front door. He turned, and for a moment, Ray saw fear and horror in his eyes. Daniel came over to him and put a hand on his shoulder.

"Guess both of our daddies are in the Army now."

Buster blinked and tried to look brave. "Dad is going to fly airplanes like Uncle Frank. But, maybe bombers."

"Could be."

"He's going to be bombing the stink out of those Nazis. What do you think of that?"

Daniel looked a little bewildered. "I don't know, Buster. I guess it's a good idea."

Buster reached up and pulled off his aviation hat and goggles and let them drop on the floor. "Good idea! Hey, you're just sore because you're not the only boy with a father for a hero around here. You just wait! My Daddy will bomb more Nazis than your Dad ever will. You just watch!"

"Oh, yeah?" A muscle twitched in Daniel's cheek, and his lip quivered.

"Yeah!" Buster shoved Daniel's hand off his shoulder.

"You act like I'm the enemy."

"Maybe you are."

Buster lashed out with his fist and caught Daniel in the side of the face. They fell back, and the two of them were suddenly at each other's throats, rolling and tussling on the floor. Ray ran over and tried to separate them, but the anger and frustration that filled their minds had given them incredible strength.

"Lonnie, get in here!" He screamed toward the front door. It flew open, and Lonnie ran in. His face was red, and his eyes were moist. He grabbed Buster and pulled him away from Daniel. Ray picked Daniel up and tried to hold him still.

Sue Carol stepped between them. "OK, that's enough, boys. Go wash up for dinner."

Buster struggled in his father's grasp. "But, Daniel thinks he's the only one who can have a hero for a Dad. We'll show him. Won't we Dad?"

Lonnie drew a deep breath and looked at Sue Carol. "Yeah, son, we'll show everyone." He said hoarsely.

Ann Lee wiped at her face with a handkerchief and motioned to Ray. "Why don't you take Daniel into the library until he calms down. Lonnie, you take Buster in the kitchen."

Ray nodded and pulled the struggling Daniel behind him toward the library. He pushed the boy into the room and shut the door behind him.

"Now would be the perfect time to find out where the deed was." A voice echoed in his head.

He stopped and shook his head. *"Why now? Because they're confused and vulnerable! You have to strike while the iron is hot! Kick a man while he is down!"* The voice continued.

Ray watched Daniel collapse into the chair behind Frank's desk, and he pushed the strange and troublesome thoughts away. Daniel looked up, and his eyes were wet with tears. "It's just not fair, Mr. Castle. My Daddy is gone. Nobody knows where he is. Nobody wants to talk about it. And Uncle Lawson saying all that stuff about war. I'm scared."

"Scared! A man should never be scared! It shows your weak side." Ray said gruffly. He shook his head. "No, wait a minute. I didn't mean that." He glanced at Daniel's tear-streaked face. A warm spot grew inside him. He cared for the boy like he was his own son. His own son?

"You don't have a son! You have a beautiful woman waiting for you on a sunny beach!"

He grabbed his head and squeezed it. "No! I don't want her. I want him." He shouted.

Daniel stood up and wiped the tears from his face. "Gee, Mr. Castle, are you all right? I didn't mean to upset you."

"I'm fine, Daniel. Just some painful memories trying to return."

"Something bad happened to you? Like maybe it happened to my Dad?" Daniel slumped again into the chair. "Why do bad things happen to heroes?"

Ray drew a deep breath and walked across the room and settled into the chair beside the desk. "I don't know what to say, Daniel. Sometimes, bad things happen to good people. I was wrong the other day about shades of gray. Your Daddy told you there was an evil sweeping over the world and he was right." Just like the evil that was trying to capture his every thought. "He said it was like a dark shadow falling over everything good and light. You've got to fight that evil, Daniel. I'm sorry you have to grow up and realize this, but the world is not always a good place." I should know, he thought.

"I worked against the good, and it felt wonderful!"

Daniel looked up at him, and his bright blue eyes gleamed with tears. "How did you know that was what Daddy told me?"

"I was taking a walk in the woods, and I saw you and your Daddy talking. He is a very wise man, Daniel. If there is any hope in the goodness of this world and if there is a God in heaven, your Daddy will be home by Christmas."

Daniel blinked. "Do you believe in God, Mr. Castle?"

Ray opened his mouth to answer. *"Of course, you believe in God! YOU are God!"* The voice echoed in his head.

He stood up and grabbed his head. "No! I am not God."

Daniel stood up again and rushed around the desk. "I'll get Mom."

Ray grabbed his arm as the boy walked away. "No. Not yet. Daniel, I'm fighting for my life here. Some of my memories are really, really bad. And, I don't want to be bad anymore. I don't like it. Just give me a moment to sift through my memories. Please, sit down. Don't leave me, Daniel. I need you here."

Daniel nodded and slid behind the desk again. "Sure thing, Mr. Castle."

"Ray, please call me Ray." The pain in his head subsided, and he closed his eyes. A dark figure stood between him and a long corridor. "Your grandfather brought a cedar tree home for your grandmother the day she died. It was the day Rachel was born. That's why there's a tree in the attic, Daniel. That's why your father keeps it alive. I don't understand how you can care for something so much you're willing to sacrifice every day to keep it alive even when it makes no sense. An attic tree? That's the kind of person I want to be, Daniel. But, I'm not. I would have tossed the tree into the trash and moved on."

"How come Daddy never told me that?"

"Some things are private, Daniel. Like this battle, I'm having inside of me. Some things you can't tell the world because you have to fight it yourself."

"You're not alone, Mister Ray. God can help you. He helps me every night. I pray for my Daddy and hope that he will come home. Surely you believe in God. You have to."

Ray studied the boy's wet face. What if he doesn't come home, he wanted to say. He had the distinct impression under any other circumstances he would have blurted that out. But, now, he thought of the dark, shadow man dwelling deep in his mind and in his heart and he hated him. He was the one who would have hurt those around him just for the feeling of hurting someone. But, this family; this child and his father had taught him something. Reluctantly and painfully, he realized something very important about this man that lived inside him. He no longer wanted to be that person.

Ray drew a deep breath and closed his eyes. He was back in the long, shadowy corridor with the shadow man. His fists balled up and with a sudden, violent blow, he shoved through the shadow. It dissipated in oily ashes and dispersed all around him. Ahead stretched a dusty and long deserted corridor. In his mind, he stumbled down the corridor and paused before a door locked and covered with cobwebs. He reached out and put a hand on the door facing. A golden warmth suffused his palm and ran up his arm. The spark of golden light settled in his heart, and he knew that at one time in his life, he had accepted the presence and the power of God. It warmed him now just as it warmed the heart of this dear, desperate boy and it gave him a glimmer of hope. Even as he took his hand away and returned to the present, he wondered what had made him take God and lock Him away in the most deserted corners of his life. He opened his eyes and blinked away a tear and wiped at it with his hand. He looked at the tiny drop of water on his finger. He glanced up at Daniel.

"Yes, Daniel, at one time in my life I believed in God."

Daniel reached out his hand. "Will you pray for my Daddy, Mr. Castle? Will you ask God to help my mother?"

Ray felt a cold wave pass over him. Pray? Did he even know how to pray? He swallowed nervously. "Sure, Daniel." He stood up and placed a hand on Daniel's shoulder. He felt the small but powerful shape of the man to come. He had held another such boy's hand, but it had been smaller. He bowed his head, and his mouth was suddenly dry. "Uh, hey, God. This is Ray. You know who I am even though I don't know all there is to know about me. But, whatever it is that I've done before today, I hope you can overlook it and just hear my prayer for Daniel and his family. Take care of Frank and bring him home safely. And, be with Ann Lee and Daniel until then." Ray looked up, and the boy's eyes were shut tightly.

"And, God, if I have to do it, help me to be the man of the house." He whispered.

Ray was stunned. He drew in a deep shuddering breath. Here was this tiny, defenseless boy willing to take on the mantle of responsibility of being the man of the house in the absence of his father. What had Ray ever done that could even approach the bravery of this young boy? He swallowed back his tears and muttered. "Amen. I think I'm looking at the real hero in this room."

Daniel opened his eyes, and he looked off into the distance. "Well, I don't know if I can do it."

Ray studied the boy's pale face, his blonde hair, his reddened eyes. Daniel wore his superhero costume. "Tell me about Captain Freedom."

Daniel looked at Ray. "What?"

"How did he become a hero?"

Daniel smiled. "Well, Chris Trueblood was the littlest boy in his high school. He was skinny. I mean real skinny. Other guys pushed him around and beat him up. But, his daddy was a doctor, and he kept telling him to take his vitamins. Only, the vitamins didn't seem to help. Every day when he got up he looked at himself in the mirror, and he was still a scrawny little kid. And then, one day, this kid showed up at school with one of those Nazi symbols on his shirt."

"The Swastika?"

"Yeah, that's it. The other kids were scared of him but not Chris Trueblood. No, Chris marched right up to that kid and called him a traitor. Well, it didn't take long for that kid to beat the living daylights out of Chris. He ended up in the hospital, and his daddy thought he might die. They gave him no hope. So, his daddy tried something. He had developed this new form of vitamin that was sort of a super vitamin. He snuck in at night and gave it to his son." Daniel's face was red with excitement.

"Chris Trueblood stopped breathing, and his daddy ran out to find a nurse. But, while he was gone a bright light showed up in the hospital room and an angel appeared. He was a warrior for God, and he told Chris Trueblood that this vitamin would make him a super soldier and as long as he kept his heart pure and fought against evil, he would be a hero for freedom."

Daniel smiled. "When his daddy came back in, Chris Trueblood was standing by his hospital bed. He was big and had muscles, and he was very powerful. He said he wasn't Chris anymore. He was Captain Freedom, and he would fight for those who couldn't fight for themselves. Want to know his motto?"

"Sure."

"Say something, do something, and stand for those who can't." Daniel struck his pose. "And, that is Captain Freedom."

"Wow!" Ray nodded. "A real superhero. You thought that up yourself?"

"Yeah, I did. And, there's more to the story." Daniel lowered his hands. "The Nazis tried to steal the formula for the super vitamin and they," He stopped suddenly, and his face paled. "They killed his daddy." He frowned and looked away. "The formula for Captain Freedom would only work for him and no one else. So, he was the only superhero soldier around." Daniel grew quiet. He glanced at his gloves and down at his costume. "I'm not going to let my Daddy die, Mr. Ray. But, I also gotta take care of my family. I know what I gotta do, now." Daniel looked at him. "Can I call you Uncle Ray?"

Ray blinked and felt his heart sink. "I could never replace your father, Daniel." But, before Daniel could answer there was a shriek from the living room. What was happening now?

❧ 15 ☙

Ray hurried into the living room. Peggy Lou was standing in the open front door. Her face was streaked with tears, and she was sobbing loudly. She had on a short, purple dress and a new hat. Ann Lee hurried over to her.

"Peggy Lou? What is wrong?"

Peggy Lou stumbled across the room. "He's a cad! A stinker!"

"Who?" Ann Lee asked.

"Esau Cheatwood." Peggy Lou spat the name. "I was supposed to meet him at the Stork Club, and I went a little early--"

Sue Carol was sitting at the dinner table talking quietly to Lonnie. She stood up slowly. "The Stork Club? That's over on the Bossier strip. What are you doing at the Stork Club?"

Peggy Lou paused and straightened as if to regain her composure. "It's a nice place to go and dance and hear big band music. Anyway, I got there a little early because I took the trolley and then a cab. And when I got inside, there he was, all cozied up to another woman!" She slammed the front door.

Aunt Wimpy had come across the room to soothe Peggy Lou. "Oh, poor thing! Don't worry, Peggy Lou. You'll find another boyfriend."

Peggy Lou took a compact out of her purse and started to study her face in the small mirror. "But, Esau is the one. He's the man I'm going to marry!"

"What did you do?" Ray asked.

Peggy Lou glanced up at him and for a second seemed not to recognize him. She frowned. "I walked across the room and grabbed his drink and splashed it in his face. Then, I marched right out of there and took a taxi back here."

Ann Lee put a hand to her mouth in shock. "A taxi? Do you know how much those things cost?"

"Madeline's taxi. She owed me a ride so it don't matter. I had to get away from Esau."

There was a knock at the door. Ann Lee started toward the door and then stopped. She turned back to Lonnie. "I can't. It might be, you know, bad news."

Lonnie stood up and came to the door. "I'll handle it, Ann Lee." He opened the door and glanced outside. He gently closed the door and smiled. "Oh. Peggy Lou, it's a woman looking for you."

Peggy Lou put the compact back in her purse and fished inside for something. "Oh, I thought Madeline wasn't going to charge me. Does somebody have a dollar?"

Sue Carol frowned. "A dollar? Do you know how much you could buy with a dollar?"

Lonnie shook his head in dismay and dug into his pocket. "Here. I've got a dollar. I've already gotten an advance on my first paycheck."

Peggy Lou took the dollar from Lonnie and stepped past him and out the front door. There was a loud metallic clang, and Peggy Lou screamed. She stumbled through the door, and her face was covered with red. She was screaming and wailing at the top of her lungs.

"I'm dead! I'm dead! Somebody help me."

Ann Lee and Sue Carol both bolted for her as a tall, willowy woman stepped in through the door. She wore a slinky evening gown and carried an iron skillet in her right hand. She brandished the skillet at Peggy Lou.

"And let that be a lesson to you. Esau don't need no floozy like you when he's got me. So, stay away from my man." She said in a high, nasal voice. She glared at them all and sauntered out the door, slamming it shut behind her.

Sue Carol helped Peggy Lou to the couch. "Lonnie, go get a wet cloth and some ice. Hurry."

Ann Lee fretted over Peggy Lou and shouted at Lonnie's retreating figure. "Oh, there isn't any ice. The iceman didn't come today."

"I'll just get a wet cloth, then."

Ray knelt down in front of her and tried to examine her forehead. "Now, just calm down, Peggy Lou. Let me see where the blood is coming from."

Peggy Lou wiped the red liquid from her face. "I can't believe that woman did that. I ought to call the police on her. She ruined my face. I just know it."

Ray breathed a sigh of relief. "No, she didn't, Peggy Lou. This red stuff is your lipstick that you smeared all over your face from crying. All you have is a nasty bump on your forehead."

Peggy Lou sat upright, and her eyes were wide with anger. "Really! Well, then, let me at that witch! I'll show her a thing or two." She jumped up from the couch and hurried to the front door. Just as she jerked it open, Esau Cheatwood appeared with his hand raised to knock on the door.

"Peggy Lou, what has gotten into you? Why did you act that way at the Stork Club?" He said as he pushed into the living room.

Peggy Lou took the washcloth from Lonnie as he returned from the kitchen and wiped her smeared lipstick from her face. "Now don't you go sweet talking me, Esau. I saw you with that woman."

Esau licked his lips nervously, and his eyes shifted to Ray for a second. "That woman was just my cousin, honey."

Ray's face warmed with anger. "Kissing cousin? Your 'cousin' showed up here a moment ago and hit Peggy Lou with a frying pan."

Esau glared at him. "Ah, and you came to her rescue. How noble. I see you're all gussied up and spruced up. You must think you look like a Hollywood star. Let me ask you something, Mr. Castle. Have you ever rescued anyone? Do you know anything about your past? For all we know, you may be a criminal. Oh, wait! You are!"

"You shut up, now, Mr. Cheatwood. That has nothing to do with what you just did to Peggy Lou."

"Maybe you're in the Army." Esau ignored his remark. "Were you kicked out of the service? Or maybe you ran away without leave. Maybe you're just a coward who can't fight for his country. And now, you dare to stand up for Peggy Lou. Why she doesn't deserve someone like you! She deserves someone better. Someone richer. Someone more powerful. She deserves me. Isn't that right, cupcake?" Esau reached out and grabbed her and pulled her to him.

"I wasn't much of a coward when I tackled you the other day," Ray shouted. "If your son hadn't hit me over the head, I think I would have shown you which one of us was a coward. Cowards lie. And, you lied to Peggy Lou. You were with another woman."

"Peggy Lou understands that sometimes you have to check out the competition to really appreciate what you've got. Isn't that right, honey?" Esau chuckled.

Peggy Lou seemed confused. "I guess." She looked at Ray with a new kind of interest in her eyes.

Esau hugged her tighter. "Good. That's better. Now, listen up, Mr. Castle. You get your nose out of my business, and you get out of this town and stop freeloading on Mrs. Collinsworth."

Lonnie stepped in front of Ray. "Mr. Castle is our guest, Mr. Cheatwood, unlike you. I would like for you to leave our home."

Esau looked him up and down. "Well, look at the proud soldier. Joined the Army did you? Ready to go blow up some of the enemy? Beats stuffing envelopes down at the post office, doesn't it?"

Buster looked up from the log cabin he was building with his little brother. He joined his father. "You don't talk that way about my Dad. He's a hero like my uncle."

Daniel ran from the library and slid to a stop beside Ray. "Hey, what is going on here?"

"Daniel, have you heard from your father?" Esau looked over Daniel's shoulder toward the library. "I see you haven't put up the Christmas tree, yet. Peggy Lou told me it was a family tradition that father and son would cut down the tree together." He put a hand to his mouth and raised his eyebrows. "Oh, that's right, your father isn't here.

The hero hasn't returned from the battlefield." He released Peggy Lou and stepped toward Ray. "So, who is going to replace Frank? Ray?" His mouth twisted in a lopsided leer. "Ray Castle? Man of the house! You could never replace Frank Collinsworth. Why you're only half a man with no memory."

Ray clenched his fists and fought back the anger. "You're going too far, Cheatwood."

Esau shrugged pointed to Daniel. "I guess that leaves the little boy to be the man of the house?"

Ann Lee stepped between Ray and Esau. "Ray, don't let him get to you." She patted his arm. She turned and glared at Esau. "You've got no call to speak to my son like that, Mr. Cheatwood. I want you out of my house. Now!"

Esau reached for Peggy Lou's hand. "Fine. Coming, sweetheart?"

Peggy Lou looked around at the people in the room. Her gaze fell on Ray.

"You don't have to go with him, Peggy Lou."

Peggy Lou seemed on the verge of speaking when Esau rubbed his hands together. "Before you come to the fair damsel's rescue, Mr. Castle stop and ask yourself what you've contributed to this household in the past few weeks. Huh? You're nothing but a leech. A parasite. Why you've been in the hospital and spent a week in the slammer." He pressed his face close to Ray's. "You know how to take advantage of a good situation. I can sense it in you. Fact is, we're a lot alike, Ray. Or, whatever your name really is. Look, you've lost this one, buddy. I'm the top of the world right now, not you. So, stop while you're ahead and move on to your next con."

Ray's neck burned with anger. "You have a lot of nerve lecturing me on taking advantage of people. I know what game you're playing, Cheatwood."

Esau grinned and leaned even closer, pressing his lips close to Ray's ear. "You're no angel, Ray. I have the feeling your dark side is worse than anything I could ever do. I've seen the way you look at Peggy Lou." His cold breath played over Ray's cheek. "I have a close friend with the police. He owes me. One phone call and you're in that jail cell of yours for more than just one week. So, leave now, or I'll see to it you never see the light of day again."

Esau stepped back and straightened his tie and reached for Peggy Lou's hand. "I said, are you coming, Peggy Lou? You don't want to stay here with these losers."

Peggy Lou broke her gaze with Ray and, head bowed, hurried out the door with Esau.

Ray drew a long, shuddering breath. Was Esau right? After all, he had just won a struggle with his 'dark' side. But, how long could he hold it at bay? What would happen if it triumphed and took over? What damage could he do to this family?

Ray looked around at everyone. He was as confused and angry as he had ever been. At least as long as he could remember. He had brought sorrow and confusion to this household just like Esau Cheatwood. These people didn't deserve to be deceived by the likes of either one of them.

"I'm sorry I haven't contributed much to this household. Maybe it's time I moved on." He grabbed the old, moth-eaten coat hanging on the coat rack and shrugged into it.

Ann Lee tried to stop him. "Mr. Castle, don't listen to people like Esau Cheatwood. You belong here."

Ray looked into her eyes. His hands were shaking. "Maybe I do. Maybe I don't. I need some time to think things over. I'm going for a walk."

"Just a second." Ann Lee said. She hurried to the dining table and returned with a sandwich. "Just leftovers tonight. If you're going for a walk, at least have something to eat."

Ray's stomach growled and accepted the sandwich. Here he was thinking only of himself, and Ann Lee had her thoughts squarely on him. What had one of the Golden Rules points been? Try to understand the ways and ideas of others? Well, he had failed already. He turned and stepped out into the cold, cold night.

❧ 16 ☙

Ray hurried down the sidewalk toward downtown. The lone porch light cast his shadow ahead of him. Glowing eyes gleamed from the shadow.

"Don't give in to Esau's words. Don't let the man push your buttons! Be strong! Don't be a coward! What is wrong with you?"

"No! Shut up! I got rid of you." Ray shook his head to clear the conflicting thoughts. He bit into the roast beef sandwich as his stomach growled with hunger.

"You'll never be rid of me. I'll always be there, crouching at your door, waiting for you to come to your senses. Then, I'll take over." His shadow disappeared in the darkness around him as he hurried toward town.

The downtown area was alive with banners hanging from the streetlights and colored lights strung along the storefronts. Shoppers hurried about carrying packages of bright colors and ribbons. It was almost idyllic if it had not been for the pall of the war that hung over the world. Ray seemed to be at war with himself. There was the old Ray, something dark and manipulative that Esau recognized. But, there was also another version of him he had discovered; a version that centered more on the God of the universe than the god that was Ray Castle. He liked this newer version much better than the other. But, who would win? He finished the sandwich and longed for something warm to drink. Perhaps a Starbucks? What? What was that?

Snow still fell and piled up along the sidewalks. On a nearby corner, four people wearing Victorian-era costumes were singing Christmas Carols. At a nearby table, an electric coffee urn steamed and a sign said. "Free spiced cider." He paused and listened to the singers as an elderly lady with red cheeks filled a thick, paper cup with cider. He thanked her and sipped the warm drink. It was pungent and sweet and just what he needed. It was Christmas! The cider warmed him. The sweet music washed over him, filling him with a longing for something he had lost. Family. Love. A wife, perhaps? A son? Like Daniel? Forget about Esau and Peggy Lou. Maybe instead of running away and buying into Esau's lies, he should do whatever he could to help Ann Lee and the friends in the boarding house.

Ray froze as the words echoed through his mind. He had friends? They had become his friends, hadn't they? Lonnie had set him up for a job at the post office. Perhaps it was time to settle in, lean into this new life.

"I can't believe she slapped me." Rachel rushed past him with Penelope and Gwen close behind her. They stopped in the cone of light from a streetlight.

"You had it coming," Penelope said.

"Whose side are you on?"

"You said some really harsh things to your mother. Can't you see she's upset about your father?" Penelope said.

Rachel looked away and spied Ray. "Oh, hi, Mr. Castle. You look different. Really nice."

"I got a haircut and a shave. I feel like a new man." He stepped into the cone of light and the swirling cloud of snowflakes. He finished his cider. "You were saying?"

"I'm sorry for that showdown with my mother. I know she's on edge without my father." Rachel bit a fingernail and looked back at Penelope. "But, I'm upset about my father, too. It's just that my mother doesn't understand me."

Gwendolyn had pulled a scarf up around her billowing blonde hair. She rubbed her hands together in the cold. "Maybe she understands you better than you think. After all, she tried to be in show business once, and I'm sure it hurt pretty bad when she realized her dream wasn't coming true. Maybe she doesn't want to see you hurt, either."

"She makes a lot of sense," Ray said.

"I guess you're right. I shouldn't have been so mad. But, Daddy told me to go after my dream. And, I am. If for nothing else, then for him. Oh, I'm so afraid he isn't coming home."

Penelope reached out and hugged her. "Rachel, listen to the words of your song. I believe your Daddy is coming home."

"And, I'll help you find the perfect dress to greet him when he comes in the door," Gwendolyn said.

"And, I'll design you a very special Christmas card with 'The Homecoming Tree' on it," Penelope said.

"Homecoming tree?" Ray said.

"My song. I wrote it for my Daddy. And, we may not have a tree at the house, but I will have this song to sing whether I'm in the contest by then or not."

Ray smiled as a warm feeling came over him. "Well, if the three of you are that determined to see Frank Collinsworth come home by Christmas, we can't stand by and let the house go without a Christmas tree. If you'll excuse me, girls, I have something I must do."

Ray hurried back toward the house and hoped he could remember how to navigate the dark woods back to the tree. He made his way up the winding path, and as he approached the hearing, he saw a glimmer of light. The lantern from weeks before was sitting on the stump. Daniel was standing in the center of the hearing with the ax in his hands studying the tree in front of him.

"Okay, Daddy, it's time for me to grow up and do what has to be done."

Ray paused just outside the clearing and watched as Daniel began chopping at the base of the tree. It shuddered and creaked with each blow and snow showered from its upper branches. *Shouldn't I help him?*

"Why? Daddy never helped us." The shadow man appeared on the periphery of his vision. *"He threw us to wolves, didn't he? Kill or be killed!*

Maim or be maimed! Survival of the fittest! We have to learn to be our own man, don't we? We'll never amount to anything if we're cowards!"

Ray grabbed his head and whispered. "Shut up! Just, shut up!"

His thoughts were interrupted by a loud cracking sound. The tree began to teeter and suddenly toppled over, catching Daniel in the face and burying him under its branches. He disappeared beneath the fallen tree. Ray gasped and was about to run into the clearing when he felt a restraining hand on his shoulder. His heart raced. The shadow man had become real! He whirled, and the figure in the shadows took off his hat and smiled.

"Mikey?" He said.

"You don't want to interfere with this, Ray. This is something that's got to happen."

Ray blinked in confusion. "But, Daniel might be hurt!"

Mikey, the cab driver, raised an eyebrow. "So, you do care about the boy?"

"Of course. What makes you think I don't?"

"Every father should love his son more than anything. More than the world. More than himself. Just watch, and you might learn something."

The air grew still, and Mikey stepped backward into the shadows and disappeared. Ray leaned against the trunk of a nearby tree. What had just happened? Why was Mikey here? Where had he gone? Ray whirled and stared at the fallen tree. An eerie luminescence appeared on the far side of the clearing. The snow suddenly stopped falling, and the air became clear and crisp. His breath grew frigid in the night air, and someone moved in the center of the diffuse light.

Daniel climbed out from under the tree and stood up shakily. He wiped at his head and pulled away some blood. "Golly, I could have been hurt real bad. Hey, it stopped snowing! What's going on here?"

Ray watched in horror as a bloody figure stepped out of the light into the center of the clearing. He was tall and thin and wore a tattered Army Air Corp uniform streaked with ashes, soot, and clotted blood. His hair was standing on end, and his eyes were fixed and wide in shock. Daniel caught sight of the man just as Ray did. He turned to run away, and the man spoke.

"Son, don't run away." The voice echoed eerily through the clearing. Ray felt his heart race, and he froze in horror. Who was this man?

Daniel turned. "Daddy, is that you?"

Ray squinted and realized he was looking at a ghostly image of Frank Collinsworth. Frank nodded. "I see you finally cut down the tree. That means you're the man of the house now."

Daniel was shaking and stepped back away from the fallen tree and the ghostly figure before him. "Daddy, where are you?"

Frank stepped closer, and the light began to fade behind him. "I may not be coming home, son. You've got to take care of your mother and sister, do you understand?"

"No, Daddy, don't say that."

Frank started backing away toward the dwindling light. "I may be seeing Jesus soon, so you do as I ask, OK?"

Daniel took a step toward the receding figure and froze. "Daddy, please. Don't say those things."

Frank's face was deep in shadow now as the light faded behind him. "Promise me, Daniel. Promise me."

Daniel collapsed onto the snowy ground, and the light disappeared. Only the thin, wan light of the overturned lantern lit the clearing. Snow began to spiral down again, and the air filled with whirling flakes. Ray realized he was gripping the trunk of a tree so tightly his hands were numb. He exhaled and tried to slow his racing heart. What had he just seen? How could Frank have appeared here thousands of miles from Hawaii? Ray did not believe in ghosts but this night had pushed him to the limits of his sanity.

Daniel was still crying with his face hidden in his hands. "Daddy, please don't say those things. Please."

Ray took a slow step into the clearing and Daniel sat up. He looked at Ray with confusion. "Uncle Ray?"

"I was going to come cut down the tree so we could have Christmas. But, you beat me to it." He whispered.

Daniel wiped his nose and the tears from his eyes. He stood up and straightened. "I cut down the tree, and it fell on me."

"You cut it down all by yourself. You're a real hero."

Daniel breathed heavily, and his misting breath filled the air along with the snowflakes. "I have to get it back to the house. By myself. You understand, Uncle Ray, don't you?"

"Yes, I do." He did not understand what he had just seen. But, he did understand the transition that had come over Daniel Collinsworth. "I don't know where to go, Daniel. I was hoping to bring the tree back, and maybe everyone would see the real me."

Daniel moved toward him. "Golly, Uncle Ray, I see the real you. You stood up to that mean Mr. Cheatwood, and you stood up for Peggy Lou even when she didn't deserve it." He reached beneath his red cape and slid his father's medal from the lapel of his shirt. "I'm not a hero. My Daddy is. Are you a Daddy, Uncle Ray?"

Ray stepped back. "I don't know. I think I might be. I'm scared I might not be as good a Daddy as yours."

Daniel wiped his nose with the back of his hand. He shrugged out of his red cape. He crossed the distance between them and reached up to Ray's shirt lapel peeking out from beneath his coat. He pinned the medal to the lapel. "I tell you what, Uncle Ray; you be the hero until my Daddy gets back and I'll be the man of the house." He stepped back and held out his hand. "Deal?"

Ray felt moisture in his eyes and glanced down at the medal. It seemed to weigh a ton. "Deal." He shook the boy's wet hand. "I'll see you back at the house." He turned to go.

"Uncle Ray?"

"Yes?"

Daniel handed Ray his red cape and took off his mask. "I won't be needing these anymore. Can you take my costume back to the house?"

Ray took the items. "Yes."

"I made my Daddy a promise. I'm going to keep it and do the best I can."

Ray nodded and looked at the cape and the mask in his hands. "I think Frank's son is just like him. You're both heroes." He turned and left Daniel to his task.

$\approx$ 17 $\approx$

Headlines The Shreveport Times
Saturday, December 13, 1941

U. S. still holds Wake, Midway as the heroic defenders of Wake and Midway islands, tiny Pacific islets, continue to hold the Japanese at bay while on the Philippine island of Luzon, American land, sea, and air forces joined in a terrific struggle to smash repeated Japanese attacks.

Harmony swept through Centenary College last night as the board of directors voted overwhelmingly to place all student activities and discipline under the direction of the president and faculty while athletic committees voted to discontinue all inter-collegiate athletics for the period of the war.

In London, King George and President Roosevelt exchanged messages shortly after the United States declared war on Japan, the foreign office announced today.

Derailed engine stacked up cars in the local yards of the K.C.S. railway near Southern Avenue when a switch engine derailed early Friday morning. A fireman was killed and the engineer burnt.

Santa Claus says, "Hey kiddies, I'll be at the Master Shoe Store at Phelps, Shoe Co, Ltd. Today and every day until Christmas. Come to see me!"

Listed in today's paper on page 8 are the regularly scheduled news broadcasts now heard on KTBS and KWKH. These are greatly supplemented daily by unexpected and unannounced newscasts from both networks. This listing of networks is printed for your convenience, keep it posted near your radio!

In spite of the war, football fans across the nation will get their usual quota of "bowl" games on New Year's Day unless present plans are changed by unexpected military developments.

◈

R ay arose early Saturday morning and headed out the front door with his seedy coat and his crumpled fedora. He caught the trolley downtown and transferred to a bus headed over the Red River bridge into Bossier City. He disembarked a short distance from the west gate to Barksdale Air Field. The sun had risen and the day would be warm and sunny. He drew a deep breath and walked up to the white stone guard house. Beyond the guard house, the wide open "grand" boulevard led up to the headquarters visible in the distance. The tall standpipe towered over the headquarters. Ray understood that once, the standpipe had been unsightly and checkerboard in appearance before being wrapped in French Revival Colonial stone to fit in with the "Parisian" style of Barksdale Air Field's physical layout. Two soldiers stood in a guardhouse. During the hot Louisiana summers, they wore white pith helmets but now that the war began, the pith helmets had been exchanged for battle style helmets.

"Sir, may I help you?" The taller one said as he stepped forward. His hand rested unsteadily on a pistol in a holster.

"Sorry to bother you. I'm trying to find out about a, well, a friend of mine stationed at Hickham Field. His family hasn't heard from him and, well, I'm afraid he might be badly injured. Or, worse."

The taller guard glanced over his shoulder at the shorter man. The other man stepped forward. "Sir, we don't handle that kind of information. You can have your friend's loved one call the main number for information."

Ray felt his face warm with anger. How dare they speak to him this way? Wait! That's the shadow man speaking! "Look, I don't want to start any trouble. I'm just trying to find out information about Frank Collinsworth."

The taller man stiffened and pushed his helmet up onto his head. "You're friends with Frank?"

"Yes. Well, sort of. I'm living at his boarding house."

The other soldier stepped closer. "You wouldn't be Ray, would you?"

Ray raised an eyebrow. "How do you know my name?"

"He told us about you. Said you had been shot and left on his front porch."

Both soldiers seemed to relax. The taller one moved his hand off the pistol. A dark Ford staff car pulled up beside Ray, and he stepped back away from the driveway. The rounded roof sloped down from the high roof across the trunk. Both soldiers snapped to attention, and the back passenger seat window rolled down. A severe looking man in uniform glared at Ray. "What is this man doing loitering at the gate, soldier?"

The taller soldier stiffened. "Sir, he's a friend of Frank Collinsworth."

The officer in the backseat relaxed. "A friend, huh?"

"Yes, sir."

"What's your name?"

"Ray Castle," Ray said.

"Carl B. McDaniel. I'm commanding officer of the Air Corps Flying School. That's how I know Frank. Why are you here?"

Ray leaned forward. "Sir, I'm trying to find out what I can about Frank. His family hasn't heard from him since last Sunday." Ray's tattered coat fell open, and Frank's medal dangled into view. McDaniel raised an eyebrow.

"Why are you wearing his medal?"

Ray glanced down. "Oh, his son, Daniel pinned it on me. It's a long story. He thinks I'm some kind of hero."

McDaniel motioned to the other side of the car. "Well, get in. I'll buy you breakfast and see what we can find out."

Ray smiled and ran around the back of the car. He paused and saluted the two soldiers before opening the door and settling onto the seat beside McDaniel. "Thank you, sir."

McDaniel nodded, and they rode quietly down the paved roadway toward the heart of Barksdale Air Field. They passed tall, white stone clad buildings and the driver pulled up to a two-story building with the tall standpipe behind it. A wide-open lawn surrounded the headquarters. A flag flew from a tall flagpole. Something about the flag seemed off. The stars. There weren't enough stars?

McDaniel hopped out of the back seat and motioned for Ray to follow. Nearby, a group of soldiers standing at attention saluted as he passed. A young man in uniform appeared down the long walkway and pressed a clipboard toward the man's hands.

"Sir, uh, General Doolittle just called. He wants to talk to you about training."

McDaniel put a hand on the aide's mouth. "Mitchell, loose lips!"

Mitchell glanced at Ray. "Sorry, sir. It can wait until we get inside."

"My office. Now. Get him on the phone." McDaniel said to Mitchell as they passed through the front doors of headquarters. McDaniel led Ray through the hallways filled with bustling people until he came to a break room. "Make yourself at home. Coffee and Southern Maid donuts. I'll be back in a few minutes." McDaniel took off his officer's cap and then paused and glared at Ray again. "Don't leave this room. Understand?"

"Yes, sir," Ray said.

"Are you going to let him talk to you like that?" The voice whispered in his ear. Ray drew a deep breath and ignored the voice as he poured himself a cup of black coffee. The white and green box containing donuts was familiar. He took a donut and bit into it. It was heavenly. Just like he remembered! No, he shook his head and looked at the half-eaten donut. The donut tasted much better when it was piping hot. As he washed the donut down with a sip of coffee, he savored the memory. The smell of vanilla; the hint of yeast. Familiarity. He closed his eyes and saw the same green and white box in a

different setting. For a second, he almost had the memory, but it drifted away.

"Manna from heaven, eh?"

Ray opened his eyes and glanced at McDaniel as he entered the room. He had taken off his coat and rolled up his sleeves. "Sorry for the secrecy."

"Yes, sir, I understand," Ray said. Secrecy he valued.

"Now, Frank's a good pilot. One of the best. Until he rubbed shoulders with Chennault. I don't like spies." McDaniel grabbed a porcelain cup and poured coffee. "Normally I get Mitchell to do this for me, but it's best we talk in private." He shut the door to the break room and plucked a donut from the box. "Have a seat."

Ray sat at a round table and finished his donut. "Thank you, sir. I don't mean to be ungracious, but you don't know me. I could be a spy."

"No, sir. I've had two snipers with a bead on you all the way to the front door. After you got in my car, McCoy, the tall one at the gate, called Mrs. Collinsworth's house and talked to our newest recruit, Lonnie Britt and confirmed who you were. I understand you have no I.D. Right before Frank shipped out, he told me about you."

"Does everyone know about me?" Ray placed his cup on the table.

McDaniel bit into the donut. "Well, it's not every day a stranger is shot and left on your front porch. Frank had you checked out. Couldn't find anything on you with the local police."

Ray sighed. "I'm a stranger to myself. Listen, you called Frank a spy?"

"He told you about Burma?"

"Yes, sir. Said he'd been sent to check on Chennault."

"A spy," McDaniel said. "Frank would be right here at Barksdale training pilots if he hadn't of ruffled some Army Air Corp feathers. Some of us really like Chennault. But then, some of us don't like loose cannons. Frank paid for it by being assigned to what we thought was the most boring place on the planet, Hawaii. Turns out we were wrong. Wish he was back here right now. Doolittle could use him."

"Doolittle?"

"Loose lips, Mr. Castle." McDaniel finished his donut. The door opened, and Mitchell came in with a ream of papers. "Sir, I've tried my best contacts. No one seems to know the whereabouts of Lieutenant Collinsworth. Things are still pretty chaotic on the islands. There was that second Japanese raid on Monday, you know."

Ray stiffened. "Second raid?"

McDaniel's face reddened, and he jerked the papers out of Mitchell's hands. "Keep your mouth closed around civilians, Mitchell." He glared at Ray. "You didn't hear that, understand?"

Ray nodded, and now he understood why there had been more problems communicating with Hawaii. A second raid the day after? That hadn't been in Lawson's precious Shreveport Times! "I'll keep it to myself, sir."

McDaniel studied the papers. "Mr. Castle, I'm afraid I can't help you today. I'm leaving tomorrow to take over the Air Corps Basic Flying School in Sebring, Florida. But, I'll have Mitchell keep a close eye on things after I'm gone. Might even get Chennault involved if I have to. But, we have our hands full with a new war, you understand? Unfortunately, the fate of one simple man in the midst of this night-marish war is just not important enough to the powers that be." He stood up, and Ray found himself rising also. "Well, give Mrs. Collinsworth my regards. Tell her what you want to about this visit. But, remember how important hope is, Mr. Castle. If Mitchell hears anything, we'll send a couple of soldiers to the front door to deliver the news. Good or bad."

McDaniel threw back the rest of his coffee and handed the empty mug to Mitchell. "Mitchell, get this man a ride home." Without another word, McDaniel marched out of the break room.

❧

THE DRIVER DROPPED RAY OFF A BLOCK FROM THE COLLINSWORTH house. Ray didn't want Ann Lee to know he had tried to find out about Frank. McDaniel told him to keep hope alive. He would do his best.

Ray walked through the front door shortly before lunch. The living room was alive with activity. Daniel's tree stood next to the piano, and it's pine fragrance filled the room along with the aroma of spiced apple cider.

Lonnie met him at the door. "Find out anything?"

Ray shook his head. "Nothing. But, McDaniel promised he'd get in touch with Chennault if he had to."

"What? You talked to the commander?"

"Yes."

"I don't understand."

Ray slipped out of his coat. "I'll tell you later. We can't let Ann Lee know they haven't heard anything. Where's your uniform?"

"I've got the weekend off. Good thing so we can get the house decorated. Should lift Ann Lee's spirits. Did you get breakfast?"

"Southern Maid donuts."

Lonnie sighed and closed his eyes. "Tell me they were hot and fresh."

"No, but that didn't matter." Ray smiled and went into the kitchen to get a cup of coffee. He poured himself a cup and turned to the kitchen door. A shadow moved between him and the door.

"Don't even think about it," Ray said to the shadow and shoved right through the inkiness and back into the living room. He settled onto the couch to watch the festivities. A dark shape filled the emptiness on the couch beside him.

"*You're no one's hero, you know.*" The shadow man whispered. "*You are a vicious traitorous man with venal desires.*"

Ray shook his head and watched the members of Daniel's family hover around the Christmas tree. "I could be, you know." He said to the shadows beside him. "But, these are good people around me. Just look how they treated Daniel when he dragged that tree through the front door. He's the hero. He's the man of the house."

The shadows shifted beside him. "*The man of the house would have made someone else cut down that tree. Don't you get it? You're above this kind of sentimental trivialities. You're a man of power! A man of action! A man in charge!*"

Ray laughed and sipped more coffee. The three sisters had turned the radio louder, and Christmas carols filled the living room. Rachel and her three friends were stringing together popcorn on a string. Daniel and Buster sat before a large trunk. Ann Lee popped the latches on the trunk.

"Now boys, you be careful with these decorations. Your father brought them home from one of his missions, and they are very delicate." She said.

"I'm seeing that the best things in life are fragile. They deserve my protection. Not my abuse. You might as well go away. I'm done with you." Ray said to the shadow man. He tapped the medal pinned to his shirt. "I'm the hero, now. Not the villain."

Ann Lee reached into the open trunk and took out a white cardboard box. Daniel reached into the box and took out a shiny glass globe. "Just like I remembered from last year, Mom. Can I hang it on the tree?"

Ann Lee smiled, and a tear glittered at the corner of her eye. "Of course, Daniel. You've grown up so fast. I think if you can cut down our Christmas tree, you can hang up these special ornaments."

Ray smiled at the sight of Sue Carol and Lonnie hanging paper chains on the tree. Little Lonnie sat in the middle of the floor with a stubby pair of scissors and tin foil. He held up a lopsided star. "Daddy, can we put this star at the top of the tree?"

"Look at that thing!" The Shadow man wheezed. *"Pathetic!"*

Ray shook his head. "No, *you're* pathetic. Why did I ever want to be you? What possessed me? This is what I want to be. These ordinary people surrounded by love and joy. You can go now. I don't need you anymore."

The shadow man wheezed some more, and the shadows shifted beside Ray. He glanced to his left. The couch was empty.

Rachel plopped down beside Ray. She wore a loose sweater over a skirt. "Mister Ray, thank you for helping out the other night."

"Of course, Rachel. It's so important you sing your song. So, this is the Homecoming Tree?" He pointed to the tree.

"Yes."

"Well, why don't we get some twinkle lights?"

Lawson lowered his newspaper and glared at Ray. "Lights? Want to know how much Christmas tree lights cost? Twelve dollars for a ten-foot string!"

Wimpy appeared behind him with a bowl of popcorn. "How would you know what anything costs? You never spend your money. Oh, wait, you don't have any!" She thumped him on the head.

"I wish we did have some lights to put on the tree. They could light the way for Daddy to find his way home." Rachel said.

"We need to string some more popcorn, Rachel," Wimpy said. She handed the bowl to Ray and placed a small bowl filled with thread and a red pincushion shaped like a tomato.

"Here, I'll help." Penelope sat on the other side of Ray. Ray popped a piece of popcorn into his mouth and chewed.

"This tastes so good. What kind is it?"

Wimpy halted as she turned away. "What do you mean?"

"You know, Orville Reddenbacher or Pop Secret?" Ray said.

All three women looked at him, and his face paled. What was he saying? "Never mind. There goes my mind again. Don't worry if I eat it all. We can put another bag in the microwave."

Lawson lowered his paper again and raised an eyebrow. "Micro what?"

Ray sat forward and studied their puzzled faces. What was he talking about? For a moment, he visualized a boxy, black appliance with glowing dials and then it was gone. "My faulty memory." He shrugged. He grabbed a needle and started stringing popcorn.

The Sisters' radio blared with big band Christmas music, and the boys hurried around the tree hanging the delicate glass balls on the limbs. Gwendolyn and Buster had made a paper chain from construction paper and hung the red and green chain around the tree. Rachel and Penelope took the growing string of popcorn and hung it across the branches. Little Lonnie had cut out several lopsided snowflakes and Lonnie and Sue Carol helped him hang them on the ends of the branches. Ann Lee reached into the big box of ornaments and took out a shoebox.

"And, for the final item, I've saved lots of strands of tinfoil to hang on the branches like icicles." The girls and the boys huddled around the box and started draping the irregular strands of shiny material on the branches. Ann Lee stood back and watched and when all of the homemade tinsel was hung she stooped down to remove one last item. She held up a shiny metal star six inches across. "And, here is the topper for the tree." She glanced at Ray. "Ray, would you like to put the star on the top of the tree?"

Ray felt his mouth grow dry and his heart race. "I would be honored."

Ann Lee handed the shiny, metal star to him. "Be careful and don't cut yourself. Frank made that star out of some scrap metal that came from a crashed airplane." She paused and looked away and dabbed at her eyes.

Ray climbed up onto a chair and stuck the open bottom of the star on the spindly branches at the very top of the tree. He stepped back, and everyone applauded. Rachel touched him on the shoulder.

"Mr. Ray. I found something on the mantle and Mom said it belonged to you. Can we put it on the tree?"

She held out her hand. Ray looked down from her eager face to the thing sitting on her palm. The small, wooden angel looked back at him. He drew a deep breath and felt his heart skip a beat. It was filled with familiarity, and yet he was afraid of it. He reached out to touch it and stopped, pulling back his hand. "It's an angel?"

"Every Christmas tree needs an angel. Especially our homecoming tree."

"Homecoming tree?" Ann Lee said.

"Yes, mother, a tree to hang our hopes and prayers on as we wait for Daddy to come home." Rachel said.

Ann Lee put her hands up to her eyes, and Sue Carol hugged her. Rachel's eyes betrayed her sense of loss. She leaned over to whisper in Ray's ear. "Remember my song? And now, we have a real homecoming tree." She nodded and turned back to the rest of the family. "If God hears my prayers, he'll send a guardian angel to watch over my Daddy and make sure he gets home. Until then, this tree will remind us of his homecoming."

Ray nodded and glanced again at the angel. "Sure, Rachel, put that angel on the tree." The ghostly figure of Daniel's father standing in the eerily quiet forest haunted his memory. Frank Collinsworth was going to need all the help he could to get home.

❦ 18 ❦

Headlines The Shreveport Times
   Saturday, December 20, 1941

Caddo Parish is slow to answer the Civilian Defense call evidenced by a lagging spirit in the registration of civilian defense volunteers. This was noted yesterday by civilian defense chiefs, and the calls were issued for more volunteers to take up the slack on the final day of registration.

The Russian offensive, extending from the Leningrad front south to Crimea, continued yesterday to drive the Germans back in many points along the front. One division of Nazis was wiped out to the last man for a total of 37,000 killed or wounded.

From London, news that the fate of Hong Kong's outnumbered garrison still was not definitely known in any quarter this morning, but military observers made no attempt to conceal their fears that the entire colony either was in Japanese hands or would be in the next few hours.

Joe Gerard, 73, one of the oldest engineers on the Santa Fe railroad lines doesn't know why but the railroad has asked that he not make his famous "Santa Fe

Santa Claus" Christmas run this year. "I think it has something to do with the war." He said.

Seven Louisiana men were arrested Saturday night on Black Lake and Saline Lake in Natchitoches Parish on charges of shooting ducks coming in to roost. Federal charges for shooting ducks after 4 p.m. were filed in U. S. district court against the men.

Barksdale cuts red tape to speed acceptance of aviation cadets. This was done as a means of meeting the acute demand which the war has brought for combat pilots, bombardiers and navigators in the armed forces of the U. S. A.

Jack Dempsey, former world's heavyweight champion, heads the lists of guests on Dave Elman's "Hobby Lobby" on CBS-KWKH tonight at 7:30 p.m. He now lectures at army training centers and will talk about teaching youngsters boxing and other healthful exercises.

"King Tarz" the sensational lion actor will be presented in two free shows in front of the Strand theater Saturday in connection with the forthcoming opening of "Tarzan's Secret Treasure" and will be held at noon and 4 p.m.

Ray had settled into his routine at the downtown Post Office. He had taken over Lonnie's old job of sorting letters. With the combination of Christmas and the war, letters and packages had increased in huge numbers. Saturday morning found Ray in the backyard splitting logs. His hands had toughened up over the last weeks, and he had lost weight. He felt like he was putting on more muscle and he enjoyed the physical labor. He waited for the voice of the shadow man to whisper in his ear, but he had been absent the past week.

"Mister Ray, you don't have to split any more firewood," Daniel said as he joined Ray in the backyard.

Ray wiped sweat from his brow. "Feels good, Daniel. I need the aerobic exercise."

Daniel laughed. "There you go with one of your new words, Mister Ray."

Ray shrugged. "One day, I'll remember what all of these words mean. What can I do for you?"

Daniel wore his corduroy pants and a flannel shirt underneath his jacket. No Captain Freedom costume. "Well, Buster and I want to go down to the Strand to see the lion."

Ray placed his ax on the ground and leaned against the handle. "You lost me."

"King Tarz is a big ole lion that's gonna be in the next Tarzan movie, and we can go see him for free at the Strand. Can you take us?"

Ray chuckled. "A big ole lion? If you're sure we don't need more firewood, I don't see why I can't. When do we need to go?"

"There's a show at noon and one at 4 p.m. It's almost eleven now, and you gotta take a bath."

Ray wrinkled his nose. "You're right about that. Let's head downtown after lunch and do some Christmas shopping, and we'll stop off and see this big ole lion of yours."

"Yippee!" Daniel jumped up and down. "I'll go tell Buster."

"And, your Mom," Ray said at his receding figure.

"Feels weird, doesn't it?" The voice whispered in his ear.

"Ah, you're back. Can't say I missed you. Yeah, it does feel weird," Ray said. "But, this time, weird is good."

"You think you can act like a father to Daniel?"

"Sure. Frank may not be coming home, and the boy needs someone to look up to." Ray said.

"What makes you think you're the one for that?"

"Listen, I don't know why you think you have to tell me what to do and what to think. I know you're a remnant of my lost memories. But, I can't think like you anymore. I've made my choices. Daniel needs a hero in his life. He needs his father. I may not have been much of a father in your world, but I can be a good father figure in this one."

"What do you know about being a good father figure?"

"It's simple. I will do everything right that our father did wrong." Ray raised the ax above his head and rammed it into a log. "Now, beat it."

Ray took the boys to the soda fountain at Woolsworth diner for ice cream even though it was in the forties outside and he finally got his piece of apple pie. Then, they wandered around Sears looking at the Christmas toys and other "manly" things on sale. Daniel seemed somewhat distant and less enthusiastic than Buster. Buster played with toy guns and "spy" toys. But, Daniel only watched.

King Tarz did not disappoint. A lion tamer led the big lion out of his cage on a makeshift stage in front of the Strand Theater. A huge crowd had gathered, and Ray helped the boys climb up onto a low wall across the street. The lion growled and roared on cue. He pawed at his trainer and did several tricks. Finally, a tough-looking man in a suit and fedora stepped up to a microphone.

"Welcome to this audacious sight, citizens of Shreveport. I am Chief of Police Williamson and to show how 'fearless' your law enforcement men are; I will climb into the cage with King Tarz."

"Golly, he'll get eaten alive!" Buster said adjusting his aviator cap.

"Naw, the lion is tame." Daniel yawned doing his best to remain nonchalant.

The man stepped into the cage with the lion, and King Tarz regarded the man with an interested look. He leaned forward and nudged Williamson's chest with his nose. Williamson stepped back, and for a moment, fear clouded his face, and then he smiled. King Tarz opened his mouth, and everyone gasped expecting a huge roar. Instead, the lion yawned and rolled onto his side. Laughter passed through the crowd.

"See, what did I tell you?" Daniel poked Buster. "He's just a big pussycat."

As the sun fell below the horizon, the air chilled and Ray shivered. "Okay, guys, time to head home for supper." Someone tapped Ray on the shoulder. He turned to see Lazarus Cheatwood rubbing his hands together to keep them warm.

"Lazarus? What do you want?" Ray said testily.

Lazarus eyed the boys and pointed down the street. "You fellas go ahead and take the trolley back home. I need to talk to Mr. Castle."

Daniel crossed his arms. "I'm not going anywhere."

Ray watched something desperate cross Lazarus' face and the

young man leaned toward. "Look, I don't like to admit it, but I need your help. Please."

"Daniel, I think I can handle Lazarus alone. Why don't you head on back to the house and make sure Buster makes it safely. If King Tarz gets loose, he might purr him to death."

Buster gasped. "What? Swell, then! I'm not taking any more of this." He ran down the sidewalk and Daniel glanced at Ray.

"Go on, Daniel. Let me handle this."

"Okay, Mister Ray. But, if you need help, you call the house, and I'll come running." He headed off after Daniel and disappeared into the midst of the dispersing crowd.

"Okay, Lazarus, what is so important you have to talk to me without your father pulling your strings?"

Lazarus ignored the insult and looked around. "He don't know I'm talking to you. But, I'm worried."

"About?"

"Peggy Lou."

Ray blinked. He hadn't seen that coming. "What?"

"Well, I thought he was taken with her and then he started acting all mean and nasty." Lazarus paused and looked around expecting his father to show up any minute. He rubbed the back of his head. "But, that ain't unusual, you know."

"So, why are you worried about Peggy Lou?"

"She don't deserve to be treated that way."

"Then, tell your father."

Lazarus' eyes widened, and he shook his head. "Oh, no, Mr. Castle. You don't tell my father anything. He tells at you and then there's the smack on the back of my head." He rubbed his head.

Ray crossed his arms and leaned up against the wall. "What is it you want me to do, Lazarus?"

"Peggy Lou lost her job at the Saenger Theater, and she hasn't told anyone."

Ray straightened. "She hasn't been at the house the past few nights. We thought she was working."

"No, she's been over at the Zephyr Room at the Washington Youree Hotel looking for Esau and his new girlfriend," Lazarus said.

"Mister Castle, you got to go help her out of this. She don't deserve to be treated this way. She's got a good heart."

Ray rolled his eyes. "The Zephyr Room?"

"Yeah, Tony DiPardo and his orchestra are playing tonight. Can you go get her, Mister Castle? Bring her home, so she doesn't do anything stupid?"

Ray studied the young man's face etched in worry. A voice whispered in his ear. *"Nightclub? Now, that's more your style."* He ignored the voice.

"I'm proud of you, Lazarus. You should stand up to your father more often. Be a real man. Don't let him knock you around. I should know. My father knocked me around. A lot! I never stood up to him and look where it got me." The shadow man!

Lazarus put out his hand, and Ray regarded it as if it were a poisonous snake. He reluctantly shook the young man's cold hand.

"Thanks, Mister Castle." Lazarus glanced around once more and put a hand on the back of his head he hurried down the sidewalk.

Ray walked down the street toward the hotel. The Washington Youree hotel sat on the corner of Texas and Market street. Peacock Alley connected the Washington and the Youree hotels, and Sam's barber shop was located in the connecting hall so he had been here before.

The eight-story structure filled the corner of Texas and Market with its beautiful front façade. A doorman opened the massive glass doors and ushered Ray into the lobby.

Two massive marble staircases dominated the lobby of the hotel leading up to a graceful balcony. A fountain surrounding plants sat between the stairways. On the second level, beautiful paintings of an outdoor scene covered the back wall. Big band music echoed across the lobby from the Zephyr Room.

Ray paused at the entrance to the nightclub. Fortunately, he had donned the pants and nice shirt he had worn on the day he had been found on Frank's front porch. It seemed an age ago! He had also worn a jacket nicer than the seedy coat he usually wore. A placard on an easel proclaimed the night's entertainment.

"Now Playing at the Zephyr Room, Tony DiPardo, 'The Showman

of the Trumpet' and his orchestra. Featuring Anne Ryan soloist and Masters and Scher 'Dancing Moods'. Cover 50 cents."

He dug in his pocket and pulled a handful of coins. Since working for the Post Office, he had accumulated a small fortune, emphasis on the "small." A nattily dressed man at the door held out his hand, and Ray dropped two quarters. The man ushered him into the Zephyr Club.

Tables surrounded a dance floor alive with uniformed soldiers and their dates. Cigarette smoke hung in the air. A far stage held the orchestra, and a tall man filled the air with his trumpeting tunes. Wait a minute? Tony DiPardo? Didn't he have something to do with professional football? Kansas City, wasn't it? But, the memory faded as quickly as it came.

Foil Christmas bells hung from the chandeliers and a Christmas tree festooned with Lawson's expensive lights sat next to the stage. The soloist, Ann Ryan backed by two other women sang "Boogie Woogie Bugle Boy of Company B" to DiPardo's trumpet. Ray's eyes finally adjusted to the dim interior and he looked around the tables. He spied Peggy Lou sitting alone at a table in the far corner.

"Remember this?" The voice whispered again. *"This is where you first thought about leaving your wife for her, remember? In a nightclub. In the dark. Away from prying eyes."*

Ray brushed at his ear as if a mosquito buzzed. The old, sick feeling of guilt gripped his stomach. He made his way through the dancing soldiers and their lady friends and paused across the small table from Peggy Lou. Her head lolled on her neck and tears dripped into a half-empty martini glass.

"Peggy Lou?" He said.

She looked up, and her eyes widened. "Mr. Castle?" She rubbed mascara from around her eyes and smiled. "Fancy meeting you here. I was just waiting for Esau."

Ray pulled the chair away from the table and sat down. "Esau isn't coming, is he, Peggy Lou?"

She studied him with her red-rimmed eyes and then her wail caught him by surprise. She sobbed and pushed aside her martini banging her head against the table. Nearby couples looked their way, and Ray reached over and tried to grab her head.

"Peggy Lou, stop that! You'll hurt yourself."

Peggy Lou laid her head on the table and continued to sob. A waiter appeared by the table. "Is there a problem, sir?"

Ray shook his head. "Maybe too many martinis?"

The waiter lifted an eyebrow. "She's had only one. Would you like a martini?"

Ray glanced around at the milling crowd. "An appletini?"

The waiter smirked and shook his head. "An apple what?"

A new wave of sobbing grabbed his attention. "Never mind. Just a bourbon and coke."

The waiter sniffed and turned away. Ray slid around the table in his chair and took Peggy Lou by the shoulders. "Peggy Lou, you have to get a hold of yourself."

She raised her mascara-stained face and looked at him. "Why? What good will it do? I lost Esau. He left me for that floozy with the frying pan. I can't use a frying pan. I burn water."

Ray nodded and took a napkin. He gently wiped the tears and mascara from her face. Her bright, blue eyes gleamed wetly. For a moment, she was someone else; a blonde with equally electrifying eyes.

"Listen, honey, I've been your secretary for an entire year, and I've been trying to get your undivided attention. You are one clueless man, aren't you? So, I'm going to lay it out straight for you. We can be good together. I know how unhappy you are chained to your wife and kid. I see the frowns every day when you start home. I can make you happy, you know. Just give me a chance. Take me away from this place to a beach somewhere, and I'll show you what happiness is really like."

Ray blinked away the image and the sight of Peggy Lou's tear-stained face returned. Who was the other woman?

"See, I told you what kind of man you really are. Go for it. Take care of yourself. Forget the other people in your life. They only hold you back. They don't care about your happiness." The shadow man sat in the darkness at a nearby table. Ray tried to ignore the green eyes.

"I thought I got rid of you." He hissed.

"Not yet."

"What did you say?" Peggy Lou sat up and looked right at him. "You want to get rid of me?"

Ray shook his head. "No, not you. Esau. You need to get rid of Esau, Peggy Lou. You're better than that man. He is using you. He doesn't care about you."

Peggy Lou grabbed the napkin from Ray's hand and dabbed at her tears. "Men! You're all alike. First, Esau tries to dump me and then you. I don't even know you."

"I'm not trying to dump you, Peggy Lou. I'm here to help you. You didn't tell anyone at the house you lost your job."

Peggy Lou froze and cut her eyes toward him. "I know. How am I going to pay the rent? I'll never hear the end of it from Lawson."

Ray reached out and took her hand. It was warm and moist with her tears. "I've got some money from working at the Post Office. I'll pay your rent until you can find a new job. There are lots of places you could work. Sears, Rubenstein's, Selber Bros."

She gently pulled her hand away. "Well, I ain't going to become a welder, that's for sure. I hear some women are doing men's jobs because of the war. My fingernails aren't cut out for it."

Ray smiled. "Now, that's the Peggy Lou we all know and love."

Peggy Lou paused from examining her fingernails and slowly looked at him. She really looked at him, her eyes roving over his face and his hair and his hands. "Do you really mean it?"

"Mean what?"

"That people love me?"

"What's not to love?" Ray tried to smile. "Okay, Peggy Lou, you're different. So am I. We're both misfits at the Collinsworth boarding house. But, there isn't any doubt you are YOU and nobody else. There's only one Peggy Lou!"

Peggy Lou sat up and straightened her curls. She smiled. "Yeah, that's right. There ain't but one of me. Hey, Mister Castle, what do you say we dance the night away? Huh? Drown our misery on the dance floor?"

Ray studied her bright, blue alluring eyes. Throw caution to the wind. Seize the day. Why not? The bourbon and coke had arrived and he gulped half of it down for courage.

"That's my boy." The voice whispered in his ear. He reached out his hand and took hers.

"Shall we dance?"

Peggy Lou giggled and she followed him out toward the dance floor. But, it became painfully apparent her balance was not what it should be. She stumbled a few times as they snaked their through the crowded tables. She paused at the edge of the dance floor and put a hand to her mouth.

"Ray, I'm going to be sick." She ran toward the restrooms. He followed her down the dark corridor to the restrooms and waited patiently outside the restroom door.

"Now, pal of mine, this is more like the real you."

Ray glanced over his shoulder. Clothed in darkness, the shadow man's glittering green eyes glowed. "I got rid of you."

"Well, that was before you reacquainted yourself with forbidden fruit." The shadow was becoming solid. A slightly portly man in a snappy suit became barely visible in the darkness. *"Remember your secretary? Off to an island? White beaches and blue water? She's still waiting for you."*

A pain stabbed into Ray's temple and for a moment, he saw the blonde woman in a skimpy bathing suit again. She had tilted her sunglasses down to expose her bright, blue eyes and she winked at him.

"No! Go away!"

"But, you're the one who brought me back, Ray. You just can't leave your old life behind. You cannot escape it. Choices, Ray. You've made your choices, remember?" The man's faced gelled and Ray stared into his own eyes.

"No!" Ray held his head.

For a moment, the shadow man's face twisted in anger and fury as the image of a dark haired woman eclipsed the shadow man's face.

"Where are you? I love you. Come home to me. Please." Her familiar voice pleaded.

Guilt! Shame! They warred against the familiar sensation of lust. Lust for power! Lust for the blonde haired woman! No! The pain in his head shot into his stomach and nausea gripped hime. He ran into the men's restroom. He lost the bourbon and coke into the sink. He looked at his sweaty face in the mirror. The eyes were the same as the shadow man. Was he that man? Had he deserted his wife?

"No! That's wrong! Not me. I wouldn't do that?"

The shadow man coalesced behind him and peeked over his shoulder. *"But, it is you."*

It was then he heard the whispers of another voice, childish and small; pleading and plaintive.

"Dear God, please find my Daddy. I love him and want him to come home."

He recognized the voice. A young boy. His son? His son was praying for him? To come home? Yes! Somewhere out there in the confusing world of war and chaos someone loved HIM! Someone wanted HIM to come home! Somewhere, there was a homecoming tree for Ray Castle!

Ray whirled and faced the inky darkness of the shadow man and smiled. "Get out of my life! I'm done with you! Someday, somehow, somewhere, I will find my family again and when I do, I won't need you anymore! Get lost!"

Ray walked right through the shadow man and he dissipated with a barely audible shriek. In the hallway outside, Peggy Lou waited for him.

"There you are. Sorry for that, but I had too much to drink."

Ray smiled. "Peggy Lou, I think I am married and my wife and son are waiting for me somewhere. It's been fun talking with you this evening, but I think it's time we both went home."

Peggy Lou smiled weakly. "You're such a nice man, Ray. My loss, sweetheart. Can you take me home, now?"

Ray nodded. "Yes I will. And, Peggy Lou? Don't settle for the likes of Esau Cheatwood. Somewhere the good Lord has someone special just for you. Be patient."

Peggy Lou blinked quickly and dabbed at her eyes. "That's the nicest thing anyone has ever said to me. Ray, will you pray for me to find that person?"

Ray offered his arm. "Gladly. Let's go home."

❦ 19 ❦

Winston Churchill, prime minister of Great Britain, seated at the side of President Roosevelt at the White House, told American newsmen that recent events – the German defeat in Russia and America's entry into the war – had produced a turning point in the tide of the worldwide conflict.

Barksdale Field underwent its first test blackout for half an hour last night, and officials said, "The lights went off a lot quicker than they came back on."

Laura Ingalls, noted American aviatrix who allegedly was a paid German propagandist, was indicted by a federal grand jury yesterday as a foreign agent.

The immediate availability of Long Distance telephone facilities is vital to the communication needs of our government. We urge everyone who plans to exchange seasons' greetings to please refrain from calls on Christmas or New Year's Day. Southern Bell Telephone and Telegraph Company.

Loretta Young, Eddie Cantor, Irving Berlin, Dinah Shore, and many other stars will join hands in a full hour broadcast on behalf of the American Red Cross' $50,000,000 drive on NBC-KTBS tonight at 8 o'clock.

Bobby Riggs and Frank Kovaks, No. 1 and No. 2 in the amateur tennis world have joined the ranks of professional tennis players and will tour for $25,000 each for 22 weeks.

A grand scale "emergency" may be created in the East Texas oil field as part of plans to safeguard the field. An "air raid" will serve as a test for civilian defense workers and their ability to coordinate a response to protect our valuable oil fields.

❦

Ray found work at the Post Office boring and tedious. As he sorted through the envelopes and cards, he wished; no, he KNEW there was a better way. Some kind of code to separate the nation into sections. This code could even separate the city into sections. One quick glance at the code would allow you to sort the letters into sections and then they would zip across the country. Ray blinked as he put the last card into its slot. The letters could be scanned by something. And the code could be a set of bars? Was that it? Again, the elusive nature of his lost memories mocked him, and he felt the old anger boil. It was Christmas Eve, and he was no nearer to recovering his memory. The nation had moved into war mode, and the world had changed and shifted around him. But, he remained the same.

At least, he thought he remained the same. He paused and touched the medal still pinned to his lapel. He no longer wanted to find the deed and claim it for himself and his own advantage. Rather, he wanted to stop Esau Cheatwood from reaching his endgame, whatever that was. The Monday after the trip to the Zephyr Room with Peggy Lou, she had found a job at the cosmetic counter at J. C. Penney. It suited her perfectly. And, there had been no more visits from Esau. Which worried Ray. What was the man up to?

Lonnie had been off to Barksdale Air Field for preliminary training, and the day after Christmas he would ship out to Europe. And, there had been no news about Frank. After what he had seen in the clearing, real or not, Ray feared the worst.

He was finishing up the last of the mail when his supervisor, a short, portly man with no hair on his head wheezed around the corner with a box of mail bundled in rubber bands.

"Hey, Castle, I got something for you to do. Now." He plopped the box down on the counter, and Ray felt a sinking sensation.

"What's this?"

"Mail for the courthouse. It needs to be sorted and quickly. Some of it is government business, Castle. You'll get overtime so get to it so I don't have to pay you too much." He turned and shuffled away.

Ray glanced up at the clock and sighed. He had been so close. He started shuffling letters and dividing them into piles based on the departments at the courthouse. There were official letters from the Army Air Corp. There were communiqués for the mayor. And, there was a growing stack of official letters he knew could only come from the armed forces. Death notifications! The parish police would contact the officials at Barksdale and escort them to the relative's house. There, the notification would take place.

He tried to imagine what it would be like to have someone appear at his door. What if one of these letters was about Frank? He finished with most of the box, and his curiosity got the better of him. He sifted through the letters and paid closer attention to the addresses. The Collinsworth boarding house was not one of the addresses. He breathed a sigh of relief. After all, he didn't want Frank to be dead. In spite of the incident in the clearing, he still felt a faint hope the man was alive.

Ray picked up the final handful of letters and was stacking the last of the letters in a pile when something caught his eye. The name 'Esau Cheatwood' embellished a large envelope. The return address said something about the national tax agency. But, what drove a chill down his spine was the title under Cheatwood's name. It clearly said 'Chairman of the Tax Board.'

Ray looked grimly at the envelope and recalled the words on the card from the records department. He went over to his overcoat and fished through the pockets. He pulled out the index card he had kept from that day at the courthouse. He had originally intended to use it as leverage on Esau for his own personal advancement. But, things had changed. Did Cheatwood know about the back taxes on the Collinsworth property? Go ahead. Open it! He was so tempted to open the envelope. But, to do so was a federal offense, especially by a postal employee. He tossed the envelope onto the pile of courthouse mail and loaded the piles into an old, leather satchel. He picked up the phone and called one of the letter mail carriers and arranged for him to come by and take the separated mail to the courthouse mailroom.

Ray glanced up at the clock on the wall and realized he had worked an extra hour. He checked out for the day and made his weary way down the sidewalk of downtown Shreveport to the nearest trolley stop. He looked up and saw the three girls hurrying down the sidewalk. Following close behind them was Ann Lee bundled up in a scarf and heavy coat. The air was crisp and cold and the ground covered with a few inches of crunchy snow. Rachel was in the lead of the three girls, and she stopped in front of the building with the radio studio. Ray paused just out of sight.

"I can't believe I was able to sneak out of the house while mother was in the kitchen. It's Christmas Eve. She'll notice I'm not there." Rachel said as she rubbed her mittens together for warmth.

"You're not the only one sneaking around, Rachel. Our moms think we're over at your house for dinner." Penelope said.

Gwendolyn glared at her heavy overcoat. "And, I had the loveliest dress planned for dinner. It was a deep forest green with sequins down the seam."

"Enough about your dress, Gwendolyn. I had to be at the studio in the next thirty minutes, or I was out of the contest. I had no choice." Rachel said.

Ann Lee had paused just outside of earshot and seemed to be in deep thought. Ray stepped up behind her. "Mrs. Collinsworth?"

Ann Lee whirled in shock and gasped. "Mr. Castle? What are you doing out here?"

"I work at the post office, remember. The question is: what are you doing following your daughter and her friends?"

Ann Lee turned back to study her daughter. "I just had to find out what she was doing. I seemed to have made a mess out of things."

Ray took her arm, and they started toward Rachel. "Then, let's make things right."

Ann Lee paused and then Rachel saw them. "Mother?" She said.

Ann Lee pulled gently out of Ray's grasp. "Rachel, forgive me for following you but it is Christmas Eve, and dinner will be ready soon. I just had to know where you were going."

Rachel looked at Ray and shook her head. "You wouldn't approve."

Ann Lee glanced at Ray, and he smiled at her. She drew a deep breath. "Rachel, I'm sorry for what happened the other day. I was under a lot of stress. This afternoon I found this." She pulled a folded sheet of paper out of her purse dangling from the crook of her arm. She unfolded the paper and read it. "We are honored to inform you that you are a finalist in the Piney Woods Holiday Singing Contest. Rachel, I thought we decided you weren't going to have anything to do with this."

"Mother, let's not fight. I told you I wanted to try and make my dream come true. Please don't stop me now. I'm one of the five finalists."

"But, I told you not to enter this contest. You deliberately disobeyed me."

Rachel glanced at Penelope and Gwendolyn. She closed her eyes in thought and then stood up straight and firm. "Father said I could do it."

Ann Lee gasped and shoved a gloved hand over her mouth. Her eyes filled with tears. "Your father said you could? What was he thinking?"

Rachel stepped closer to her mother and glanced once at Ray. Ray nodded encouragingly. "He told me to try and make my dream come true."

Ann Lee looked around desperately for help. "Well, he's not here right now. I'm in charge. And, I will not allow you to continue with this."

Penelope stepped forward. "Mrs. Collinsworth, you really ought to hear Rachel sing. She has a beautiful voice."

"I thought I had a beautiful voice, too. But, I was wrong."

Rachel reached out tentatively and touched her mother's arm. "Mother, I know you don't want to see me hurt. But, I'm almost grown up. I've got to take my chances. I've got to make my own decisions. And, I've got to have my own failures. You can't live my life for me."

Ann Lee shook her head. "That is exactly what I told Frank when I auditioned for a movie."

Penelope looked over at Gwendolyn and laughed. "You auditioned for a movie role?"

"Yes. These filmmakers had come to Louisiana to shoot a western, and they needed a woman who could sing to play a small part." Ann Lee said. "Rachel's father and I were dating at the time, and when he found out the part I was trying out for, he had a fit."

Gwendolyn was suddenly very interested. "What kind of a part was it?"

Ann Lee looked at Gwendolyn and then glanced at Ray. "A saloon girl."

Rachel gasped. "Saloon girl? Mother, how dare you? What if you'd gotten the part? My friends would never speak to me. They'd say, 'There goes your mother, the saloon girl. Can she do the can-can?'"

Ann Lee looked at Rachel and suddenly laughed. She shook her head. "You know what? We're both being silly about this. I didn't get the part because of my voice. They were switching over to talkies, and I couldn't get by on my looks alone. You father had come to Shreveport from the farm to sell watermelons. So, he told his father. But, truth be known, he wanted to sneak onto the movie set and surprise me. He saw the whole fiasco of my audition. I thought it was the end of my world. And then, your father took me in his arms and told me that I was too beautiful to be a saloon girl and that's when he asked me to marry him. Right there on that movie set in front of all those camera people."

Rachel glanced at Gwendolyn, and they giggled. "Mother, you did more than just try out for a part. You made your dream come true when father asked you to marry him. Isn't your life better than being a saloon girl in a movie?"

Ann Lee was speechless for a moment. She glanced at Ray and frowned. "It would be if your father was here." She handed the notification to Rachel. "Rachel, go ahead and finish the contest. We'll turn the radio on and be listening."

Rachel took the paper and grabbed her mother in a hug. "Mother, thank you. I love you. Well, girls, let's go win this contest." She hurried through the door into the building.

Ray put an arm around Ann Lee. "I'm glad you came to your senses. It's about time you let go. Rachel will do fine. Let the Lord take care of her dreams."

Ann Lee looked at him. "So now you're fine with doing the Lord's work?"

"What makes you think I never was?"

"Oh, I don't know. Sometimes, you seem to be two different people. And, I haven't heard you talk about God very much. But, I like it when you're more like you are right now. Now, come on, I've got to get back and finish dinner so we can listen to the contest results on the radio." Ann Lee hurried down the sidewalk, and Ray had to run to keep up with her. He was almost to the corner across from the church downtown when he saw Esau Cheatwood coming out of the court-house down the street. He called out to Ann Lee.

"Mrs. Collinsworth, I forgot something at work. I'll be along in a minute." Ann Lee nodded and continued on her way.

Ray rushed back down the sidewalk and followed Esau up to the front of an old building. Esau pushed through the door and into the reception office of the building. Ray followed him.

"Cheatwood?" Ray called out.

Esau Cheatwood paused and turned around. He carried the enve-lope in his hand from the post office. Esau's eyes narrowed as he studied Ray.

"Is that you, Mr. Castle?" He said.

"Yes, it is." Ray paused trying to decide what to say. He didn't want to give too much away. "I work at the post office, you know."

Esau stepped toward him and raised an eyebrow. "Well, I'm glad someone took Lonnie's place. I'm glad you found a source of income instead of mooching off the Collinsworths."

"Now, listen here, Cheatwood. Ann Lee was kind enough to take me in when she found me on the sidewalk. I can't help it that I lost my memory. I'm going to pay her back for taking care of me. I'm not a moocher. I'm proud of who I am."

Esau smiled and his thin, little mustache curled upon his lip. "So, you remember who you are?"

Ray opened his mouth and then shook his head. "No."

"Ah, then you are a man with no identity. Mr. Castle, a man with no identity, is an empty shell; a worthless ghost. It is only when the world stands up and takes notice of who and what we are that our worth is established." Esau started to turn away, and Ray grabbed his arm.

"What are you looking for on Frank's property?"

Esau jerked his arm out of Ray's grasp. "What?"

"I was there in the woods. I heard you tell Lazarus you wanted the property so you could find 'buried treasure.' I know what you've been up to the whole time." Ray said.

Esau studied him and then smiled. "And, I'm sure you told Ann Lee everything, right?"

Ray felt a rush of guilt. He looked away. "No."

"Oh, and why not?" Esau stepped closer.

"Well, I . . ." Ray couldn't finish the sentence.

Esau stood taller and straighter. "I'll tell you why Mr. Castle. You thought maybe you could work an angle in this thing for yourself. I talked to the lady at the courthouse, and she said you came by looking through the deeds. You were interested in the Collinsworth property." Esau stepped closer. "In fact, she said you asked her about taxes. Now, if you intended on protecting Ann Lee and her family, then why were you snooping around down at the courthouse? Huh? I know why, Mr. Castle. It's because you are a hypocrite. You are a man used to taking advantage of any situation for his own good. You know how I know this? Because it takes one to know one. Don't stand there and be so sanctimonious as to accuse me of wrongdoing when you've hidden this fact from Ann Lee for weeks. You could have stopped me long before now, but you've been busy on your own."

Esau reached out and shoved him back toward the door. Ray stumbled and didn't have the strength to stand up to the man. "You had your own little plan in place. What happened? Did the good Lord melt your heart? Did you find forgiveness? Well, Mr. Castle, only the strong survive in this world. And, now that the United States is going to war, I will benefit from the 'buried treasure' on that property. And, I have you to thank for the angle I needed to make certain the property would become mine."

Ray felt a chill run over him. "What do you mean?"

Esau held up the envelope. "I'm taking this upstairs to Mr. Stanton to verify the contents of this envelope. And, if it is what I think it is, then I'll soon be visiting the Collinsworth boarding house. And, don't think you can stop me. Because, Mr. Castle, I have the law on my side." He shoved Ray out the door and onto the cold sidewalk. "Merry Christmas!"

❧ 2 0 ☙

Ray hurried to the boarding house, his mind racing. He had to think of something to stop Esau Cheatwood. But, all he could think about was how he had messed up things so very badly. He should have never tried to find his angle. He should have recognized the old, selfish man he had been long before tonight. And, the worst of it was, he had no idea when Esau Cheatwood would show up and put his final plan into place.

He stepped into the living room and took off his coat. The aroma of candy and cakes filled the room. He felt so much a part of this now. He would not ruin this Christmas Eve with bad news. He would wait until later to tell Ann Lee about Esau's plan. Whatever it might be!

Ann Lee surveyed the table along with Sue Carol. "Now, that should be enough place settings for everyone."

Sue Carol was wearing a deep red sweater with Santa Claus embroidered on the front pocket. "Assuming Peggy Lou hasn't made up with Mr. Cheatwood and drags him along."

Ann Lee looked over at Ray. "And, if he does, Mr. Castle, you keep your distance. I don't want another roast ruined by a wrestling match in my living room."

"I'll try and restrain myself, Ann Lee." No need to worry, he thought. He and Peggy Lou were just casual acquaintances.

Daniel was sitting in Uncle Lawson's place holding up his newspaper. He put it down, and Ray was shocked to see Lonnie's pipe in his mouth. Ray's eyes widened, and he motioned to the pipe.

"What are you doing?" He whispered.

"Being the man of the house," Daniel whispered back with a bit of a lisp. The pipe fell out of his mouth and clattered across his lap and onto the floor. Fortunately, it wasn't lit. Daniel stood up and placed the newspaper back in the chair. He marched across the living room and up to Ann Lee.

"Is there anything I can do to help, Ann Lee?" His voice seemed to be a bit lower than usual.

Ann Lee turned and studied her son with a strange look on her face. She ruffled his hair and finally smiled. "No, son. You've done enough already. You brought us our Christmas tree, and you brought some wood for the fireplace. You've become a regular man about the house."

Buster appeared from the stairway wearing his aviator goggles and his cap. "Yeah, I can't even get him to chase Nazis anymore."

"Sorry, Buster. But, I've got more important things to do. Ann Lee, can I talk to you?"

"Sure, son. But, you can't call me by my first name. I'm your mother."

"Of course." Daniel looked at Ray. "Can you come with me and Uncle Ray to the library?"

Ann Lee glanced over at Ray. Ray shrugged in confusion. "To the library?"

Daniel nodded. "We need some privacy."

"Well, of course." Ann Lee raised an eyebrow at Ray.

Ray followed them to the library. Daniel motioned to the chair beside the desk, and his mother sat there. He turned to Ray.

"I just wanted you to be here, Uncle Ray, because you know what happened when I cut down the tree." Daniel moved around and settled behind his father's desk. Ray moved across the room to his cot and sat down. He leaned back into the shadows. What was Daniel up to?

Daniel leaned forward across the desk and smoothed back his unruly hair. For a second, Ray saw Frank Collinsworth in the boy's stature and his determination. He had grown up in the last few days. He looked older, and for a second an elderly man seemed to be sitting in the chair with his jaw set and his eyes alive with power and determination. Ray blinked, and the image was gone.

"Have you heard any more news from father?" Daniel asked.

"You mean, your Daddy?" Ann Lee looked down at her hands. She looked back at her son. "No, I haven't. I've made phone calls, checked the mail, and your Uncle Lonnie even went to try and find out something at Barksdale Air Field. I'm hoping and praying your father is fine. It's just so confusing after the attack and all."

Daniel nodded. He glanced once at Ray and then back at his mother. "Mommy, do you believe in visions?"

"Visions? What on earth are you talking about?"

Daniel drew a deep breath. "Something happened in the woods when I cut down the tree."

Ann Lee sat forward. "What?"

Daniel blinked rapidly as if reliving the event. "It fell on me, and I think I passed out. And, when I woke up--"

"Daniel, tell me what happened."

"I saw Daddy."

Ann Lee stood up quickly, and her face was twisted in horror. "Don't tell me any more. I'm sure it was because you were hit in the head by the tree. You probably had a concussion like Ray, is all."

"But, Mommy, it was so real. He was standing there just looking at me."

Ann Lee paced toward the door to the living room. She whirled and shook her finger at Daniel. "Daniel, you stop this nonsense right now! I don't want to hear anything else about your Daddy appearing in a vision. You just had a nasty bump on the head. Just a nasty bump. Do you understand?"

Daniel stood up and looked over at Ray. He swallowed and looked back at his mother. "But, Mommy, he told me--"

Ann Lee put her hands over her ears. "No, I won't hear any more. Your Daddy is fine, you understand? He's coming home! You just imagined things. Now, go on outside and play with Buster. Put on your superhero costume and play outside. I want you to be Captain Liberty again."

Daniel came around the desk and seemed to gain a few inches in height. He stood right behind his mother. "I was Captain Freedom. Mommy, I can't do that anymore. Daddy told me to be the man of the house."

Ann Lee jerked as if he had slapped her. She put her back to the closed door. "No, *he's* the man of this house. Not you. You're just a boy. Just a boy. Do you understand?"

Tears glistened on Daniel's cheek. "But, Daddy told me--"

Ann Lee shook her head. "No! You're just a boy, I told you. Don't say any more. Don't say it."

Daniel backed away and seemed to shrink. His face reddened and tears poured from his eyes. "Mommy, I'm sorry I told you. I'm sorry I can't be the man of the house."

Ann Lee gasped for breath and seemed, for the first time, to see Ray sitting on the cot.

Ray stood up and swallowed. "I was there. He's telling the truth."

"No. You've had a concussion, too. Both of you. I know he's not dead. He's coming home, I tell you." Ann Lee was gasping for breath.

"We all just need hope, Mrs. Collinsworth." Ray managed to say. Just a little hope because he knew what was coming. Esau Cheatwood. "Daniel needs hope. We all do."

Ann Lee nodded and straightened up. She forced a smile on her face and wiped tears from her eyes and drew a deep breath. "Daniel, I tell you what. Until your father gets here, you can be the man of the house. You cut down that tree all by yourself."

Daniel backed away and wiped the tears off his cheek. "Daddy told me he planted it on the day I was born and when I could cut it down by myself, I was growing into a man."

Ann Lee's lip quivered, and she tried to be strong. "He's right. Why just look at you. All tall and handsome. You've grown up so much in the past few weeks. I don't guess you've had much of a choice but to grow up. We live in evil times. There just isn't time left for being a child anymore."

Daniel turned and went back to the chair behind the desk. He sat down and drew in a deep breath. "Mommy, I feel different. I don't want to play Captain Freedom anymore. It seems silly. I want to help you out around the house. I want things to be right again."

"I know. You've had a great responsibility put on your shoulders. A young man your age should never have to worry about such things. But, we don't seem to have much of a choice, do we?"

Daniel shook his head. "I guess not. Mommy, why would God let such bad things happen?"

Ann Lee came and sat in the chair beside the desk. She looked once at Ray with a pleading expression on her face. She drew a deep breath. "Now, that's a real deep question. I really don't know. But, I know one thing. All the evil that is in this world didn't just show up out of the blue. It comes from men who have evil thoughts and do evil things."

Ray felt his heart race. Was he one of the evil men? There was something rotten and dead inside of him. There was something evil within, and he hoped he had destroyed it. He sat forward out of the shadows to catch Ann Lee's words.

Ann Lee put a hand on Daniel's arm. "These evil men bring it into this world. There's good all around us. God put it there. But, it's like when you block the sun with your hand, and you make a shadow. The shadow is the absence of light. Evil is the absence of good. Men and women make decisions that aren't good and the shadow they leave across our world is evil. What we have to do is stand up for the good that God has put into our hearts. We are the light in this world of darkness."

Daniel smiled. "Then, we are all heroes for God, aren't we?"

Ann Lee smiled back. "Yes. We are heroes for God."

Daniel gestured at Ray. "Even Uncle Ray. He talked to me in the clearing. He helped make sense of it all. He's a good man, isn't he?"

Ann Lee nodded. "Yes, he is, Daniel."

Ray grew cold and pale. He closed his eyes. He walked down a long, dark corridor. Shadows writhed beside him. One of them could be the shadow man. Hadn't he chased him away? At the end of the corridor an old, beaten wooden door creaked as it opened. Dim, crimson light poured out from the room beyond. Ray stepped across the threshold.

The room beyond was small and dark. Orange light flickered from a small fireplace. His father sat in a recliner, his head tilted to the side. His stomach protruded from beneath a stained tee shirt. Behind the sleeping figure of his father, the front door opened slowly. Ray's heart raced. He knew who was at the door.

The young man who stepped through the door was tall and thin. He wore a skinny tie over a dark, blue shirt. His hair was long and touched his shoulders. Behind him, a younger man peeked into the room. He was short and awkward at his age of sixteen. Ray recognized the eyes.

"Sir, may I speak to you?" The man in the tie said as he paused in front of the recliner. Ray's father snorted and gasped for breath as he looked up with a clouded visage toward the young man.

"Who are you?"

"I'm the youth minister at the church. Your son told you about me. I'm here to talk to you about your son." The young man's voice was strong and unhesitating.

Ray's father slowly lumbered to his feet and towered more than six inches over the younger man. "Well, listen to me you con man. My son is not going to get hoodwinked by the likes of you. He's not going to become some pasty, cowardly Christian. No sir! Not him!"

Ray's younger self stepped into the room and paused behind the recliner. "But, Dad, I'm a new person. I gave my life to Christ."

Ray's father whirled, his belly bouncing with the movement. His face reddened. "You want to be a Christian? Well, if you do, son, you'll be living on the street. I will not have you in this house. Not some muling, puking coward."

Ray's younger self shrunk away from the man's hulking figure. His youth minister moved closer to his father. "Sir, if you would just let me explain."

Ray's father spun and with one, slow movement drove a fist into the young man's face. Blood splattered across the tie and the shirt, and he collapsed like an empty sack. Ray's father kicked the motionless young man. "You leave my son alone, you hear?"

The younger Ray ran around the recliner and knelt beside his youth minister. "Dad, leave him alone! He means no harm!"

Ray flinched as his father drove his foot into the younger Ray's face. The boy fell back onto the recliner, and his arm raked across the empty beer cans on the side table. The recliner tilted backward and the boy slid onto the floor. Ray's father hunkered over the boy.

"You got a choice to make, you hear? Be strong and take charge. Or, be a sheep and get led to the slaughter. If you stay in my house, you ain't going to be no sheep. You're going to be the butcher. Understand?"

Ray backed away from the living room, his heart racing. This was a memory he did not want. He knew what choice he had made that night. It had started him down a path that had led to the shadow man. There, in that moment, he had made a choice that had ruled his life for decades. He opened his eyes and watched Ann Lee hug her son. Now, he sat here in a different world, a different place. Could he choose differently this time? Could he turn his back on the creature he had become to please his father?

Somewhere in a corner of the dusty attic of his memories, he had shuttered away his connection to God. He reached back down those dark, dusty corridors and reached back to the boxes shut away from his mind and found the one with light leaking around the edges. Just as Ann Lee had opened the trunk on a fragile possession, he gingerly touched a latch on the side of the box.

"God, forgive me." He whispered in the quiet corner of his mind. The latch fell open, and the lid of the box slammed back as light gushed out filling the corridors and the rooms of his mind. He gasped as the light penetrated him, chasing away the shadows and the mist of darkness. Almost, he saw the memories he had lost. But, it no longer mattered who he had been or where he had been. Now was what mattered. He was here in the presence of the light of the Lord. He gasped and felt tears pour down his cheeks. He blinked and was back in the library. Daniel and Ann Lee were oblivious to his transformation.

Daniel sat forward and took his mother's hand in his own. "Thanks, Mommy. Thanks for helping me understand. I'll try my best to be the man of the house, but now and then I feel like crying. Did Daddy ever cry?"

Ann Lee's eyes were wet with tears. "Honey, the day you were born, he cried like a baby. Tears of joy."

Daniel nodded. He looked at Ray. "Are you okay, Uncle Ray?"

Ray was almost speechless. He saw a baby wrapped in a blue blanket. He felt the touch of the child's soft skin. He opened his mouth and tasted the tears on his cheeks. "Never better, son."

❧ 21 ❧

Ray followed Ann Lee and Daniel back into the living room. Lonnie had come home since they had gone into the library. He was sitting on the couch with his pipe in his mouth.

"Lonnie, welcome back," Ray said.

Lonnie was frowning as he studied the stem of his pipe. "Oh, uh, thanks, Ray. It's been brutal the last few days. They call it boot camp. Must have affected my taste buds. This pipe tastes like bubble gum."

Daniel laughed, and Ray smiled. "I'm sure you'll get your taste back."

Uncle Lawson had taken his place in his chair with his newspaper. "Hopefully we'll get to taste supper pretty soon. I'm starved."

Aunt Wimpy was over at the table arranging plates. "I don't think you're going to starve, Lawson. You've got plenty to hibernate on. Especially in your feet."

Ray smiled. It seemed all so perfect, so right. Peggy Lou was standing in front of the mirror checking her hair. Sue Carol and Wimpy were fussing with dinner just as Ann Lee showed up to supervise. Buster was playing on the floor with Little Lonnie. Daniel was standing next to him, tall and strong and certainly now more of a man than at any point in his life. Ray sighed. That was also now true of him.

He was more of a complete man than he had ever been. He was sure of it. If his memory ever returned, he knew he would no longer recognize the thing he had once been. He was a new creature, transformed by the power of God. Even though the world around him was filling with the evil of Hitler and the Japanese Empire of the sun, he was basking in the glow of God's love and light. He turned to study the Homecoming Tree. The tree glittered with light. Presents poured out from under the tree. The world seemed almost perfect.

Evil stepped in through the front door without even knocking. Esau Cheatwood appeared from the darkness outside followed by Lazarus. Everyone stopped as he stepped into the living room. Peggy Lou gasped as she looked away from her reflection in the mirror. "Esau, you came back."

Esau's eyes were wild and bright. He licked his upper lip, and his mustache glimmered with the sheen of his sweat. "I'm not here to see you, sweetheart."

Peggy Lou put her hand on her hip and rubbed the spot on her forehead with the other hand where she had been hit with the skillet. "Ah, hanging out with that floozy? You know what, she can keep you! I've moved on!"

Esau glared at her with a look of utter contempt on his face. "Yeah, I hear you've been hanging out with a real loser." He cut his eyes towards Ray and smiled. He winked. "No, sweetheart, I've got business with Mrs. Collinsworth."

Ann Lee shook her head in confusion. "Business? What are you talking about?"

Esau pulled a folded sheet of paper out of his coat pocket and shoved it into Ann Lee's hands. "I'm talking about this court order."

Ann Lee looked at the paper as if it were a snake. "I don't understand."

Esau laughed and started pacing around the room. "Years ago, my father sold this house and all of its property to Frank Collinsworth's father, Samuel. But, as you can plainly read in the order, the deed for this property was never registered at the courthouse. Now, I have discovered as of today that the back taxes on this property were never paid. If I pay those taxes this house and the property it sits on are mine." He held up a check. "And, once I hand this to the authorities, you're out on the street."

Lazarus was watching his father pace. "Uh, Dad, you didn't tell me this was what we were coming for. Do we have to do this on Christmas Eve?"

Esau shoved the young man away from him. "You stay out of this, boy. Just watch and learn how to handle a business transaction."

Lazarus stepped back into the fray. "But, Dad--"

Esau slapped him on the side of the head. "I said for you to shut up!"

Ray flinched, feeling the blow. He saw his father's red-rimmed eyes and the spittle running from his lips. His heart pounded, and he smelled the stale alcohol breath of the monster that had almost ruined his life. He realized for the first time how over the years, he had looked at God through the lens of his hatred for his father. No wonder he had become the shadow man. His father had dwelled in darkness, and this was how he saw God. But, God was not darkness. God was light. And life. And love. And hope.

Esau grinned and massaged his pencil thin mustache. "Now, Mrs. Collinsworth, unless you can produce the deed to this property, I will have to ask you and your tenants to leave."

Ray felt the anger burn within him. This was worse than anything that had happened in the last few weeks. This was a Pearl Harbor sneak attack. Before he could say anything, Peggy Lou rushed across the room.

"Esau, how can you do this?"

Esau glared at her. "Peggy Lou, don't try and understand what I'm doing. Just put your little mind to work on finding your next boyfriend. Oh, silly of me, you already have found him."

"There was a time when I thought you and I had something special."

Esau shook his head in dismay. "Why would I want to waste my time with a washed-up dame like you? I just needed you to get into this house and try and find that deed. Since no one can find it, no one can prove this property belongs to Frank Collinsworth."

Tears filled Peggy Lou's eyes. "You no good, two-timing jerk! Oh, I ought to sock you in the nose!"

Esau ducked her feeble attempt at striking him in the face. But, her fist caught Lazarus on the cheek just as he turned back to help his father. Lazarus stumbled away, and Peggy Lou almost fell.

"Why don't you go get a frying pan instead?" Esau laughed. "You're familiar enough with frying pans. Now get lost."

Peggy Lou stumbled backward into the edge of Uncle Lawson's chair. Ray had had enough. He grabbed Peggy Lou and kept her from falling. He winked at her and stepped between her and Esau.

"I'm not going to let him treat you this way."

Esau's face lit up with interest. "So, you think you can mess with a real man? A whole man, Mr. Castle?"

Lonnie appeared beside Peggy Lou. "Now, listen up Mr. Cheatwood, you can't come into this house and pull this stunt. It's Christmas Eve, and you're not going to get away with this."

Uncle Lawson wadded his newspaper and tossed it across the room. He stood up from his chair and stood on the other side of Peggy Lou from Lonnie. "Listen to the man, Mr. Cheatwood."

Lonnie glanced at him. "You're standing up for me?"

Uncle Lawson nodded, and a severe, deadly look came into his eyes. "No. I'm standing beside you. Soldiers always stand by their comrades."

Esau licked his lip again. "Well, you guys can come at me all you want. I'll treat Peggy Lou anyway I see fit! Lazarus, see if Mr. Stanton is here yet."

Lazarus was rubbing his cheek, and he stepped out through the open front door. Cold air and wind were coming into the living room. Mikey, the cabbie walked in.

"How long you want me to wait, Mr. Cheatwood?"

"Not long. But, you might want to get a few more cabs to haul away this riff-raff from MY house." Esau said.

A man in a long, black overcoat and fedora stepped into the living room. Esau motioned to him. Mikey whistled. "Ain't you a somber sight? Well, Mr. Cheatwood, seeing as how this may take a while, I have another ride to pick up. I'll be back shortly." He slipped out through the door and left it wide open.

"This is Mr. Stanton, a representative of the court. He is here to see that you understand the nature of this eviction notice." Esau said.

Mr. Stanton took off his hat and frowned at Ann Lee. "I'm sorry, Mrs. Collinsworth. I wish there were something I could do. But unless you can produce the deed and pay the back taxes, Mr. Cheatwood will own this property."

Ann Lee was suddenly surrounded by Sue Carol and Aunt Wimpy. Her face was pale. "I can't believe you're doing this, Mr. Cheatwood. It's Christmas Eve. And, Frank may be—"

Esau chuckled. "Mrs. Collinsworth, I think it is time for you to face the reality of your husband's death."

Lonnie clenched his fists. "That's enough, Cheatwood."

Esau looked down at Lonnie's fists. "Are we going to resort to fisticuffs, Mr. Britt? You've wanted to beat up on the Nazis for weeks."

"You'll be a decent substitute," Lonnie growled.

Sue Carol ran over and grabbed his hand. "Wait a minute, Lonnie. Don't do this. He'll just have you arrested."

Esau nodded. "Your wife is right, Lonnie. I even a have a representative of the court as a witness."

Uncle Lawson rolled up his sleeves, and his huge, beefy hands coiled into fists. "I've seen worse than the inside of a jail cell and wouldn't mind giving you a knuckle sandwich."

Esau rolled his eyes. "Aunt Wimpy, you had better hold back your husband."

Aunt Wimpy had a wicked gleam in her eye as she joined her husband. "Why? How about a double-decker sandwich?" She raised her fist.

Ray stepped in front of them all, positioning himself between Esau and his friends. "Well, I don't care if you throw me in jail. Been there. Done that. Got the coveralls. You leave these people alone!"

Esau laughed at him. "What? You don't even know who you are! You're a pathetic failure just like the whole lot of you. I mean, just look at all of you. Three daft sisters who peddle their moonshine as a Remedy for what ails you. An old, burned out veteran of the Great

War who can't do anything but read the newspaper and whine and complain about everything and a wife who hasn't the guts to tell him to shut up. And, you, Lonnie. You think the answer to everything is to beat the living daylights out of someone."

Lazarus reached out and grabbed his father's shoulder. "Dad, that's enough!"

Esau shrugged away his son's hand. His eyes were on fire with maniacal power. "I haven't even begun, son. Step back. And, Mrs. Collinsworth. You've raised a son who believes he's some kind of superhero. And, what's worst, believes his father is a hero. Yes, let's talk about Frank Collinsworth. A simple farmer who learned how to fly a biplane and now he thinks he is the champion of the Army Air Corps! Where is he now? It's Christmas, and you don't even know if he's dead or alive."

Daniel jerked Esau's coat. "You stop talking about my Daddy that way; you mean old man."

Buster joined him. "Yeah, my uncle is a real hero. Right, Daniel?"

Esau looked at them as if they were insects. "Oh, I'm sorry. I shouldn't have spoken the truth about your father. He's no hero. He saved drunken volunteer flyers who didn't know their rudders from their flaps. You think he's some kind of a Messiah? Huh, do you think he's like Jesus or something? Well, I guess in a way he is. Let's see; he taught you everything you know like you're one of his disciples. And then, he goes off and dies on a heroic mission. I suppose you expect him to rise from the dead! Maybe he'll show up here."

Something clicked in Ray's mind. Frank. A hero. The medal. Yes, in the book safe!

He smiled and pushed Daniel and Buster aside. He leaned over and whispered in Daniel's ear. Then, he stood up and shoved his face into Esau's. "How dare you talk that way about Frank Collinsworth! How can you be so callous, so mean? Can't you see Ann Lee is stricken with grief and loss? Have you no humanity?"

Ray watched as Daniel and Buster ran across the living room, past the Christmas tree, and into the library.

Esau backed up in sudden fear. "I'm a realist, Mr. Castle. I know what's happening out there. We are at war, and the strongest will survive. I plan to be the strongest. It's every man for himself. Once I get my hands on this property, I'll run the lot of you out of here and uncap that oil well my father buried. And, then, I'll rake in the money by the millions selling oil to the government. You should have stuck with your original plan to look out for only yourself." Esau glanced down at the medal on Ray's lapel. "Well, looky here! You think you're some kind of hero? You are a loser, Ray. A pathetic loser."

Ray blanched and touched the medal. He saw his drunken father. He felt the kick in his face. He saw his youth minister bleeding as he stumbled from their house and his father slammed the door on his new life. No, he would not be that man. Daniel had shown him the way. Become the man of the house. Be the man his father never was.

"Daniel taught me otherwise. He made me realize that he could be as much of a hero as his father. And, as much as I want to bust you in the chops, I've got to do what the Lord has laid on my heart. I'm going to forgive your miserable little carcass."

Lazarus grabbed his father again. For the first time, Ray saw the conflict that warred in the young man's features. "Father, let's go. Forget about the deed."

Esau glared at him. "I told you to step back and be quiet. You will learn how to be a man, Lazarus. You can't bow down to this riff-raff, you weakling. Got that yellow streak from your mother's side of the family. She was weak, too. That's why she died from tuberculosis. Now shut up, and a let a real man take care of this!"

Daniel and Buster ran past Ray and handed a sheaf of papers to Ann Lee. She looked at them, and her face was lit up with joy. "Mr. Cheatwood, the boys seem to have found something. It's the deed to this property, and it is signed by your father, Frank's father, and Frank."

Esau's eyes widened. He grabbed the papers out of her grasp. "Let me see that." He read the papers and a sly smile crept over his face. "There is one problem. It is not witnessed. And unless Frank Collinsworth walks through that door, there is no one to swear to the authenticity of these signatures. I'm afraid you have done nothing but proven my case for me."

Ray was vaguely aware of the telephone ringing behind her. He heard Ophelia mumble something and then place the headset back in its receptacle. Ann Lee paled, and she turned toward her.

"Who was that?"

Ophelia was, for once, speechless. Her face was paler than ever. "Ann Lee, that was Mikey, the cabbie. He said he's bringing some Army officers over."

Ann Lee gasped and stepped toward the telephone. "What?"

Ophelia reached out and took Ann Lee's hand. "They said they needed to talk to you."

Esau handed the deed to Mr. Stanton and rubbed his hands together. "See, Mrs. Collinsworth, there is the answer to your undying hope. This officer is coming to tell you of your husband's death. I'm afraid there is no hope anymore."

Ann Lee almost collapsed, and Ray rushed over to catch her. He pulled her up against his chest.

"NO! It can't be. Where's Rachel? I've got to tell her before she finds out." Ann Lee said.

"She's at the radio station, Ann Lee. Remember?" Ray said quietly.

Ophelia turned back to the radio station. "I do believe they are about to let her sing, Ann Lee. She's a finalist in the contest."

Ann Lee drew a deep breath and motioned to Daniel. "Come here, son. Let's at least hear Rachel sing before we get the bad news. Turn it up, sister."

The volume on the radio increased as Ophelia twisted the dial. "This is the Voice bringing you the last contestant in our Piney Woods Holiday Contest. Miss Rachel Collinsworth will sing a special song for you that she has written just for this occasion. Miss Collinsworth."

Ann Lee gasped as she heard Rachel's voice over the speaker. "Thank you, Mr. Voice. I'm very pleased to have made it this far in the contest. When I had the dream of singing this song, my mother didn't understand. But, she and my father both want me to be able to live out the dream the Lord has placed in my heart. So, I wrote this song for my father. I know that somewhere tonight, he is listening and I want so badly for him to come home for Christmas. Daddy, this song is for you."

The music began, and Rachel's voice echoed out over the speaker strong and powerful.

❧

The sky is filled with stars tonight as far as I can see
The brightest star shines down its light for all the world to see
My Daddy is so far away but still that star he'll see
I wish that star would come and land upon my Christmas tree
My prayer this night is with that star my Dad will finally see
His way home on Christmas Eve to see his special tree

We gather around a special tree
It glows with love and light
We pray around our special tree
For God's protecting might
Bring back our loved ones to family
Who gather in hope with songs of love
Around the Homecoming Tree.

The angels sang their song of praise for all the world to hear
Those angels hovered in the sky and to the earth came near
But maybe if those angels see my Daddy in his fear
They'll sing a song of love and hope and draw his heart so near
I pray that angel comes and hovers near our special tree
And brings my Daddy back home to see his special tree

We gather around a special tree
It glows with love and light
We pray around our special tree
For God's protecting might
Bring back our loved ones to family
Who gather in hope with songs of love
Around the Homecoming Tree.

Love came down from heaven on high for all the world to see

The Son shown brighter in the sky than any star could be
And still our hopes and still our prayers were answered for free
When the Son hung upon the cross; it was his special tree
My prayer this night is with that love my Daddy will be
Led through the fear and through the night and see his special
tree

We gather around a special tree
It glows with love and light
We pray around our special tree
For God's protecting might
Bring back our loved ones to family
Who gather in hope with songs of love
Around the Homecoming Tree.

RAY BACKED AWAY FROM ANN LEE AND DANIEL AND ALLOWED THEM to have this special moment together. Something stirred in the doorway, and he turned to see two soldiers standing at attention. In the distance, supported by Mikey, leaning on a cane was another soldier listening to the song. He hobbled toward the living room and stepped inside just as the last verse of the song faded.

"That was excellent, Miss Collinsworth. We now await the decision of the judges. Miss Collinsworth?" The Voice seemed distracted. "You can't leave, or you forfeit your chances."

Rachel's voice was heard in the background. "I just got a call from the Army looking for me. There's news of my father at home. I must go."

Ann Lee gasped and hugged Daniel even tighter. "I knew it was bad news. Even Rachel can't escape the bad news."

The figure in the doorway laughed. "What bad news?"

Frank Collinsworth moved further into the living room. Ann Lee spun around and screamed. Daniel yelled.

"Frank?" Ann Lee was motionless. "Are you real? Or, are you a ghost?"

Frank looked down at his cane. "I don't think ghosts limp."

Ann Lee ran to him and embraced him. He groaned once she hugged him. Daniel joined them.

Frank kissed Ann Lee and reached out to hug Daniel. "I've been trying to get in touch for weeks. But, they shut down all communications from the island. So, McDaniel at Barksdale called up General Chennault and he pulled some strings on the island. Found a way to get me home. I'm sorry I haven't been able to get here before now."

Ann Lee wiped tears from her eyes. "Oh, none of that matters. What matters is that you're alive."

Frank shifted his weight on the cane. "In pain, but alive."

Ray drew a deep breath. He had so doubted that things would turn out this way. But, God had worked it out. All but the deed, of course. Lazarus was watching the reunion with a strange look in his eyes. He glanced once at his father's glaring face and seemed to reach a decision. He pulled the deed out of Mr. Stanton's hand and carried it over to Frank.

"Mr. Collinsworth, is this your signature?"

Frank looked at the deed. "Hey, that's the deed to the property. Of course, it's my signature."

Mr. Stanton tapped the papers with his hat. "Then you swear that you signed this deed on the occasion of your father's death?"

Frank looked around in puzzlement. "Yes. What is going on here?"

Lazarus walked over to the kitchen table and pulled a fountain pen out of his pocket. He scrawled his name on the deed. "There. An official witness to the deed. It seems my father has to eat a lot of crow."

Esau's mouth fell open, and his face grew beet red. "You traitor! Turning against your own father! Just wait until I get finished with you."

Lazarus handed the deed to Mr. Stanton and put a hand on his father's chest. "You are finished with me, father." He pushed him backward and Esau stepped closer to the door. "From now on, I'll learn on my own." He shoved him again. "It seems your way of doing things just doesn't work." He shoved him out the open door. "Now, get out of here and leave this family in peace."

Esau was shaking with anger. "I'm not finished with you,

Collinsworth. You may have come back from the dead, but it's far from over. I will have this land. You just wait and see."

Lazarus slammed the door in his father's face, and the two soldiers standing outside jumped out of the way. Lazarus brushed his hands together and smiled. "I think I've decided I want to be a better son than my father. And, as bad as he is, he did do one thing right. He paid your back taxes. Merry Christmas!" He handed the check to Mister Stanton, laughed out loud and bowed as he walked out the front door.

"Would someone tell me what is going on?" Frank said.

Ann Lee walked over and hugged Frank around the neck. "Esau Cheatwood was going to take our home away from us. But you showed up just in time. You saved the day. You're my hero."

Frank smiled and pointed his cane at the Christmas tree. "Daniel, it looks like someone has finally grown up into a young man."

Daniel nodded. "Yes, Daddy. I cut the tree down and brought it home for our Christmas tree." He paused and poked his father in the arm. Frank groaned in pain. "But, I saw you in the woods. You talked to me. I thought you were a spirit or something. Even Mr. Castle saw you."

Frank looked at Ray. Ray nodded. "I was there. It was eerie, Mr. Collinsworth. Do you remember anything like that happening to you?"

Frank looked down at the floor and massaged his chin. "I seem to remember something weird happening. I was injured in the attack and a few days ago I started bleeding. They thought I was a goner for sure. I lost a lot of blood. The doctors said I died for a few minutes and I remember seeing Daniel in the woods." He looked up at Daniel. "You had cut down the tree. I wasn't sure I was coming home or not. Yes, it's all coming back to me. But, then, I woke up in the hospital and I was strong enough to come home. Come here, my little hero." Frank and Daniel embraced. "Now, where's Rachel?" Frank turned and searched the room.

Ann Lee came over to him and put her arm around him. "She's at the radio station at that singing contest."

Frank smiled. "I thought I heard her singing from outside. That was quite a song she wrote. I hope she won. Have they chosen a winner?"

Ann Lee shook her head. "I don't know. I can't believe you told her she could sing in the contest and didn't bother to tell me."

Frank laughed. "I knew you wouldn't understand, dear. She's a wonderful singer. Why shouldn't she use her talents to better herself? Just think what God may have planned for her and her singing."

The door burst open in a flurry of cold, snowy wind. Rachel ran into the living room and slid to a stop when she saw her father. She blinked in disbelief.

"They told me you were dead! There was a telegram that arrived at the radio station. It didn't make any sense." Rachel babbled.

Frank hobbled over to her and put an arm around her neck. "Well, the Army officers probably weren't very specific when they sent that telegram. They have to be secretive. We're at war, now."

Rachel kept looking at him as if he couldn't possibly be real. "Daddy, when I thought you were dead, I couldn't stay for the judging. I had to come here and with Mother. I decided to put my dream behind me."

There was a knock at the door, and Uncle Lawson collapsed into his chair. "Well if this ain't Grand Central Station."

The door opened, and the man known as the Voice stepped in. Three men with stacks of equipment followed him. The Voice carried a microphone. He looked at Frank and smiled.

"My dear Rachel looks like your dream is far from over. In spite of you leaving the studios, the judges have chosen you as the winner of the contest."

Rachel squealed as Penelope and Gwendolyn hurried in from outside. Rachel looked at the men bustling around the room. "What? But, what are you doing here?"

The Voice smiled. "We are doing something unprecedented. We can run this live to the studio over shortwave. Rachel Collinsworth, we can't let this opportunity pass. You have written an extraordinary song. And, the good Lord has seen fit to make it come true. I heard your father made it home by Christmas just like the song proclaimed."

Rachel jumped up and down. "You mean I won the contest?"

The Voice nodded and one of the men gave him a 'go ahead' signal. He put the microphone up to his mouth and began speaking. "This is the Voice coming to you live from the home of Frank Collinsworth. Just now, the heroic pilot has returned from Pearl Harbor to spend Christmas with his family. And tonight, we are going to bring you a very special treat. We want you to put aside the fears and concerns of this war and remember the reason for this Christmas season. Tonight, we want to bring you peace and goodwill for all men. Therefore, I am proud to announce the winner of our 1941 Piney Woods Holiday Singing Contest is Rachel Collinsworth. Miss Collinsworth."

Rachel swallowed hard as Frank, and Ann Lee hugged her from each side. She took the microphone. "I want to thank everyone at the radio station for giving me this chance. And, I want to thank my father for encouraging me and thank my mother for loving me. And, I want to thank God for bringing my Daddy home for Christmas."

The Voice motioned to everyone. "Now, let's get some photographs for the newspaper. Just Rachel and her immediate family." A photographer came out of the knot of men near the front door, and Rachel and Frank and Ann Lee and Daniel posed for the photograph. The Voice then motioned to everyone. "Now, let's get the whole bunch of you here at the Collinsworth Family Boarding House."

Ann Lee motioned to Ray. "Come on, Ray. You're part of this family now."

Ray stepped behind Daniel and tried to smile. He didn't belong here. These were friends, not family. He had a family. Somewhere, he had a family. Flashbulbs fired, and he squinted.

"Sir." One of the photographers pointed to Ray. "Don't squint. Your eyes will be closed on the final photo. Everyone, look here, smile and open those peepers wide enough to see the whites of your eyes."

Ray opened his eyes, and the flashbulbs ignited. He blinked and grabbed his head as pain lanced down the middle of his skull. He stumbled away from Daniel and leaned against the living room wall. He glanced around and huge purple blobs obscured his vision. He rubbed his eyes, and the pain came again. He rolled along the wall, trying to get away from the flashing lights and the throbbing pain.

He fell up against the piano, and discordant notes rang through the air, crashing against his eardrums. He groaned with the pain.

"Help me! What is happening?"

He blinked away the blobs of purple, and his hands hit the keyboard again. The room was filled with people. People frozen in mid-motion. He shook his head in confusion.

"What is going on? What is wrong with everyone?"

From the library, he heard a voice. "Dad? Where are you? We're looking for you."

Ray froze. The voice was so familiar, young and male. His son? Didn't he have a son? His head throbbed again, and he whirled in horror toward the library. Inside, the shadows writhed, and for a moment, he saw the face of a small boy with blonde curls and a tear streaked face.

"Dad? Come back. Please."

Ray stumbled around the Homecoming tree toward the library, but by the time he got to the door, the room was empty. He turned. The living room was empty. Where had everyone gone? Dead. They were all dead! The horrific feeling of doom fell over him, and his head throbbed again. He fell to his knees clutching his head.

"Wait! This isn't 1941! It's 2001. I'm not there. I'm here!"

Echoes of memories surged through his brain. Deb, his wife, a tall brunette. David, his son. His faced warm at the thought of a woman in a bikini. A tall, office building. Cheatwood, his financial officer. The park. The bench. The mugger.

"Mr. Collinsworth!" He screamed. "Where are you? Where is everyone? What's going on? Oh, it's all coming back to me. I can remember! My son! My wife! My plans! Oh God, I'm so sorry. Please forgive me. Please! I just want my family back. I want my wife and my son. Please let me go home. Please let me go home."

He stood up shakily and stumbled into the library. Through the shifting shadows, he spied the cot and collapsed in pain onto the canvass. "I just want my family back. Please, God. Please."

22

"Here's some water and some ibuprofen for your headache." A gruff voice said from the shadows. The lamp burst into light and Ray squinted. He was lying on a couch in the library, and the shadow man stood over him.

"No! Go away! I'm not you anymore. I've made my choices."

"Roy! It's me. Mr. Collinsworth." The man stepped into the light. His gray hair was awry, and he leaned heavily on his cane as he handed Ray a glass of water. "It seems that glancing bullet may have knocked some sense into your head. And, I'm fine, by the way. No thanks to that mugger."

Ray sat up abruptly, and his head swam. "What? It's you! I'm back!

Mr. Collinsworth placed the glass on the side table and took a bottle of pills from his pocket. "Yeah, you were unconscious there for a bit. So was I, I think. I had Mikey drop us off at my house, but maybe we should go on to the hospital. I figured with all your sneaking about; you didn't want your wife to find out you'd been mugged."

Ray looked around at the library. He stood up and pushed past Collinsworth and stepped into the living room. It was almost identical to his memories. "This is your house? This is your house! But, where is everyone?"

"In Hawaii waiting for me. We go there every Thanksgiving to commemorate a special event." Collinsworth followed him into the living room.

"I know. Your father's homecoming! Yes, I know. And, there's the tree." He pointed to a Christmas tree covered in popcorn strands and paper chains.

"How do you know that?"

Ray studied the old man's wrinkled face. The hair was gray but still as unruly as he remembered. The eyes were tired but still held the bright light of the little boy who had become a hero. "Daniel, I was there. I was in this house when your father came home. I sat on that couch. I took a coat from that coat rack."

Collinsworth pulled a cell phone from his pocket. "That's it. I'm calling 911."

"911? We have 911!" Ray laughed. "Hey, we have 911, and you have a cell phone! I'm back! Hurray, I'm back!" He froze. The woman in the bikini! "I'm back? Oh no! I have to call Deb and David. I have to let them know I'm okay. I have a lot of explaining to do."

Collinsworth held the cell phone in his hand. "What about your trip to the Caribbean?"

Ray drew a deep breath. He grabbed the phone from Collinsworth. "Forget 911. Look, Mr. Collinsworth, Daniel, I have been so wrong. You tried to show me, and I wouldn't listen. Somehow God let me see your past. I saw it all. I know what you mean about family and integrity and loyalty and love. I'm so sorry for treating you the way I did. I'll meet with the board. You can be CEO again. We'll, YES; we'll save the park! We can't possibly plow it under! What was I thinking?"

Collinsworth rubbed his face. "Let me get this straight. You claim that somehow you went back in time?"

Ray nodded. "I was there, Daniel. The Homecoming Tree. Rachel's song. Esau Cheatwood trying to take this house. I was there."

Collinsworth reached for his phone. "Let *me* call your wife. This is more serious than I thought."

Ray shoved the phone back into Collinsworth's hands. "Yes! You do that! Great! But, we were right here when your father walked through that door, and Rachel won the singing contest." He looked around the empty room. "Daniel, what happened to them all?"

Collinsworth mumbled something into the phone and then studied Ray's face. "My family?"

"Yes. My friends. What happened to them?"

Collinsworth sighed. "Well, my Daddy went on to join the new Air Force and taught pilots how to fly until he retired. He died at the ripe old age of 87 right after Mother went on to be with Jesus. Uncle Lonnie disappeared on D Day, and I'm afraid that story is too sad to tell right now. There's a cross over there with his name on it. Peggy Lou found the man of her dreams, got married and raised a good family. Buster went on to become a doctor and is retired living out by the lake. We have coffee every week at the park bench. Lawson and Wimpy took over the boarding house after Mother and Daddy moved to the housing at Barksdale Air Force Base. Lawson worked in the kitchen and never stopped bellyaching. The three sisters ended up patenting their Remedy and made a fortune after the war. Esau ended up in an insane asylum, and Lazarus took over the business and made an honest man of himself. Rachel went on to serve in the USO and met the man of her dreams. She got married and lives in Dallas. She's waiting for me in Hawaii."

Ray felt the tears run down his cheeks. He nodded. "I miss them, Daniel."

"I miss them, too," Collinsworth whispered. The doorbell rang, and the front door burst open. A small, blonde haired boy ran into the room.

"David!" Ray shouted. He squatted and opened his arms as the boy ran into his hug. He held him close and kissed his face. "My son! Oh, my son! I have missed you so much. I'm never going to let you go." He pushed the boy back, and David's eyes widened.

"Dad, are you okay?"

"I couldn't be better! Son, I have so much to tell you. We need to go for a walk in the woods, and I need to tell you all about the Home-coming Tree."

A woman stepped through the door and stood quietly. Ray glanced up at her, and his heart sank. He stood up and paused.

"Roy?" She said. "You've lost weight. How?"

His name was Roy. Yes, not Ray. Roy. But, in his heart, he would forever now be Ray. Roy was gone, banished to the shadows never to return. He walked across the cold living room and knelt before his wife.

"Deb, I almost did something horrible, terrible. I've been a bad husband and an absent father. Can you forgive me, Deb? I've done some terrible things. Things we need to work through. But, God has brought me home. I'm back, and I'm staying forever."

Deb reached out. "I know what has been going on, Roy. I'm not blind."

"I almost ruined everything. But, we can work through this. I realize now just how much I love you and need you. I've let my past with my father ruin our present and almost ruin our future. Will you give me a chance?"

Deb nodded and tears filled her eyes. "Yes."

"Dad, look at this picture." David stood on his knees on the couch and pointed to a large photograph hanging above the piano.

Roy came to him and smiled. "Those are my friends. I mean, that is Mr. Collinsworth's family. That picture was taken on Christmas Eve, 1941."

"Hey, Dad, that man looks just like you."

Roy's heart leaped, and he moved around the couch and stood before the photograph. There, standing behind the young Daniel Collinsworth was a man in a threadbare shirt and suspenders, his hair slightly mussed. The man's eyes were wide in surprise. There was no mistaking who it was. It wasn't the shadow man. It was Ray Castle.

"How? They're gone now. I don't understand."

Collinsworth stood beside him. "Well, it's not the end, you know. The world was swamped with evil, and it still is. Man thinks he'll rise above that evil side but he never will. That's why the good Lord sent his Son to show us the way and to die on a tree for our sins." He pointed to the Christmas tree nearby. "Hmmm, die on a tree. His death and resurrection will one day lead us to spend eternity in heaven with God. I guess that tree will lead us home. Roy, the cross is the real homecoming tree. And one day, there will be a glorious homecoming in heaven." He wiped a tear from his eye. "Roy, I guess I can't pretend anymore."

Roy pointed to the photograph. "But, it's me! Daniel, I'm in the picture."

"Yeah, I know. I've known for a long time."

"But, how?" Roy said.

The old man shrugged. "God works in mysterious ways. Now, if you don't mind, I'll take my father's medal. I've been waiting for you to return it to me for 60 years."

Roy glanced down at his shirt. Pinned on his pocket was the medal given to him by the younger Daniel. He removed it with shaking hands.

Collinsworth took the medal from Roy's trembling hands. "I don't question the miraculous works of God anymore, Roy." The old man walked slowly across to the Christmas tree and placed the medal on one of its branches. "And, you might want this back."

He took something from the tree and held it out in an open palm. David ran over to the old man and snared the object from his hand.

"Hey, this is the angel I gave you, Dad."

David handed the wooden angel to his father. Roy studied the wooden angel, now gray with age. "Yes, I had it in my pocket."

David smiled. "Then he did his job."

Roy looked down at his son. "What job?"

"I prayed for God to send you a guardian angel. That's why I carved the angel. I prayed for God to help you. So, God told me He would send an angel to look after you."

Roy felt the tears run down his cheeks. A hand slid beneath his arm, and Deb leaned against him. "Welcome home, Roy."

"Yeah, Dad, welcome home." David took the angel and kissed it. "And, thanks to Michael for letting the Lord bring back my Dad."

"Michael?"

"The Archangel Michael. Mom said you were in a battle and I thought Michael would be the best warrior to fight for you. See, I wrote his name right here on the bottom."

David held the angel bottom up. Through the prism of his tears, Roy barely made out a name written in a childish scrawl. Though the years had discolored the wood and the writing was faded he had no problem seeing the name, "Mikey" written by his son.

"Mikey?" He looked upward toward heaven. "Hey, thanks Mikey for the homecoming."

EPILOGUE

October, 2018
Homecoming Tree Park
Shreveport, Louisiana

DAVID PUSHED INTO THE SOFT SOIL AND TURNED ANOTHER SHOVEL full of dirt. He paused and looked at his father. "Dad, is that deep enough?"

Roy Anderson leaned over the hole in the ground. "Should be. But, we can't do it just yet."

David leaned against the shovel. "What are we waiting for?"

"You'll see." Roy tilted his head to look down the winding path leading into the park from the street. In the years since Collinsworth Industries had completely redesigned the park, the trees had grown so high most of the cityscape of Shreveport was barely visible above the tree line.

"Ah, here he comes." Roy said and ran his hand through his salt and pepper hair.

David turned and squinted down the pathway into the setting sun. The sound of an electric motor filled the air undercut by the chirping of birds. The old man drove his electric scooter with alarming speed up the winding path until he halted at the edge of the walkway. He stood slowly and pulled off his old, black fedora. He snared a walking cane from where it was clipped to the back of his seat. He hobbled toward them, his thin, white hair stirring in the breeze. "Evening David."

"Mr. Collinsworth?" David said. "How did you get away from the nursing home?"

Collinsworth paused and planted his cane in the grass. "Assisted living, David. I'm only 89." The man turned his rheumy, bright blue eyes toward Roy. "Ray, how are you?"

Roy beamed and slowly embraced the older man. They hugged for a few seconds and Roy felt the water moisten his eye. He stepped back. "You look great, Daniel."

"I should. We built that assisted living center to be state of the art. And, state of the heart." He chuckled. "So, David, has your father explained to you why we are here?"

David motioned with the shovel tip to a black, plastic bucket containing a short fir tree. "Planting a tree, right?"

"You got a picture?" Daniel asked as he ran a gnarled hand through his thin hair.

Daniel pulled out his cell phone and the screen filled with the image of a newborn. "Rachel Ann Anderson." Daniel smiled.

"You did well, son." Daniel pointed to the trees around them. "See these fir trees?"

David studied the circle of fir trees ranging in size from two feet to over ten feet tall. "Yes, sir. I know all about the Circle of Trees. But, Dad has never told me what this is all about. It seems to be a secret."

Daniel chuckled and nudged Roy. "You and your secrets."

"David, when Daniel Collinsworth was born way back in the twentieth century, his father planted a fir tree on the day he was born." Roy said. "Then, in time that tree would grow. And, the day Daniel was big enough to cut down that tree for the family Christmas tree was the day Daniel began his journey into adulthood."

David raised an eyebrow. He looked around the circle. "These trees?"

"Yes." Roy said. "Family and friends of ours who have had children these past seventeen years. Some of them have been cut down. Some of them are still growing because those children are no longer with us. Now, it's your turn to plant this tree for your daughter."

David looked at his father. "Where is *my* tree?"

"I didn't learn about the Homecoming Tree until you were seven."

David opened his mouth and nodded. "Oh, yeah. The photograph in Mr. Collinsworth's house. I thought that was just a story. So, this is my Homecoming Tree?"

"No, son, it is your daughter's Homecoming Tree. And, yes, what I told you was more than a story. But, before you put that tree in the hole there is one other person who must be present." He pointed over David's shoulder.

Out from between two trees, the dark figure appeared and walked toward them. He wore the same black driver's jacket and his cap was tilted back on his head in at a jaunty angle. His eyes glittered in the light of the setting sun.

"Do I know you?" David asked.

The man stopped and took off his hat and winked. "Michael's the name. But, I think you know me by another name?"

David dropped the shovel. "Mikey?"

"Good to see you again, David." Mikey smiled and the clearing filled with light. "The Good Lord let me come by today to wish you congratulations." He reached into his jacket pocket and pulled out a small figure. "And, to give you this."

David took the object and studied the small, hand carved wooden angel. "This is my angel!"

"Yep. I sort of restored it for you." Mikey winked at Roy. "Now, you have something to give to your daughter to remind her a guardian angel will always be looking out for her."

David wiped a tear from his eye and looked at his father. "Thanks, Dad."

Roy put an arm around Daniel Collinsworth and the other arm around Mikey. "No, thank God."

SOURCES

SOURCES

Shreveport (Images of America), Eric J. Brock, Acadia Publishing, June, 1998

Barksdale Air Force Base (Images of America) by H. D. Buck Rigg, John Andrew Prime, and Shawn Bohannon, Acadia Publishing, June, 2002

Oral History of life in Shreveport during World War II from Slayton and Lena Hennigan and their son, Ronald.

Additional information from Sue Hammack and Gwen Ennis, daughters of Slayton and Lena Hennigan.

AFTERWORD

The Homecoming Tree was performed at Brookwood Baptist Church November 10 – 12, 2005. My father, age 91, helped paint the sets for the play. He passed away in 2012 at the age of 98. My mother passed away in August 2004 and never got to see the play. Many of the characters and much of the story are based on their lives living in Shreveport at the start of World War II. Relatives came and went through their home while mothers and wives of men deployed overseas looked for jobs to support their families. While the Hennigan house on Buckner Street was not a true boarding house, it functioned like one. In 1999 I interviewed my parents and my brother, Ronald, who passed away in 2008, about life during World War II. That live interview is recorded and served as a background for much of this story.

My father also sang for the play, recording a version of "There's a Star Bangled Banner Waving Somewhere," a song made popular by Kate Smith. It was a joy to see his reaction as the play was performed. After the play became a success, I decided to adapt it as a novel. I changed the main character in the play to a modern businessman seen in an opening video that set the stage for the play. Inspired by the movie, "It's a Wonderful Life," I chose to put a modern man in the world of 1941. How would you act? How would any us act in a world where God was still important to most people, and the concept of good and evil was a given, and truth ruled America? How, indeed, would we act if we were to live out the days and nights of America's Greatest Generation? That is the story I chose for Roy/Ray to experience and I hope you have enjoyed it. Below are notes from the play. I want to honor those men, women, boys, and girls who made the play a success so many years ago and I want to thank my friend and pastor (now retired) Mark Sutton for allowing us to honor the men and women of our military with this play on the week of Veteran's Day.

Below are notes from the program for the play as well as information given to the cast in preparation for portraying a person living in Shreveport, Louisiana in late 1941.

Bruce Hennigan, 2018

❦

Welcome to The Brookwood Company's presentation of "The Homecoming Tree." The drama is set in Shreveport, Louisiana between Thanksgiving and Christmas of 1941. The cast and crew have spent many wonder-filled weeks reliving the past from the days just before World War II. We want to pay tribute to those men and women who have sacrificed so much for our freedom. We want to honor the service and the willing sacrifice of all our armed forces wherever they may find themselves this Christmas.

We also want to invite you to participate in a very special prayer program. During tonight's intermission and after the production, please stop by our table in the Gathering Area and place the name or names of loved ones you would like to pray for this Christmas. Maybe it is for them to come home. Perhaps it is for their continued safety until they can come home. Or, you may have someone not in the services who needs a special prayer this Christmas. Just place their name on an ornament and hang it on our "Homecoming Tree" and we will lift their names in prayer this season.

Again, thank you for your presence, and we hope you will find tonight's presentation uplifting and inspiring at this special time of the year.

Bruce Hennigan
>   Director of The Brookwood Company

❦

SCENES:

>   Prologue – A park in Shreveport present day.

>   Radio Spots – The studios of KWTT, Shreveport, Louisiana Thanksgiving Day, 1941

>   Act 1 Scene 1 – The library of the Collinsworth boarding house on Thanksgiving Day, 1941.

>   Act 1 Scene 2 – The living room and dining room of the Collinsworth home on Thanksgiving Day

>   Act 1 Scene 3 – The woods on the Collinsworth property on Thanksgiving Day.

>   Radio Spots – The studios of KWTT, Sunday, December 7, 1941.

>   Act 2 Scene 1 – The living room and dining room of the Collinsworth home on Sunday, December 7, 1941

>   Act 2 Scene 2 – The living room and dining room of the Collinsworth home two weeks after the attack on Pearl Harbor

>   Act 2 Scene 3 – The woods on the Collinsworth property the same day.

>   Intermission – Ten Minutes

>   Radio Spot – The studios of KWTT on December 24, 1941.

>   Act 3 Scene 1 and 2 – The Collinsworth home on December 24, 1941.

❦

CAST AND CREW

CAST

Frank Collinsworth: Jason Howard
    Ann Lee Collinsworth: Jean Brown
    Daniel Collinsworth: Randle Milliken
    Rachel Collinsworth: Angelique Milliken
    Lonnie Britt: Steve Brown
    Sue Carol Britt: Bennetta Smith
    Buster Britt: Heath Garner and Chris Hussein
    Little Lonnie Britt: Grey Thomas
    Aunt Wimpy: Donna Nix
    Uncle Lawson: Rodney Milliken
    Sister Ophelia: Theresa Gatti
    Sister Theophila: Deanna Cassity
    Sister Evelia: Chrissie Purcell
    J. D. Cummings: Ronnie Page
    Esau Cheatwood: Lance E. Ray
    Lazarus Cheatwood: Justin Brown
    Peggy Lou: Alissa Reed
    Sissy LeBeau: Tywana Keller
    Penelope: Casey Hennigan
    Gwendolyn: Hillary Garner
    Soldier: Mitch Bailey
    Mr. Stanton (and Roy Anderson): Bruce Hennigan
    Older Daniel Collinsworth: Larry Robison
    The Voice: Mark Riser
    Announcer: Heather Alonzo
    The Milliken Sisters: Rosalyn Milliken, Amy Ricketts, and Jennifer
English
    Additional Singer Tonya Sipes

CREW

Produced, Directed, and Written by Bruce Hennigan
    Assistant Director: Ronnie Page
    2nd Unit Director: Mark Riser
    Assistant to Mark Riser: Heather Alonzo

The Song, "The Homecoming Prayer" lyrics and composition by Philip Wade

Costumes: Donna Nix and Bruce Hennigan

Set Design: Debbie Oliver

Set Construction: Alan Young

Video and Graphic Design: Chris Lyon of Perennial Media and Jeremy Johnson

Hair Styling: Tywana Keller of True Colors

Makeup: Deanna Cassity

Sound: Shane Reed

Gathering Area Décor: Angie Hazel

Program and Poster Design: Jeremy Johnson

Stage Crew:

Sam Hussein

Jerry Garner

Jared Barber

LIFE IN 1941

LIFE IN 1941

1941 Prices

Bread: $.08 a loaf
　　Milk: $.34 a gallon
　　Eggs: $.60 a dozen
　　Car: $750 to 925
　　Gas: $.19 a gallon
　　House: $6,954
　　Stamp: $.03
　　Average income: $2059 a year
　　Minimum wage: $.30 an hour
　　Dow average: 111
　　A live Christmas Tree: $.75
　　To decorate the tree: $10
　　A ride on the Shreveport trolley: $.25 round trip
　　Movie: $.09
　　A coke at the movie: $.05
　　Popcorn at the movie: $.10

Rent on the house on Buckner street: $35 a month

Most wanted toys for Christmas:

Erector Set
    Lionel Train
    Monopoly
    Teddy Bear
    Lincoln Logs
    Radio Flyer "Streak-O-Lite"
    Duncan Yo-Yo
    Parker Brothers "Sorry"
    Crayola crayons
    Raggedy Ann
    Tinkertoy
    View-Master
    Foto-Electric Football

SPORTS:

Ted Williams (Boston) bats .406 with 37 homers
    Joe DiMaggio (NY,AL) hits 56 consecutive games, 91 hits in a streak
    Left Gomez (NY,AL) pitches 15 − 5
    World Series New York, AL 4 −Boston, NL, 1
    College Football champion is Minnesota

TOP SONGS:

You and I by Glenn Miller
    Amapola by Jimmy Dorsey
    Daddy by Sammy Kaye
    There'll Be Some Changes Made by Benny Goodman
    There I Go by Vaughn Monroe
    Chattanooga Choo Choo by Glenn Miller
    I Don't Want to Set the World on Fire by Horace Heidt

Piano Concerto in B Flat by Freddy Martin
Maria Elena by Jimmy Dorsey
Green Eyes by Jimmy Dorsey
I'm Walking the Floor Over You by Ernest Tubbs

TOP MOVIES:

Dumbo
    Citizen Kane
    The Maltese Falcon
    Suspicion
    How Green Was My Valley
    Sergeant York
    Meet John Doe
    Never Give a Sucker an Even Break
    The Little Foxes
    Sullivan's Travels
    The Wolf Man
    The Devil and Daniel Webster
    Here Comes Mr. Jordan
    Hold Back the Dawn
    The Lady Eve

MOVIE THEATERS IN SHREVEPORT:

Rex Theater (Highland and Kings Hwy)
    The Capitol Theater
    The Don Theater
    The Saenger Theater (Capri)
    The Star on Texas Avenue
    The Glenwood on Line Ave.
    The New Venus on Lakeshore
    The Centenary on Centenary Blvd.
    The Broadmoor on Youree
    The Southland on Barksdale Blvd.

DOWNTOWN

The Trolley ran back and forth downtown

The Commercial National Bank was the tallest building at 17 stories

Washington Youree Hotel was the sight of many band dances

Those who performed there: Jan Garber, Jimmy and Tommy Dorsey, Xavier Cugat, Bob Hope, Jimmy Durante, Perry Como, and Victor Borge.

The Charity Hospital was at 1200 Texas Ave.

The Texas and Pacific Railroad Station was at 201 Market built in 1940

The Big Chain Grocery Company opened Shreveport's first true supermarket in 1941 at 3950 Ockley Dr. This became a model for supermarkets all over the nation.

MILITARY

Barksdale Air Field was the home of the United States Air Corps Bombardier School from 1940 – 1941

The Louisiana Maneuvers took place in the fall of 1941. The planners of strategy in the games were Dwight Eisenhower and George Patton. Patton took Shreveport in mock fighting which ended on Dec. 3, 1941.

One interesting note: On December 24, 1941, Bing Crosby sang a song on the NBC radio program that was largely ignored in the aftermath of Pearl Harbor. This song would one day become an enormous hit once he featured the song in a hit movie by the same name, "White Christmas."

SHREVEPORT 1941

Shreveport and World War II

In my efforts to keep this play as historically accurate as possible, I researched the role that Shreveport and Bossier City played in the war. Barksdale Air Field was the headquarters for many training missions at the start of the war. General George Patton did indeed win the "Louisiana Maneuvers" and was proclaimed the winner on December 3, 1941. Dwight Eisenhower visited the area during these maneuvers. General Chennault was from Louisiana and the story of his "Fighting Tigers" is the stuff of legends. Only, it is all true. My character, Frank Collinsworth never really served with Chennault, but the background information regarding Chennault's American Volunteer Group is all true. There are many excellent books by local authors on Shreveport and Bossier City during the twentieth century as well as the history of Barksdale Air Field. I encourage you to read these books and learn more about our local history during the war.

Bruce Hennigan

ABOUT THE AUTHOR

Bruce Hennigan grew up in the deep pine forests of northwest Louisiana. There wasn't much to do in the country for a young boy with an active imagination and acres of pastures and woods unless imagination opened the door to another reality. Bruce spent his childhood chasing dinosaurs, giant robots, aliens from Alpha Centauri, and an occasional cow through this vast land of imagination.

In the eighth grade, he saved up his meager allowance and bought a teal blue portable typewriter and began to write his own stories. He was doomed; captured; enslaved by Story! Bruce wanted to write for the rest of his life.

But, God intervened. He called Bruce to another profession in the medical field to become the very last thing in the world he wanted to be, a doctor. He continued to write through college and medical school and found success in, of all places, the theater. For 15 years, Bruce was the drama director at a local church and wrote over 150 plays. Challenged by questions from fellow scientists regarding his faith, Bruce explored the field of Christian apologetics, the defense of the truthfulness of the Christian faith. He became a Volunteer Apologist with Reasons to Believe and a Certified Apologetic Instructor with the North American Mission Board.

After suffering through a severe depression, Bruce co-authored *"Conquering Depression: A Thirty Day Plan to Finding Happiness"* with Mark Sutton published by Broadman & Holman Publishing in 2001. After the success of that book, he fulfilled his life long dream of writing supernatural thrillers in the series, "The Chronicles of Jonathan Steel", currently at 10 books. He has also published "Our Darkness, His Light" and "Shadow Merchant" a medical mystery.

In 2014, Bruce and Mark Sutton updated their depression book with the release of *"Hope Again: A 30 Day Plan for Conquering Depression"* through B&H Publishing. Mark and Bruce have produced a short seminar, "Conquering Depression Seminar" to accompany the book. For more information go to **conqueringdepression.com**.

He has two grown children and lives in Shreveport with his wife, Sherry. Bruce continues to speak on the topics of apologetics, creative writing, depression, and drama. For more information, check out his website at **brucehennigan.com**. For information on the Jonathan Steel Chronicles go to hopeagainbooks.com.

ALSO BY BRUCE HENNIGAN

The Chronicles of Jonathan Steel

Death By Darwin

The 13th Demon: Altar of the Spiral Eye

The 12th Demon: Mark of the Wolf Dragon

The 11th Demon: The Ark of Chaos

The 10th Demon: Children of the Bloodstone

The 9th Demon: Time of the Cross

The 8th Demon: A Wicked Numinosity

The 7th Demon: The Pandora Stone

The 5th Demon: Demoneyes

The 4th Demon: The Trial of the 3rd Demon

The 2nd Demon: Tales of the Grimvox

The Conquest Series

Conquering Depression: A 30-Day Plan to Finding Happiness

Hope Again: A 30 Day Plan for Conquering Depression

The Homecoming Tree

Our Darkness, His Light

Shadow Merchant (A Jack Merchant Medica Mystery)

Merchant of Justice

www.ingramcontent.com/pod-product-compliance
Lightning Source LLC
Chambersburg PA
CBHW070432120726
47910CB00003B/747